*The Village of Stepanchikovo
and Its Inhabitants*

Fyodor Dostoevsky

Translated by Roger Cockrell

ALMA CLASSICS

ALMA CLASSICS
an imprint of

ALMA BOOKS LTD
Thornton House
Thornton Road
Wimbledon Village
London SW19 4NG
United Kingdom
www.almaclassics.com

The Village of Stepanchikovo and Its Inhabitants
first published in Russian in 1859
This edition first published by Alma Classics in 2023

Translation © Roger Cockrell, 2023

Cover: Nathan Burton

Extra Material and Notes © Alma Books Ltd

Printed in Great Britain by CPI Group (UK) Ltd, Croydon CR0 4YY

ISBN: 978-1-84749-908-0

Contents

Translator's Introduction

In 1854 the thirty-three-year-old Dostoevsky, having spent four years in a penal colony in Omsk, was compelled to spend the remaining five years of his exile as a private in the Russian army. Based in the Siberian town of Semipalatinsk (now in north-eastern Kazakhstan), he was all too keenly aware of his isolation from the social and cultural life of St Petersburg and Moscow. As someone who, before captivity, had lived an intensely rich inner life, as the first Russian translator of Honoré de Balzac's *Eugénie Grandet* and the published author of three novels and a number of stories, he had found the lack of literary culture and the almost total absence of books in prison exceptionally torturous. Anxious for his name to reappear in print after an absence of many years (his last work, the unfinished novel *Netochka Nezvanova*, had been published in 1849), he began the search for suitable new ideas and themes.

This was not an easy task: however urgent his desire to "return to literature", the theme and content of any new work required considerable thought. He could of course have written about his experiences in prison – something that would have been relevant and topical, with prison reform very much under discussion. Yet, fearful of the censor's response, he decided to wait – for the moment at least: he was to publish the semi-fictionalized account of his experiences, the sensational work that was to become *The House of the Dead*, a few years later, in 1861. But the basic problem remained: what could he write about? He was certain of one point: he knew that it needed "to be better than *Poor People*" – his very first novel, which had burst onto the scene in 1846, with the critics hailing the arrival of a bright new talent. But new ideas and concerns relating to radical social reforms, most particularly the emancipation of the serfs (which was to come into law in 1861), were now beginning to make themselves felt. It was not, however, simply the times that had moved on: he himself had fundamentally changed, as a result of his experiences in jail. His interests and instincts were now shifting away from a desire for socio-political reform towards the need for spiritual and moral awareness.

It was against the background of such concerns that Dostoevsky embarked on two stories, more or less simultaneously: *Uncle's Dream* and *The Village of Stepanchikovo and Its Inhabitants*. As far as it is possible to glean from available sources, Dostoevsky started to work seriously on *The Village of Stepanchikovo* no earlier than the autumn of 1857. Despite a number of interruptions, arising from the need to deliver his manuscript of *Uncle's Dream* to the publisher, by the spring of 1859 he had completed three quarters of the story, and by June he was in a position to send the final chapters to his brother Mikhail. Should the story prove to be a success (and he firmly believed that it would), he was counting on the fact that this would enable him to establish a firm literary position, to demand increased fees from his publisher and perhaps even to produce a collected edition of his works. As he wrote to Mikhail on 9th May, "This work is not without its faults, of course, not least because it's rather too long, but it's my firm opinion that it possesses some truly great qualities – in fact that it is my very best work... but I must confess that, if the reading public doesn't like it, then I may well become extremely upset. My very best hopes and, most importantly, my future literary career depend on it. I have been writing it for the last two years (with an interruption in the middle, because of *Uncle's Dream*). I have now reworked the beginning and middle, and it has a rather hasty conclusion. But I have put my whole soul, my flesh and blood into it. I can't say I've been able to express absolutely everything I wanted to... but it includes two immensely typical figures, which I have been thinking about and jotting down in my notebooks for over five years and which, in my opinion, have been impeccably realized – two totally Russian characters that, moreover, have hitherto been inadequately represented in Russian literature." After a few failed negotiations with various publishers, the story was eventually published in the journal *Notes of the Fatherland (Otechestvenniye Zapiski)* in November and December 1859.

Characteristically for Dostoevsky, literary references abound. There is a constant dialogue, largely hidden and often critical, with Dostoevsky's great predecessor, Nikolai Gogol, and even a nod to the person who was to become his ideological arch-opponent, Ivan Turgenev. Yet, as has often been observed, it is in the central confrontation between these two "immensely typical" figures – the hypocritical and despotic Foma and the self-effacing and gullible colonel – that Dostoevsky draws most heavily on a literary antecedent: Molière's *Tartuffe, or The Impostor* (1664). Any analysis of the two works shows the close links between them, but Dostoevsky's characters remain archetypically his own, to be used and developed in his later novels. Many of Foma's traits, for example, can be detected in the grotesque Fyodor Karamazov, while Rostanev is an embryonic forerunner of the "positively good" figure of Prince Myshkin in *The Idiot*.

Unlike *Uncle's Dream*, in which we find ourselves only partly in the hands of an unreliable narrator, who disappears entirely from the scene for whole episodes, *Stepanchikovo* is told throughout, in the first person, by an omnipresent but naive and far from omniscient figure. Once the action starts, he very soon finds himself plunged into a totally incomprehensible world, thrust as it were at random into a household that, with very few exceptions, seems collectively to have taken leave of its senses, the bedrock of normality apparently shattered beyond repair. The quirky (not to say deranged) behaviour of the majority of the house's denizens is enough on its own to give *Stepanchikovo* a decidedly theatrical flavour. Strip it of its introductory chapter and its concluding paragraphs and you are left with a succession of highly charged, confrontational scenes, rising to an extraordinary climax at the height of a violent thunderstorm. Just like the narrator, we find ourselves in a world of unexpected arrivals and departures, overwhelming emotions and indescribable agitation.

Eyes brim with tears, faces are overcome by paroxysms of joy, the room is filled with choruses of shrieks and wails, as people collapse in a swoon into conveniently placed armchairs. Add to all this the *mises-en-scène* and romantic tropes (a self-contained provincial country house, secret trysts in a summer-house, unexplained events, a neglected, stagnant pond), the "dumb scenes", almost certainly inspired by the final moments of Gogol's *The Government Inspector*, and the ultimate triumph of true love against seemingly impossible odds, and we have the makings of pure theatre, combined, for the discerning reader, with elements of a morality play. It is hardly surprising that, although Dostoevsky himself may never have written a play, his stories and novels, including *Stepanchikovo*, should frequently have been adapted very successfully for the stage.

Interestingly, and perhaps rather disappointingly, once Dostoevsky has told his story, he feels the need to add a fairly lengthy conclusion in which practically all the characters are seen in a compassionate and sympathetic light (with the possible exception of the grisly Perepelitsyna). Even though Foma Opiskin (the name comes from the Russian *opiska*, "misprint", "slip of the pen") remains as obnoxious as ever, he is not only forgiven, but fully restored to his pride of place as at least the nominal head of the family. The tone of this concluding section is markedly different from that of the earlier chapters, creating a far more sober and conventional effect.

Dostoevsky was anxious to see how *Stepanchikovo* would be received, both by the critics and by the general public. In his correspondence to Mikhail he is constantly asking his brother to tell him everything that everybody is saying about his story. In the event, the story went practically unnoticed in the critical press, receiving no reviews at all in *Notes of the Fatherland*, the journal in which it had been published. When reviews did eventually appear, after the story was reissued in volume form in 1860, they were mixed, ranging from the positive to the extremely critical. Nikolai Dobrolyubov, for example, took Dostoevsky to task for creating totally "unrealistic" characters, with Foma Fomich, on the one hand, being exaggeratedly negative, and Nastenka, the governess, on the other, implausibly positive, and therefore colourless. It was not until some twenty years later, in an article published in 1882, a year after Dostoevsky's death, that the literary critic Nikolai Mikhailovsky acknowledged the full force of Dostoevsky's genius in creating a monstrous character such as Foma Fomich.

Despite many disappointments, Dostoevsky could justifiably look back on his achievements since leaving prison with some pride. Whatever other people might have thought, he had been able to prove, at least to himself, that he was capable of creating new and highly effective narrative forms such as *The Village of Stepanchikovo* and *Uncle's Dream*. This, in turn, was to give him renewed confidence for the future, a confidence that, with the publication of *Notes from Underground* and *Crime and Punishment* within a few short years, would be fully borne out. His was now a voice that would be difficult to ignore.

I should like to thank Alessandro Gallenzi for all his encouragement and his meticulous and sympathetic editing of the text.

– Roger Cockrell, 2023

Table of Ranks

Civil Service	Military	Court
1) Chancellor	Field Marshal/ Admiral	
2) Active Privy Councillor	General	Chief Chamberlain
3) Privy Councillor	Lieutenant General	Marshal of the House
4) Active State Councillor	Major General	Chamberlain
5) State Councillor	Brigadier	Master of Ceremonies
6) Collegiate Councillor	Colonel	Chamber Fourrier
7) Court Councillor	Lieutenant Colonel	
8) Collegiate Assessor	Major	House Fourrier
9) Titular Councillor	Staff Captain	
10) Collegiate Secretary	Lieutenant	
11) Ship Secretary*	*Kammerjunker*	
12) Government Secretary	Sub-Lieutenant	
13) Provincial Secretary*		
14) Collegiate Registrar	Senior Ensign	

* *(abolished in 1834)*

The Village of Stepanchikovo and Its Inhabitants

FROM AN ANONYMOUS NOTEBOOK

List of Characters

Colonel Yegor Ilyich Rostanev (Yegorushka)

Foma Fomich Opiskin

Praskovya Ilyinichna Rostaneva, the colonel's sister

The colonel's children: Ilyusha and Sasha (Sashenka, Sashurka, Alexandra Yegorovna)

Sergei Alexandrovich (Seryozha), the colonel's nephew and the narrator

Agafya Timofeyevna Krakhotkina (the "general's lady"), the colonel's mother

Nastasya Yevgrafovna Yezhevikina (Nastenka, Nastya), the children's governess

Yevgraf Larionovich Yezhevikin, Nastenka's father

Anna Nilovna Perepelitsyna, confidante to the general's lady

Pavel Semyonovich Obnoskin (Paul)

Anfisa Petrovna Obnoskina, Pavel's mother

Ivan Ivanovich Mizinchikov

Tatyana Ivanovna, distant relative of the colonel

Stepan Alexeyevich Bakhcheyev, neighbouring landowner

Falaley, house boy

Grigory Vidoplyasov, the colonel's lackey

Gavrila, the colonel's personal valet

FIRST PART

I

Introduction

When my uncle, Colonel Yegor Ilyich Rostanev, retired, he went to live in the village of Stepanchikovo, which he had inherited and where he settled down so effortlessly that it seemed as if he had spent his entire life on the estate without ever once having left it. There are certain particular natures for whom life holds no challenges whatsoever, and who are able to adapt to any circumstance; the retired colonel possessed just such a nature. It was difficult to conceive of a more submissive and compliant person. If someone had asked him in all seriousness to give him a ride on his back for several hundred yards or so, he would probably have agreed: he was such an obliging man that, as the occasion arose, he would not have been averse to parting with anything as soon as he were asked, down almost to his very last shirt. He was very powerfully built: tall, slim, ruddy-cheeked, with teeth as white as ivory, a full, reddish-brown moustache, a strong, resonant voice and a natural, booming laugh; whenever he spoke, it was always in a rather abrupt, hurried way. When he retired, he was about forty years old, and he had spent his entire life, from the age of sixteen practically, serving in the hussars. He had married at a very young age and been head over heels in love with his wife, but she had died, leaving him with a heart full of lasting, very pleasant memories. Finally, having inherited Stepanchikovo – increasing his estate to six hundred serfs – he retired from army service and, as has already been said, settled down in the village with his children: eight-year-old Ilyusha (whose arrival in the world had cost his mother her life) and his daughter Sashenka, a girl of about fifteen, who, on her mother's death, had been educated in a boarding school in Moscow. But very soon my uncle's house turned into a veritable Noah's ark. This was what happened.

At the time he inherited the estate and went into retirement, his mother, the wife of General Krakhotkin, lost her husband. This had been her second marriage, which had taken place some sixteen years earlier, when my uncle had still been a cornet, but nevertheless thinking of getting married himself. His mother had been very reluctant to give her blessing to such an idea, weeping bitter tears for ages, reproaching him for his selfishness, ingratitude and lack of respect. She was determined to prove to him that even his estate of two hundred and fifty serfs was barely sufficient to support his family (to support, that is, his mother, together with her clique of hangers-on, pug dogs, spitzes, Chinese cats and so on) – and then suddenly, totally unexpectedly, while engaged in all these rebukes, reproaches and hysterical outbursts, she herself got married, at the age of forty-two, before her son did. But even here she was able to find a pretext to attack my poor uncle, maintaining she was getting married only to guarantee herself some security in her old age – something which was denied her by her disrespectful, selfish son, who had behaved with such unpardonable insolence by setting up his own home.

I have never been able to understand what it was exactly that persuaded such an apparently sensible person as the late General Krakhotkin to marry a forty-two-year-old widow. It can only be assumed that he suspected her of having money. There were some who thought he simply needed someone to take care of him, as even then he could foresee the myriad of illnesses which would beset him later, in his old age. One thing was certain: the general demonstrated a profound lack of respect for his wife during the whole of their married life together and callously mocked her at every available opportunity. He was a strange man. Semi-educated but far from stupid, he had a decided contempt for all and sundry, living entirely without principle, jeering at everything and everybody, and as the result of ill health – the consequence of a not entirely correct and upright life – turning into a malevolent, irritable and ruthless old man. He had had a successful army career, but, following an "unpleasant incident", he had been forced to resign his commission in a very untimely fashion, only just managing to avoid being taken to court and stripped of his pension. He was never to get over the feeling of embitterment. Almost totally penniless, the owner of a hundred or so impoverished serfs, he simply gave up, spending the rest of his life, an entire twelve years, never bothering to enquire what he was living on or who was providing for him, and yet insisting on enjoying all life's comforts, maintaining his expensive lifestyle and keeping a carriage. He soon lost the use of his legs, and spent the remaining ten years of his life in a wheelchair, rocked whenever necessary by two enormous lackeys, who never heard a single word from him, apart from all kinds of profanities. The carriage, lackeys and wheelchairs were the responsibility of the insolent son, who sent his mother all that he possessed, constantly mortgaging and remortgaging his estate, denying himself essentials, incurring debts which he had hardly any hope of repaying from his income at the time, while continuing to be regarded by his mother as an incorrigibly selfish and ungrateful son. But my uncle's character was such that he himself finally came to believe in his own egotism, and so, in self-flagellation and in order to prove he was not selfish at all, he carried on sending more and more money.

The "general's lady", as she came to be known, worshipped her husband. But most of all she liked the fact that he was a general and that she, as a result, was a general's wife. She had her own part of the house where, throughout the whole of her husband's semi-existence, she led a flourishing life, surrounded by her hangers-on, gossips and lapdogs. In her little town she was a figure of some consequence. Tittle-tattle, invitations to christenings and weddings, games of preference for trivial stakes – all such activities, combined with the respect shown to her as the wife of a general, more than compensated for the constraints of her domestic existence. Gossips visited her regularly with all the latest rumours; everywhere she went, she was always given pride of place – in short, she was able to exploit to the full all the advantages that her husband's title entailed. Although the general himself didn't interfere in any of this, he taunted her heartlessly in public, openly asking himself, for example, why he had ever married "such a holier-than-thou prig of a woman". And nobody ever dared to stand up for her. Gradually, one after the other, all his acquaintances abandoned him – and yet, at the same time, he craved other people's company: he loved to chat and argue and relished the fact that there was always someone there, sitting and listening to him. As a freethinker and atheist of the old school, he much enjoyed holding forth on lofty matters.

But the numbers of people from the town of N—— who had any time at all to listen to lofty matters grew smaller and smaller. There was an attempt to introduce preference whist to members of the household, but each game usually ended with the general having such fits of rage that his terrified good lady and her minions would light candles and offer up prayers, divine fortunes from beads and cards, distribute alms outside prisons and anxiously await the after-dinner hour, when they would once again have to make up a party for whist and prepare for every mistake to be met by shouts, yells, curses and practically physical assault. Every time the general found something not to his liking, he could never contain himself: he would shriek like an old woman, swear like a coachman, and sometimes even, as he ripped up the cards and hurled them down on the floor, chasing his partners out of the room, burst into tears from irritation and anger, merely because someone had put down a jack instead of a nine. Eventually, as his sight deteriorated, he needed someone who would read to him. This signalled the arrival on the scene of Foma Fomich Opiskin.

I must confess that it is with a certain sense of awe that I introduce this new figure. He is, without any doubt, one of the most important characters in my story. But I will not begin to conjecture the extent to which he claims the reader's attention: it would be more proper to leave the reader to make up his own mind on the subject.

Foma Fomich became part of General Krakhotkin's household as a sponger, in need of a crust of bread – no more, no less. Exactly where he came from is shrouded in mystery. I have nonetheless deliberately made some enquiries and found out one or two details about this remarkable man's earlier life. People said, in the first place, that he had once been in government service, and that he had endured some kind of hardship – for a "good cause", naturally. It was also said that he had once embarked on a literary career in Moscow. There is nothing surprising in that: the fact that Foma Fomich was appallingly ignorant could not of course in any way have served as an impediment to such a pursuit. All that has been established beyond doubt was that he had been a failure at everything and that he had finally been compelled to endure the ordeal of becoming the general's reader. There wasn't a humiliation he didn't have to suffer for the sake of his board and lodging. True, subsequently, once the general had died and Foma himself had totally unexpectedly become a figure of extraordinary significance, he would keep on assuring us all that, in agreeing to act as a clown, he had magnanimously sacrificed himself for the sake of friendship; that the general had been his benefactor, someone who had in fact been an exceptional person, misunderstood by all, and that he alone, Foma, had been privy to the innermost secrets of the general's soul; and, finally, that if he, Foma, had been forced to play the role of various wild beasts and so on, it had been only to entertain and amuse a dear suffering friend who had become depressed by his illnesses. But such assurances and explanations on Foma's part must be taken with a pinch of salt. While playing the fool, this very same Foma Fomich was acting out a very different role in the women's section of the general's house. How he managed to do this is difficult for the non-specialist in such matters to imagine. The general's wife regarded him with a particular kind of mystical reverence – why this should have been so, I have no idea. Little by little he managed to wheedle himself into a position of astonishing dominance over the entire female section of the general's house, not dissimilar to that of the sundry Ivan Yakovleviches* and other such sages and soothsayers, whom certain well-born lady admirers like to visit in lunatic asylums. He would read them edifying books aloud, and expound, his eyes filled with eloquent tears, the various Christian virtues; tell them all about his life and his achievements; attend church services, such as vespers and even matins, and partly foretell the future. The general had some idea of what was going on in the rooms at the back of the house and adopted an even more tyrannical and callous attitude towards his hapless victim. But Foma's tortured suffering only increased the respect shown him by the general's wife and all her retinue.

Finally everything changed – with the death of the general. His death was rather out of the ordinary. As a one-time freethinker, this atheist was an extraordinary coward. He wept, repented, raised icons to his lips, summoned priests. Liturgies were held, extreme unctions administered. The poor wretch shouted that he didn't want to die, and even tearfully begged Foma Fomich for forgiveness – thereby lending considerable weight to the latter's prestige. However, just before the general's soul departed from his body, the following incident occurred. The general's wife's daughter from her first marriage, my aunt Praskovya Ilyinichna – a confirmed spinster and long-time resident in the general's house, one of the general's favourite victims throughout the whole of his ten-year wheelchair-bound existence, someone who, in her simple-hearted and humble way, was the only person capable of pleasing him by attending to his every need – approached his bedside weeping bitterly and was just attempting to straighten the pillow under the invalid's head when he managed to grab her hair and tug at it three times, practically foaming with rage. Ten minutes or so later he was dead. The colonel was informed, although the general's wife declared she didn't wish to see him and that she would rather die than allow him to be anywhere near her at such a moment. There was a magnificent funeral – paid for, naturally, by the impertinent son, the very person she didn't want to let into her sight.

In the bankrupt estate of Knyazyovka, the joint possession of a number of landowners, including the general with his hundred or so serfs, stands a mausoleum of white marble, the walls covered in inscriptions, testifying to the wit, talent, nobility of soul, awards and military exploits of the general. Foma Fomich was to a large extent responsible for these inscriptions. For a long time after the general's death, his widow persisted in refusing to forgive her disobedient son. Surrounded by her cohort of minions and lapdogs, she continued to declare, sobbing and shrieking, that she would sooner resort to living on dry crusts (washed down, naturally, "by her tears"), sooner go round people's houses hobbling on a stick and begging for alms, than agree to the request of "that disobedient man" to move to Stepanchikovo – and that she would never, never so much as *set foot* in his house! That expression, *set foot*, when used in a general sense, can be uttered in a particularly effective way by some well-born ladies. The general's widow used it with unsurpassed artistry... In short, there were no limits to her eloquence. It would, however, be remiss to forget to mention that, in the midst of all this shrieking and raving, the preparations were gradually being put into place for her move to Stepanchikovo. The colonel wore all his horses out, going back and forth practically every day, covering the twenty-five miles or so from Stepanchikovo to the town, and it wasn't until two weeks after the general's funeral that he was allowed to appear in front of his indignant parent. Foma Fomich was charged with overseeing the discussions. Throughout these two weeks he reproached and attacked the reprobate son for his "heartless" behaviour, reducing him to real tears, almost to despair. This marked the beginning of Foma Fomich's incomprehensible and inhumanly despotic domination of my poor uncle. Foma intuitively grasped the kind of person he was dealing with, immediately realizing that his role as a clown was over and that in the land of the blind even he, Foma, could be king. It was now, indeed, that he could make up for the past.

"Just imagine what you would feel," Foma would say to him, "if your own mother, the very person responsible for your existence, so to speak, actually had to hobble around everywhere clutching a stick and, leaning on it with her trembling hands, withered from starvation, asking for charity? Would that not be a monstrous thought, bearing in mind, in the first place, her status as a general's wife and, in the second, her many virtues? What would you feel if she were suddenly to come – mistakenly, of course (but after all, such a thing could happen) – to your window, holding out her hand begging for charity, while you, her very own son, were perhaps at that very moment lounging in some feather bed? How awful that would be – so awful! But the worst thing of all, if I may be quite frank, colonel, the worst thing of all is that you are now standing here in front of me like some mindless block of wood, your mouth hanging open and your eyes popping out – it's positively indecent, when just the thought of such a circumstance should be making you tear your hair out and weep floods of tears... yes, I'm telling you: rivers, lakes, seas, oceans of tears!..."

In short, Foma would get carried away by the heat of the moment. But that always happened whenever he waxed eloquent. The outcome of it all, of course, was that the general's lady, together with her entire entourage of minions and lapdogs, with Foma Fomich and her main confidante Miss Perepelitsyna, finally graced Stepanchikovo with her presence. She announced that her decision to live with her son was only a *test* to see if he was truly devoted to her. You can imagine what the colonel had to endure in undergoing such an appraisal of his devotion to her! At first, as befitting someone who has been recently widowed, the general's lady saw it as her duty to collapse in despair two or three times a week as she remembered her departed husband, and each time it was always the colonel who was on the receiving end. On certain occasions, especially when there were visitors present, the general's lady would summon her little grandson Ilyusha and her fifteen-year-old granddaughter Sashenka, sit them down by her side, look at them fixedly with her sad, tormented eyes, as at children who had been ruined at the hands of *such a father*, give a deep, heavy sigh and finally burst into floods of silent and inexplicable tears for a whole hour at the very least. Woe to the colonel, if he should prove unable to *understand* these tears! But he, the poor man, could almost never understand their import, and, in his naivety, would happen to turn up practically every time at such tearful moments and find himself perforce subject to her scrutiny. But his respectful devotion for her remained as strong as ever, eventually breaking all bounds. In short, both of them, the general's widow and Foma Fomich, had finally grasped that the storm in the shape of General Krakhotkin that had been threatening them for so many years had passed – passed, never to return. There were occasions when the general's widow would suddenly, for no reason, collapse in a fainting fit onto the sofa, turning the whole place into confusion and uproar. The colonel would stand there dumbfounded, trembling like an aspen leaf.

"You heartless son, you!" the general's widow would cry as she came to. "You have ripped out my entrails... *mes entrailles, mes entrailles!*"

"But how on earth, Mother, could I have ripped out your entrails?" the colonel would object meekly.

"But you have, you have positively ripped them out! Listen to him, making excuses! Such insolence! You cruel, heartless man! I'm dying!..."

The colonel of course would be totally shattered.

But somehow or other the general's lady would always recover. And within half an hour the colonel would be buttonholing someone and giving his version of events:

"But you need to understand, my dear fellow, that she is a *grande dame*, the wife of a general! She's such a kind old lady – it's just that she's used to living such a refined life, you see... I'm nothing but a bumptious clod in comparison! She's now really angry with me. It's all my fault, of course. I've still no idea, my dear chap, exactly what it is I've done wrong, but I'm certainly to blame..."

On occasion it would be the spinster Miss Perepelitsyna – a crabbed and petulant old woman well past her prime, with her hair done up in a chignon, with sharp, predatory little eyes without eyebrows, thin pursed lips, hands that had been washed in pickled-gherkin juice – on occasion she would be the one who saw it as her duty to lecture the colonel:

"It is all because you show her no respect. It is because you think only of yourself, and therefore you insult your dear mother, sir; her ladyship is not accustomed to such behaviour, sir. She is the wife of a general, and you, sir, are still only a mere colonel."

"That Miss Perepelitsyna, my dear chap, is the most excellent of women, the most wonderful support for Mother! Such an admirable lady! Don't you go thinking that she's some sponger or other; she herself, my dear fellow, is a lieutenant colonel's daughter. Yes, really!"

But, of course, these were only the opening shots. That very same general's lady, who was capable of playing such silly tricks, would in her turn shake like a little mouse in fear before the person who was once dependent on her. She had fallen under the spell of Foma Fomich once and for all. She hung on his every word, heard everything through his ears, saw everything through his eyes. One of my distant cousins, also a retired hussar, still a young man but unbelievably worn out by years of reckless behaviour, and who at one time had taken refuge in my uncle's house, confided in me his profound conviction that the general's lady was in an improper relationship with Foma Fomich. Naturally, at the time I angrily rejected such an idea as being far too coarse and naive. No, it was something else – something I could only explain by making some preliminary remarks to the reader concerning the character of Foma Fomich, as I myself was subsequently to come to know it.

Picture to yourself the most insignificant, the most faint-hearted little man, an outcast from society, superfluous to requirements, utterly useless, totally vile, but immeasurably vain and, moreover, endowed with precisely nothing that could remotely justify his pathologically warped vanity. I must warn you in advance: Foma Fomich is the embodiment of the most boundless (yet very special) kind of vanity – in other words, a vanity that goes hand in hand with the uttermost insignificance, and, as is usually the case in such instances, an aggrieved vanity that has long been festering in someone who has been crushed by a string of past failures and who ever since has been exuding a particularly toxic form of envy at any human contact and whenever anyone else meets with any success. Needless to say, all this was seasoned by the most outrageous tetchiness and the most insane oversensitivity. What was the source of such vanity, people may ask? How could it have arisen in such a worthless, pathetic person – someone who, because of his social position, should have been duty-bound to know his place in life? How can one answer this question? Who knows, perhaps there are exceptions, of which my hero is an example. And he is indeed an exception to the rule, as will become clear later. Allow me, however, to ask: are you sure that those people who have totally humbled themselves and who consider it an honour and a matter of good fortune to be able to play the fool for you and ingratiatingly indulge your every request – are you sure that they have totally renounced all vanity? What about envy, or tittle-tattle, or double-crossing, or backbiting, or clandestine defamatory comments in the hidden corners of your house, somewhere right next to you, at your very table in fact?... Who knows, perhaps when it comes to some of these hapless misfits, to your buffoons and holy fools, vanity is not merely the result of humiliation, but becomes even more inflamed precisely because of this very humiliation, this playing the fool and buffoonery, this ingratiating behaviour and the constantly enforced obligation to serve others and suppress one's own personality. Who knows, perhaps such monstrously heightened vanity is merely the deceptive and initially distorted manifestation of a sense of one's own worth, a sense that might have first become humiliatingly apparent as a child, living maybe in circumstances marked by oppression, poverty, dirt – perhaps even become debased in the future outcast's parents themselves, in front of his very eyes. But, as I have already said, Foma Fomich was an exception to the general rule. And that was indeed the case. At one time he had embarked on a literary career and had been disappointed and rejected – but literature (rejected literature, naturally) can destroy the life of not only the Foma Fomiches of this world. I can't say for certain, but Foma Fomich's life could well already have been a failure even before his foray into literature – maybe, in whatever career he embarked upon, he received a slap in the face rather than a salary, or something even worse. I could of course be mistaken about this. But when I made some enquiries later, I found out for sure that Foma had indeed once produced a novel of sorts in Moscow, very similar to the kind of thing that was being concocted there every year during the Thirties by scores of people along the lines of such works as *The Liberation of Moscow*, *The Storm of the Atamans*, *The Sons of Love*, or *Russians in 1104*, etc. etc.* – novels which provided such tasty dishes for the wit of Baron Brambeus.* That was all a long time ago, of course, but the serpent of literary vanity sometimes has very sharp fangs that can inflict mortal wounds on people, especially on the worthless and the feeble-minded. Having been humiliated by his first venture into literature, Foma Fomich became at a stroke a member of that enormous legion of embittered people who are subsequently to emerge as holy fools, misfits and outcasts. That, I believe, was the moment that witnessed the beginning of his grotesque swollen-headedness, his craving to be acclaimed and distinguished from other people, to be admired and appreciated. Even as a clown he managed to surround himself with a whole clique of sycophantic idiots. Simply so that he could somehow, somewhere, behave as the dominant figure, act as the oracle, embroider a little and puff himself up – that, above all, was what he needed to do! If others didn't praise him, then he would set about praising himself. I can clearly remember what Foma said in my uncle's house in Stepanchikovo when he had already become the undisputed master and prophet. "I am not a lodger here," he would sometimes cryptically and portentously say, "not a lodger at all! I will see what needs to be done, set you all to rights, show you and teach you everything, and then *adieu*: I'm off to Moscow, to publish a journal. Thirty thousand people will throng to my lectures every month. I will become famous, and then... woe to my enemies!" But his genius, even before its fame had become fully established, demanded an immediate reward. If it is gratifying in general to receive a payment in advance, in this case it was especially so. I know that he assured my uncle in all seriousness that he, Foma, was destined to perform an extraordinarily great feat, a feat for which he had been summoned to this world and which he was being urged to accomplish by some winged figure who appeared to him at night, or something of the sort. And the feat? To write a work of particular significance of a spiritually uplifting nature that would hit everywhere like a thunderclap and confound all Russia. And once Russia had been confounded, then he, Foma, brushing aside any thought of glory, would go to a monastery and spend night and day in the Kievan caves* praying for the salvation of his motherland. My uncle, naturally, found this all deeply impressive.

And now picture to yourself what is going to become of Foma, the man who has spent all his life downtrodden and cowed, even perhaps actually beaten into submission – Foma, the secretively libidinous and arrogant Foma; Foma, the embittered literary figure; the Foma forced into buffoonery for the sake of a crust of bread; Foma who was at heart a despot, notwithstanding all his aforementioned worthlessness; Foma the bragger, whose boasting turns to insolence whenever he actually achieves anything; Foma who has suddenly fallen upon honour and glory, who is nurtured and praised to the skies thanks to his idiot benefactress and his enthralled, always obliging benefactor, in whose house he has finally found shelter after long years of rootless drifting. I shall of course need to say more about my uncle in greater detail – otherwise Foma Fomich's success becomes incomprehensible. But for now I shall merely comment that Foma is a perfect illustration of the old proverb "Seat someone down at a table and he will put his foot on it." And he certainly more than made up for his past! Weak, worthless characters who have been tyrannized will always go on to tyrannize others. Foma had been tyrannized, so he immediately felt the urge to tyrannize others; he had been bullied, so he himself began to bully others; he had been a clown, so he too immediately felt the need to be surrounded by his own coterie of clowns. He was an incredible braggart, an unbelievable swank, someone who demanded the impossible and who terrorized others so overbearingly that any decent, God-fearing people who had never witnessed any such behaviour for themselves and only heard accounts of it looked on it all as some inexplicable phenomenon, crossed themselves and spat with disgust whenever they heard his name.

I have already said something about my uncle. I repeat: without attempting to shed some light on this remarkable character, Foma Fomich's achievement in rising to such dominant heights of insolence in someone else's household and his metamorphosis from clown to a person of considerable stature can never be understood. To say that my uncle was an astonishingly kind-hearted man is only the half of it: belying his rather rugged outward appearance, he was a man of the most delicate sensitivity, the most exalted nobility of soul and of tried-and-tested courage. I do not hesitate to use the word "courage": he never shirked his duties or responsibilities, no matter what obstacles lay in his way. Spiritually, he had the innocence of a child. Indeed, he was a forty-year-old child, exuberant to the highest degree, always in good spirits, seeing everyone as angels, accusing himself of possessing other people's faults and exaggerating other people's good qualities to an extreme extent, even attributing them when they didn't exist. He was one of those most generous and at heart most incorruptible people who are even ashamed to see any bad in others and who are quick to endow their fellow creatures with all the virtues, to rejoice at other people's successes, and who therefore live in an ideal world, seeing themselves above all as responsible for any failures. Such people regard it as their life work to sacrifice their own interests for the sake of others. There are some who might have seen my uncle as spineless, weak, lacking in character. He *was* weak, of course, and definitely too soft-hearted, but it wasn't because of any lack of courage and determination, but because he was afraid of giving offence, of acting harshly. This stemmed from a disproportionate respect for others and for mankind in general. If, moreover, he was weak and lacking in character, it was solely insofar as his own personal interests were concerned, of which he was extremely dismissive – something for which he was mocked throughout his life, often even by those people for whom he sacrificed his own interests. He never, however, believed he had any enemies, even though they did in fact exist: somehow he never seemed to be aware of them. He feared any untoward noise and shouting in his house like the plague, and immediately gave way to everyone else, always doing whatever he was told. He would yield to others out of a self-effacing kind-heartedness: "All I want," he would say, brushing aside any suggestion of partiality or weakness, "all I want… is for everyone to be content and happy!" It goes without saying that he was always willing to agree with any noble cause – meaning of course that any cunning reprobate could completely hoodwink him and even lure him into doing something wrong, naturally masking it as a good deed. My uncle was an extraordinarily gullible man, and in this he was certainly not faultless. But even when, after much agonizing, he finally concluded that the person who had deceived him was dishonest, he would first of all blame himself, and very often no one but himself. Now, picture to yourself the sudden arrival in his quiet household of a domineering, wilful and totally scatty idiot of a woman in league with another idiot, her idol – a woman who hitherto had been afraid only of her general, and who now was afraid of nothing and felt the need to make up for everything that had happened in the past – an idiot of a woman whom my uncle considered it his duty to revere, if only for the fact she was his mother. They both began by immediately impressing on my uncle that he was vulgar, intolerant and ignorant – and, above all, to the highest degree selfish. Remarkably, the idiotic old woman actually believed what she preached. What's more, I think Foma Fomich did so as well, at least partly. Between them they succeeded in convincing my uncle that Foma had been sent down by God in order to save his soul and to suppress his unbridled passions – and that he, my uncle, was an arrogant man who flaunted his wealth and who was perfectly capable of accusing Foma Fomich of abusing his position simply for a crust of bread. My poor uncle very quickly became convinced just how far he had fallen from grace, and was ready to tear out his hair and ask for forgiveness...

"You see, my good fellow," he would say to one of his acquaintances, "it's all my fault! You have to be doubly considerate to someone who is beholden to you... that is... what am I on about? Beholden to me indeed... I'm talking nonsense again! He's not beholden to me at all. Just the contrary: *I'm* beholden to *him*, simply for the fact that he's staying here, with me, in this house! And I resented him living here for free!... That is to say, I never resented him at all, it was just a slip of the tongue – that often happens with me... Anyway, the long and short of it is that the man has had a difficult life, but has nevertheless managed to achieve so much; he spent ten years caring for a sick friend, regardless of the many insults he received along the way; all so deserving of a reward! And then he's such an erudite man... a writer! So educated! In short, the noblest of souls..."

The image of Foma as an erudite and unhappy man, once a clown to a capricious and heartless master, filled my uncle's generous heart with pity and a sense of anger. My uncle quickly explained away all Foma's meanness and quirky behaviour, saying it was a result of what he'd had to go through, of his resentment at having been humiliated... In his compassionate and generous soul he immediately arrived at the conclusion that someone who had suffered in life should be viewed differently from a normal person; that one should not only forgive such a person, but, in addition, set out to heal his wounds with gentleness and consideration, to restore him and reconcile him with the rest of humanity. Once he had set himself this task, he became passionately and excessively fired with enthusiasm for the idea, yet at the same time totally unable to understand that his new friend was no more than a lascivious, capricious, selfish, idle and lazy brute. He nevertheless believed implicitly in Foma's erudition and genius. I should say here at this point that my uncle reacted to the very mention of the words "science" or "literature" with a feeling of the most naive and disinterested awe, even though he himself had never studied anything.

That was one of his most striking and innocent traits.

"He's writing an article!" he would say, tiptoeing towards Foma's study, still as many as two rooms away. "No idea what it's about," he would add proudly with an air of mystery, "just some mash-up probably... that is, mash-up in the very best sense. Some people will understand what he's saying, but as far as you and I are concerned, my good fellow, it's just plain gibberish... Seems to be about some productive forces or other, so he said. Something political, no doubt. It'll make his name! And then, because of him, you and I will become famous. He told me so himself, my good fellow..."

I know for a fact that, on Foma's orders, my uncle was forced to shave off his magnificent reddish-brown side whiskers. Foma seemed to think that my uncle's side whiskers made him look like a Frenchman, and therefore unpatriotic. Little by little Foma began to interfere in the running of the estate and give people the benefit of his wisdom – with disastrous results. The serfs very quickly grasped what was what and who their real master was, leading to much scratching of heads. I myself later heard one conversation Foma Fomich had with the serfs, a conversation on which, I must confess, I eavesdropped. Foma had already let it be known how much he loved talking to an intelligent Russian peasant. One day he had gone onto the threshing floor and started lecturing the peasants on the management of the estate, even though he couldn't tell the difference between oats and wheat. Then, having suavely given his opinion concerning the sacred obligations of a serf towards his master, touching on the questions of electricity and the division of labour (about which of course he hadn't the faintest notion), and having explained to his listeners the manner in which the earth goes round the sun, totally enraptured by the force of his own eloquence, he turned to the subject of ministers of the Crown. I could understand that: after all, didn't Pushkin himself talk about a certain father who impressed on his four-year-old son that he, his father, was "such a brave man that the Tsar loved him"?* And didn't this demonstrate just how much this father needed a four-year-old listener? The serfs themselves hung slavishly on Foma Fomich's every word.

"So, master, did the Tsar pay you well?" one grey-haired old man, Arkhip Korotky by name, asked him suddenly, clearly attempting, among all those present, to ingratiate himself. But Foma Fomich found this question overfamiliar – something he couldn't abide.

"So what business is that of yours, you imbecile?" he replied, eyeing the poor man up and down with contempt. "And stop thrusting that ugly mug at me, or I'll spit on it."

Foma Fomich always adopted that tone when talking to "your shrewd Russian peasant".*

"But master," intervened another peasant, "we're an ignorant lot of people. You may be a major, or a colonel, or p'raps Your Highness – we don't know what to call you!"

"You imbecile!" Foma Fomich repeated, but now rather less harshly. "There are salaries and there are salaries, you blockhead! There are generals who don't get paid a thing – no point, because they're no use to the Tsar. But I used to be paid twenty thousand when I worked at the ministry, yet I didn't take a single copeck, because I served for the honour of it; in any case, I had sufficient money of my own. I used to give what I earned to state education and to the victims of the Kazan fire."*

"Well I never! So you helped to rebuild Kazan, master?"

The serfs' general feeling towards Foma Fomich was one of astonishment.

"Well yes, I did have a hand in that," Foma replied, as if reluctantly, seemingly annoyed with himself for condescending to talk on *such* matters with *such* an imbecile.

Conversations with my uncle took quite a different turn.

"So what kind of a person were you before?" Foma would ask, for example, as he sat spread out in the deceased general's chair after a substantial dinner, while a servant stood behind him fanning away the flies with a newly plucked lime branch. "I mean, what were you like before I came on the scene? But when I did, I lit that spark of divine fire which now blazes in your heart. Tell me, did I light that spark in you or not? Well, answer me: did I or didn't I?"

Truth to tell, Foma Fomich himself had no idea why he had asked such a question. But he became suddenly incensed by my uncle's lack of response and evident embarrassment. Once so self-effacing and downtrodden, he would now flare up like a tinderbox at the slightest affront. He found my uncle's silence highly insulting, and he would insist on an answer.

"Come on then, answer me: did you have a spark lit in you, or not?"

My uncle would hum and haw, not knowing which way to turn.

"Permit me to observe that I'm waiting for an answer," Foma remarked, thoroughly offended.

"*Mais répondez donc*,* Yegorushka!" the general's lady would interpose, with a shrug of her shoulders.

"I'm asking you: is there a spark alight in you or not?" Foma would repeat loftily, taking a sweet from the box which was always placed in front of him on the table. That was something the general's lady had ordered to be done.

"Really and truly I don't know, Foma," my uncle would answer finally, with a despairing look in his eyes. "It would really be better not to ask such things, otherwise I might admit to something I don't believe..."

"Right! I see... you think I'm such a worthless person that I don't even deserve an answer – is that what you mean? Well, let that be the case then – let me be a nobody."

"Of course not, Foma, Heaven forbid! Whenever have I said anything of the sort?"

"No, that is precisely what you meant."

"But I swear to you I didn't mean that!"

"Right, then! So I'm a liar, am I? So I'm someone who, according to you, deliberately sets out to pick a quarrel, am I? Doesn't matter what kind of insult, does it? I can put up with anything…"

"*Mais, mon fils…*"* shrieked the terrified general's lady.

"Foma Fomich! Mother!" my uncle exclaimed in despair. "Really and truly I'm not to blame! It was just a slip of the tongue, that's all!… Don't look at me like that, Foma: I know I'm stupid, I can feel how stupid I am – I can hear myself saying absurd things… I know, Foma, I know everything! You don't need to tell me!" he continued, with a dismissive wave of his hand. "I've been alive for forty years, and for the whole of that time, right up until I first got to know you, I've always thought of myself as someone who… you know, as someone quite normal. It had never crossed my mind, until now, what a wicked man, an unsurpassed egoist I am. I have done so many outrageous things it's a wonder the earth has been able to bear the weight of it all."

"Yes, that's right: you're such an egoist!" commented a now pacified Foma.

"And I realize that now myself! But enough! I will turn over a new leaf, and from now on I will be a much better person."

"May God grant that to be so!" Foma remarked, concluding the conversation with a pious sigh and getting up from his chair to take his postprandial nap. Foma Fomich always had a nap after the evening meal.

As a conclusion to this chapter of my story, permit me to say something in particular about my relationship with my uncle and to explain how it was I came to meet face to face with Foma Fomich and to become totally unexpectedly caught up in the maelstrom of the most momentous events that were ever to take place in the blessed village of Stepanchikovo. With this I will conclude my introduction and proceed directly to the telling of my story.

I was orphaned as a young child and quite alone in the world when my uncle took the place of my father, raising me at his expense and, in short, taking care of me in a way that even a real father might not have done. I became totally attached to him from the very first day he took me into his house. I was ten years old at the time, and I can remember us almost immediately forming a very special bond and arriving at a complete understanding of one another. We used to play games such as spinning tops together, and once stole a bonnet from one extremely tetchy old lady who was a relative of ours. I immediately tied the bonnet to the tail of a paper kite and launched it skywards. Many years later I briefly met my uncle in St Petersburg, where I was finishing my studies (for which he was paying). I was once again drawn towards him with the full fervour of youth: there was something about his nature – generous, unassuming, honourable and naive to a fault – that I found particularly striking and that cast everyone under his spell. After graduating I lived for a time in St Petersburg, for the moment unemployed and, as is so often the case with callow youth, convinced that in the not-so-distant future I was destined for remarkable, even great things. I didn't want to leave St Petersburg. I wrote to my uncle relatively rarely, and then only when I needed money – something that he never refused me. And then one of my uncle's house servants, who had come to St Petersburg on business, told me that, back in Stepanchikovo, astonishing things were going on. I was very intrigued and amazed by these first reports. I started writing to my uncle with greater care and attention. Whenever he replied, it was always in guarded and rather strange terms, referring in his letters merely to the sciences, saying how extraordinarily much he was expecting of me in the field of learning and expressing his pride in my future achievements. Suddenly, after a fairly lengthy period of silence, I received an extraordinary letter from him, quite unlike anything he had sent before. It was replete with such weird insinuations, such a mass of contradictions, that at first I had no idea what he was talking about. All that was obvious was that the writer had been in a highly unusual state of alarm. There was one point, however, that was absolutely clear: my uncle was in all seriousness suggesting, practically imploring, that I get married as soon as possible to one of his former wards, the daughter of

an impoverished provincial civil servant named Yezhevikin; she
had received an excellent education in a Moscow boarding school
at my uncle's expense, and had now become a governess to his
children. He told me that she was unhappy, that I could make her
happy, that I would even be performing a noble act, appealing
to my generosity of heart and promising to provide her with a
dowry. With regard to the dowry, however, he spoke in rather veiled
and anxious terms, concluding his letter by entreating me not to
breathe a single word about any of it. I found the whole letter so
astonishing that by the end of it my head had begun to spin. And,
indeed, how could such a romantic-sounding proposition not have
an effect on a young man such as me, someone just beginning to
make his way in the world? And besides, I had heard that the young
governess in question was extremely attractive. Although I had
no idea what my decision would be, I nevertheless wrote to my
uncle telling him I would set off for Stepanchikovo immediately. In
this same letter, my uncle had enclosed the money for the journey.
Despite that, I was sufficiently doubtful and anxious about the
whole idea to delay matters for three weeks before finally leaving
St Petersburg. And then, suddenly, I chanced to come across one
of Uncle's former colleagues, who had called in at Stepanchikovo
while on his way back from the Caucasus to St Petersburg. He was
an elderly, down-to-earth man, a lifelong bachelor. He spoke of
Foma Fomich with considerable indignation, informing me of one
circumstance which was entirely new to me: that Foma Fomich and
the general's lady had thought up the idea of marrying my uncle
off to one extremely eccentric, almost half-witted lady well past
her prime, with an unconventional background and a dowry of
close on half a million; that the general's lady had already been
able to convince her that they were related, thereby luring her to
come and live with them; that although my uncle, of course, was
in a state of despair about it all, it seemed that it would end with
him getting married on account of the half-million dowry; and
that, finally, those two brilliant people, Foma Fomich and the general's lady, had begun a terrible campaign of persecution against

my uncle's children's poor, defenceless governess, straining every sinew to get her out of the house, no doubt afraid that he might fall in love with her – might, indeed, already have fallen in love with her. I found this last possibility very concerning. And yet, however much I tried to find out whether my uncle had truly fallen in love, the man could not or did not want to give me a precise answer, and had generally spoken rather tersely and reluctantly, noticeably unwilling to go into any more detailed explanation. It left me with a great deal to think about: the news was so strangely at variance with my uncle's letter and his proposal… But there was no time to be lost. I resolved to go to Stepanchikovo, wishing not only to knock some sense into my uncle and put his mind at rest, but even to rescue him as best I could – that is, to drive Foma out of the house, to call a halt to the hated marriage with the elderly lady and, finally – since, in my considered view, the idea of my uncle being in love was merely a figment of Foma's pernicious imagination – to bring happiness to the unfortunate but highly desirable young lady by offering her my hand in marriage, etc., etc. Little by little I became so inspired and carried away by the idea that, having nothing to do and being still such a young man, I leapt from doubt to its absolute opposite: I was now consumed by the desire to perform all kinds of wondrous deeds. I even felt that in so nobly sacrificing myself for the sake of an innocent and charming creature I would be demonstrating my exceptional magnanimity – in short, I spent the whole journey congratulating myself. It was June; the sun was shining brightly; all around me I could see fields of ripening corn extending as far as the horizon… I had spent so long cooped up in St Petersburg that I seemed to be looking at God's earth properly for the first time in my life!

2

Mr Bakhcheyev

I was already approaching the end of my journey. While passing through the little town of B——, only some six or so miles from Stepanchikovo, I was forced to stop at the smithy, close to the town gate, as the rim on one of the front wheels of my tarantass had broken. Since only a temporary repair would be needed for such a short distance, it wouldn't take very long. I therefore decided to wait where I was while the men got on with their work. Getting out of my tarantass, I spotted a rather large gentleman who, just like me, had been forced to stop for repairs to his carriage. He had already been standing in the intolerable heat for a whole hour, shouting and cursing and urging on the workmen, who were bustling around his impressive carriage, with exasperated impatience. I only needed to take one look at this gentleman to see what an extraordinarily ill-tempered man he was. He was about forty-five years old, of medium height, very plump and with a pockmarked face. His sizeable belly, prominent Adam's apple and puffy, baggy cheeks all spoke of the pampered life of a country landowner. I was immediately struck by his rather womanish manner. He was neatly dressed in loose-fitting, but not at all fashionable, clothes.

For some reason, he was angry with me too – no idea why, since he had never seen me before in his life or, indeed, spoken a single word to me. I was aware of his unusually angry looks as soon as I stepped out of my tarantass. And yet I nonetheless really wanted to make his acquaintance. From what his servants were saying I deduced he had just come from Stepanchikovo, from my uncle's estate. I started raising my cap and remarking with all due civility what a nuisance it was sometimes to have to delay one's journey, but the plump gentleman rather reluctantly looked me up and down with a displeased and grumpy expression, muttered something to himself and deliberately turned his large, solid-looking back on me. While this part of his anatomy may well have been of considerable visual interest, it offered of course no prospect of any pleasant conversation.

"Grishka! Stop muttering to yourself like that! You'll get yourself a thrashing!" he suddenly yelled at his valet, as if he hadn't heard my remark about delaying one's journey at all.

This "Grishka" was a grey-haired, elderly servant, dressed in a long frock coat and sporting a pair of very imposing side whiskers. From the expression on his face he too was in quite a temper, and he was muttering something angrily under his breath. An argument between master and servant immediately ensued.

"Go ahead and give me a thrashing, then! You old windbag!" muttered Grishka as if to himself, but loud enough for everyone to hear. And he turned away irritably to rearrange something in the carriage.

"What's that? What did you say? 'You old windbag'?... Want to be insolent, do you?" the fat man yelled, growing purple in the face.

"Why are you flying off the handle like that, might I ask? Can't say a word!"

"Why am *I* flying off the handle? Never heard the like! *You're* the one griping at me – why should I gripe at you?"

"So why should I gripe at you?"

"What do you mean?... So you think you haven't been griping, do you? It's perfectly obvious why: it's because I left before we'd had any dinner – that's why."

"Why should I care about that? I wouldn't care if you never had any dinner. I'm not griping at you – I was just having a word with the smiths."

"The smiths?... What, gripe at them?"

"No, not at them – at the carriage."

"What's the matter with the carriage?"

"Well, why's it broken down? Shouldn't have done that, should it? Make sure you don't do that again!"

"At the carriage... No, you're having a go at me, not the carriage at all. He's the one who's at fault, and yet he's blaming someone else!"

"Stop picking on me, will you, sir? Just leave me alone!"

"Why did you have to sit there like that the whole way here, with a face as black as thunder, not saying a word to me? You just can't keep your mouth shut, can you?"

"A fly flew into my mouth – that was why I simply sat there looking like that. What do you want me to do? Tell you fairy tales or something? Get yourself a nanny to tell you fairy tales, if you're so fond of them!"

The fat man opened his mouth, about to answer back, but said nothing, evidently at a loss for words. For his part, his servant, delighted with his command of the language and the fact that he had been able to demonstrate his power over his master in the presence of witnesses, turned back to the workmen with a redoubled sense of importance and began showing them what to do.

My attempts to introduce myself remained fruitless, partly as a result, no doubt, of my awkwardness, but something quite unforeseen came to my aid: suddenly a sleepy-looking, dirty, unwashed face with a shock of uncombed hair appeared in the window of an old, enclosed coach cab that had been standing, without any wheels, in the smithy since time immemorial, waiting day after day, in vain, to be repaired. At the sight of this face all the workmen burst into laughter. It transpired that the man looking out of the cab window had found himself locked firmly in the cab, unable to get out. Having spent the night there in a drunken state, he was now begging to be released. Finally, he asked someone to go and fetch him his tools. Everyone found the whole matter extraordinarily amusing.

There are people who find the strangest things especially pleasurable. The faces made by a drunken peasant, someone tripping over in the street, two women having a row about something, etc., etc. – for some reason such things seem to provoke the most good-natured hilarity in some people. The fat landowner was just such a person. The morose and louring expression on his face was gradually transformed into something much more mellow and cordial, until he was finally positively beaming.

"That can't be Vasilyev, can it?" he asked with a concerned tone. "What on earth's he doing there?"

"He's on a bender, sir," explained one of the workmen, a tall, gaunt, elderly man, with a severe, rather portentous expression on his face, clearly seeing himself as superior to the rest of them. "Went on a bender, sir, left his master a couple of days ago and hid himself away here ever since – been a right pest! Now he's asking us for a chisel. What do you want a chisel for now, you idiot? He'd pawn his last tool for money!"

"Oh, Arkhipushka, money's here one minute and the next it's gone – flown away like a bird. Let me out, for Heaven's sake!" Vasilyev implored in a thin, high-pitched voice, his head poking out of the carriage.

"Once you're there, you prize chump, you might as well stay there!" Arkhip replied severely. "Been on the bottle for two days now; he was dragged here from the street early this morning; we were able to hide him, thank the Lord, telling Matvei Ilyich he'd been taken ill, saying he'd been laid low by 'these stabbing pains'."

Everyone burst out laughing again.

"Yes, but where's my chisel?"

"Our Zuy's got it! Just listen to him! Off his head with drink as usual, Stepan Alexeich, sir!"

"Ha-ha-ha! What a scoundrel! So this is what you've been up to in town: pawning your tools!" the fat man wheezed, choking with laughter, now totally content, his mood suddenly transformed into one of extraordinary geniality.

"As a craftsman, you won't find a better one this side of Moscow! That's what he always says about himself, at any rate, the rogue," he added, turning to me totally unexpectedly. "Let him out, Arkhip; he may need something."

They did as their master said. The nail they had banged into the carriage door, mainly to have a bit of fun at Vasilyev's expense when he woke up, was removed, and a dirty, unkempt and ragged-looking Vasilyev emerged into the light of day. Blinking from the sun, he sneezed and swayed unsteadily on his feet. Then, shielding his eyes from the sun, he took a look around him.

"Goodness, so many people!" he said, with a shake of his head. "And all per-fect-ly sober, it seems," he continued pensively, dragging out his words as if reproaching himself. "So, lads, good morning, top of the morning to you!"

General laughter once again.

"'Top of the morning'! Can't you see how late it is already, you imbecile?"

"Tell us another one!"

"For me, an hour's as good as a day."

"Ha-ha-ha! What a windbag!" the fat man shouted, doubled up with laughter once more, and again giving me a friendly look. "Aren't you ashamed of yourself, Vasilyev?"

"I've had some bad news, Stepan Alexeich... bad news," Vasilyev answered with a wave of his hand, putting all joking aside – clearly glad of the opportunity to bring up the subject of his misfortune.

"What bad news is that, you idiot?"

"Never known nothing like it: Foma Fomich's to be our new owner."

"Who? When?" the fat man shouted, now extremely agitated.

I took a step forward as well: this was a matter that directly concerned me.

"Well, all the Kapitonovka people. Our master, the colonel, may God bless him, wants to hand over the entire Kapitonovka estate, all the ancestral lands, to Foma Fomich – no less than seventy serfs in all. 'There you are, Foma,' he says, 'you've hardly got a thing – a couple of little fish in Lake Ladoga, so to speak – that's all the workforce you inherited from your father. And your father himself,'" Vasilyev went on, as if maliciously seizing on the chance to have a dig at anything concerning Foma Fomich, "'your father inherited an estate, no one knows where, or who from, but he too, like you, had to beg for a living, making do on scraps in the kitchens of his lords and masters. But now, when I hand over Kapitonovka to you, you too will become a landowner, an entitled nobleman, with your very own serfs, and you will be able to live a life of luxury, enjoying your estate…'"

But Stepan Alexeyevich was no longer listening. He had been extraordinarily affected by Vasilyev's semi-inebriated story. The fat man was so irritated that he had even turned purple in the face. His Adam's apple shook, his little eyes became bloodshot. It looked as if he was going to have a stroke at any moment.

"That's all I need!" he said, catching his breath. "That good-for-nothing, useless parasite, Foma, becoming a landowner! My God! You can go to hell, the lot of you! Hey, you – get a move on! We're going home!"

"If I might ask," I began to say, hesitantly taking a step forward, "you said something about Foma Fomich just now; his surname, I think, is Opiskin, if I'm not mistaken. You see, I would like to… in short, I have my own special reasons to be interested in this person, and, for my part, I would really like to know how far one can believe what this good man is saying – that his lord and master, Yegor Ilyich Rostanev, wishes to hand over one of his villages to Foma Fomich. I find this extremely interesting, and I—"

"And might I ask you in turn," the fat man interrupted, "why exactly you should be so interested in this person, as you put it? As far as I'm concerned, he shouldn't be called a person at all, but a damned scoundrel! He has the face of a louse, not a human being! Just a walking disgrace, not a person!"

I commented that I was as yet unacquainted with his appearance, but that Yegor Ilyich Rostanev happened to be my uncle, and that my own name was Sergei Alexandrovich Such-and-Such.

"Ah, you must be the man of learning! But good God, they're so looking forward to seeing you!" shouted the fat man, genuinely overjoyed. "I've just come from there myself, from Stepanchikovo; I was having dinner there, but got up and left during the dessert – couldn't stand the sight of Foma a moment longer! Almost came to blows with everyone because of that blasted little man…

Fancy meeting you! You must forgive me, my good sir. My name is Stepan Alexeich Bakhcheyev, and I can remember you when you were this height... Well, who would have thought?... If you will allow me..."

And the fat man reached out to give me a warm embrace.

After the initial moments of excitement, I immediately proceeded to ask questions: there would never be a better opportunity to do so.

"But who *is* this Foma?" I asked. "How has he managed to take over the entire household? Why hasn't he been chased away with a broom? I must confess—"

"Chase Foma away? Have you gone off your head? With the colonel, Yegor Ilyich, obeying his every whim? One week, you know, Foma decreed that the Thursday should be a Wednesday, and they all, without exception, agreed that that Thursday would be a Wednesday. 'I don't want it to be Thursday today, so let it be Wednesday!' So that week there were two Wednesdays. You think I'm making this up? Not a bit of it! Even Captain Cook couldn't have managed that!"

"Yes, I did hear something about that, and yet I must admit—"

"Admit... admit! The things people say! What's the point of admitting? No, you'd be better off asking me questions. You wouldn't believe everything I told you – although I could certainly tell you what forests I came through to get here. Let's take the colonel's mother: a very worthy lady, no doubt, the wife of a general to boot, but, in my opinion, she's gone totally out of her mind: she absolutely adores Fomka, may he be thrice accursed. She's the one to blame for it all: it was because of her that he was able to establish himself in the household. He's so bamboozled her with his erudition that she can no longer speak for herself – even though she has the title of 'Your Excellency' and leapt into fame by getting married to General Krakhotkin! As for Yegor Ilyich's sister, Praskovya Ilyinichna, who has been an old maid for forty years, I really don't want to say anything about her. Oohing and ahing the whole time, clucking away like a hen – she bores me stiff... well, to hell with her! The only thing in her favour, I suppose, is the fact that she's a woman – and people are supposed to respect her just because of that! Pouf! I should hold my tongue: she is your aunt, after all. There's just one person of any worth there, and that's Alexandra Yegorovna, the colonel's daughter. She may still be a little thing, only fifteen years old, but she's brighter than any of them, in my opinion. She has no respect for Foma at all – it was such fun to see them together! Such a sweet girl! And what is there about him to respect? After all, Foma simply acted as a buffoon for the general, pretending to be wild animals! But where Vanya plays the fool, he has now begun to rule. And the colonel, your uncle, looks up to this retired clown as if he were his own father, setting him up on a pedestal, the crook, and grovelling in his presence – when he's nothing but a sponger in your uncle's household! Good God!"

"Poverty is not a crime, however... and... I have to say... if I might ask, is he perhaps handsome, or clever?"

"Foma?! Handsome?" Bakhcheyev replied, his voice quivering with an especial kind of malice. (He was finding my questions irritating, and he had already begun to regard me with some suspicion.) "Handsome! Do you hear that, everyone? He thinks he's found a handsome prince! He is actually like a wild animal, my good sir, if you would really like to know. Wouldn't be so bad if he had a head on his shoulders, if he had a scrap of wit about him, the rascal – if he had, then I'd perhaps hold my nose and accept him for what he was, but there's nothing there at all, a complete blank! He's a quack who's simply drugged everyone with something or other! That's quite enough of that, damn it! Let's just spit at him, and leave it at that. You've put me out of sorts, my dear sir, with your questions! Hey, you! Are you done or not?"

"Blackie needs reshoeing," Grigory said morosely.

"Blackie. I'll give you Blackie!... Yes, sir, I could tell you things that would make you gasp, and you'd stand there with your mouth open until doomsday. I myself, you know, used to respect him. You don't believe me? I admit it, admit quite openly that I was an idiot

– he bamboozled me as well. What a know-all! Knew absolutely everything, mastered all the sciences! Used to give me drops – I'm a sick man, you see, my good fellow, a bit overweight. Believe it or not, I'm not well. Anyway, those drops of his knocked me out cold. No, don't say anything – just listen! When you get there, you'll be able to see everything for yourself. He'll have the colonel weeping tears of blood – yes, that's what he'll make the colonel do, but it will already be too late. The whole neighbourhood is now shunning them because of Foma, damn him to hell. Anyone who shows his face in the house gets roundly abused. What do I care if that includes me? Even top-notch people get the same treatment! Everyone is subjected to a sermon. He's become obsessed with morality, the scoundrel. 'I'm wiser than anyone,' he says. 'You have to listen to me, and only me.' 'I am,' he says, 'a man of learning.' Well, so what if you are? Does that mean you have to make life hell for anyone who's not very learned?… And you should hear how he bangs on and on with that learned tongue of his… blah, blah, blah, blah, blah, blah! Such a chatty tongue that, if you were to cut it off and toss it into a dung heap, it would carry on and on chattering away, until the crows pecked it up. The conceit of the man! As puffed-up as a mouse in a granary! Totally out of his depth. What do you think? He's now had the idea of teaching the servants French! Yes, really! 'It will do that ignorant boor of a servant good!' he says. Heavens above! He's nothing but a barefaced scoundrel! I ask you: why on earth should a peasant need to know French? Why would any of us want to be able to speak French, for that matter? So that we could canoodle with young ladies dancing the mazurka? Prance about with other people's wives? Sheer debauchery! That's what I think of your French language! You can speak French, too, I should imagine: lah-di-dah, lah-di-dah! Hey diddle, diddle, the cat and the fiddle…" Bakhcheyev added, giving me a withering look. "You're a man of culture, aren't you, my dear fellow? Eh? Know a few things, don't you?"

"Well, yes… I suppose so, one or two."

"Mastered all the sciences, no doubt?"

"Yes... I mean, no... I have to confess I'm more of an observer at the moment. I've been in St Petersburg all this time and am now hurrying to see my uncle..."

"But who enticed you to do that? You should have stayed where you were, wherever that may have been! No, my dear chap, your learning won't be of much use here, I tell you, and that uncle of yours won't be of any help – you'll find yourself trapped! Take me: I lost weight, after just one night there. Well, do you believe me when I say I lost weight? No, I can see you don't. Well, see if I care: don't believe me, then."

"No, my dear sir, of course I believe you – it's just that I still don't understand," I replied, becoming more and more confused.

"Yes, I believe, no, I don't believe! You're like butterflies, all you brainy types: you just need to flash your wings to show off! Can't abide all that brainy stuff myself, my dear fellow! I know you St Petersburg types: what an immoral bunch! Freemasons, the lot of them; spread their atheist views, scared of a drop of vodka: they think it might bite them... I ask you! You've made me cross, my dear fellow, and I don't want to tell you a thing! After all, I'm not actually obliged to tell you anything, am I? In any case, I'm tired of talking to you. You can't find fault with everybody, my dear chap – anyway, shame on you for doing so... I think you should know that your uncle's valet, Vidoplyasov, has been turned into practically an idiot by your man of science! He's gone off his head, has Vidoplyasov, thanks to Foma Fomich."

"Well, I'd take this Vidoplyasov," put in Grigory, who up to this point had been listening respectfully to the conversation in strict silence, "I'd take him and give him a proper hiding. If I'd bumped into him I'd have knocked all that idiotic German nonsense out of him! I'd have given him such a walloping he wouldn't know what had hit him."

"Keep quiet! Just hold your tongue, will you? Nobody asked for your opinion!"

"Vidoplyasov," I said, now totally confused, not knowing what to say. "Vidoplyasov... that's an odd name, isn't it?"

"What's odd about it? What are you on about, you egghead?"
At that I lost my patience.

"Excuse me," I said, "but why are you getting so angry with me? What have I done wrong, for Heaven's sake? I have to say I've been listening to you for a whole half-hour, and I've no idea what you're talking about…"

"But you don't need to take offence like that, my dear chap," the fat man replied. "No need at all! I'm talking to you as a friend. I can see you're thinking I do nothing but shout at people – I've just had a go at my Grigory here, for example. He may be an absolute wretch, my Grishka, but that's precisely what I love about him, the scoundrel. Too kind-hearted: that's the trouble with me. And it's all Foma's fault! He'll be the ruin of me – I swear he will! It's his fault that I've been baking here in the sun now for two hours. I wanted to drop in on the archdeacon while these idiots were fiddling about with their repairs. First-class fellow, that archdeacon. But that Foma has so upset me I never want to go and see him again! To hell with them, every last one! There isn't even a decent innkeeper around here. They're all absolute scoundrels, I tell you, the lot of them! Now, if he had some sort of important rank," Mr Bakhcheyev continued, reverting to the subject of Foma Fomich, evidently unable to drive him from his mind, "then that at least would be something… but he hasn't got any sort of rank, even the most miserable one* – I know that for a fact. True, he says that some while back, in the '40s, he went through a bad time, for which we're supposed to bow down and grovel to him! Good God! At the drop of a hat he'll be up on his feet, yelling he's been insulted because of his poverty, and not being shown the respect he's due. Don't anyone dare sit down at table before Foma puts in an appearance… but then he doesn't come himself. 'You have insulted me,' he says, 'me, a poverty-stricken, homeless vagabond, reduced to eating a crust of bread.' Then, no sooner has everyone sat down than he appears. Once again the violin starts sawing away: 'How dare you sit down at table without me! It shows you have no regard for me at all.' In a word, such a merry occasion! As for me, my dear chap, I kept quiet, not saying anything for ages. He thought I would dance in front of him like a dog on its hind legs! You can think what you like, my friend! No, you may have your hand on the bridle, but I'm sitting in the cart! I served in the same regiment as Yegor Ilyich, you know. I retired still a cadet, but he carried on until last year, when he inherited the estate as a colonel. So I say to him: 'Come on, you're destroying yourself – stop pandering to Foma! You'll regret it!' 'No,' he replies, 'he's the most wonderful man (Foma, that is!), he's my friend – he tells me how I should behave.' Well, I think, you can't argue against that, can you? Once you've started to teach people how they should behave, that's the end of the matter. And what do you think today's excitement was? Tomorrow is St Ilya's Day, the day of Elijah the Prophet" – as he said this, Bakhcheyev crossed himself – "the name day, that is, of your uncle's son, little Ilyusha. I was thinking I'd spend the day there, and at dinner give Ilyusha the present I'd ordered from the capital: a clockwork German kissing his bride's hand with her wiping away a tear with a handkerchief – wonderful little piece! But I can't give it to him now: out of the question! Look, it's lying there in the carriage, with the nose broken off. I'm going to take it back. Yegor Ilyich himself wanted to mark the day with a little celebration, but Foma was against the idea: 'Why,' he said, 'why are you bothering about Ilyusha? You're ignoring me again, aren't you?' What about that, eh? Begrudging an eight-year-old lad his name-day celebration! 'That's not right,' he says. 'It's my name day too!' But it will be St Ilya's Day and not Foma's! 'No,' he says, 'it's my name day as well!' Here I am observing all this as patiently as I can. And what do you think happens? There they all are walking about on tiptoe and whispering to each other. Should they congratulate Foma on St Ilya's Day or not? Not to do so would possibly be to insult him, while to do so would possibly make them appear ridiculous. To hell with it! An absolute disaster! We sat down to dinner... Are you listening to me, my dear fellow?"

"Yes I am listening, really – I'm absolutely riveted by what you're saying, because, thanks to you, I now know... and... I must confess—"

"'Riveted', you say? You and your 'riveted'! You're not saying that just to make fun of me, I trust, are you?"

"Make fun of you? For goodness' sake! As if I would do that! In any case, you have... such an unusual way of expressing yourself that I'd like to make a note of it all."

"What do you mean, my dear fellow, 'make a note of it all'?" asked Mr Bakhcheyev in some alarm, eyeing me suspiciously.

"Well, maybe not 'make a note of it all'... it was just a figure of speech."

"You're not trying to get me to say something, by any chance, are you?"

"What on earth do you mean, 'get you to say something'?" I asked in astonishment.

"Just that. You're trying to bamboozle me into telling you everything, like some prize idiot, and you'll write it all down and then put it in some journal or other."

Although I immediately hastened to assure Mr Bakhcheyev that I wasn't that sort of person at all, he continued to eye me suspiciously.

"I see, 'not that sort of person', eh? But I don't know you, do I? Maybe that's not the half of it: Foma's threatened to write something about me and publish it as well."

"If I might ask," I interrupted, wishing partly to change the subject, "can you tell me if it's true that my uncle wishes to get married?"

"Well, what if he is? Nothing wrong with that. Let him get married, if that's what he wants to do. That's not the problem, however..." Mr Bakhcheyev added pensively. "Hmm... I can't really give you a satisfactory answer to that. All kinds of womenfolk are clustering there, like bees buzzing round a honeypot – no idea which of them is the marrying kind. But let me tell you quite openly, as a friend: I don't like women! The only thing they have going for them is that they're human, but actually they're nothing but a disgrace, a pernicious influence on your soul. But that your uncle is head over heels in love, like some Siberian cat, there can be absolutely no doubt. But for now, my dear fellow, I'll say no more: you'll be able to see for yourself, but it's not at all a good sign that he keeps on putting it off. If you want to get married, then get on with it, I say. But he's afraid to tell Foma, afraid to tell the old lady – she'll take Foma's side and start screeching at everyone and kicking up a mighty fuss. 'What!' she'll say. 'Foma Fomich will be really upset if there's a wife in the household!' Of course he'd be upset, since he wouldn't last for more than a couple of hours there. She, this new wife, would grab him by the scruff of the neck and, if she had any sense at all, give him such a boot up the behind he wouldn't dare to show his face anywhere in the district again! So he and Mother are scheming to fob him off on some other woman… But why did you interrupt me, my dear chap? I was just getting to my most important point when you go and interrupt me! I'm older than you – you shouldn't interrupt an old man…"

I apologized.

"No need to apologize! I simply wanted you, as a man of learning, to judge the extent to which he insulted me today. So tell me what you think, as a fair-minded man. There we were, sitting down to dinner, and there and then he goes and literally gobbles me up, I tell you, my dear chap! It's clear from the very start that he's so angry he's practically boiling with rage; he'd drown me in a spoonful of water if he could, the snake! The man's so vain he can barely contain himself! Anyway, he decides to pick on me and begins lecturing me on good behaviour. Why, he asks, am I so fat? Starts nagging me: 'Why are you fat and not thin?' Well, tell me, my dear chap, what sort of a question is that? Is there anything remotely logical about it? So I answer him perfectly reasonably: 'That's the way God made me, Foma Fomich: one man's fat, the next one's thin. We mortals have to accept whatever benign Providence decides.' Pretty good, eh? What do you think? 'Not at all,' he says. 'You own five hundred serfs, you have everything provided for, but you are of no use to your country. You should get yourself some government job, yet all you do is sit about and play your harmonium.' And it's true: whenever I'm a little out of sorts, I do like to tootle on my harmonium. Anyway, I once again come up with quite a sensible answer: 'What government job, Foma Fomich? What uniform would fit such a fat body? What if I were to squeeze myself into a uniform and then sneeze? Well, all the buttons would fly off, possibly in the presence of important people, and, God forbid, they'd take it as an insult. What then?' So tell me, my dear chap, there was nothing so hilarious about that, was there? But no, they start rolling about, giggling and cackling at my expense... so, he's totally lacking in any kind of decency, I tell you, and, what's more, he starts abusing me in French, calling me '*cochon*'.* Well, I happen to know what *cochon* means. 'Right,' I think, 'you damned boffin, so you think I'm an idiot, do you? I put up with it and put up with it, until I could take no more. I got up from the table, in front of all those good people and snapped: 'I must confess I've been totally wrong about you, Foma Fomich, my good man: I thought you were a cultured man with a good education, but it turns out, my friend, that you are just as much a swine as everyone else.' Having said that, I got up from the table, in the middle of the dessert they were just serving. 'To hell with your pudding!...'"

"Forgive me," I said, having heard everything Mr Bakhcheyev had to say, "I am of course prepared to agree with everything you say. But the main thing is that I still have very little idea what you're talking about... But, you must understand, I have just formed my own ideas on the subject."

"And what ideas might they be, my dear chap?" asked Mr Bakhcheyev distrustfully.

"Well, you see," I began in some confusion, "I may be talking out of turn here, but maybe you ought to know what I think. So, here we go. We may possibly both be mistaken about Foma Fomich: maybe all this strange behaviour is a mask for a very special, even gifted nature... who knows? Possibly we are talking about someone who has become embittered, having suffered so much in life that he's been broken, wishing to wreak his vengeance on all mankind. I've heard he was once something of a clown – maybe he felt humiliated, insulted, crushed by that?... A noble, generous soul, you see, very self-aware... and then suddenly he becomes a clown!... And so he comes to distrust mankind in general and... and perhaps, so as to reconcile himself with humanity... with people, that is... maybe, as a result, he would become a very special, even quite remarkable person, and... and... there must be something to him, after all, mustn't there? Surely there must be some reason why everyone idolizes him as they do?"

In short, I felt that I may have terribly let my tongue run away with me – something for which, as a young man, I might possibly have been forgiven. But Mr Bakhcheyev was not in a forgiving mood. Looking me straight in the eye with a serious and severe expression, he suddenly turned as purple as a turkey.

"That Foma a very special person?" he shouted.

"Look, I myself hardly believe in anything I've just said. It was simply an idea on my part..."

"Allow me, my dear fellow, to ask you a question out of sheer curiosity: have you, or have you not, studied philosophy?"

"In what sense do you mean?" I asked, nonplussed by this question.

"Never mind 'what sense'. Just answer my question, my dear fellow, directly, without worrying about the sense: have you studied philosophy or not?"

"I must confess, I intend to do so, but—"

"Right, I thought as much!" cried Mr Bakhcheyev, giving full rein to his sense of indignation. "Even before you opened your mouth, my dear fellow, I just knew you must have studied philosophy! Not a chance! You can't fool me! I can sniff out a philosopher a couple of miles away! Off you go and kiss your Foma Fomich! A 'remarkable fellow' indeed! Bah! To hell with the lot of you! There was

I thinking you were a sensible person, but it seems you… Right, then," he shouted to his coachman, who was clambering up onto the box of the newly repaired carriage. "Home!"

After a lot of effort I somehow managed to calm him down, and finally, somehow or other, he relented. But it was a long time before his anger gave way to a more amiable mood. By then he had already climbed into his carriage, with the assistance of Grigory and Arkhip – the person who had earlier rebuked Vasilyev.

"Might I ask," I said, going up to the carriage, "if you're intending never to go and see my uncle again?"

"Never see your uncle again? May he be cursed whoever put that idea into your head! Do you really think I'm the sort of person who sticks to his word, and that I'll not go back there? That's precisely my trouble: I'm actually a wet rag, and not a human being at all! I'll be dragging myself there again before the week's out. And why's that? I've absolutely no idea, but I will be going back and have a fight with Foma again. That, my dear chap, is the burden I have to bear! The good Lord has sent this Foma to me as a punishment for my sins. I'm like an old woman: no backbone at all! I'm such a coward, my dear fellow…"

In spite of all, we parted on friendly terms. He even invited me to have dinner with him.

"Please come, my dear man, come for dinner. I've got vodka that's walked all the way from Kiev, and my cook's been to Paris. The scoundrel will regale you with such wonderful *fines herbes*, such meat pies, that you'll be on your knees begging him for more. Such an educated man! I haven't flogged him for a long time now, been pampering him… thank you for reminding me of him… Please come! I would have invited you today, but I'm quite out of sorts today, I'm very feeble – can't move from exhaustion. I'm a sick man, you see, gone to seed. You don't believe me, perhaps… Anyway, goodbye, my dear fellow! It's time my boat set sail. There you are, you see: your tarantass is ready. And tell that Fomka he'd best stay clear of me, otherwise I'll give him such a welcome that he'll…"

But his final words were no longer audible. His carriage, drawn smoothly along by four powerful horses, disappeared in a cloud of dust. My own carriage was brought up; I got in and, within a flash, we had left the little town behind. "That man was exaggerating, of course," I thought. "He's too angry to be impartial. Yet everything he was saying about my uncle was so interesting. So now we have two people agreeing that he's in love with this girl... Hmm! Am I going to get married or not?" This really set me thinking.

3

My Uncle

I was, I must confess, a little apprehensive. As I drove into Stepanchikovo, my ideas of romantic love suddenly seemed to be really odd, even rather stupid. It was about five o'clock in the afternoon. The road ran along the garden of the manor house. Once again, after many years, I was seeing that enormous garden where I had spent a few brief days as a child and which had formed part of my dreams later, in the dormitories of the schools where I was being educated. I jumped out of the cab and set off straight across the garden towards the manor house. I was really anxious to arrive unnoticed, to find out things for myself, to elicit information on the sly and, most importantly, to have a full and frank conversation with my uncle. I was not to be disappointed. I walked along the avenue of ancient lime trees and came out onto the terrace, where a French window led into the house. The terrace was ringed by flowerbeds and brimming with pots of exotic plants. Here I met one of the servants, old Gavrila, who had looked after me when I was a child and who was now my uncle's valet. The old man was wearing glasses and clutching an exercise book, to which he kept on referring with particular attention. I had met him two years earlier, in St Petersburg, where he had come, together with my uncle, and so he now recognized me immediately. With tears of joy in his eyes he rushed over to kiss my hand, his glasses slipping off his nose onto the floor as he did so. I was very moved by such a show of loyal devotion. However, I had been so disturbed by Mr Bakhcheyev's story that my attention was directed first of all at the exercise book Gavrila was clutching.

"What's that, Gavrila? Surely they're not teaching you French as well, are they?" I asked the old man.

"They teach me, sir, old as I am, as if I'm a parrot."

"Foma does the teaching himself?"

"Foma himself, sir. Such a clever man, clearly."

"Obviously! He gives you lessons?"

"No, sir, he uses this grammar book."

"The one you're holding here? Ah, I can see! French words written in the Cyrillic alphabet – how clever of him! Are you not ashamed, Gavrila, to allow this blockhead, this prize idiot, to do what he wants with you?" I shouted, instantly forgetting all the generous-hearted ideas for which I had just been severely rebuked by Mr Bakhcheyev.

"But how, sir," the old man replied, "how can he be such an idiot, when he runs the entire household?"

"Hmm! Maybe you're right, Gavrila," I mumbled, taken aback by this remark. "But please, would you take me to my uncle?"

"Good Heavens above, sir! I cannot, dare not so much as show my face there – I'm even scared of him now. So I sit here brooding, darting behind the flowerbeds whenever he appears."

"But what is it you're scared of exactly?"

"I did badly at French the other day. Foma Fomich wanted me to kneel, but I refused. I'm too old, Sergei Alexandrovich, sir, to have to do that kind of thing! My master got cross with me for not doing as Foma Fomich had ordered. 'You silly old fool,' he said. 'He cares about your education; he wants to teach you to speak properly.' So here I am, swotting up on my vocabulary. Foma Fomich said he was going to test me again this evening."

I felt that there was something not quite right here. There was something behind this French-language business, I thought, which the old man was unwilling, or unable, to divulge.

"One question, Gavrila: what does he look like? Handsome, tall?"

"Foma Fomich, you mean? No, he's rather a plain little man."

"Hmm! Hold on, Gavrila: this all might sort itself out yet – it will definitely sort itself out, I promise you! But... where on earth's my uncle?"

"He's meeting the serfs behind the stables. The old Kapitonovka men have come with a petition. They've heard that Foma Fomich is planning to enlist them. They've come to plead for mercy."

"Yes, but why behind the stables?"

"He's scared, sir..."

And, indeed, I found my uncle behind the stables. He was standing there, in the yard, confronting a group of peasants, who were respectfully but forcefully presenting a petition. My uncle was heatedly trying to explain something to them. I went up to them and called out to him. He turned and saw me, and we rushed to embrace one another.

He was extraordinarily pleased to see me; his joy seemed to know no bounds. He embraced me, shook my hands... It was as if his own favourite son had been restored to him from some mortal danger. It was almost as if the mere fact of my appearance had delivered him from mortal danger as well, and that I had somehow brought with me the solution to all his problems, ensuring his future happiness and that of all his loved ones. My uncle would never have agreed to a happiness that was just for him. After the first ecstatic outbursts of delight, he suddenly grew agitated – so much so that he became utterly confused and bewildered. He bombarded me with questions and wanted to take me straight away to see his family. We were about to do just that, but then he turned back, wishing to introduce me at first to the Kapitonovka peasants. Then, I remember, he suddenly changed the subject and started talking for some reason about a certain Mr Korovkin, a very unusual man, whom he had met three days before somewhere on the high road and whom he was now anxiously expecting to arrive on a visit. Then, throwing all thought of Korovkin to one side, he launched into another topic of conversation altogether. I watched him the whole time in absolute delight. In answer to his hurried questions I told him I had no wish to enter government service, but to continue my scientific studies. As soon as the subject of science came up, my uncle frowned and adopted an unusually serious expression. On learning that I had most recently turned to the study of mineralogy, he threw his head up and looked around him proudly, as if he alone, without anyone's assistance, had written all that there was to know about mineralogy. I have already mentioned that he would always react to the word "science" in a particularly reverential way – all the more so because he knew absolutely nothing about the subject.

"You see, my boy, there are people in the world who know all there is to know about everything!" he had once said to me, his eyes radiant with joy. "You sit in their presence and listen to them, and though you know you don't understand a word they're saying, it's nonetheless a joy simply to listen to them. And why should that be? Well, it's because it's good, it's wise, it means universal happiness! *That* I can understand. Take me, for example: I can now travel by train, but my little Ilyushka may well be able to fly through the air... And then there is trade, industry... all those connecting links and branches, as it were... what I'm trying to say is that whichever way you look at it, it's beneficial... Yes, beneficial – I'm right, aren't I?"

To return to our meeting, however.

"Just you wait, my boy, just you wait," he prattled on, rubbing his hands with glee, "and you'll see a real man! Someone very special, I tell you – a learned man, a man of science, who will make his mark for years to come... 'Make his mark for years to come'? That's a ringing phrase, isn't it? Foma explained it to me... Just wait a moment, and I'll introduce you."

"What, you mean Foma Fomich, Uncle?"

"No, no, my boy! I'm talking about Korovkin now... that is, about Foma as well, him as well... But I had Korovkin in mind just now," he added, blushing for some reason and looking somehow embarrassed at the sound of Foma's name.

"What's his particular area of study, Uncle?"

"Just the sciences, my boy, the sciences, sciences in general! It's just that I can't say which sciences exactly: I only know that it's sciences in general. Spoke so well about the railways! And, you know," he added in a half-whisper, screwing up his right eye in a conspiratorial gesture, "a little bit of freethinking, so to speak! I noted that, especially when he got on to the subject of family happiness... such a pity that I wasn't able to understand very much at all myself (there was no time), or I'd be able to explain it to you in great detail. And what's more, the nicest of gentleman! I have invited him here. Expecting him at any moment!"

All this time the peasants had been looking at me with their mouths wide open and their eyes on stalks, as if I'd been some freak of nature.

"Listen, Uncle," I interrupted, "it seems I've stopped these people from talking to you. They clearly need to talk to you. What have they come here to say? I have to confess that I suspect what it could be, and would really like to listen to whatever it is..."

My uncle suddenly became agitated and uneasy again.

"Ah, yes, of course! I forgot! Well, you see... what is one to do with them? They've got it into their heads – and I'd really like to know who was the first to do so... they've got this idea that I'm going to sign over the whole of the Kapitonovka estate – you remember Kapitonovka, don't you? We used to go walking there in the evening with Katya, God rest her soul... anyway, the entire Kapitonovka estate, all sixty-eight serfs, to Foma Fomich! 'We don't want to leave you,' they say, 'and that's the end of it!'"

"So it's not true, Uncle? You're not going to hand over Kapitonovka?" I cried almost exultingly.

"Never came into my head! But who told you that? I let something slip just the once, and now it's on everyone's lips. And why should they all have taken against Foma so? Just wait, Sergei, and I'll introduce you," he added, giving me a wary look, as if already sensing my possible dislike of Foma Fomich. "You know, my boy, he's such a—"

"We don't want anyone but you, only you!" the whole group of peasants suddenly chorused as one. "You are our father, and we are your children!"

"Listen, Uncle," I said in response. "I've never met this Foma Fomich, but... you see... I've heard one or two things about him.

You should know that I met a certain Mr Bakhcheyev today. However, for the time being, I've formed my own ideas about him. Anyway, Uncle, why don't you let these men go, so that you and I can have a little talk on our own, without anyone around? After all, that's really why I came…"

"Absolutely, absolutely," my uncle agreed, "absolutely! Let's send them on their way, and then we can have a little talk, you know, just a friendly, pleasant, down-to-earth little chat! So!" he said, quickly turning to the peasants. "Be off with you, my friends. And whenever you feel the need, make sure to come and see me, only me – come straight to me, whenever you want."

"Thank you, kind sir! You are our lord and master, and we are your children! Don't let Foma Fomich control our lives! We're just poor people, and we beg you not to let him do that!"

"You silly things! I'm telling you: I'm not going to do that!"

"All that there studying will finish us off, master! Already 'appened to quite a few round these parts."

"He hasn't really made you study French, has he?" I cried out almost in alarm.

"Not yet, sir, thank the Lord!" one of the men replied, very probably someone who loved to shoot his mouth off, a ginger-haired man with a huge bald patch on the back of his head and a long, wedge-shaped beard which jiggled around so much when he spoke it seemed as if it had a life of its own. "Not yet, sir, thank the Lord."

"So what on earth does he teach you, then?"

"Well, sir, it's like buying a gold casket and then filling it with copper coins."

"What do you mean 'copper coins'?"

"Seryozha! You're wrong; that's just slander!" cried my uncle, going red in the face, acutely embarrassed. "They simply haven't understood what he said, that's all, the fools! He simply… copper coins indeed!… And as for you," my uncle continued, turning reproachfully to the peasant who had spoken, "you had no need to shoot your mouth off like that – it was for your own good, you fool, so better not to shout out like that if you don't understand!"

"But I'm sorry, Uncle, what about the French lessons?"

"It's simply to improve their pronunciation, simply for that," my uncle said in a rather placatory tone. "He himself says it's for their pronunciation... Besides, there's something particular that's happened here – you don't know, so you can't judge. You need, my boy, to find out the facts first, before starting to criticize... It's easy to criticize!"

"But why are you acting so dumb?" I shouted, turning angrily to the peasants again. "Why don't you tell him straight out, 'See here, Foma Fomich, you can't behave like this' – that's what you should do! Have you lost your tongues?"

"But the mice can't bell the cat, sir! 'I'm teaching you,' he says, 'how to live a clean, orderly life, you oaf. Why is your shirt so filthy?' Cos it's soaked in sweat! I can't change it every day, can I? You won't go to heaven just cos you're clean, any more than being dirty will get you to hell!"

"Just the other day, see, 'e comes to the threshing barn," put in another peasant, a tall, rather gaunt man, in patched clothing and with the skimpiest bast shoes imaginable on his feet, evidently the type of man who is constantly grumbling and always ready to make some poisonous, venomous comment. Up to that point he had stood hidden behind the backs of his fellows, listening to everything that was being said in sullen silence, his lips twisted into an ironic, sarcastic smile. "'E comes to the threshing barn and asks: 'Do you know 'ow far it is to the sun?' Now, 'ow are we to know something like that? We ain't scientists, are we? That's toffs' business. 'Of course you don't,' 'e says, 'you're just an idiot, a country bumpkin, no idea what's good for you – but I, I'm a astrolomer! I know every one of God's planids!'"

"Well, did he tell you how far it is to the sun?" my uncle interposed, suddenly livening up and giving me a sly wink, as if to say: "Just see what happens now!"

"Well, 'e did tell us, I s'pose," the man answered reluctantly, not expecting this question.

"Well, what did he say, then? How many miles was it precisely?"

"People such as yourself, sir, will know better than us – we're ignorant folk."

"Yes, I know how far it is, my man, but do *you* remember what he said?"

"Well, 'e said it'd be several 'undred or a thousand, like – summat of the sort. More than three cartloads, any road."

"Come on, my good man, what did he say exactly? I suppose you thought it would be about a mile, a stone's throw away? No, my good man, the earth's a big round ball, like this, do you see?" my uncle went on, describing a ball with his hands.

The man gave an incredulous smile.

"Yes, like a ball! It hangs up there in the sky of its own accord and goes round the sun. And the sun stays where it is. It only appears to you to be moving. That's quite something, isn't it? It was Captain Cook, the navigator, who found all that out... The devil knows who it was, actually," he added in a half-whisper, turning to me. "I don't know a thing, myself, my boy... Do *you* know how far it is to the sun?"

"I do, Uncle," I replied, observing the whole scene with astonishment. "But here's what I think: ignorance is on a par with scruffiness; on the other hand, however, to teach peasants astronomy..."

"You're right: it's scruffiness – scruffiness, without a doubt!" exclaimed my uncle, seizing delightedly on my expression, which struck him as so felicitous. "What a splendid thought! Scruffiness! That's precisely what I've always said... that is, I've never actually said it, but have always felt it to be true. Do you hear that?" he called out to the peasants. "Ignorance is no different from scruffiness – they're both filthy! That's why Foma wanted to educate you. He did it for your own good, and that's such a grand idea! So, you see, my good man, it's like government or military service: it can lead to all kinds of honour or promotion. So that's science for you! Well, all right, all right, my friends! May God be with you, and I'm glad, so glad that... don't worry, I won't abandon you."

"Protect us, dear father!"

"Look after us, master!"

And the peasants fell on their knees at his feet.

"Come on, what nonsense is this? Bow down to the Tsar or to God, but not to me... Do you know," he said, suddenly turning to me as soon as the peasants had gone, beaming with joy, "peasants love to be spoken to kindly, and a little present for them will never do any harm. I think I'll give them a little present... eh? What do you think? In honour of your arrival... Shall I do that?"

"Oh yes, Uncle! I can see you're a veritable Frol Silin,* a really generous man."

"No need for that, my dear boy, no need at all – it's nothing. I've long wanted to give them something," he added, as if apologetically. "Why did you think it so amusing, me lecturing the peasants on science like that? No, my boy, it was simply because I was so pleased to see you, Seryozha. I merely wanted that peasant to find out how far it was to the sun and watch him open his mouth with amazement. It's such fun, my boy, to see him do that... it's as though you rejoice with him. Nonetheless, my friend, you're not to tell anybody there in the drawing room about my little chat with the peasants. I deliberately arranged to meet them here behind the stables so that no one would see. Quite impossible to do anything of the sort there, my dear chap – very tricky business – and they themselves came without telling anyone. It was more for their sake, in any case..."

"So, Uncle, here I am: I've arrived!" I said, changing the subject and wishing to get on to the most important matter as soon as possible. "I must confess, Uncle, I found your letter so astonishing that I..."

"That's quite enough, my dear boy!" my uncle interrupted, as if highly alarmed, and even dropping his voice. "Later, leave it for later, when all will become clear. I may need to say how much I have wronged you, how very much I have wronged you, but..."

"Wronged me, Uncle?"

"Later, not now, my dear boy, later! All will become clear. My, what a splendid fellow you've become! My dear chap! I've been so looking forward to seeing you! So much I've been wanting to say, as it were... You're a real scholar, the only one I know... you and Korovkin. I ought to tell you that everyone here is angry with you. So make sure you take care, watch your step!"

"Angry with me?" I asked, looking at my uncle in astonishment, not understanding how I could have angered a group of total strangers. "Angry with me?"

"With you, my boy. What can we do? Foma Fomich just a little bit... well, Mother as well. So in general you need to take care – show everyone respect, don't contradict, but above all, be respectful..."

"You mean towards Foma Fomich, Uncle?"

"What else is there to do, my friend? I'm not defending him, you understand? He may indeed have his faults, and perhaps even now, this very minute he... Oh, Seryozha, my dear boy, I find this all so worrying! How I wish all this could be sorted out, and that we could all be contented and happy!... Yet find me the person who is without fault! We're hardly paragons of virtue, are we?"

"But really, Uncle! Look at the sort of thing he does!"

"Oh, my boy, it's just petty squabbling, that's all! Take what's happening at the moment, for example: he's cross with me about something, and do you know why? In any case, it could be my fault... Better to leave it there for now..."

"But do you know, Uncle, I've come to my own conclusions on the subject," I interrupted, hastening to express my opinion. And, indeed, we were both in a hurry. "Firstly, he was a clown – he was aggrieved and wounded by this; his sense of the ideal was crushed and warped; and so an embittered and pathologically insecure figure emerged, wishing, so to speak, to take his revenge on everyone else... But if he were to be reconciled with others, if he were to be restored to his former self..."

"Exactly, exactly that!" my uncle cried in rapture. "Exactly that! What a noble thought! How shameful, how ungenerous it would be on our part to criticize him! Precisely!... Oh, my friend, you understand me – you have made me so happy! If only it could all be sorted out there! I'm now afraid to show my face there, you know. And now that you've arrived, I'm definitely going to be in real trouble!"

"But Uncle, if that's the case..." I started to say, taken aback by such an admission.

"No, no, no, absolutely not!" he shouted, grabbing me by the hand. "You are my guest, and that's the way I want it to be!"

I found all this extraordinarily astonishing.

"Uncle, please, will you tell me right this minute," I insisted, "why you asked me to come? What are you expecting me to do – and, most importantly, why do you think you have wronged me?"

"Please don't ask, my dear boy! Later, not now! All will become clear in good time! I may well have done you a great wrong, but I wanted to behave like an honest man and... and... and you will marry her! You will marry her, if you possess a grain of decency!" he added, blushing bright red from a sudden onrush of emotion and fervently clasping my hand. "But that's enough, not another word! You'll find everything out for yourself very shortly. It will all depend on you... You must do your best to please them there – that's the main thing: do your very best to make a good impression. And, above all, keep a cool head."

"But tell me, Uncle, who is it who's going to be there? I'm so unused to company, you see, that—"

"So you're a little scared, are you?" my uncle interrupted with a smile. "Goodness, don't worry! You'll be among friends, so cheer up! Above all, cheer up, don't be afraid! I'm a little concerned about you, though. You want to know who's going to be there? Well, let me see... Firstly, there's Mother," he began hastily. "Do you remember her or not? The kindest, most generous-hearted old lady. Totally unpretentious, one could even say. A little old-fashioned, but that's not such a bad thing. Has these strange ideas sometimes, makes some very odd remarks – she's cross with me at the moment, but it's my own fault... I know it is! Anyway, she is what's known as a *grande dame*, a general's wife... her husband was such a splendid fellow: firstly, he was a general, such an erudite man – left no fortune, but was terribly battle-scarred...

in short, he was constantly seeking to earn the respect of others! Then we have Miss Perepelitsyna. Well, she... I don't know... has somehow been... rather strange lately... However, we mustn't criticize everybody... I wish her the best of luck... But please don't get the idea that she is some sort of sponger. She, my boy, is herself the daughter of a lieutenant colonel, a confidante and friend to Mother! Then there is my sister, Praskovya Ilyinichna. Well, there is not very much one can say about her: unsophisticated, good-natured, gets worked up about things, but then what a heart!... above all look for the heart... she is an elderly woman, but apparently that weird fellow Bakhcheyev is trying to gain her affections, wants to marry her. But mum's the word – keep that to yourself, it's a secret! So, who else is there? I won't say anything about the children: you'll see for yourself. It's Ilyushka's name day tomorrow... Goodness! I nearly forgot! There's also Ivan Ivanych Mizinchikov, who's been staying here with us for a whole month now, a distant cousin of yours, it seems! Lieutenant, recently retired from the hussars, still a young chap. The kindest of souls! Mired himself so deeply in debt, however, that I've no idea how he managed it, even though he hardly ever had any money... He's now staying here, with me. I didn't know him at all before: he simply came and introduced himself. A dear, kind fellow, unassuming and respectful. Has anyone here heard him say a single word about anything? Quiet as a mouse. Foma mockingly calls him 'the silent stranger', but he doesn't mind, doesn't let it rile him. That pleases Foma; he looks on Ivan as a bit of a simpleton. True, Ivan never stands up to him about anything, agrees with everything he says. Hmm! He's so browbeaten... Well, the best of luck to him as well! You'll see for yourself. There are guests from town: Pavel Semyonych Obnoskin with his mother – he's a young man, but of the highest intellect... there's something mature about him, you know, something resolute... I'm just not very good at expressing what I mean... and, what's more, he's a man of the highest morals, a strictly moral character! Anyway, finally we have this Tatyana Ivanovna staying with us, you see, another distant relative of yours... you don't know her... she's a spinster, past her prime, one has to confess, but... with some positive qualities: she's rich enough, my dear fellow, to buy Stepanchikovo twice over... recently came into money, but before that without a copeck to her name. So Seryozha, my friend, take care: she's not quite normal... you know, she's a little prone to fantasizing. Anyway, you're a generous soul, you'll understand... she's been through difficult times. You need to be twice as careful with people who have experienced misfortune! Still, don't jump to any conclusions. She has her faults, of course: she's too hasty sometimes, doesn't stop to think, says the wrong thing – not that she lies, you understand... it all stems, my boy, from a pure and noble heart – that is to say, if she does actually tell the occasional lie, it's merely the result of a too-generous spirit... do you understand what I'm saying?"

My uncle seemed to me to be incredibly embarrassed.

"Listen, Uncle," I said, "I'm so fond of you... please forgive me for asking you so directly: are you getting married to someone here or not?"

"Who told you that?" he replied, blushing like a little child. "See here, my boy, let me tell you everything: in the first place I'm not getting married. Mother, my sister, partly, and most importantly Foma Fomich, whom Mother adores (and for good reason, for good reason: he's been so good to her) – they all want me to get married to that very same Tatyana Ivanovna... it would be such a sensible thing to do, and it would benefit the whole family. Naturally, they wish only the best for me, I can understand that, but I'm not going to get married for anything in the world – I've fully made up my mind on that. Nonetheless, I have somehow not been able to answer with a firm yes or no. I've always been like that, my boy. Anyway, they've jumped to the conclusion that I've agreed, and want me to make a definite proposal tomorrow, on the day of the family celebration... so tomorrow's going to be such a frantic day I don't know what to do! And what's more, Foma Fomich is angry with me about something for some reason – Mother also. I must confess, my boy, I have been so looking forward to seeing you and Korovkin... wanting to unburden myself of everything, as it were..."

"But how exactly is Korovkin going to be of any help here, Uncle?"

"He will be of help, my friend, he will... he's such a special person – in a word, a man of science! I see him as a solid rock, an absolutely indomitable fellow! You should hear what he has to say on family happiness! I also have to say I have been so relying on you too, hoping you'd knock some sense into them. Look at it this way: all right, I agree I may well be to blame, definitely so – I realize that, I'm not totally insensitive. But why can't I occasionally be forgiven? Oh, wouldn't life be wonderful then? Just look how my little Sasha has grown, almost ready to tie the knot! And as for Ilyusha! It's his name day tomorrow. But I'm so concerned about Sasha!..."

"Uncle! Where's my suitcase? I'll go and get changed – I'll be back in a flash, and then..."

"It's in the mezzanine, my boy, in the mezzanine. I ordered that you be taken straight to the mezzanine as soon as you arrived, so that no one would see you. Of course, of course, go and get changed! That's wonderful, absolutely wonderful! Meanwhile, I'll go and prepare everyone, as much as I possibly can. May God be with you! You know, my boy, we're going to have to watch our step... like some Talleyrand, so to speak.* Well, never mind! They'll be taking tea there at the moment. We take tea early. Foma Fomich likes his tea as soon as he wakes up... it's better that way, you know... So, I'll leave you now, and you follow me as quick as you can... don't let me be on my own: I feel a little uneasy, my boy, when I'm left on my own with them... Ah! Wait! Just one other thing: don't shout at me, as you did just now, all right? Later perhaps, if you really need to say something, when it's just the two of us together, but for the moment hold back, bide your time! I've really done all sorts of stupid things there, you see. They're cross with me..."

"Listen, Uncle, from everything I've heard and seen, it seems to me that you—"

"That I'm just a doormat, you mean? Go on, say it!" he inter-rupted me quite unexpectedly. "What can be done, my boy? I'm fully aware of it already. So, you'll come? Come as soon as you possibly can, please!"

I went upstairs and hurriedly opened my suitcase, not forget-ting that my uncle wanted me to go down as soon as possible. As I was changing, it occurred to me that, although I had been talking to him for a whole hour, I had still found out hardly anything I wanted to find out. I was struck by this fact. There was just one thing that had become more or less clear to me: my uncle really did still want me to get married, and consequently all rumours to the contrary – that he was in love with that very same person – were unfounded. I can remember how alarmed I felt. At the same time, the thought occurred to me that, in arriv-ing the way I had and in saying practically nothing to my uncle, I had to all intents and purposes signalled my agreement, given my word, bound myself for life. "How easy it is," I thought, "to let yourself be bound hand and foot merely by making a promise. And I hadn't even set eyes on my bride-to-be!" And another thing: why this animosity towards me on the part of the whole family? Why did they have to look on my arrival, as my uncle had assured me was the case, in such a hostile way? And why was my uncle behaving so strangely, in his own house? Why was he being so mysterious? Why all these fears and anxieties? I must confess that I suddenly found it all quite ridiculous – all my romantic and heroic dreams had vanished into thin air, at the first brush with reality. It was only now, after my conversation with my uncle, that I realized just how incongruous and absurd his proposal had been, and it became clear that such an idea, in such circumstances, could have only come from him. It was also obvious that, in responding immediately to his request by dash-ing here post-haste in such a state of ecstasy at his proposal, I had made myself look like an idiot. As I hurriedly got dressed, I was so engrossed in my doubts that I wasn't at first aware of the manservant in attendance.

"Which necktie would you prefer to wear, sir: the Adelaide blue or this small-checked one?" the manservant suddenly asked, turning to me with an exaggeratedly cloying, deferential manner.

I glanced at him, and it became apparent that he too merited further scrutiny. He was still a young man, remarkably well dressed for a lackey, making him look at least the equal of any provincial dandy. His brown tailcoat, white trousers, straw-coloured waistcoat, patent-leather ankle boots and pink necktie had evidently been chosen with particular care, so as to draw attention to the young fop's refined taste. His watch chain was prominently displayed, clearly with the same purpose in mind. He had a pale face which was even a little greenish in colour; he had a large, aquiline nose, slender and unusually white, as if made of marble. The smile on his thin lips betrayed a certain melancholy – but it was a refined melancholy. His large, slightly protruding, glassy eyes bore an especially dull expression, and yet they too possessed something of the same refinement. His thin, soft ears were blocked with cotton wool – so that he could hear everything in a refined way. His long, thin hair was curled and pomaded. His hands were white and spotlessly clean, having probably been washed in rose water; the tips of his fingers displayed impossibly long, elegant pink nails. All this pointed to a pampered, indolent fop. He had a slight speech defect – he was unable to pronounce the letter "r" correctly – and he kept on fluttering his eyes, sighing and talking in a contrived way the whole time. There was the smell of perfume about him. He was a short, rather flabby and puny man who, when he walked, kept on bobbing up and down in a special kind of way, probably considering this to be an expression of the height of refinement – in short, the man was the very embodiment of refinement and sophistication, inordinately aware of his own self-importance. For some reason, this last characteristic annoyed me intensely.

"So this necktie is Adelaide blue, then?" I asked, giving the young lackey a severe look.

"Yes, sir," he replied in a self-assured, refined way.

"Not Agatha purple, then?"

"No, sir, no such colour can be possible, sir."

"Why not?"

"Agatha's not a decent name, sir."

"What do you mean? Why isn't it?"

"It's a well-known fact, sir, that Adelaide, at least, is a foreign name, and therefore highly distinguished, whereas Agatha can be the name of any old washerwoman."

"Have you lost your mind?"

"Not at all, sir – I have all my wits about me, sir. You can of course call me all sorts of names, if you so desire, sir, but many a general and even some counts from the capital have been most contented with my manner of speaking, sir."

"So, what is your name?"

"Vidoplyasov."

"Aha! So *you're* Vidoplyasov?"

"Precisely so, sir."

"I see. Well, we'll meet again sometime, no doubt."

"But this is close to bedlam," I thought to myself, as I went downstairs.

4

At Tea

The room where tea was being served was the very same room with its door leading out onto the terrace where I had just met Gavrila. My uncle's mysterious misgivings concerning the reception that awaited me made me very anxious. Young people are sometimes prone to disproportionate pride, and youthful pride is almost invariably pusillanimous. That would explain the utter distress I felt when, on entering the room and seeing everyone sitting around the table, I suddenly tripped on the carpet, stumbled and, striving to keep my balance, unexpectedly flew into the middle of the room. I stood there motionless, mortified, looking at the assembled company, my face as red as a beetroot, feeling that I must have ruined my entire future prospects, honour and good name at a single stroke. I am only mentioning this incident, so trivial in itself, because of the extraordinary way it affected my state of mind – and consequently my attitude towards some of the characters who form part of my story – for almost the whole of the rest of that day. I attempted a bow, without success, grew even redder in the face, dashed over to my uncle and seized his hand.

"Hello, Uncle," I said, struggling to breathe and wishing to say something quite different and much more original, but, quite unexpectedly, managing nothing more than a hello.

"Hello, hello, my boy," my uncle answered, suffering on my behalf. "But we've already greeted each other, haven't we? But please, don't be embarrassed," he added in a whisper, "it's the sort of thing, my boy, that could of course happen to anybody! Whenever such things happen, you'd like to disappear off the face of the earth!... Anyway, Mother, allow me to introduce you: this is the young man I told you about; he's a little embarrassed at the moment, but I'm sure you'll come to like him. My nephew, Sergei Alexandrovich," he added, turning to address everyone present.

But before continuing with my story, permit me, dear reader, to describe, one by one, the entire company of people in whose presence I suddenly now found myself. This will be an essential prerequisite for a proper understanding of what is to follow.

The entire assembled company consisted of several ladies and only two men, apart from my uncle and myself. Foma Fomich – the person I so desperately wanted to see and whom I had already sensed to be the undisputed master of the house – wasn't among them; he was, indeed, conspicuous by his absence, as if he had taken some of the light in the room with him as he had departed. They all looked despondent and immersed in their own cares – something that became perfectly obvious after only one glance; despite my own extremely confused and distressed state, I could see that my uncle was almost as upset as I was, although he was evidently making every effort to conceal his agitation with a pretence of indifference. It was as if a leaden weight lay on his heart. One of the two men in the room was still extremely young, aged about twenty-five – the very same Obnoskin about whom my uncle had just spoken very highly, praising him for his intelligence and integrity. But I didn't take to him at all: everything about him spoke of modishness and bad taste; his suit, despite its outward elegance, was somehow shabby and unprepossessing; there was something rather shabby about his face as well. His sparse, tow-haired, rather cockroach-like whiskers and his pathetic, scruffy little beard were clearly intended to denote a man of independence, perhaps even of free thought. He kept on screwing up his eyes as he sat there in his chair, surveying me through his lorgnette with a feigned and rather unpleasant smile on his face; but whenever I looked in his direction, he immediately seemed to take fright and to drop his lorgnette. The other man in the room, also young, some twenty-eight years old, was my distant relative, Mizinchikov. And it was true: he was an unusually silent person. The whole time we were at tea he didn't utter a word, or even laugh when everyone else did. But I was unable to detect a trace of the subservient manner which my uncle had observed in him. Quite the opposite: there was a determination in his light-brown eyes that spoke of a man of definite character. Mizinchikov was rather handsome, with dark hair and a swarthy complexion. He was very smartly dressed – thanks to my uncle, as I was later to find out. Of the ladies present, the first to catch my eye, because of the unusually malevolent, bloodless expression on her face, was Miss Perepelitsyna. She was sitting close to the general's lady – of whom in particular there will be more later – not right next to her, but a little behind her, as a sign of respect; she was forever leaning forwards and whispering something in the ear of her benefactress. There were two or three elderly ladies, impoverished members of the household, sitting in a row by the window, respectfully waiting for their tea and gaping mutely at the general's lady. My attention was also caught by the sight of a very large, elephantine woman of about fifty, tastelessly and flamboyantly dressed, with rouged cheeks, whose teeth had been reduced to blackened, broken stumps – which didn't, however, prevent her from squeaking away and showing off the whole time, in a display that was not far short of flirtation. She was bedecked in little chains, and she kept on levelling her lorgnette at me, like Monsieur Obnoskin. She turned out to be his mother. My aunt, Praskovya Ilyinichna, was meekly pouring the tea. Although she clearly wanted to embrace me and, quite naturally, to burst into tears, as she had not seen me for such a long time, she was too timid to do so. It was as if everything in the room had been subjected to some kind of prohibition. Next to her sat an extremely pretty, dark-eyed girl of fifteen, who couldn't stop staring at me out of childish curiosity – my cousin Sasha. Finally, and perhaps most strikingly, there was an extremely odd-looking lady, sumptuously attired with a youthful extravagance that was quite at odds with her age, which could not have been any less than thirty-five years. She had a very pale, pinched face with a rather haggard, but nevertheless unusually animated expression. Her pallid cheeks would constantly flush crimson, almost at every movement she made, at every new emotion. She seemed to be in a perpetually agitated state, shifting around in her chair, as if incapable of sitting still even for a moment. She kept on staring at me with a kind of eager curiosity and leaning forward to whisper something into the ear of Sashenka, or that of her other neighbour, and then bursting into fits of the most unaffected, childlike, carefree laughter. But, to my astonishment, nobody seemed to pay any attention at all to such eccentric behaviour, as if by general agreement. I guessed that this had to be Tatyana Ivanovna, the person referred to by my uncle as being "a little prone to fantasizing", and who was being foisted on him as a bride, and who almost everyone in the house was pursuing for her wealth. I was however particularly struck by her gentle blue eyes, and although little crow's feet were already beginning to show at their corners, they radiated such innocence, joie de vivre and kindness that it was such a pleasure to become aware of them. But of Tatyana Ivanovna, one of the real "heroines" of my story, I shall have much more to say later: the story of her life is quite remarkable. Some five minutes after I'd first come into the room, a strikingly good-looking boy, my cousin Ilyusha, whose name day it was on the following day, came running in; both his pockets were crammed full of knucklebones, and he had a spinning top in his hands. He was followed in by a young, slender girl, with a rather tired expression on her pale face, but extremely attractive. Casting an inquisitive, mistrustful and even timid glance round the entire assembled company, she gave me a particularly quizzical look and sat down next to Tatyana Ivanovna. I remember my heart involuntarily missing a beat: I realized that this must be the governess... I can also remember my uncle suddenly giving me a quick glance and going bright red as she came in; then he bent down, grasped Ilyusha's hands and brought him over to me to kiss. I also noticed Madame Obnoskina first glaring at my uncle and then levelling her lorgnette at the governess with a caustic smile. Almost paralysed by embarrassment, my uncle, not knowing what to do, started to ask Sashenka to come over and introduce herself to me, but she merely stood up and silently, with a serious, dignified expression on her face, made a little curtsy; I really liked that, as it so became her. At that very moment the good-natured Praskovya Ilyinichna, unable to restrain herself any longer, stopped serving tea and rushed over to kiss me. But I hardly had time to say a couple of words to her before I heard Miss Perepelitsyna's shrill voice echoing throughout the room, squeaking: "Praskovya Ilyinichna must clearly have forgotten about Mother" – that is, the general's lady. "Mother wants her tea, but you are not serving her any, and she is waiting." At which, Praskovya Ilyinichna immediately abandoned me and dashed off at top speed to do her duty.

This general's lady, the most important figure in the entire assembled company, and on whom everyone danced attendance, was a gaunt, cantankerous old woman, dressed entirely in black – her evil temper clearly stemming from her advanced age and the loss of her remaining mental faculties, which had never been particularly impressive at the best of times – she had, in fact, been an exceptionally silly woman. On marrying the general, she had become even more stupid and overbearingly arrogant. Whenever she lost her temper, the whole household turned into a version of hell. The old woman had two ways of demonstrating her foul temper. The first was to say absolutely nothing, keeping her lips obstinately sealed for whole days at a time and pushing away or sometimes even hurling anything that was presented her onto the floor. The second was the complete opposite: to become particularly loquacious. It usually began with Grandmother – for that, indeed, was what she was to me – becoming unusually depressed, expecting the end of the world and of her entire household at any moment, anticipating dire poverty and every kind of grief, becoming totally absorbed in her own premonitions, beginning to enumerate on her fingers future disasters, even taking a kind of rapturous delight in doing so. Naturally, it turned out that she had long seen it all coming in advance, and that she had only kept quiet about it all because "the household" had forced her into silence. Yet, if only people had shown her any respect, if only they had listened to her earlier, then... and so on and so on. In saying all this, she would immediately be backed up by the coterie of hangers-on, by Miss Perepelitsyna, finally eliciting the triumphant approval of Foma Fomich. At the particular moment I was introduced to her, she was in the throes of a terrible rage, apparently of the silent, horrendously silent, type. Everybody was looking at her full of trepidation. Only Tatyana Ivanovna, who was given full rein to do exactly what she wanted, was in the highest of spirits. My uncle made a special point, even with some solemnity, of taking me up to Grandmother, but she made a sour face and angrily pushed her cup away from her.

"So that's the *vol-ti-geur*, is it?" she asked through clenched teeth, in a sing-song voice, turning to Perepelitsyna.

This idiotic question totally nonplussed me. I have no idea why she should have referred to me as a *voltigeur*.* But such questions were run-of-the-mill to her. Miss Perepelitsyna bent down and whispered something in her ear, but the old woman angrily gestured her away. I stood there with my mouth open, looking questioningly at my uncle. Everyone exchanged glances, and Madame Obnoskina even bared her teeth, which struck me as being particularly unpleasant.

"She can sometimes get carried away, my boy," my uncle whispered to me. He, too, was a little disconcerted. "But it's nothing, she says such things sometimes, through the kindness of her heart – the heart... that's the most important thing."

"Yes, the heart, the heart!" suddenly rang out Tatyana Ivanovna's clarion voice; she had never taken her eyes off me, as she kept on shifting around restlessly in her chair; she had evidently picked up the word "heart", even though it had been uttered in a whisper.

Despite clearly wanting, however, to say something else, she wasn't able to. Whether from embarrassment or for some other reason, she abruptly fell silent, went bright red in the face, quickly bent over to the governess to whisper something in her ear, and then suddenly covered her face with her handkerchief, leant back in her chair and burst out into an apparently hysterical fit of laughter. I looked round the room in utter consternation. But, to my astonishment, everyone stayed perfectly calm, looking as though nothing untoward had happened. I understood of course what kind of person Tatyana Ivanovna was. Eventually I was served tea, and I was able to recover a little. I don't quite know why, but it suddenly occurred to me that I ought to enter into polite conversation with the ladies.

"You were right, Uncle," I began, "when you told me just now how easy it is to get embarrassed about things. I have to confess… I can't hide the fact," I continued, turning to Madame Obnoskina with an ingratiating smile, "that I have hitherto had very little knowledge of female company, and that when I made such a clumsy entrance just now I must have cut a very comic figure, standing there in the middle of the room like that, looking like some sort of simpleton, do you agree? Have you read *The Simpleton*?"* I concluded, losing my way in ever greater desperation, blushing at the thought of my ingratiatingly candid manner and giving Monsieur Obnoskin a defiant look; he, for his part, continued to look me up and down from head to toe, with his teeth bared.

"That's right, that's right, absolutely right!" my uncle suddenly exclaimed with extraordinary emotion, genuinely overjoyed that some sort of conversation was finally under way, and that I was recovering my poise. "All right, my boy, you were embarrassed, as you said just now, but it's of no consequence at all. Yes, you were embarrassed, but that's water under the bridge now! Believe it or not, when I first entered society I lied! No, really, Anfisa Petrovna, this is an interesting story, I tell you! I had just become a cadet, newly arrived in Moscow bearing a letter of introduction to a highly important lady – an extremely haughty woman, but with an essentially kind heart, whatever else people might have been saying about her. Anyway I come in, together with the other guests being received. The drawing room is packed with people, for the most part out of the top drawer. I bow and sit down. Almost immediately she asks: 'Have you, my good man, any estates?'

What on earth am I to say? Naturally I hadn't got a single chicken to my name. Everyone is looking at me (as if to say, 'Well, come on then, you little cadet!'). Why couldn't I simply have replied 'I haven't got any'? It would have been far better to have done that, as it would have been the truth! But I couldn't stop myself from crowing about the fact that I had an estate of seventeen serfs. Why 'seventeen' serfs, for goodness' sake? If I had to make something up, I could have used a round number, couldn't I? A moment later and the letter of introduction I had brought with me made it clear that I hadn't a bean to my name – and, what's more, I had lied about it! Well, what could I do? I beat it out of there as fast as I could, and have never set foot in the place since. I really was penniless at the time. Everything I now own has been inherited since: three hundred serfs from my uncle Afanasy Matveich, together with the two hundred before that from the Kapitonovka estate, belonging to my grandmother, Akulina Panfilovna – that's a total of some five hundred. That's wonderful! And I vowed never to lie again, and I never have!"

"Well, if I were in your place, I would never have made such a vow. You never know, do you?" Obnoskin remarked with a sneer on his lips.

"Yes, yes, that's true, very true! You never know!" my uncle agreed ingenuously.

Obnoskin roared with laughter, leaning back in his chair; his mother smiled; Miss Perepelitsyna, too, tittered in a somehow really repellent way; Tatyana Ivanovna also burst into laughter, without knowing why, and even clapped her hands – in a word, it was obvious that my uncle counted for precisely nothing in this household. Sashenka stared at Obnoskin, her eyes flashing angrily. The governess went red in the face and looked down at her feet. My uncle was astonished.

"What's all this? What's wrong?" he asked, looking at everyone with a puzzled expression.

All this time my cousin, Mizinchikov, had been sitting some distance away, saying nothing, not even smiling when everyone else had burst into laughter. He was engrossed in his tea, studying everyone present philosophically, and several times, as if finding it all profoundly boring, he would start whistling, out of habit, but then almost immediately check himself. I noticed that Obnoskin, who took such pleasure in crossing swords with my uncle and needling me, was too scared to glance across at Mizinchikov. I also noticed that my silent cousin kept on looking at me with evident curiosity, as if wanting to find out exactly what kind of a person I was.

"I have no doubt," Madame Obnoskina suddenly piped up, "I have no doubt at all, Monsieur Serge – that's right, isn't it? – that in that St Petersburg of yours you weren't really the one for the ladies. I know that there are many, very many young men there now who go out of their way to avoid female society. But, in my view, they are just a lot of freethinkers. In my view, this is nothing but an unforgivable example of freethinking. And, I must confess, I find that astonishing, young man, simply astonishing!"

"I have never been in society at all," I replied with unusual animation. "But that's... in my opinion at least, there's nothing wrong with that... I lived... that is to say, I had rooms there... but that's perfectly normal, I can assure you. I shall get to know people – it's just that up until now I have simply stayed in my rooms..."

"Studying the sciences," observed my uncle, drawing himself up to his full height.

"Oh, Uncle, you're always going on about those sciences!... Just imagine," I continued in a very casual tone, once again turning to madame Obnoskina with an eager-to-please smile, "my dear uncle is so devoted to the cause of science that he has unearthed, somewhere out on the highway, some miracle-working practical philosopher, a Mr Korovkin – and his first words to me when we met today, after so many years apart, were that he was looking forward to meeting this phenomenal miracle-worker with feverish, so to speak, impatience... all out of love for science, naturally..."

And I began to giggle, hoping that everyone would start laughing, applauding my wit.

"Who's that? Who's that he's talking about?" the general's lady asked tartly, turning to Miss Perepelitsyna.

"A guest, madam, invited by Yegor Ilyich, madam, some scientist. Yegor Ilyich has been going up and down the highways looking for scientists, so that he could bring them here, to this house, madam," squeaked the spinster, with obvious delight.

My uncle was completely flummoxed by this.

"Ah, you're right! I'd quite forgotten!" he cried, flashing me a reproachful look. "I *am* waiting for Korovkin. A man of science, a man of the century..."

He broke off and fell silent. The general's lady threw her arms in the air, this time succeeding in sending her teacup flying from the table and crashing into bits on the floor. There was general consternation.

"She always does that, whenever she gets angry... she gets hold of something and hurls it on the floor," my uncle whispered sheepishly to me. "But only... when she gets angry, mind... Don't take any notice, my boy, look away... But why did you have to bring Korovkin up?..."

But I was looking away, in any case: at that very moment I had caught sight of the expression in the governess's eyes as she looked at me, and it seemed to contain a hint of a reproach, even something of scorn; her pale cheeks flushed with irritation. I understood why: I realized that my pathetic, vile wish to make my uncle appear a laughing stock, so as to divert attention away from my own ludicrous behaviour, had not particularly disposed her in my favour. I cannot express just how ashamed I felt!

"But we were talking about St Petersburg," trilled Anfisa Petrovna again, when the excitement caused by the broken teacup had died down. "I have such, so to speak, en-joy-able memories of our life in that enchanting capital... We got to know one particular family so well – do you remember, Paul? General Polovitsyn... Oh, and Madame Polovitsyna was such a delightful, de-light-ful person! Well, you know, the aristocratic lifestyle, the beau monde... Do tell me... you no doubt must have met... I must confess I have been so looking forward to meeting you – I have been waiting to hear so much from you about our dear St Petersburg friends…"

"I'm very sorry that I'm unable to… forgive me… I have already said that society life wasn't really for me, and I don't know General Polovitsyn at all – never even heard the name," I answered brusquely, abruptly switching from politeness to an extremely irritated and piqued frame of mind.

"He used to study mineralogy!" my incorrigible uncle remarked proudly. "That's what mineralogy is, my boy, isn't it? Looking at pebbles, that sort of thing?"

"Yes, Uncle, pebbles…"

"Hmm… so many different sciences, and all so useful! But you know, my boy, I really had no idea what mineralogy was! Just gibberish, as far as I was concerned. In one or two other things I can hold my head above water, but I have to admit openly that as far as the sciences are concerned, I'm hopeless!"

"You openly admit that, do you?" interposed Obnoskin, with a sneer.

"Papa!" Sasha cried out, giving her father a reproachful look.

"What, my darling? Oh, good Heavens, I keep on interrupting you, Anfisa Petrovna," exclaimed my uncle with a start, failing to grasp the point of Sasha's comment entirely. "Please forgive me, for the Lord's sake!"

"Oh, please don't worry!" answered Anfisa Petrovna with a sour smile. "In any case, I have already conveyed everything I want to say to your nephew, and I will merely conclude by saying that you, Monsieur Serge – that is right, isn't it? – really have to mend your ways. I am sure that the sciences, the arts… sculpture, for example… well, in short, all such high ideas can be absolutely fascinating, so to speak, but they are no replacement for the fairer sex!… It's women, women, young man, that will be the making of you, and you cannot, cannot, ab-so-lute-ly cannot do without them, young man!"

"Absolutely cannot!" echoed Tatyana Ivanovna in her somewhat shrill voice. "Listen," she began to say, rather hurriedly, like a little child, and, naturally, going bright red in the face, "listen, I would like to ask you…"

"Please go ahead," I replied, giving her an intent look.

"I wanted to ask whether you intend to stay for long?"

"I don't know – really I don't… business matters, you know…"

"Business matters! What business matters? Oh, you madman!" And Tatyana Ivanovna, going as purple as a beetroot and shielding her face behind her fan, leant over to the governess and immediately began whispering something to her. Then she suddenly burst out laughing and clapped her hands.

"Wait! Wait!" she exclaimed, tearing herself away from her confidante and hurriedly turning to me again, as if afraid I might have gone. "Listen, guess what I'm going to say! You are awfully, terribly like a certain young man, an en-chant-ing young man! Sashenka, Nastenka, you remember? He's the spitting image of that madman… you remember, Sashenka? We were out for a drive and we met him… he was on horseback, in a white waist-coat… and he turned his eyeglass on me, the impudent fellow! You remember… I'd hidden my face in my veil, but couldn't stop myself from leaning out of the carriage and yelling 'How dare you!' – and then I threw my bunch of flowers on the road… You remember, don't you, Nastenka?"

And the semi-besotted spinster, trembling all over from excitement, buried her face in her hands. Then, suddenly, she leapt up from her chair, darted over to the window, plucked a rose from a flowerpot, tossed it down onto the floor close to me and dashed out of the room, with everyone's eyes on her! This time there was quite a lot of confusion in the room, although the general's lady remained totally calm, as before. Anfisa Petrovna didn't seem unduly surprised, either, but she was clearly concerned about something and gave her son a concerned look; the young ladies blushed, while Paul Obnoskin stood up with an irritated expression, which I did not understand at the time, and walked over to the window. My uncle began to make signals to me, but at that moment someone new entered the room, capturing everyone's attention.

"Aha! Here's Yevgraf Larionych! Speak of the Devil!" my uncle shouted, genuinely overjoyed. "Come straight from town, have you?"

"What a weird lot of people! And they all seem to have deliberately conspired to come together here, in this room!" I thought to myself, still unable to grasp entirely what I'd seen, and not suspecting that I myself, in appearing here, was merely adding to their number.

5

Yezhevikin

The person who had now entered the room (or, rather, squeezed his way through what was in fact an extremely wide doorway) was a little figure of a man who bobbed up and down in the entrance, bowing and baring his teeth as he looked round at everyone present with an air of the utmost curiosity. He was a little balding old man with a pockmarked face, darting, rather furtive eyes and a slight, somewhat vague smile on his fairly thick lips. He was wearing a very tattered, almost certainly second-hand, frock coat. One button hung on a single thread, while a couple of others were missing altogether. His worn-out boots and greasy peak cap completed the impression of a generally scruffily dressed individual. In his hands he was holding a check cotton handkerchief that was covered in snot, with which he kept on wiping away the sweat from his forehead and temples. I noticed the governess blushing slightly and giving me a quick glance, containing, it seemed to me, a hint of pride and defiance.

"I've come straight from town, generous and bountiful sir! Yes, straight from town, kind sir! I'll tell you all about it, but let me first pay my respects," the old man said, and immediately started going over to the general's lady, but, stopping halfway, he turned and addressed my uncle once again:

"You are naturally already acquainted, generous and bountiful sir, with the sort of person I am: I am a scoundrel, a veritable scoundrel! Look at me: no sooner do I come into the room than I make straight for the most important person in the house to solicit her favour and protection. A scoundrel, my dear man, a scoundrel, kind sir! Allow me, my dear lady, to kiss the hem of Your Grace's dress, so that I do not sully Your Grace's precious hand with my lips."

To my astonishment, the general's lady obliged him by offering him her hand.

"And my respectful greetings to you as well, beautiful lady," he went on, turning to Miss Perepelitsyna. "No help for it, gracious lady: a scoundrel! As long ago as 1841 it was determined that I would be a scoundrel, when I was dismissed from the service – at precisely the same time as Valentin Ignatych Tikhontsov was promoted and made an assessor; he became an assessor and I a scoundrel. I am so constituted that I openly confess everything. What was I to do? I tried to live an honest life, I really did; now I must try to do things differently... Alexandra Yegorovna, delectable apple of all our lives," he continued, as he made his way round the table towards Sashenka, "permit me to kiss the hem of your dress; you are filling the air, my darling girl, with the sweet smell of apples and all kinds of delicious things. My greetings and respects to our name-day boy – here, I've brought a bow and arrow for you, my boy, spent the whole morning making it... my lads helped me. So we'll have a go at shooting it together. And when you grow up, you can become an officer and chop a Turk's head off. Tatyana Ivanovna... aha, I see my generous and bountiful lady is not here! Had she been here, I would have kissed the hem of her dress as well. Praskovya Ilyinichna, my dear, dear lady... I can't squeeze my way through to get to you, otherwise I would have kissed not only your hand, but also your foot – that's what I would have done! Anfisa Petrovna, my deepest, deepest respects to you. I was down on my knees only this morning, praying to God for you, my generous and bountiful lady, and for your dear son, with tears in my eyes, so that He can bless him with every advancement in rank and with every kind of talent – above all, talent! And while I'm on the subject, Ivan Ivanovich Mizinchikov, please accept our humblest of greetings and respects. May the Almighty grant you all that you desire for yourself – although it is not easy, my dear sir, to know what exactly it is you desire for yourself, since you say so little... Greetings, Nastya: all my little ones send their respects to you; they think of you every day. And now my deepest respects to the master of the house. I've come straight from town, sir, straight from town. And this must be your nephew, fresh from his science studies? My deepest, deepest respects to you, sir – please, offer your hand."

There was an outburst of laughter in the room. The old man was clearly adopting the role of a self-appointed clown. Everyone had cheered up at his arrival in the room. Many had missed the sarcasm in his remarks, even though he had been round to practically everybody. Only the governess – whom, to my surprise, he had addressed as simply Nastya – stood there blushing and frowning. I tried to withdraw my hand, but it seemed that was precisely what the old man had been waiting for.

"But I was only wanting to shake it, my dear sir, with your permission – not to kiss it. Did you think I was going to kiss it? No, sir, for the time being I shall only shake it. You, kind sir, take me for the house clown, no doubt?" he said, looking at me mockingly.

"N... no, not at all, I..."

"Precisely so, sir! I may be a clown, but I'm not the only one around here! And you ought to respect me, you know: I'm not such a scoundrel as you might think... although I may of course be a clown. I am a slave, as is my wife, but flatter, flatter, I say: that's the thing to do – at the very least it means something extra for the little ones. Add a little sugar, above all sugar, to everything, and it's very good for the constitution. I'm telling you that, my dear sir, in confidence – it may come in useful. Fate has not been good to me, kind sir – that's why I always play the fool."

"Ha-ha-ha! Such a funny old man! He always makes me laugh!" squeaked Anfisa Petrovna.

"But, my dear generous and bountiful lady, you get through life much better if you're a fool! Had I known that as a young man I would have become one much earlier in life. Who knows, I might have ended up as a wise man now. It's because I wanted to be so clever early on in life that I've now become such an idiot in my old age."

"Tell me, please," intervened Obnoskin (clearly not best pleased at the comment about talent), making a particular point of sprawling in his chair and scrutinizing the old man through his eyeglass, as if examining a leech, "tell me, if you would be so kind... I keep on forgetting your name... let me see, that would be?..."

"Ah, my dear sir! My name, for what it's worth, would be Yezhevikin. I have now been out of work for over eight years, and I live simply according to the laws of nature. And as for children – well, I have as many children as the Kholmsky family!* As the saying has it: the rich man has cattle, and the poor man... children..."

"Well, yes... cattle... but let's put that to one side. Anyway, listen, I keep on meaning to ask why, whenever you come into a room, you immediately take a look behind you. It's such a funny thing to do."

"Why do I take a look behind me? Because I keep on thinking that someone's going to creep up on me and swat me like a fly, that's why. I've become an obsessive, sir."

Once again everyone laughed. The governess got up from her seat as if wanting to leave, and then sat down again. Despite the colour in her cheeks, she looked pained and miserable.

"Do you know who that is, my boy?" my uncle whispered to me. "Well, he's *her* father!"

I looked at my uncle in absolute astonishment. The name Yezhevikin had gone completely out of my head. During the whole journey to Stepanchikovo I had been building myself up, devising all kinds of heroic and wonderful plans for my intended, and had completely forgotten her surname – or, rather, had never paid any attention to it from the very start.

"What do you mean her father?" I replied, also in a whisper. "But I thought she was an orphan!"

"Her father, my boy, her father. And, you know, the most honest and honourable of men – doesn't drink, merely plays the fool sometimes. Absolutely destitute, my boy, eight children!

82

Lives on Nastenka's salary. Sacked from his job for shooting his mouth off. Comes here every week. Extraordinarily proud – won't accept a thing. Gives the whole time, but never takes! An embittered man!"

"So tell me, Yevgraf Larionych old chap, what's new?" my uncle asked, giving him a hearty slap on the shoulder, noticing that the suspicious old man was already beginning to listen in to our conversation.

"What's new, my kind sir? Valentin Ignatych has been giving evidence in the Trishin case. Some of Trishin's bags of flour turned out to be underweight. Trishin, by the way, dear lady, is the one who looks at you as if he's trying to blow on the coals under a samovar. You may remember him, dear lady? Anyway, this is what Valentin Ignatych has to say about Trishin: 'If,' he says, 'the aforementioned Trishin was unable to guard the honour of his own niece – she was the one who ran away with that officer last year – then he's hardly likely,' he says, 'to take good care of government property, is he?' That's what he wrote in his affidavit – no, really, that's what he said."

"Pah! Tell us another one!" exclaimed Anfisa Petrovna.

"Exactly, exactly, exactly! You've let your tongue run away with you, Yevgraf, old boy," my uncle agreed. "That tongue of yours will be the undoing of you! You may be an honest, straightforward and decent fellow, but you have a poisonous tongue, let me tell you! And I am astonished you can't get on with them! They seem to be such simple, good-natured people…"

"My dear, kind, generous sir – the simpler the person, the more I'm afraid!" the old man cried with especial fervour.

I liked that answer. I quickly went up to Yezhevikin and firmly shook him by the hand. If truth be told, I wanted somehow to show how much I disagreed with everyone else by expressing my feeling of solidarity for the old man. And perhaps – who knows? – perhaps I wanted to raise myself in Nastasya Yevgrafovna's estimation. But my action had none of the intended effect.

"Permit me to ask," I said, blushing and stumbling over my words as usual, "have you heard of the Jesuits?"

"No, my dear sir, I have not... or maybe something, on one occasion. But then I'm hardly the person to know about such things, am I? Why do you ask?"

"Well, I just... I just, you know, wanted to say... Never mind, you must remind me some other time. But for now please be assured that I understand you and... can appreciate..."

And, in total confusion, I grabbed his hand once again.

"Of course, my dear fellow, of course I'll remind you! I'll inscribe it in golden letters on my heart. Here, you see, I'm tying a knot, to remind myself."

And, indeed, finding a clean part of his dirty, tobacco-stained handkerchief, he tied a knot in it.

"Please have some tea, Yevgraf Larionych," said Praskovya Ilyinichna.

"At once, my beautiful lady, at once – my princess, that is, not lady! Thank you for the tea. I met Stepan Alexeich Bakhcheyev on the way here, madam. In *such* high spirits! He's not getting married by any chance, is he? Flatter them, flatter them!" he said in a half-whisper to me, as he walked past me, carrying his tea, winking at me and screwing up his eyes. "But why is the most generous and bountiful person of all, Foma Fomich, not here? Surely he'll be joining us for tea, won't he?"

My uncle winced as if he'd been stung, and glanced timidly at the general's lady.

"He's been told, but he... I'm really not sure, maybe he's not in the mood. I have already asked Vidoplyasov to... but why don't I go myself?"

"I dropped in on him just now," Yezhevikin announced mysteriously.

"Really?" my uncle exclaimed anxiously. "And?..."

"I called in on him first of all, to convey my respects. He said he wanted to take his tea on his own, adding that a crust of dry bread would totally suffice – that's what he said, sir."

These words seemed to strike real terror into my uncle.

"But you should have explained to him, Yevgraf Larionych, you should have told him…" my uncle said finally, looking at the old man in anguished reproach.

"But I did, sir, I did."

"Well?"

"He didn't deign to answer me for a long time, sir. He was absorbed in trying to resolve some mathematical problem – something obviously really baffling. He was sketching out Pythagoras's theorem, in front of me. I tried three times to speak to him, and it was only then, at my fourth attempt, that he looked up and seemed to see me for the first time. 'I'm not coming down – apparently some *scholar* or other has shown up, so what kind of figure will I cut next to such a luminary?' That was the expression he saw fit to use: 'next to such a luminary'."

And the old man gave me a sideways, rather mocking glance.

"Well, that was just what I expected!" my uncle exclaimed, throwing his hands up in the air. "Just what I thought! By 'luminary' he clearly meant you, Sergei. So what do we do now, then?"

"I must confess, Uncle," I replied, with a dignified shrug of the shoulders, "in my opinion that was such an absurd remark that it's not worth paying it any attention, and I have to say I'm astonished you should be so affected by it."

"Oh, my boy, you don't have the first idea, do you?" he cried, with a vigorous gesture.

"Well, it's a bit late to be concerned about it now," Miss Perepelitsyna suddenly interposed, "seeing that it was all your fault in the first place, Yegor Ilyich, sir. Once the head's chopped off, there's no point in crying over the hair. If you'd listened to your mother, you wouldn't be weeping now, sir."

"But for the love of God, why on earth is it my fault, Anna Nilovna?" my uncle pleaded, as if imploring her for an explanation.

"Well, I certainly love God, Yegor Ilyich, but all this has come about because you are selfish and you don't love your mother, sir," Miss Perepelitsyna replied regally. "What made you disobey her in the first place? She is your mother, sir. And I am not about to lie to you, sir. I am a lieutenant colonel's daughter, sir, not just anybody."

It occurred to me that the only reason Miss Perepelitsyna had become involved in the conversation was so that she could let everyone know, and especially me as the newcomer, that she was a lieutenant colonel's daughter, and not just anyone.

"It's all because he insults his own mother," the general's lady said finally and menacingly.

"But Mother, why do you say such things? How have I insulted you?"

"By being such a wretched egoist, Yegorushka," insisted the general's lady, becoming more and more animated.

"But Mother, Mother, in what way have I been a wretched egoist?" my uncle exclaimed, close to despair. "You've been cross with me for five days – a whole five days – and refused to say a word to me! But why? What for? Let people judge me, let the whole world judge me! But let my side of the story be finally heard as well! I have kept quiet for far too long, Mother – you've refused to listen to me, so let everyone hear me now, Anfisa Petrovna! Pavel Semyonych, dearest Pavel Semyonych! Sergei, my dear boy! You are an outsider, an impartial witness, as it were, so you'll be able to give an unbiased opinion…"

"Calm down, Yegor Ilyich, calm down," cried Anfisa Petrovna. "You'll be the death of your mother!"

"No I won't, Anfisa Petrovna, but here is my chest – go on, punch me!" my uncle went on, now in an emotionally overwrought state, as sometimes happens to weak-willed people when they are driven to the limits of their endurance, even though their passion is merely just a flash in the pan. "I would like it to be known, Anfisa Petrovna, that I never insult anyone. And let me begin by saying that Foma Fomich is the most honest and honourable of men – and, moreover, someone of the highest qualities – but in this instance he was less than fair to me."

"Hmm!" muttered Obnoskin, as if wishing to provoke my uncle even more.

"Pavel Semyonych, my dearest Pavel Semyonych! Surely you don't think that I'm just an unfeeling block of wood, do you? Of course I can see, of course I understand, with a tearful heart, so to speak, that all misunderstandings come about because of *his* love for me. But, think what you like, in this instance he is genuinely and truly being unfair. I'll tell you the whole story. I want to tell the whole story now, Anfisa Petrovna, as clearly and as thoroughly as possible, so that you can see for yourself how it all began, and whether Mother is being fair when she blames me for offending Foma Fomich. You must listen to this as well, Seryozha," he added, turning to me – something he kept on doing throughout the rest of his story, as if worried the other listeners might not be so sympathetic. "You must listen, too, and decide for yourself whether I'm right or not. You see, this is how it all began: a week ago – yes, that's right, it was no more than a week ago – my former commanding officer, General Rusapyetov, accompanied by his wife and sister-in-law, happened to be passing through town, where they stopped off for a short time. When I heard about this, I was astounded, and determined not to let the opportunity slip. So I dashed off, introduced myself and invited them here to dinner. He promised to come, if at all possible. He's an absolute gentleman, a shining example of rectitude and integrity, and, what's more, someone of real eminence! So kind to his sister-in-law, arranging matters so that she, an orphan girl, married a wonderful young man (now an attorney in Malinov, still young but with an all-round education, so to speak!) – in short, the very example of what a good general should be! Naturally, it meant the house was turned upside down, hustle and bustle everywhere, discussions, cooks, fricassees... Anyway, I hire an orchestra, and naturally start going about everywhere, looking as pleased as punch! But Foma Fomich doesn't like that! There we were, I remember, at dinner, with his favourite dish, blancmange and cream, being served up; he was sitting there without saying a word, when he suddenly jumped to his feet and exclaimed: 'It's an insult! An absolute insult!' 'What do you mean, Foma Fomich,'

I say, 'an "insult"?' 'You're set on ignoring me,' he said. 'With
you, it's nothing but generals now – you're more bothered about
generals than you are with me!' I'm cutting a long story short
here, of course, giving you just the essence, as it were, but if you
knew what he went on to say... I was absolutely shattered! What
was I to do? I was of course very depressed, shaken to the core,
I would say, and went around the place looking like a wet rag.
Anyway, the momentous day arrived. The general sends someone
to say he's sorry, but is unable to come – the whole thing was
off, in other words. So I go to Foma and say: 'There's no need to
worry, Foma: he's not coming!' And what do you think? Do you
think he forgave me? Not a bit of it. 'You've offended me,' he says,
'that's what you've done.' When I demurred, he simply said: 'Go
on, off you go to your generals – you've more time for them than
for me... you have destroyed the bonds of friendship between
us.' Oh, my friend! Of course I could understand why he was
so angry with me. I'm not some block of wood, not some idiot,
some idle parasite! No, he did it because he loved me so much,
because he was, so to speak, jealous, jealous of the general, afraid
I might stop loving him, testing me to find out what I might be
prepared to give up for his sake. 'No,' he says, 'you have to look
on me as the equivalent of a general, you have to address me as
"Your Excellency"! Harmony can only be restored between us
when you can demonstrate your respect for me.' 'But how can
I do that, Foma Fomich?' 'You are to address me every day as
"Your Excellency" – that will be the only way of demonstrating
your respect for me.' I was lost for words! You can imagine how
astonished I was! 'And let that serve as a lesson to you,' he says,
'not to allow yourself to be carried away by generals, when there
are other people who are probably worth so much more than all
your generals put together!' But this was the final straw, I have
to admit – admit quite openly! 'Foma Fomich,' I say, 'that's not
really possible, is it? How could I bring myself to do anything
like that? How could I possibly make you a general, how would
I have the right to do so? Think about it: who has the authority

to make someone a general? So how can I possibly address you as "Your Excellency"? After all, that would be, so to speak, a violation of the supreme laws governing the destiny of individuals! A general serves as a shining example to his country! A general has fought for his country, he has shed blood on the battlefield for the honour of his country! How can I possibly address you as "Your Excellency"?' Does he back down? Not in the least! 'I'll do whatever you want me to do, Foma,' I say. 'You once ordered me to shave off my sideboards because they weren't very patriotic, so I shaved them off – under protest, but I went ahead and shaved them off anyway. In short, I'll do anything you want me to do, but you have to give up this idea of becoming a general!' 'No,' he replies, 'there will be no harmony between us until you start addressing me as "Your Excellency"! That,' he says, 'will be an edifying exercise for you – it will humble your spirit!' he says. And now a week, a whole week has gone by, during which he hasn't said a single word to me. Whenever anyone comes to the house, he rips into them. When he heard you were a man of science – that was my fault: I got overexcited, got carried away – he said that, as soon as you arrived, he would make himself scarce. 'So,' he says, 'you no longer consider me a scholar, then, I suppose?' What he'll do when he hears about Korovkin I simply can't imagine! Please, I ask you, you be the judge: in what way can I possibly be at fault here? How on earth can I bring myself to start addressing him as "Your Excellency"? How can I go on living like this? Why did he drive that poor fellow Bakhcheyev away from the table today? All right, he's not a founding father of astronomy, but then neither am I, nor you, for that matter... So then why did he do that – why?"

"Why? It's because you're jealous, Yegorushka," the general's lady muttered again.

"But Mother!" my uncle cried in total despair. "You're driving me out of my mind! You're just parroting what other people are saying, Mother! I'm just a lump of wood, a tree stump, a lamppost, and not your son!"

"I heard, Uncle," I interrupted, totally bowled over by what he had said, "I heard from Bakhcheyev – I don't know whether it's true or not – that Foma Fomich is jealous of the fact that it's Ilyusha's name day, and maintains that it's his name day too tomorrow. I have to confess, I was so astonished by this particular manifestation of his character that I—"

"Birthday, my boy, birthday, not name day, but birthday!" my uncle hurriedly interrupted me. "It was just a slip of the tongue, but he's right, insofar as tomorrow actually is his birthday. Truth, my boy, above all…"

"It's not his birthday at all!" Sashenka exclaimed.

"What do you mean, 'not his birthday'?" my uncle exclaimed, taken aback by this.

"It's not his birthday at all, Papa! You're simply saying something that's not true, deceiving yourself just to placate Foma Fomich. His birthday was actually in March – if you remember – we went to the service at the monastery just before, and he made life so uncomfortable for everyone in the carriage, shouting the whole time that the cushion was *pressing* against his ribs, and he kept on pinching people: he pinched Auntie twice – he was so cross! And then, when we came to celebrate his birthday, he flew into a rage, complaining there had been no camelias in our bouquet of flowers. 'I love camelias,' he said, 'because I have the highest possible taste, and you objected to me picking some from the greenhouse.' And he spent the whole day sulking and complaining, refusing to talk to anyone…"

I think that if a bomb had fallen into the middle of the room, it would have caused less shock and fright than this rebellious outburst – and this, moreover, from a young girl who had been forbidden from ever speaking loudly in her grandmother's presence! The general's lady, unable to speak from astonishment and fury, sat up and glared at her insolent granddaughter in disbelief. My uncle was stricken with terror.

"What absolute cheek! This will be the death of Grandmother!" shouted Miss Perepelitsyna.

"Sasha, Sasha, think what you're saying! What's got into you, Sasha?" cried my uncle, dashing over now to one, now to the other, now to his mother, now to Sashenka, to stop her talking.

"No, I won't be quiet, Papa!" Sasha shouted back, suddenly jumping up from her chair and stamping her feet, her eyes flashing. "I won't be quiet! We have all had to put up with Foma Fomich, that vile, horrid Foma Fomich of yours, for far too long! He'll be the undoing of us all – everybody keeps on telling him what a brilliant, generous-hearted, distinguished scholar he is, someone who combines every virtue as in a potpourri, and Foma Fomich, the fool, drinks it all in! He's been served so many wonderful dishes that it would put anyone else to shame, but Foma Fomich guzzles everything put in front of him, and then asks for more! He'll gobble us all up, you'll see, and it's all Papa's fault! Horrid, horrid Foma Fomich, I say, and I don't care what you think! He's a stupid, fickle, ungrateful, cruel and despotic man, a gossip and a squalid little liar... Oh, if it were up to me, I'd kick him out of this house this minute, but Papa adores him, thinks he's absolutely wonderful!..."

"Oh my God!" shrieked the general's lady, and collapsed back onto the sofa in a swoon.

"My darling, Agafya Timofeyevna, my angel!" cried Anfisa Petrovna. "Here, take my scent bottle! Water, quick, water!"

"Water, water!" my uncle shouted. "Mother, Mother, please calm down. I'm begging you, on my knees, to calm down!"

"You should be confined to a dark room and given only bread and water... you murderess, you!" Miss Perepelitsyna hissed at Sashenka, beside herself with rage.

"Lock me in with only bread and water, see if I care!" shouted Sasha, also at the end of her tether. "I'm defending Papa, because he's not capable of defending himself. Who is this man, who is he, your Foma Fomich, compared to Papa? He eats Papa's bread and then goes and humiliates him, the ungrateful man! I would rip him into little pieces, that Foma Fomich of yours! I would challenge him to a duel and then kill him on the spot with both pistols..."

"Sasha! Sasha!" shouted my uncle in despair. "One more word from you and I'm lost, lost for ever!"

"Papa!" exclaimed Sasha, suddenly rushing headlong over to her father and vigorously throwing her arms around him. "Papa! You're such a kind, wonderful, cheerful, clever man, why are you allowing yourself to be destroyed in this way? Why are you putting up with this vile, ungrateful man, letting yourself be his plaything, becoming everybody's laughing stock like this? Papa, my precious, wonderful Papa!"

She broke into sobs, covered her face in her hands and dashed out of the room.

A terrible commotion ensued. The general's lady was lying in a swoon. My uncle was kneeling in front of her, kissing her hands. Miss Perepelitsyna was hovering nearby, looking across at us with an angry but triumphant expression. Anfisa Petrovna was mopping the general's lady's brow and fussily administering the contents of her scent bottle. Praskovya Ilyinichna was trembling, with the tears pouring down her cheeks; Yezhevikin was searching around for a corner in which to hide, while the governess simply stood there with a pale face, totally petrified. Only Mizinchikov remained completely unconcerned by it all. He stood up, went up to the window and became utterly absorbed by what was going on outside, deliberately ignoring what was happening in the room.

Suddenly the general's lady sat up straight and looked at me menacingly.

"Get out!" she cried, stamping her foot at me.

I hadn't expected that at all, I must confess.

"Get out! Get out of this house! What's he doing here? Get out of my sight! Get out!"

"Mother, Mother, what are you saying? But this is Seryozha," my uncle mumbled, his whole body quaking with fear. "He's come here as our guest, Mother."

"What Seryozha? Nonsense! I'm convinced it's Korovkin. I know I'm right. He's come to kick Foma Fomich out – he's been specially engaged for that purpose. My heart never deceives me… Get out of the house, you scoundrel!"

"If that's how it is, Uncle," I said, choking with righteous indignation, "if that's how it is, then… you'll have to excuse me…" And I grabbed my hat.

"Sergei, Sergei, what are you doing?… But really, Mother, this is Sergei!… Sergei, I beg you!" he shouted, dashing after me and trying to take my hat away from me. "You are my guest, you're not going anywhere – I insist!… She's like this sometimes," he added in a whisper. "She only does this when she's angry… Best go and find somewhere to hide for now… stay there for a bit, and everything will turn out all right. She'll forgive you, I can assure you! She's a kind-hearted lady, really – just gets carried away sometimes… She's taken you for Korovkin, you see, but she'll come to her senses, I know she will… What do you want?" he shouted at Gavrila, who had just come into the room, quaking with fear.

There was someone else with Gavrila: he was accompanied by one of the serf boys, a very handsome lad of about sixteen, who had been taken on in the house precisely for his good looks, as I was later to discover. His name was Falaley. He was dressed in a very striking costume: a red silk shirt, with braiding around the collar, a gold lace belt and black velveteen baggy trousers with red turn-ups. This costume had been the general's lady's idea. The boy was sobbing his heart out, the tears running down his cheeks from his large blue eyes.

"What now?" exclaimed my uncle. "What's happened? Come on, say something, you devil!"

"Foma Fomich told us to come – he'll be here himself very shortly," replied Gavrila. "I've got this examindation, see, and he…"

"And he?"

"Dancing, sir," Gavrila replied mournfully.

"Dancing!" my uncle exclaimed in horror.

"Dancing!" howled Falaley through his tears.

"The Kamarinskaya?"*

"The Ka-ma-rinskaya!"

"And Foma Fomich caught him at it?"

"Yes, sir!"

"I've had it!" my uncle cried. "I'm done for!" And he clutched his head in his hands.

"Foma Fomich!" announced Vidoplyasov, coming into the room.

The door opened to reveal Foma Fomich himself, in person, standing in front of the bewildered assembly.

6

Apropos of a White Bull
and the "Peasant from Kamarin"

But before I have the honour of personally introducing Foma
Fomich to the reader, I think I should first definitely say a few
words about Falaley and explain what it was precisely that was so
terrible about the fact that he had been dancing the Kamarinskaya
and that Foma Fomich had caught him doing it. Falaley was a
house boy, an orphan from the cradle up and the godchild of my
uncle's deceased wife. My uncle was very fond of him. This of
itself was quite enough to explain why Foma Fomich, once he had
settled in Stepanchikovo and started to tyrannize my uncle, should
have taken such a strong dislike to his favourite boy, Falaley. But
the general's lady nonetheless became very fond of the lad, who,
despite Foma Fomich's angry protests, remained upstairs, in the
family part of the house – something the general's lady herself
insisted upon. In this instance Foma had yielded to her wishes,
while remaining mortally offended by it (he saw everything as a
personal offence) and taking his revenge on my totally innocent
uncle at every available opportunity. Falaley was a remarkably
good-looking lad. He had a girl's features, the face of a village
beauty. The general's lady watched over him, pampered him,
treasured him as if he were some rare, precious toy, and no one
knew for certain which she more doted on: her small curly-haired
bitch Ami or Falaley. We have already mentioned his costume,
which she herself had created. The young ladies would provide
him with pomade, while the barber Kuzma was tasked with curling
his hair on feast days. This lad was a rather curious individual.
You couldn't really call him a complete idiot or a holy fool,* but
he was such a naive, honest and ingenuous character that he could

at times genuinely be considered a simpleton. If he had a dream, he would immediately go and tell his masters about it. He would interrupt their conversation, without being in the least concerned he was doing so. He would tell them things which were totally inappropriate. He would burst into floods of tears whenever his mistress fainted or someone was giving his master a too-severe telling-off. He would sympathize with everyone else's misfortune. Sometimes he would go to the general's lady, kiss her hands and ask her not to be angry with him – and she would magnanimously forgive him for such a liberty. He was an extraordinarily sensitive person, as kind and as gentle as a lamb, as happy as a young child. At table he would be rewarded with titbits.

He always stood behind the general's lady's chair. He had a particular partiality for sugar, and whenever he was given a sugar lump, he would immediately gnaw at it with his strong, pearly white teeth, his animated blue eyes and his handsome little face lighting up with inexpressible pleasure.

Foma Fomich took a long time to calm down. But, finally concluding that anger wouldn't get him anywhere, he suddenly resolved to become Falaley's benefactor. Having taken my uncle to task in no uncertain terms for neglecting the education of the house serfs, he there and then decided he would teach the poor lad correct moral behaviour, good manners and the French language.

"Think about it," he would exclaim, in defence of his absurd idea (an idea which has occurred to others besides Foma Fomich, as the author of these lines can testify), "think about it! He spends the whole time upstairs, in his mistress's room – what if she, forgetting he doesn't understand French, were suddenly to say to him, for example, '*Donnez-moi mon mouchoir*',* and he finds himself in the position of having to do what she asks?" But it transpired that not only was it impossible to teach Falaley French, but that his uncle, the cook Andron, who, out of the goodness of his heart, had tried to instil in him the basics of Russian grammar, had long ago given up the attempt and returned the textbook to the shelf! Falaley had proved so hopeless at anything involving studying from a book that he had been unable to understand a single thing. This led, moreover, to another little incident. When the other house serfs began teasing Falaley, calling him "Froggie", old Gavrila, my uncle's trustworthy valet, openly dared to question the value of studying Russian grammar. When Foma Fomich heard about this, he flew into a rage, and, as a punishment, forced the wayward Gavrila to take up the study of French himself. That was how the whole matter relating to the French language that had so incensed Mr Bakhcheyev had started. As far as manners were concerned, things took an even worse turn: Foma proved to be totally incapable of reforming Falaley, and the lad, despite being told not to, persisted in appearing each morning with an account of his dream – something that Foma, for his part, considered highly unbecoming and presumptuous. But Falaley stubbornly refused to change his ways. And naturally it was my uncle who was the first to suffer as a result.

"Do you know, do you know what he did today?" Foma shouted one day, choosing the moment of maximum effect when everyone was present. "Are you aware, colonel, just what effect your systematic pampering has had? Earlier today he devoured a piece of pie which you'd given him at the table, and do you know what he said? Come here, come here, you ridiculous little man, come here, you red-faced imbecile!"

Falaley went up to Foma, crying and wiping away the tears with both hands.

"What did you say when you'd gulped down that piece of pie? Repeat what you said, so that everyone can hear!"

Falaley stayed silent, with the tears streaming down his cheeks.

"All right then, I'll answer on your behalf. You said, slapping yourself on your full, indecent belly: 'I stuffed myself with pie, just like Martin with soap!'* I ask you, colonel: is that how people talk in educated society? Not to say in exalted company? Did you or did you not say that? Come on, speak up!"

"Yes, I did say that," Falaley confirmed, still sobbing.

"Right! So now tell me: does Martin really eat soap? Where precisely have you seen anyone called Martin eating soap? Come on, say something: tell me about this legendary Martin!"

Silence.

"I'm asking you," persisted Foma, "who precisely is this Martin fellow? I would like to meet him, get to know him. Come on, for goodness' sake, who is he? Is he a clerk, an astronomer, some country bumpkin, a poet, a captain at arms, a household serf?... He's got to be someone or other. Come on, answer me!"

"A household serf," Falaley answered eventually, the tears still running down his cheeks.

"Whose serf? Who does he belong to?"

But Falaley couldn't say who Martin's owner was. The whole matter ended of course with an enraged Foma running out of the room shouting that he'd been insulted, the general's lady having one of her attacks and my uncle cursing the fact he'd ever been born, asking everybody's forgiveness and spending the rest of the day tiptoeing around in his part of the house.

This was bad enough, but what happened on the very next day after the Martin's soap story was even worse: when bringing Foma Fomich his tea in the morning, Falaley told him he had had a dream about a white bull, having totally forgotten all about Martin and the previous day's unhappy episode. That was the final straw! Incandescent with rage, Foma Fomich immediately summoned my uncle and started taking him to task for the vulgarity of Falaley's dream. On this occasion strict measures were taken: Falaley was punished by being made to kneel in a corner and expressly forbidden from ever having such coarse peasant's dreams. "It makes me so angry!" Foma said. "How dare he even think of coming to me with his dreams like that – and about a white bull! Besides, you will be the first to agree, colonel, that this white bull merely demonstrates just what a vulgar, ignorant peasant your uncouth Falaley is! What you think determines what you dream. Anyway, haven't I already made it clear that he's a hopeless case and should never have been allowed to wait on his masters upstairs? You will never ever be able to make this useless country bumpkin conceive lofty poetic ideas. Why can't you," he continued, turning to Falaley, "why can't you dream about something refined, delicate, uplifting, some scene or other from polite society – your lords and masters playing cards, for example, or ladies taking a stroll in a beautiful garden?" Falaley promised that the very next night he would dream about his lords and masters, or ladies taking a stroll in a beautiful garden.

As he lay down to sleep, Falaley prayed tearfully to God, asking for help in this matter, and for a long time concentrated his thoughts so as to avoid dreaming about that cursed white bull. But human hopes are fickle. Awaking the next morning, he recalled with horror that once again he had dreamt about that hated white bull, and not about any lady going for a stroll in a beautiful garden. This time the consequences were particularly serious. Foma Fomich absolutely refused to believe there could have been any repetition of such a dream, and was convinced that someone in the household, possibly even the colonel himself, had told Falaley what to say simply in order to annoy him. The house erupted in shouts, reproaches and tears. By that evening the general's lady had fallen ill, and everyone was walking around with a long face. There was still the faint hope that the next (that is the third) night high society would undoubtedly feature in Falaley's dream. You can imagine the general consternation when every night, for a whole week running, Falaley dreamt about a white bull, and nothing but a white bull! Not even a peep into high society.

But the most intriguing point about all this was that it never occurred to Falaley to tell a lie – simply to say, for instance, that he hadn't dreamt about a white bull, but of a carriage driving along full of ladies together with Foma Fomich, particularly since, to tell a lie in such extreme circumstances would hardly have been considered a sin. But Falaley was such an honest person that he could never have told a lie, even if he had wanted to. Nobody had even suggested that he should. Everyone knew that he would give himself away the instant he opened his mouth, and that Foma would immediately know he was lying. What was to be done? My uncle's position became intolerable: Falaley was clearly incorrigible. The poor lad even began to lose weight, he was so depressed. The housekeeper, Malanya, maintained he had the evil eye and sprinkled on him coal dipped in water. In this valuable operation she was assisted by the kind-hearted Praskovya Ilyinichna. But even this was of no help. Nothing was of any help!

"Damn the blasted creature!" Falaley would complain. "I dream about it every night! Every evening I pray: 'Don't dream about the white bull, don't dream about the white bull!' But there he is as plain as anything standing in front of me, the damn thing – as large as life, with horns, thick-lipped… oh my Lord!"

My uncle was in despair. But, happily, Foma Fomich suddenly seemed to completely forget about the white bull. Naturally no one believed that such a significant circumstance could have slipped Foma Fomich's mind. Everyone simply reckoned, in trepidation, that he was merely keeping the white bull in reserve so that he could produce it again at the first convenient moment. It subsequently became apparent that, at that particular moment, white bulls were the last thing in Foma Fomich's mind: he had other matters, other concerns to think about; other ideas were blossoming in his productive and fertile brain. That was why he allowed Falaley to breathe a sigh of relief. Everyone, together with Falaley, could relax. The lad cheered up and even began to forget about what had happened – even the white bull started appearing less and less frequently in his dreams, although it would continue every so often to remind him of its phantom existence. In short, all would have been well, had it not been for the Kamarinskaya.

It should be noted that Falaley was an excellent dancer; it was what he was best at, something even of a vocation; he danced with energetic abandon, with real enjoyment, being especially fond of the dance of the "peasant from Kamarin". He liked it not so much because of the frivolous and in any case incomprehensible behaviour of this empty-headed peasant, but solely because he was totally incapable of hearing the music of the Kamarinskaya and not dancing to it. Sometimes, in the evening, a couple of servants, the coachman, the gardener, who played the fiddle, and even some of the women of the household would assemble in a circle somewhere in an extremely remote part of the estate, as far away as possible from Foma Fomich. The music would strike up, the dancing would begin, until finally the Kamarinskaya would take its rightful place in the proceedings. The band would consist of two balalaikas, a guitar, a violin and a tambourine,* played with real skill by the postilion Mityushka. Falaley's behaviour now was a sight to behold: he would dance himself into a state of total oblivion and exhaustion, encouraged by the cheers and laughter of those watching. He would shriek, yell, laugh and clap his hands; he danced as if inspired by some mysterious, inscrutable force which he was unable to control, as he stamped his heels and strained every sinew to keep up with the accelerating tempo of the audacious tune. For him, those were moments of pure delight. And it would all have been fine and wonderful had not the rumours of the Kamarinskaya finally reached Foma Fomich's ears.

Horrified by what he'd heard, Foma Fomich immediately sent for the colonel.

"Would you be so kind as to tell me one thing, colonel," Foma began. "Is it or is it not your avowed intention to completely ruin that unfortunate idiot? If it is, then here and now I shall do nothing about it – if not, then..."

"What are you talking about? What's happened?" my uncle exclaimed in alarm.

"What's happened, you ask? Don't you know he's been dancing the Kamarinskaya?"

"Well? What of it?"

"What of it!?" shrieked Foma. "How can you say that – you, their master and, in a certain sense, their father! Do you really have no idea what the Kamarinskaya actually is? That it's a song about a loathsome, inebriated peasant on the brink of committing a highly immoral act? Do you know what that depraved peasant did? He violated the most sacred of bonds – trampled, as it were, on them with his clodhopping boots, accustomed only to stamping on tavern floors! And don't you realize that, by replying like that, you have insulted my noblest feelings? Don't you understand that you have personally insulted me by that reply? Do you understand that or not?"

"But, Foma... it's only a song, isn't it, Foma?"

"What do you mean 'only a song'? And you're not ashamed to admit that you know this song? You, a member of the highest echelons of society, the father of fine, innocent children and, what's more, a colonel! 'Only a song' indeed! But I am convinced that this song has been taken from real life! 'Only a song'! How can anyone with any sense of decency admit he knows this song, ever even heard it, without dying from shame? How? Tell me, how?"

"Well, you have for one, Foma, if you want to know," my uncle replied in all simplicity and mired in confusion.

"What's that? *I* know it, you're saying? Me... me... you really mean me? That's such an insult!" Foma suddenly yelled, leaping up from his chair, choking with anger. He had never expected such a jaw-dropping reply.

I cannot begin to describe just how angry Foma Fomich was. The colonel was ignominiously expelled from the presence of the guardian of morality for the impropriety and *inappropriateness* of his reply. But from then on Foma made a promise to himself that he would catch Falaley red-handed at the scene of the crime, dancing the Kamarinskaya. In the evenings, when everyone presumed he was busy with something, he would make a point of going out quietly into the garden, skirting the vegetable beds and concealing himself in the hemp, from where, a little distance away, there was a good view of the place where the dances were taking place. There he lay in wait for the unfortunate Falaley, like a hunter waiting for his prey to appear and licking his lips at the thought of the reaction, in the event of success, on the part of the whole household and, in particular, of the colonel. Eventually his tireless efforts were crowned with success: he observed the Kamarinskaya in action! It was hardly surprising therefore that my uncle was so beside himself with anxiety when he saw Falaley in tears and heard Vidoplyasov announcing the arrival of Foma Fomich, who was just about to make an unexpected appearance at such a fraught moment.

7

Foma Fomich

I scrutinized this gentleman with particular curiosity. Gavrila had been right in describing him as an unprepossessing little man. Foma was short in stature, with greying fair hair, a hook nose and his face covered in little wrinkles. There was a large mole on his chin. He was some fifty years old. He had come into the room quietly, taking measured strides, his eyes fixed on the ground. But the expression on his face and his entire pompous little figure spoke of arrogant self-confidence. He was wearing a dressing gown – admittedly of foreign cut, but nevertheless quite clearly a dressing gown – and, what's more, slippers on his feet. The collar of his open-necked shirt was fashioned *à l'enfant,** giving him a highly ridiculous appearance. He went up to an empty chair, moved it close to the table and sat down, without a word to anyone. All the excitement and commotion that had filled the room a moment earlier disappeared in an instant. The silence was such that you could hear a pin drop. The general's lady went as quiet as a little lamb – the full extent of this poor imbecilic woman's deferential attitude towards Foma Fomich was now quite apparent. She looked admiringly at her little angel, unable to take her eyes off him. Miss Perepelitsyna rubbed her hands in glee, showing her teeth with a contented smile, while poor Praskovya Ilyinichna was visibly shaking with terror. My uncle immediately clapped his hands.

"Tea, tea, sister, dear! Lots of sugar, don't forget, my dear; after his sleep Foma Fomich likes his tea as sweet as possible. That's right, isn't it, Foma?"

"I've no time for tea just now!" Foma pronounced in an unhurried and dignified tone, making a dismissive gesture. "That's all you seem to care about – whether something's sweet enough or not!"

I found these words, together with Foma Fomich's ludicrously pompous entry, extraordinarily fascinating. I was curious to find out exactly how far the insolence of this stuck-up little man would extend.

"Foma!" my uncle exclaimed. "Allow me to introduce you: my nephew, Sergei Alexandrovich! Only just arrived."

Foma Fomich gave him a withering look.

"I never cease to be astonished at the deliberate way you always love to interrupt me, colonel," he said after a significant pause, not paying me the slightest attention. "Here I am talking to you about something important, and you... you start *rambling* on about something... goodness know what. Have you seen Falaley?"

"I have, Foma..."

"Oh, you have, have you? Well, in that case I'll let you take another look at him. Have a good look at your masterpiece... in the moral sense, that is. Come here, you imbecile! Come here, you ugly Dutch mug! Well, come on then, come on! Don't be afraid!"

Falaley went up to him, sobbing, his mouth wide open as he swallowed his tears. Foma Fomich looked at him with particular relish.

"I called him an ugly Dutch mug deliberately, Pavel Semyonych," he remarked, lolling back in his chair and partly turning to Obnoskin, who was sitting next to him, "and in general, you know, I don't find it necessary to mince my words. The truth will always be out. And no matter how hard you try to conceal dirt, it will always remain dirt. So why bother beating about the bush – all you do is deceive yourself and other people! Only a society idiot could conceive of such senseless niceties.* Tell me – I'm asking you to judge – do you find anything beautiful in that face of his? What I mean, of course, is: does it contain anything refined, beautiful, uplifting, or is it just an ugly red mug?"

Foma Fomich spoke quietly, in measured tones, and with a kind of disdainful indifference.

"Anything beautiful in him?" Obnoskin replied, with a contemptuous sneer. "As far as I'm concerned, he's just a nice piece of roast beef."

"Went up to the mirror today and took a close look," Foma went on, portentously omitting the pronoun "I". "I would hardly call myself handsome, but I was nonetheless forced to conclude that there was something in those grey eyes of mine that distinguished me from any old Falaley. There was thought, there was life, there was wit in those eyes! I'm not just speaking about myself: I'm speaking about our class of people in general. So tell me: do you think that this living piece of roast beef could possibly possess the least trace, even the tiniest particle, of a soul? No, indeed not, Pavel Semyonych: note the total absence of thought and imagination in these so-called *people*, with their partiality for roast beef, and their disgustingly fresh complexion, their stupidly coarse fresh complexion! Would you like to find out just what a genius we have here? Hey, you! Come closer, let's have a good look at you! Why's your mouth wide open like that? Want to swallow a whale, do you? Are you beautiful? Tell me: are you beautiful?"

"Beau-ti-ful," answered Falaley, choking down his sobs.

Obnoskin rolled about in his chair from laughter. I felt myself beginning to seethe with anger.

"Did you hear that?" Foma continued, turning triumphantly to Obnoskin. "And there's more: I've come to give him a little test. You see, Pavel Semyonych, there are people who like to corrupt and ruin this pathetic moron. Maybe I'm being too harsh, maybe I'm wrong, but I speak out of love for mankind. Just now he danced the lewdest of dances. Nobody here seems to be bothered by it. But just listen for yourself. So tell me: what did you do just now? Come on, tell me, tell me this instant – do you hear?"

"I danced..." said Falaley, with redoubled sobs.

"And what did you dance? What dance was it? Come on, tell me!"

"The Kamarinskaya."

"The Kamarinskaya! And who is this man from Kamarin that gives it its name? What is this Kamarinskaya? How on earth am I to make sense of such a reply? Well then? Give us some idea: who is this man from Kamarin?"

"A peas-ant..."

"A peasant! Just a peasant? I'm astonished. So he must be a very special peasant! He must be a famous peasant then, if people write poems and make up dances in his honour? Come on, answer me!"

Foma had this need to wear others down by questioning them into a state of exhaustion. He played with his victim like a cat with a mouse. But Falaley remained silent, snivelling and not understanding the question.

"Come on, will you? Answer me!" insisted Foma. "I'm asking you: what kind of peasant was he exactly? Speak up, then! Did he belong to a manor house or to the Crown? Was he free, or tied to the land, or perhaps he was owned by a monastery?"

"Monas-te-ry..."

"Ah, is that so? Do you hear that, Pavel Semyonych? A new historical fact: the peasant from Kamarin was owned by a monastery. Hmm!... So, what did this peasant owned by a monastery do then? What did he achieve that was so wonderful for him to be so celebrated in song... and dance?"

The question was a tricky one, and one fraught with danger, inasmuch as it was directed at Falaley.

"I say... look here... you..." Obnoskin began, looking across at his mother, who was beginning to shift around uneasily in her chair. But there wasn't really anything she could do about it: Foma Fomich's whims were regarded as laws to be obeyed.

"Please, Uncle... if you don't calm this idiot down, he'll... Do you see what he's trying to do? Falaley will make something up, I can absolutely assure you..." I whispered to my uncle, who was in a state of utter confusion, undecided what to do.

"But Foma, perhaps it would be better if you..." he began to say. "Foma, may I introduce you to my nephew, a young man, a one-time student of mineralogy..."

"Might I ask, colonel, that you don't interrupt me with your talk of mineralogy, about which, to the best of my knowledge, you haven't the slightest notion – and that goes for the *others* too. I am not a child. He'll answer me by saying that this peasant, instead of working for the good of his family, became totally intoxicated, sold his sheepskin coat for drink and then ran down the road in an inebriated state. That, as everyone knows, is the entire content of a poem in praise of drunkenness. Don't worry: he knows how to reply *now*. Well, come on, answer me... What did that peasant do? Haven't I already told you, put the words into your mouth? What I want is for you to tell me, in your own words, what it is that he did, what it was exactly he did to deserve such immortal glory that the troubadours sing of it even now. Well?"

Poor Falaley looked around at everybody in despair, searching frantically for something to say, his mouth opening and closing like a carp hauled out of the water onto the sand.

"I'm too a... ashamed to say!" he mumbled finally, in total despair.

"Ah! 'Ashamed to say'!" repeated Foma Fomich, seizing on Falaley's words in triumph. "*That* was the answer I was looking for, colonel! Too ashamed to say, but not to perform! That is the morality which you have sown, which has sprouted and which you are now... watering. But that's enough talk! Off you go now, Falaley, to the kitchen. I'm not going to say anything to you for now, out of respect for those present, but sometime today, definitely today, you are going to be severely punished, punished so hard that it hurts. But if not, if you replace me as the centre of attention and stay here entertaining your masters by dancing the Kamarinskaya, then I shall be out of this house this very day! That's enough. I have spoken. Be off with you!"

"Well, that seems a little... harsh," mumbled Obnoskin.

"Exactly so – exactly, indeed!" my uncle started to say, but broke off and fell silent. Foma gave him a withering look.

"I'm amazed, Pavel Semyonych," he went on. "What is it exactly that all our men of letters, our poets, scholars and thinkers do? Why do they turn a deaf ear to the songs that the Russian people sing and the songs that they dance to? What have all these Pushkins, Lermontovs, Borozdnas* been doing up until now? I am amazed! The Russian people dance the Kamarinskaya, that apotheosis of drunkenness, and all they can do is sing the praises of some forget-me-nots or other! Why can't they write more edifying songs for the Russian public and throw away their forget-me-nots? It's a social question! If they are to portray a peasant, then let it be not so much a peasant, but a villager, so to speak, of real distinction. Let them portray a rural sage in all his simplicity, even one in bast boots, if you like (I would have no objection to that, even), but replete with all the virtues, which would be – I say this quite openly – the envy even of some highly overrated Alexander the Great. I know Mother Russia, and Mother Russia knows me: that's precisely why I'm saying this. Let them portray this peasant, if you like, weighed down by family responsibilities, of advancing age, living, if you like, in a cramped, airless hut, hungry but contented, giving thanks for (rather than complaining about) poverty and indifferent to the rich man's gold. Let this very same rich man, out of the kindness of his heart, finally bring him his gold – let this even be the occasion for the fusion of the peasant's virtue, if you like, with that of his lord and master. Villager and lord, streets apart in social status, are now finally joined together in high-minded probity – such an elevating notion! But what do we see? On the one hand, forget-me-nots, on the other, some unkempt ne'er-do-well reeling out of a tavern and running down the street! So I ask you: is there anything poetic about that? Anything to admire? Where is the wit? The grace? The morality? I'm lost for words!"

"I owe you a hundred roubles, Foma Fomich, for what you've just said!" Yezhevikin exclaimed, with an enraptured expression on his face.

"He won't get a damned thing from me," he whispered to me quietly. "Flattery, flattery!"

"Well, yes… that was a nice picture you painted," muttered Obnoskin.

"Exactly, exactly, exactly!" my uncle exclaimed, giving me a triumphant look.

"Some topic, that!" he whispered, rubbing his hands together. "Such a wide-ranging conversation, damn it! Foma Fomich, this is my nephew," he added, overcome with emotion. "He, too, has studied literature – let me introduce you."

As before, Foma Fomich totally ignored my uncle's attempt to introduce me.

"For God's sake, stop introducing me! No, I mean it!" I whispered sternly.

"Ivan Ivanych!" Foma suddenly began again, turning to Mizinchikov with a penetrating gaze. "What would your view be on what we've just been talking about?"

"Me? You're asking me?" Mizinchikov responded with astonishment, looking as though someone had just woken him up.

"Yes, you, sir. I'm asking you because I value the opinion of truly clever people, and not any old supposed intellectuals who are clever only because they are *constantly being touted* as such, as *scholars*, even sometimes being especially singled out to be paraded at a fairground or something of the sort."

That was a shot aimed directly at me. And there couldn't be the slightest doubt that Foma Fomich, while totally ignoring me, had initiated this entire conversation about literature solely for my benefit, so that he could at one fell swoop blind, annihilate and crush the scholar and clever man from St Petersburg. That was my considered view, at least.

"If you want to know my opinion, then I... I agree with what you've said," Mizinchikov replied rather listlessly and reluctantly.

"You do nothing but agree with me! This is all becoming rather sickening," Foma observed. "I'll tell you quite frankly, Pavel Semyonych," he continued after a moment's or so pause and turning once again to Obnoskin, "if I respect the immortal Karamzin for anything, it's not for his *History*, not for his *Martha the Mayoress* or his *Memoir on Ancient and Modern Russia*, but particularly for his *Frol Silin** – that is a grand epic, a work truly of the people, destined to live for ever! The grandest of epics!"

"Exactly, exactly, exactly! A grand *epoch*! Frol Silin, such a charitable figure! I can remember reading that book: having ransomed two *more* young maidens, he then looks up at the sky and weeps. So sublime!" concurred my uncle, beaming with delight.

Poor uncle! He could never ever resist becoming involved in *scholarly* conversations. Foma merely sneered.

"Yet there is still some entertaining writing today," Anfisa Petrovna interposed cautiously. "Take *The Mysteries of Brussels*,* for example."

"I don't know about that," Foma remarked, as if regretfully. "I recently read one rather long poem... And what do you think? Just another forget-me-not! But if you want my opinion, of today's writers the one I like most is 'the Scribe'* – such a light touch!"

"The Scribe!" cried Anfisa Petrovna. "The one who writes letters for that periodical? Oh, yes, such entrancing writing! Such wordplay!"

"Precisely: wordplay – he plays with his pen, so to speak. A writer with an unusually light touch."

"Yes, but he's a pedant," Obnoskin remarked nonchalantly.

"Pedant, pedant – I don't disagree... but a charming pedant, a likeable pedant! Of course not a single idea will stand up to serious criticism, but he has such a winning lightness of style! A windbag – I agree, but a delightful windbag, a graceful windbag! You remember, for example, his announcement in one of his articles that he's the owner of some estates?"

"Estates?" my uncle said, seizing on the word. "That's wonderful! Which province?"

Foma paused, stared at my uncle for a moment and carried on in the same tone:

"So then, tell me straight out, why should I, the reader, want to know that he's an estate owner? Yes, he is – all right, good luck to him! But it's all so delightfully, so amusingly told! He dazzles, sparkles, bubbles over with wit! He is a soda fountain of wit! Yes, that's how people ought to write! That's exactly how I would have written, I feel, if I had agreed to write for such publications..."

"Perhaps even better, sir," Yezhevikin observed politely.

"There is something so melodious about the way he writes!" my uncle assented.

That was the final straw for Foma Fomich.

"Colonel," he said, "might I ask you – with all due respect, naturally – not to interrupt and to allow us to conclude our conversation in peace? You have nothing to say of any value, nothing at all! So please stop poking your nose into our congenial literary discussion. Look after the affairs of the household, drink your tea, but... leave literature in peace. It won't be to its detriment, I can assure you!"

This was now beyond the bounds of all decency! I didn't know what to think.

"But, Foma, didn't you yourself say that there was something melodious about it?" my uncle responded dejectedly, now totally confused.

"I did indeed, sir. But I spoke as someone who knew what he was talking about, to the point. Unlike you!"

"That's right, sir, we talked sense," Yezhevikin assented, dancing attendance on Foma Fomich. "Not that we're that brainy – we have to exert ourselves to achieve anything, just enough for two government departments, possibly even a third – that's the sort of people we are!"

"Well, it seems as if I've put my foot in it again!" my uncle concluded, smiling in his good-natured way.

"At least he admits it," Foma observed.

"It's nothing, Foma, don't worry, I'm not angry. I know that you took issue with what I said, as a friend, as a brother. You did it because I allowed you, asked you, to do so! And quite right too! It is for my own good! I thank you for that, and I will be guided by it!"

My patience was exhausted. All I had heard about Foma up to that point had seemed to me a little exaggerated. But now, having seen everything with my own eyes, in reality, I was totally flabbergasted. I was simply unable to believe it: I just couldn't comprehend the insolence, the effrontery and despotic behaviour on the one hand, and the self-effacing obsequiousness and gullible good nature on the other. My uncle, however, was clearly finding such insolence upsetting... I burned with the desire somehow to cross swords with Foma, to do battle with him, to wound him to the quick – no matter what happened! I was galvanized by the thought. All I needed was the opportunity, and in my eager expectation I completely snapped off the brim of my hat. But a suitable opportunity did not present itself: Foma persisted in refusing to take any notice of me.

"It's true, it's perfectly true what you are saying, Foma," my uncle continued, doing his very best to make up for his inappropriate behaviour and somehow smooth over any unpleasantness arising from the preceding conversation. "What you said was exactly right, Foma, for which I thank you. You need to know what you are talking about before you open your mouth. I have to confess, however, this is not the first time I've been in such a position. Just imagine, Sergei, I was once even a member of an examination panel... You find that funny? Well, there you are! Yes, really, I was an examiner, however strange it may sound. I was invited to some establishment or other to attend an examination, and they placed me on the panel of examiners as an honorary member, as there was a vacant position. I confess my heart sank, I was terrified: I didn't have a clue about any of the subjects! What could I do? What if they were to call me up to the blackboard to explain something? Well, in fact, everything turned out all right in the end. I even managed to ask a question or two myself: who was Noah? People answered brilliantly on the whole; afterwards we had lunch and drank champagne, raising our glasses to prosperity. Such an excellent establishment!"

Foma Fomich and Obnoskin were helpless with laughter.

"Yes, I myself saw the funny side afterwards," my uncle exclaimed, sharing and rejoicing in the general mirth in the most good-natured way. "So, Foma, how about this, then? Let me tell you all a really funny story, how I once came a cropper... Just imagine, Sergei, we were stationed in Krasnogorsk—"*

"If I may ask, colonel," Foma interrupted, "is this story of yours going to take very long?"

"Oh, Foma! But it's the most wonderful story... you'll simply die laughing. Just listen – it's good, really good. I'll tell you how I made a fool of myself."

"I always love it when you tell such stories," said Obnoskin with a yawn.

"There seems nothing for it, we'll have to listen," Foma pronounced.

"But it will be really good, I promise you, Foma. I want to tell you how I once made such a fool of myself, Anfisa Petrovna. You listen too, Sergei – it will be most enlightening. There we were, stationed in Krasnogorsk," my uncle began, his face beaming with pleasure, speaking too rapidly, tripping over himself and inserting countless asides, as he always did when telling some story or other for the entertainment of his listeners. "The very evening we arrived I went to the theatre. There was this most magnificent actress, Kuropatkina; later she was to run off with Cavalry Captain Zverkov in the middle of the play, and it never finished – they just lowered the curtain... he was quite a devil for drinking and gambling, that Zverkov – not that he was an actual drunkard, simply ready to live it up with his fellow officers. But when he really hit the bottle, he would lose it entirely... forget where he lived, in which country, what his name was – in short, absolutely everything, but, in essence, the most wonderful fellow... Anyway, there I am, in the theatre. In the interval I get up and find myself running into an old friend, Kornoukhov... splendid fellow, I tell you. Actually, we hadn't seen each other for about six years. Been in action, chest full of medals. He's now joined the civil service, I've heard recently, risen to the rank of active state councillor...* Naturally, we were really glad to see each other again. We talked of this and that. There were three ladies in the box sitting next to us. The one on the left was as ugly as sin... Later I was to find out that she was a most admirable woman, happily married, with a family... Anyway, like an idiot, I go and blurt out to Kornoukhov:

'Tell me, my friend, do you happen to know who that old hag is?' 'Which one's that?' 'That one, of course.' 'That's my cousin.' Damn it! You can imagine how I felt! Hastily correcting myself, I say: 'No, I don't mean her. Are you blind or something? That one, sitting opposite: who's she?' 'That's my sister.' Would you believe it? And his sister, moreover, was as lovely as a rosebud, as pretty as anything, beautifully decked out, with brooches, gloves, bracelets – in short, sitting there like a little angel; later she was to get married to the most splendid fellow by the name of Pykhtin; she ran away with him, and they got married without her parents' agreement, but now everything's fine, they're really well off, and their in-laws couldn't be happier... Anyway, be that as it may. 'No, no,' I exclaim, beside myself with embarrassment, 'not her!' 'You mean the one sitting in the middle?' 'Yes, who's she?' 'Well, my friend, she's my wife...' Between you and me, such a ravishingly beautiful lady you'd want to swallow her whole from sheer pleasure... 'Well,' I say, 'if you've never seen an idiot in your life, here's one right now, in front of you. Come on, chop off his head!' He just laughs. After the performance he introduced us, and it was clear that the absolute scoundrel had told them all about it – you could tell by the way they laughed... And, I admit, I had the time of my life with them. So that, Foma, my friend, is how people can make absolute fools of themselves sometimes! Ha-ha-ha!"

But my poor uncle's laughter fell on stony ground; he swept the room with his beaming, good-natured smile, but to no avail: his amusing story was greeted by deathly silence. Foma Fomich remained seated with a glum expression and said nothing, like everybody else. Only Obnoskin permitted himself a faint smile, as he anticipated the criticism that was to come. Overcome by confusion, my uncle went red with embarrassment. That was precisely what Foma had been waiting for.

"Have you quite finished?" he asked finally, turning portentously to my bewildered uncle.

"Yes, Foma."

"And pleased with yourself?"

"What do you mean, 'pleased', Foma?" my poor uncle responded dejectedly.

"Do you feel better now? Are you happy that you have ruined a pleasant literary discussion among friends by interrupting them and thereby satisfying your own petty vanity?"

"But really, Foma! I was only trying to entertain you all, but you——"

"Entertain?" exclaimed Foma, suddenly boiling over with indignation. "But all you're capable of doing is depressing people, not entertaining them! Entertain! But aren't you aware that your little story was practically immoral? Not to mention indecent – that goes without saying... There you were just now, betraying an incredible coarseness of feeling by announcing that you had sneered at an innocent and highborn lady simply because she did not do you the honour of being sufficiently attractive to you. And then you wanted to make us (*us*, for goodness' sake) laugh and thereby connive in your coarse and outrageous behaviour, and all merely because you are master of this house! You can do what you like, colonel: go ahead and cast about for toadies, lickspittles, accomplices, even foreigners, so that you can enrol them in your cause and increase the numbers of your followers, to the detriment of all decent and plain, honest human principles – but Foma Opiskin will never become your flatterer, lickspittle or sponger! Something else maybe, but never that, I can assure you!"

"Oh, but Foma! You misunderstood me!"

"No, colonel, I saw right through you a long time ago – I know exactly your type! You have been consumed by the most insatiable pride, in the pretentious and absurd belief that you are the soul of wit, forgetting that pretentiousness blunts the edge of wit. You——"

"But really, Foma, for Heaven's sake! Think what you're saying, in everyone's presence like this!"

"But it's all so sad, colonel, and when I see that, how can I possibly keep silent? I am not a rich man, I *get by* only through the generosity of your mother. If I say nothing, then that could well be interpreted as flattery, and I certainly don't want some *milksop* to think I'm your toady! If, perhaps, when I came in the room just now, I deliberately exaggerated my perfectly justified frankness and found myself forced to be actually rude, it was precisely because you yourself made me adopt that position. You are too overbearing with me, colonel. I could be seen as your slave, as someone who sponges off you. You enjoy humiliating me in front of *strangers*, but I am your equal, do you hear me? Your equal in every respect. It could even be *me* doing *you* a favour by living in your house, rather than the other way round. I am being humiliated – consequently, I am forced to sing my own praises... that's only to be expected! I have no choice but to speak out – I must speak out, must immediately register a protest – and I therefore directly and simply declare that you are a phenomenally jealous man! As soon as you see someone, for example, spontaneously exhibiting his knowledge, erudition, good taste during the course of a simple, friendly conversation, you get irritated that you don't possess the same qualities: 'Why can't I show off my erudition and good taste as well?' But what good taste do you have to speak of, might I ask? You have about as much appreciation of beauty and elegance – if you'll forgive me, colonel – as a bull has of the Holy Bible! Coarse and harsh, I admit, but honest and fair at least. You won't hear your toadies saying such things, colonel."

"But Foma!"

"There you go: 'But Foma'! Truth is no feather bed, is it? Well, all right, let's leave it at that for the moment, but now allow me to entertain everyone as well. After all, you don't have the exclusive rights, do you? Pavel Semyonovich, have you ever seen this sea monster in human form? I've been observing him for some time. Take a good look: he would like to gobble me up, whole, as I am, alive – wouldn't he?"

Foma was referring to Gavrila. The old servant was standing in the doorway, from where he had indeed been observing the way his master had been taken to task with considerable distress.

"I too would like to entertain you with an amusing spectacle, Pavel Semyonych. Hey, you, you old crow, come here! Do me a favour, Gavrila Ignatych, and come a bit closer! So, Pavel Semyonych, here you have Gavrila, standing right there in front of you. As a punishment for his insolence, he is studying the French language. I, like Orpheus, am setting out to improve the morals of people around here, but through the French language rather than singing.* So Frenchie, Monsieur Chematon* – he can't stand being called 'Monsieur Chematon' – have you done your homework?"

"Yes, I have," replied Gavrila, looking down at the ground.

"And, *parlez-vous français?*"

"*Oui, monsieur, je le parle un peu…*"

I don't know whether it was the sight of Gavrila talking French or simply in anticipation of Foma's obvious desire to make everyone laugh, but they all became helpless with laughter as soon as Gavrila opened his mouth. Even the general's lady deigned to join in. Anfisa Petrovna fell back on the sofa and simply shrieked with laughter, covering her face with her fan. But the general mirth redoubled when Gavrila, seeing what his French examination had turned into, spat on the ground and said indignantly: "So that's what I've come to in my old age, is it?"

Foma Fomich started up.

"What's that? What did you say? Being insolent, are you?"

"No, Foma Fomich," Gavrila replied in a dignified tone, "I wasn't being insolent, and it wouldn't be right for me, a mere servant, to be insolent to a natural-born gentleman such as yourself. But every man has been made in God's image and likeness. I am now sixty-two years old. My father remembered that monster Pugachev,* and my grandfather, together with his master, Matvei Nikitych – may their souls rest in peace – were hanged on the same aspen tree by Pugachev, for which my father was honoured more than anyone else by our late master, Afanasy Matveich: he served as his valet and ended his days as his master's butler. As for me, Foma Fomich, sir, I may be just a servant, but I have never seen such shame as this in all my born days!"

At this, Gavrila spread out his hands and hung his head. My uncle watched him with anxious eyes.

"Well, really, really, Gavrila!" he exclaimed. "You shouldn't have gone on like that – that's enough!"

"Never mind, never mind," Foma said, having turned a little pale and giving a rather forced smile. "Let him have his say... it's all your doing, in any case..."

"I want it all to come out," Gavrila said, with an unusual onrush of emotion. "I'm not going to hide anything! You can manacle someone's hands, but not his tongue! I might be standing here in front of you, Foma Fomich, a vile wretch – a slave, in a word – but even I can feel insulted! I'm bound to you in service and subservience for ever, because I was born a slave and it is my duty always to serve my master in fear and trembling. If you sit down to write a book, then I have to prevent anyone from disturbing you – that's the nature of my duty. It is my greatest pleasure to be able to serve you as and when it is necessary to do so. But to make me, at my age, bark out something in some foreign language in front of everyone is to pile shame on shame! It means I can't go into the servants' quarters now without people referring to me as the 'Frenchie!' No, Foma Fomich, sir, it's not just a fool like me, but other good people have begun to say with one voice that you have now become a very cruel and nasty man, and that our master has turned into a little child in your eyes – that you might have been the son of a general and could well have been a general yourself, but now you have turned into a real monster."

Gavrila stopped. I was beside myself with delight. Foma Fomich sat there, in the ensuing confusion, his face pale with rage, as if unable to recollect himself after Gavrila's unexpected onslaught – as though trying to decide at that moment just how far his anger could express itself. Finally, he exploded.

"How dare he insult me like that? Me! This is rebellion!" he yelled, leaping up from his chair.

The general's lady followed suit, throwing her hands in the air. Chaos ensued. My uncle dashed over to drag the delinquent Gavrila out of the room.

"Put him in chains, in chains!" shouted the general's lady. "Take him to the town and get him enlisted in the army, Yegorushka! If you don't, you'll never get my blessing. Put him in the stocks immediately and enlist him in the army!"

"What!" Foma shouted. "A slave, a yokel, a peasant dared to insult me like that! That man, that rag I wipe my boots with! He had the absolute cheek to call me a monster!"

I stepped forward with unusual determination.

"I must confess that, in this instance, I am in total agreement with Gavrila," I said, looking Foma Fomich straight in the eye and trembling with emotion.

He was so shocked by this impulsive comment that he was at first unable to believe his ears.

"What was that?" he yelled finally in an absolute frenzy, his small, bloodshot eyes boring into mine. "And who might you be?"

"Foma Fomich…" my uncle started to say, "this is Seryozha, my nephew…"

"The scholar!" screeched Foma. "So this is the scholar, is it? *Liberté, égalité, fraternité! Journal de débats!*[*] No, my man, it's all lies! You haven't the first idea what you're talking about! This isn't St Petersburg, you can't pull the wool over my eyes! I don't give a damn for your *débats*! You can have your *débats*, but we, my man, are not impressed! Scholar indeed! However much you already know I've already forgotten seven times over! That's the kind of scholar you are!"

If the others had not restrained him, it seemed he would have dashed at me and started punching me.

"The man's clearly drunk," I said, looking around at everyone in bewilderment.

"Who? Me?" yelled Foma, as if in someone else's voice.

"Yes, you!"

"Drunk?"

"Yes, drunk."

This was the final straw for Foma. He screamed as if someone had stabbed him and dashed out of the room. The general's lady, it seemed, was on the point of collapsing in a faint, but thought better of it and hurried after him. Everyone else did the same, with my uncle bringing up the rear. When I had recovered and looked around the room, I saw that only Yezhevikin was left. He was smiling and rubbing his hands together.

"That Jesuit you promised to tell us about just now..." he said deviously.

"What's that?" I asked, not understanding what he meant.

"You promised you would tell me about a Jesuit just now... a little anecdote, sir..."

I ran out onto the terrace and on into the garden. My head was spinning...

8

A Declaration of Love

I wandered around the garden for about a quarter of an hour, irritated and extremely unhappy with myself, wondering what I should do now. The sun was setting. Suddenly, at a turning into one of the dark alleyways, I came face to face with Nastenka. She had tears in her eyes, which she was wiping away with a handkerchief.

"I have been looking for you," she said.

"And I've been looking for you," I replied. "Tell me: am I in a madhouse or not?"

"It's not a madhouse at all," she said, offended by the question and giving me an intent look.

"But in that case what on earth's going on? For Heaven's sake, tell me what to do! Where has my uncle got to now? Can I go and find him, wherever he is? I'm so pleased I've met you: maybe you can suggest something."

"No, better not to go. I've just come from them myself."

"But where are they now?"

"Who knows? They might have gone to the kitchen garden again," she said irritably.

"What kitchen garden?"

"Last week Foma Fomich shouted he didn't want to stay a minute longer in the house and suddenly dashed off to the kitchen garden, grabbed a spade from the shed and began digging. We were all astonished: had he gone out of his mind? 'This is in order to stop people accusing me of living off others,' he said. 'I'll dig and produce my own food with my own hands and then I'll leave. That's what I've been reduced to!' And then everyone started crying, practically going down on their knees in front of him, trying to take the spade away from him, but he went on digging until he'd dug up all the turnips. They indulged him then, so maybe he'll do it again. It's the sort of thing he does."

"And you… and you can stand there telling me that as if you're totally unconcerned by any of it!" I exclaimed in utter exasperation.

Her eyes flashed angrily.

"Forgive me – I don't know what I'm saying! Listen, do you know why I came here?"

"N… no," she replied, blushing, with a look of some distress crossing her sweet face.

"You must forgive me," I continued, "I'm rather overwrought at the moment. I feel that I ought not to be bringing this matter up… particularly with you… But never mind! In my opinion, honesty is always the best policy. I confess… that is, I wanted to say… do you know what my uncle's plans are? He told me to propose to you…"

"What nonsense! Please, I'd rather you didn't talk about that!" she said, hastily interrupting me and going bright red.

I was nonplussed.

"What do you mean, 'nonsense'? He did write to me about that."

"So he actually wrote to you, did he?" she asked animatedly. "Oh, what a… After promising me that he wouldn't! What nonsense! Good God, what utter nonsense!"

"You must forgive me," I muttered, at a loss for words. "I may have been a little insensitive and rather abrupt… but at a time like this! Just think what's going on all around us at the moment…"

"Oh, please don't apologize, for Heaven's sake! Believe me, it's difficult enough for me to have to listen to it all as it is, but you have to understand that I wanted to talk to you myself, to see what I could find out… Oh, how annoying! So he actually wrote to you! That's what I was so afraid he would do! Good God, what an idiot! And you believed him, and came rushing here post-haste? That's all I needed!"

She was unable to conceal her irritation. I found myself in an extremely awkward position.

"I must confess," I said, by now totally embarrassed, "I didn't expect such an outcome... on the contrary, I thought..."

"Ah, that's what you thought, did you?" she said with a touch of irony, and slightly bit her lip. "So, why don't you show me that letter of his he wrote to you?"

"All right then."

"But please, don't be angry with me, don't be offended – I've got quite enough to be worried about as it is!" she said pleadingly, accompanying this, however, with a rather derisive little smile on her pretty lips.

"Oh, please, don't take me for a fool!" I responded with some heat. "But perhaps you're prejudiced against me? Perhaps someone has been talking behind my back? Perhaps because I behaved so badly in there just now? But that's neither here not there, I assure you: I can understand only too well what an idiot I am, standing here like this in front of you. Please don't laugh at me! I don't know what I'm saying... And it's all because I'm still only twenty-two, damn it!"

"Good God! What of it?"

"What do you mean, 'what of it'? When you're twenty-two, emotions are stamped on your face – take the way I pranced into the middle of the room like that just now, for example, or the way I'm standing here in front of you at this moment... It's a really loathsome age!"

"Oh no, not at all!" Nastenka replied, barely able to restrain her laughter. "I'm sure you're a kind, sweet and clever man, and I really do mean that! But... your problem is that you suffer from overbearing pride. You can do something about that, however."

"It seems to me that I am only as proud as I need to be."

"No, actually. Just now, for example, when you got all embarrassed – what was that about? It was because you stumbled as you came in the door!... What right did you have to make such a laughing stock of your kind, generous uncle, someone who's been so good to you? Why did you have to make him appear ridiculous by making yourself such a fool of yourself? That was so wrong and shameful of you! It does you no honour, and I have to say I found you very unlikeable at that moment – so there you are!"

"It's true! I behaved like an imbecile! Worse, even: I acted despicably! You saw it, and for that alone I am punished! Tear strips off me, laugh at me if you like, but listen to me – you may possibly change your mind, eventually," I added, carried away by a strange emotion. "You know me so little that perhaps, later, when you have got to know me better, you'll—"

"For goodness' sake, that's enough!" Nastenka exclaimed, with evident impatience.

"All right, all right, let's leave it at that! But... when can I see you again?"

"What do you mean?"

"Surely we've got more to say to each other, haven't we, Nastasya Yevgrafovna? For pity's sake, tell me when I can see you again – today, perhaps? However, it's already getting dark. Well, how about tomorrow morning, then, as early as possible? I'll make sure someone wakes me in very good time. There's a little summer-house over there, by the pond, as you know. I remember it, and know the way there. I used to live here as a child."

"See each other again? What on earth for? We're talking to each other now, aren't we?"

"But I know absolutely nothing, Nastasya Yevgrafovna. The first thing I need to do is to find out everything from my uncle. Sooner or later he'll simply have to tell me everything, and then I may finally be in a position to say something important to you..."

"No, no! There's no need for that, no need at all!" Nastenka exclaimed. "We must put a stop to all this, here and now, and ensure the subject never comes up again. And don't even think of going to that summer-house: you can rest assured I'm not going to be there, so please clear your head of all that nonsense – I'm being perfectly serious..."

"So my uncle treated me like an idiot, then!" I cried, in a fit of intolerable irritation. "So why on earth did he ask me to come? But listen... what's that noise?"

We were not far from the house. From the open windows came the sound of yelling and shouting.

"Oh my God!" she said, going pale. "Not again! I knew this would happen!"

"You knew? Nastasya Yevgrafovna, just one more question. I don't have the least right, of course, but I simply have to put this final question to you, for the good of all concerned. Tell me – and I promise that'll be the end of it – tell me frankly: is my uncle in love with you?"

"Oh, for God's sake, get this nonsense out of your head once and for all!" she cried, flaring up with anger. "You as well! If he were in love with me, he wouldn't have wanted to marry me off to you, would he?" she added with a bitter smile. "Where did you get that idea from, for goodness' sake? Do you really not understand what's going on? Can't you hear all that shouting?"

"But... but that's Foma Fomich!"

"Yes, of course it's Foma Fomich – but now it's all about me... they're simply going over the same rubbish we've just been talking about: they, too, suspect he's in love with me. And since I'm poor and of no significance and they can therefore blacken my name and honour whenever it suits them, and since they want to marry him off to someone else, they're insisting he drive me out of the house so that I can go and live with my father, to make everything easier for everyone. But as soon as they put that to him, he gets furious – he's quite prepared to confront Foma Fomich about it even. That's what they're shouting about in there – I'm sure I'm right."

"So it's true, then! So, he's definitely getting married to that Tatyana?"

"What Tatyana?"

"Well, that idiot woman."

"She's not an idiot at all! She's a good, kind woman. You have no right to talk about her like that! She has such a generous heart... more generous than most! It's not her fault she's so unhappy."

"Forgive me. Let's assume you're totally right about that, but aren't you wrong about the most important thing? Tell me: I've noticed they're all so considerate towards your father – how can that be? Surely, if they had been as angry with you as you claim and trying to drive you out of the house, they would have been as angry with him too and not been nearly so friendly, wouldn't they?"

"But can't you see what my father is doing on my behalf? He's playing the clown in front of everyone! If they accept him, it's precisely because he's succeeded in winning over Foma Fomich through flattery. And since Foma Fomich himself was once a clown, it flatters him to have other clowns around him now. Who do you think my father is doing all this for? He's doing it for me, for me alone. He doesn't have to do that: he'd never agree to defer to someone simply for himself. He may appear ridiculous in some people's eyes, but he's such a wonderful, wonderful man! He thinks, goodness knows why – and definitely not because I'm earning quite a good salary here, I can assure you – he thinks it's better for me to stay in this house. But now I've been able to change his mind completely, by writing to him in the strongest possible terms. He's come here to take me away, and if it's absolutely necessary, then even tomorrow – things have got that bad. They want to crush me, and I know exactly what they're shouting about in there now. They're ripping *him* to shreds because of me, and they will destroy *him*! And *he* is like a father to me, do you understand? Even more so than my own father! I don't want to wait any longer. I know more than anyone. So I shall leave tomorrow, yes, tomorrow! Who knows – perhaps, as a result, they'll put off his marriage to Tatyana Ivanovna as well, if only for a short while... So, there you are: I've told you everything. Please pass it all on to him, because I simply can't talk to him myself: they're watching our every move, especially that Perepelitsyna woman. Tell him he's not to worry about me, that I'd rather eat black bread and live in a hut with my father than be the cause of his torments here, in this house. I am poor and have no choice but to live as such. But, my God, listen to that noise! The shouting! What's going on now? No, I'm going to see for myself, no matter what! I'll tell them straight to their faces, whatever happens! I have to do it. Goodbye!"

She ran off. I stood there on the spot, fully aware of the comical role I had been forced to play, but without the least idea how it would all end. I felt sorry for the poor girl, and I was very concerned for my uncle. Suddenly Gavrila appeared at my side. He was still holding his exercise book.

"Your uncle would like to see you," he said in a mournful voice.

I gave a start.

"My uncle? But where is he? How is he?"

"In the drawing room, where they were having tea just now."

"Who's with him?"

"He's on his own, waiting."

"Who for? Me?"

"He's sent for Foma Fomich. Our golden days are over!" he added, with a deep sigh.

"For Foma Fomich? Hmm! But where's everyone else? Where is the general's lady?"

"In her room. She fainted, and she's now lying in a state of prostration, in tears."

Still talking, we reached the terrace. Outside it was already almost completely dark. My uncle really was on his own, in the same room where I had had my recent altercation with Foma Fomich. He was striding up and down the room; there were lighted candles on the tables. On seeing me he rushed over and firmly grasped my hands. He was pale and breathing heavily; his hands were trembling, and his whole body shook every so often with a nervous tremor.

9

Your Excellency

"My dear boy! It's all over, it's all been decided!" he said in a dramatic half-whisper.

"But Uncle," I said, "I heard people shouting."

"Shouting, my dear boy, shouting – all kinds of shouting! Mother's lying upstairs in a faint, and the whole world's gone mad. But I am determined to have my own way. I'm no longer afraid of anyone, Seryozha. I want to show them that I am my own person, and I intend to do just that! That's exactly why I've sent for you – so you can help me in that... My heart is in tatters, Seryozha... but I have to, I'm absolutely obliged to take drastic action. Justice shows no mercy!"

"But what's happened, Uncle?"

"Foma and I are going our own ways," my uncle announced in a determined tone.

"Uncle!" I cried, overjoyed. "You couldn't have come up with a better idea! And if I can be of any assistance in any way at all... I shall for ever be at your service."

"Thank you, my dear boy, thank you! But it's all been decided. I'm waiting for Foma. I have already sent for him. It's either him or me! We have to part company. Either Foma leaves this house tomorrow, or I swear I'll drop everything and rejoin the hussars! They'll have me back and give me a division. To hell with this way of life! From now on it's all going to change! What on earth are you doing with that French exercise book?" he shouted angrily, turning to Gavrila. "Throw it away! Burn it, trample on it, rip it up! *I* am your master, and I order you to stop studying French. Don't you dare disobey me, because *I'm* your master, and not Foma Fomich!"

"Glory be to God!" Gavrila muttered to himself. The matter had clearly taken a serious turn.

"My dear boy," my uncle continued in a state of high emotion, "they are demanding the impossible of me! You will be my judge – you will stand between them and me as an impartial arbiter. You don't know, you simply have no idea what they have demanded of me – formally demanded of me, in fact... it's all come out into the open now! But it's contrary to human decency, human dignity, honour... I'll tell you all about it, but now..."

"I know it all already, Uncle!" I exclaimed, interrupting him. "I can guess... I have just been talking to Nastasya Yevgrafovna."

"Please, my dear boy, not a word about that now, not a single word!" he hurriedly interposed, as if alarmed. "I'll tell you all about it later, but for the time being... Well?" he called out to Vidoplyasov, who had just come in. "Where's Foma Fomich, then?"

Vidoplyasov had returned to tell him that Foma Fomich didn't wish to come, as he viewed such a demand as excessively impertinent, finding it grossly insulting.

"Order him to come! Drag him here! By force!" my uncle shouted, stamping his foot.

Vidoplyasov had never seen his master in such a rage and left in a state of shock. I was astonished.

For several minutes my uncle paced around the room, evidently debating with himself what he should do.

"Perhaps it would be best not to tear the exercise book up, after all," he said at last to Gavrila. "Wait a moment – I may still need you. My dear boy," he added, turning to me, "I think I may have become overexcited just now. One needs to do things with dignity and with courage, but without shouting or insults. That's exactly how things should be done. Do you know what, Seryozha? Maybe it would be better for you not to be present? You won't mind, will you? I'll tell you all about it later, eh? What do you think? Do that as a favour for me, please."

"Are you getting cold feet, Uncle? Beginning to have second thoughts?" I said, looking at him intently.

"No, no, dear boy, I'm not having any second thoughts!" he exclaimed with redoubled fervour. "I'm not afraid of anything any longer. I have made momentous decisions, extremely momentous! You don't know, you simply have no idea what they have demanded of me! Surely I wasn't obliged to agree, was I? No, I will prove them wrong! I have rebelled, and I will prove them wrong! It was something I simply had to do, sooner or later! But do you know, my boy, I do regret asking you to come: Foma may well not like it at all if you were here, so to speak, to witness his downfall. You have to understand that I want to expel him from the house in a perfectly civil way, so that he doesn't feel in the slightest humiliated. That's easy to say, of course – it's got to the point, my boy, that no amount of honeyed phrases will stop him from feeling insulted. I am rather an uncouth person, lacking in sophistication, quite capable of blurting out something idiotic which I will later regret. Whatever you might say, he's done a lot for me... Go, my boy... But here they come, here they are! Please go, Seryozha, I beg you! I'll tell you all about it later. Go, for God's sake!"

And my uncle ushered me out onto the terrace at the very moment Foma came into the room. But I confess I stayed where I was, on the terrace, where it was very dark and consequently I was barely visible from inside the house. I had made up my mind that I was going to eavesdrop!

Without wanting to justify my decision at all, I can nevertheless state unhesitatingly that the half-hour I spent standing on that terrace, keeping my temper in check the whole time, was an ordeal. From where I was standing I was not only able to hear perfectly everything that was being said, but also to see what was going on, since the doors were of glass. So I ask you now to picture Foma Fomich *summoned* to appear in person, under the threat of physical force if he refused.

"Have I heard correctly, colonel?" screeched Foma as he came into the room. "Have I been threatened with something?"

"Yes, you have heard correctly, Foma. Calm down," my uncle replied undaunted. "Sit down. We need to have a serious talk, in a friendly, brotherly way. Do please sit down, Foma!"

Foma Fomich imperiously sat down in an armchair. My uncle paced rapidly and a little unsteadily around the room, evidently trying to decide how to begin.

"Yes, precisely – in a brotherly way," he repeated. "You will understand what I'm about to say, Foma: you are not a child... neither am I, for that matter: in short, we are both adults... Hmm! It's like this, Foma: there are certain points of difference between us... yes, that's just it, certain points of difference – and so, would it not be better, my dear man, for us to go our own ways? I am convinced you have a generous heart, that you wish me nothing but good, and so... But there's no need to go on for long, is there? Foma, I am your friend until the end of time, I swear that by all the saints! Here is fifteen thousand, in silver roubles* – that's all I have, my friend, all I've been able to scrape together, my own family's money. Come on, take it! It is my duty, my obligation to see that you are provided for! It is mostly in securities, together with a tiny bit of cash. Come on, take it, don't hesitate! You don't owe me anything, as I shall never be able to repay you for all that you've done for me. Yes, yes, that's right, that's what I feel, even though you and I differ on something fundamental right now. Tomorrow, or the day after... or whenever it suits you... we will go our separate ways. Why not move into town, Foma? It's only six or so miles from here. There's a little house in the first little alleyway just behind the church, with green shutters, a dear little house belonging to the priest's widow, as if built especially for you. She'll put it up for sale, and I will buy it, on top of the money I'm giving to you now. So why not settle down there, near us? You'll be able to study literature, science, you will become famous... The civil servants there are all, without exception, real gentlemen – kind-hearted, generous people; the local priest is a scholar. You'll be able to come and visit us on holidays – we shall have such wonderful times together, it will be like paradise! What do you think?"

"So those are the conditions for getting rid of Foma, are they?" I said to myself. "My uncle has never mentioned the money before."

For a long time nobody said a word. Foma sat in his armchair as if stunned into silence, looking at my uncle without moving a muscle. For his part, my uncle was clearly discomfited by both the silence and the expression on Foma's face.

"The money!" Foma said finally in an affectedly feeble voice. "Where is it, where is this money of yours? Give it to me, come on, give it to me at once!"

"Here it is, Foma – everything I've managed to scrape together, fifteen thousand precisely. In notes and securities – here, see for yourself!"

"Gavrila! Here, you have this money," Foma said mildly. "You might well be able to make use of it, old man. But wait! No!" he suddenly screeched, his voice rising to an unusually high pitch as he leapt up from his chair. "No, give it to me first, Gavrila, the money! Give it to me! Come on, give it to me! Give me those millions, so that I can stamp on them, scatter them to the four winds, spit on them, defile them, desecrate them!... Someone is offering me, *me*, money! They are bribing me, to get me to leave this house! Have I heard correctly? Have I lived to witness this final humiliation? Here, here they are, your millions! Look! There, there and there! *That's* how Foma Fomich behaves, in case you didn't already know, colonel!"

And Foma scattered the whole bundle of money all over the room. Remarkably, however, he didn't tear or spit on a single note, as he had boasted he would do: he merely crumpled them a little, taking some care even over that. Gavrila dashed to pick the money up from the floor – to give it to his master later, when Foma had left the room.

Foma's response had had a really devastating effect on my uncle. He, for his part, stood there in front of him, without moving, inanely, gaping at him open-mouthed. In the mean time, Foma had settled back in his chair, puffing and panting, as if in an inexpressibly agitated state.

"You are such an outstanding man, Foma!" my uncle exclaimed at last, coming to his senses. "You have no equal!"

"I know," Foma replied feebly, but with inexpressible dignity.

"Foma, forgive me! I am such a vile person, compared with you, Foma!"

"Yes, that's right," agreed Foma.

"Foma! It's not your nobility of spirit that astonishes me so much," my uncle continued rapturously, "as the fact that I could have behaved so coarsely, blindly and despicably to offer you money under such conditions! But Foma, you're wrong about one thing: I wasn't trying to bribe you at all, wasn't paying you off to leave the house – I simply wanted to ensure that you had some money, so that you wouldn't be destitute once you'd gone. I swear to you that's how it was! I am ready to go down on my knees, my knees, to ask for your forgiveness, Foma, and if you would like me to, I will do just that… you only have to say…"

"I don't need you on your knees, colonel!…"

"But, my God, Foma! Can't you see how overwrought, how worked up, how confused I was! But just tell me, you only have to say what I have to do to make up for hurting you like this. Instruct me, guide me…"

"There's no need for that, colonel, no need at all! And you can be sure that tomorrow I will be shaking the dust off my feet at the doorway of this house."

And Foma began to get up from his chair. Horrified, my uncle rushed to sit him down again.

"No, Foma, you're not going anywhere, I assure you!" he cried. "Stop all that nonsense about dust and feet, Foma! You're not going anywhere – if you do, I shall follow you to the ends of the earth, and shall carry on doing so until you forgive me… I swear to you Foma, that's what I'll do!"

"Forgive you? So you're guilty?" Foma said. "But do you understand just how guilty? Are you aware that you stand guilty before me now, not least for offering me a crust of bread in this house? Do you realize that it's only taken a single moment to poison all the previous crusts of bread I have consumed in this house? You took me to task just now for these crusts, for each morsel of bread I have ever eaten, thereby proving that I have lived as a slave in your house, as a lackey, as something you've had to wipe off your patent-leather boots! And there I've been all the time thinking, in the purity of my heart, that I was residing here as your friend and brother! Was it not you, yes, you yourself who assured me a thousand times with your serpent's tongue of our friendship and brotherhood? Why have you been secretly laying all these traps, into which I have fallen, like an idiot? Why have you been furtively digging this snake's pit, into which you yourself have now pushed me? Why haven't you picked up that club before now and felled me with a single blow? Why haven't you wrung my neck, like some farmyard cock, because… well, simply because, for example, it hasn't laid any eggs? Yes, precisely that! I stand by that example, colonel, even though it has a rustic ring to it and contains something of the trivial tone of our contemporary literature – and I stand by it, since it clearly demonstrates the entire pointless stupidity of your charges against me, for I am no more guilty before you than this presumed farmyard cock which has displeased his light-minded owner by not laying any eggs! Really, colonel! What kind of person pays off a friend or brother by offering money – and for what? That's the important point: for what? It's like saying: 'Well, my darling brother, I am in your debt, even to the point of saving my life, so take these pieces of silver, as Judas did, so long as you clear off out of here, out of my sight!' How naive of you! How crude of you to treat me like that! You thought I lusted after your gold, whereas in fact I harboured nothing but the most sublime thoughts for your well-being. Oh, look how you have shattered my heart! You have played with my most noble and generous feelings like a small boy playing a game of jacks! I have seen this coming this for ages, colonel – that's why your crusts of bread have long since stuck in my throat… I have found it difficult to breathe! That's why I feel crushed by your feather beds – crushed, rather than lulled to sleep! That's why all your sugar, all your sweets taste like cayenne pepper in my mouth, not sweets! No, colonel! You live and prosper on your own, and leave Foma to take his own forlorn path, with his bag on his back. So be it, colonel!"

"No, Foma, no! It won't be, it cannot be so!" my uncle protested, utterly destroyed.

"Yes, colonel, yes! That's precisely how it will be, because that's how it has to be. Go on, go ahead, scatter your millions, carpet my whole way with banknotes, every little bit of the road to Moscow if you like, and I will proudly and contemptuously trample them underfoot. See this foot, colonel? It will trample, defile and crush those banknotes, and Foma Opiskin will eke out his existence by living on the nobility of his spirit alone! I have spoken, and I have demonstrated it to be so. Farewell, colonel! Fare thee well, colonel!…"

And once again Foma started to get up from his chair.

"Forgive me, Foma, forgive me! Forget what I said," my uncle kept on repeating imploringly.

"Forgive you? But what would be the point of doing that? Well, all right, let us suppose that I forgive you: I am a Christian, that is something I have to do – I have almost done so already in fact, even now. But think about it: would it even be in the least in keeping with common sense and my feeling of self-esteem if I were to remain in this house a minute longer? After all, you've been wanting me to go, haven't you?"

"It would be in keeping, Foma, it would be! I assure you it would!"

"Really? But how on earth can we be equals now? Can't you understand that I have, so to speak, crushed you with my nobility of soul, and that you have crushed yourself by acting in that humiliating way? You have been flattened to the ground, and I have been raised to the sky. How then can there be equality between us? And without equality how can there be friendship? I am saying that with a broken heart, and not, as you might think, gloating over you or with any sense of triumph."

"But I have a broken heart as well, Foma, I assure you…"

"And this is the same man," Foma continued, his tone of voice ranging from severe to sanctimonious, "this is the man for whose sake I spent so many sleepless nights! How many times, unable to sleep, would I get up, light a candle and say to myself: 'He's now sound asleep, putting his trust in you. So you must stay awake, Foma, and keep watch over him… maybe you'll be able to think of something that will enhance his life.' That was what Foma was thinking during those sleepless nights! And that is how this colonel has repaid him! But enough, enough!…"

"But I will regain your friendship, Foma, I swear I will!"

"Regain it? But how can you guarantee that? As a Christian I forgive you, and will even love you, but as a man, and a man of honour, I have no choice but to despise you. I must, I am obliged to despise you… I am obliged to do this out of moral necessity, since – I repeat it – you have disgraced yourself, whereas I have acted in the most honourable way possible. Who, of *all your lot*, would have done anything similar? Who would have followed the example of the destitute and universally despised Foma and rejected such a colossal sum of money for the sake of glory? No, colonel, in order to become my equal you will now need to perform so many good deeds… And what good deeds are you capable of performing, I wonder, when you can't even address me correctly as your equal, and talk to me as if I were your servant?"

"But Foma, I was only trying to be friendly!" my uncle cried. "I had no idea it wouldn't be to your liking… My God! If only I had known…"

"You were simply unable," Foma continued, "simply unable – or rather, unwilling – to agree to the most trivial, most insignificant, of my requests when I asked you to address me, as a general, as 'Your Excellency'…"

"But, Foma, wouldn't that have been, so to speak, an extreme breach of etiquette, Foma?"

"'Extreme breach of etiquette'! That's just some bookish phrase you've learnt by heart and are now repeating like a parrot! Are you not aware, however, of the extent to which you have belittled and dishonoured me by refusing to address me as 'Your Excellency'? 'Dishonoured' because, in failing to understand my motives, you have made me look like some capricious fool who ought to be put away in a lunatic asylum! Of course I understand how ridiculous it would be for me, someone who despises all ranks and worldly honours, to want to be addressed as 'Your Excellency', unless they were sanctified by virtue. Without such virtue I would never accept a general's rank for a million roubles! And yet you thought I had gone off my head! For your benefit, I sacrificed my sense of self-esteem and allowed you, *you*, to conclude that I was a madman – you and all your clever *scholars*! The only reason I had for demanding that you address me as a general was to enlighten your mind, to develop your moral sensibility and to infuse you with the light of new ideas. In fact, what I wanted was for you to stop looking at generals as if they were the greatest luminaries on the entire planet: I wanted you to see that rank is worthless, unless accompanied by real generosity of spirit, and that the arrival of a general in your midst should not be a cause for celebration when there could well be people standing next to you shining with virtue! But you've flaunted your colonel's rank in front of me for so long that you now find it hard to address me as 'Your Excellency'. *That* is the reason – *that* is where it is to be found, *not* in any 'extreme breach of etiquette'! It's all because you are a colonel, whereas I am simply Foma…"

"No, Foma, no! I assure you you're wrong. You are a man of learning, not simply Foma… I respect—"

"Respect me! That's good! So, if that's the case, then tell me whether in your opinion I am worthy of a general's rank or not. I want a straight answer now: am I worthy or not? I want to see if your mind has made any progress."

"As regards your honesty, your selflessness, your intellect, your supreme nobility of soul, yes – you are worthy!" my uncle proudly said.

"Right, so why then do you not address me as 'Your Excellency'?"

"Foma, I will... perhaps."

"But I demand you do! I demand that you do so right now, colonel, I insist on it! I'm insisting on it because I can see you're finding it so difficult. Such a sacrifice on your part will mark merely the first step towards a truly heroic deed – for you mustn't forget that you will have to take a whole series of such steps before you can become my equal; you will have to learn to master yourself – only then will I be assured of your sincerity..."

"I'll address you as 'Your Excellency' tomorrow, Foma, I promise!"

"No, colonel, not tomorrow – tomorrow is another day. I want you to address me *now*, this very instant, as 'Your Excellency'."

"All right, Foma, I'm ready to do that... it's just that... why 'this very instant'?"

"Why not this very instant? Or are you ashamed to say it? If that is the case, I shall take offence."

"All right, Foma, I'm ready... I would even be honoured to... But, Foma, what if I were suddenly to come out with 'Hello, Your Excellency', out of the blue, just like that? It would sound silly, wouldn't it?..."

"No, not 'Hello, Your Excellency' – that would sound offensive... it would be like a joke, a farce. I will not permit such jokes at my expense. Remember who you're talking to – remember at once who you're talking, colonel! Keep a civil tongue in your head!"

"But you must be joking, Foma, surely?"

"In the first place, Yegor Ilyich, I am not 'Foma' to you, but 'Foma Fomich' – don't forget: not 'Foma', but 'Foma Fomich'."

"That makes me really and truly happy, Foma Fomich! I'll gladly make every effort... But what am I actually to say?"

"You're finding it difficult to think of what to add after "Your Excellency" – that's understandable. Why didn't you say so at the beginning? It's not a crime, particularly if you lack *creative imagination*, putting it as politely as I can. In that case, however, I can help you. Say after me: 'Your Excellency'!"

"Well, all right: 'Your Excellency'."

"No, not 'well, all right: "Your Excellency"', but simply 'Your Excellency'! Did I not tell you to watch your tone, colonel? I also trust you won't be offended if I suggest you make a slight bow, bending forward at the waist. When conversing with a general you must incline forward at the waist, thereby expressing your respect and your readiness, so to speak, to dash off and do whatever he commands. I myself have been in the company of generals, so I know exactly what one should do... So, then: 'Your Excellency'."

"Your Excellency..."

"'I can't tell you how overjoyed I am to have finally been able to ask your forgiveness for failing to recognize from the very first Your Excellency's truly spiritual nature. I venture to assure you that from henceforth I shall not spare any of my feeble efforts in the cause of the common good...' Well, that's enough for now!"

My poor uncle! He was being obliged to repeat all this nonsense, sentence by sentence, word for word! I stood there blushing, as if I were the one at fault. I was seething with anger.

"So, don't you now feel," continued his tormentor, "a sudden sense of relief, as if an angel has flown down to calm your innermost being? Can you feel the presence of that angel? Come on, answer me."

"Yes, Foma, I really do feel calmer," my uncle replied.

"As though, once you have mastered yourself, your heart has been dipped, so to speak, in some sort of balm?"

"Yes, Foma, indeed, as if rubbed with some unguent."

"Unguent, you say? Hmm... I wasn't actually talking about unguents... Anyway, never mind! That's what it means, colonel: to have fulfilled one's duty! Master yourself. You are proud, unbelievably proud."

"Yes I am, Foma, I can see that," my uncle replied with a sigh.

"You are an egoist – and a miserable egoist, at that."

"It's true, Foma, I am an egoist, I can see that; I saw that as soon as I got to know you."

"I am talking to you now as a father, as a loving mother... you are pushing everyone away from you and forgetting that a gentle calf has two mothers to suckle it."

"Yes, that's very true as well, Foma!"

"You are uncouth, someone who so crudely obtrudes into people's hearts, so arrogantly demands the attention of others, that any decent man is ready to escape to the ends of the earth to be rid of you!"

Once again my uncle gave a deep sigh.

"So then you need to be more gentle, more understanding, more loving in your dealings with other people. If you forget about yourself and think of others, then others will remember you. Live and let live – that's my motto! Fortitude, hard work, prayer and hope – those are the precepts I would like all at once to instil in every human heart! Follow them, and I will be the first to open up my heart to you – I will weep on your chest... if I have to... But with you, it's me, me and me the whole time – yes, and your airs of superiority! Good God, I can't stand your airs of superiority, if you'll permit me to say so."

"You have such a way with words!" pronounced Gavrila deferentially.

"That's so true, Foma – it's something I'm always aware of," my uncle agreed, overcome by emotion. "But it's not all my fault, Foma: it was the way I was brought up, living among soldiers. When I said goodbye to my regiment, all the hussars, the whole division, simply wept, swearing that there would never be anyone else like me! At the time I thought that perhaps I wasn't entirely a lost cause."

"Ever the egoist! I've caught you being vain again! There you are boasting about yourself while at the very same moment showing me up because I never had hussars weeping tears about me! So what if I can't brag about anyone's tears? Although I could do, of course – indeed I could."

"It was just a slip of the tongue, Foma. I simply couldn't resist thinking about the good times."

"Good times don't just fall from the skies – we have to create them ourselves; they are locked in our hearts, Yegor Ilyich. That is why I am always happy, and, despite all my suffering, contented and spiritually calm; I never annoy anyone, apart from fools, upstarts and *learned men*, whom I can't and won't tolerate. I can't stand fools! And what of these learned men – what of this 'man of science'! His so-called science is just a gigantic fraud, not science at all. What was it *he* said just now? Bring him here! Bring all those men of science here! I can refute everything – I can refute all their propositions and theories! And I'm not talking about the nobility of the soul here..."

"No, Foma, of course not – that's absolutely right."

"Only recently, for example, I demonstrated my wit, talent, extraordinary erudition, understanding of the human heart and knowledge of contemporary literature. I showed and proved with utter brilliance how someone with talent can take something like the Kamarinskaya and turn it into a subject for high-minded debate. And what happened? Did anyone present appreciate me as I deserved to be appreciated? No, they turned their backs on me! I bet you he's told you that I am a great ignoramus. But it could have been Machiavelli himself or a Mercadante* sitting there right in front of him – my only fault is that I am poor and obscure... No, they won't get away with it!... And then there's this Korovkin fellow. What kind of a goose is he?"

"He's a clever man, Foma, a man of science... I'm expecting him. He really is an excellent chap, Foma!"

"Hmm! I doubt it. Some idiot with modern ideas, probably... up to his ears in books. They've no soul, these people, colonel, no heart! And what good is knowledge without virtue?!"

"No, Foma, no! He spoke so well about family happiness! Straight from the heart, Foma!"

"Hmm! We'll see... we'll give Korovkin a good going over as well. But enough," concluded Foma, getting up from his chair. "I still can't totally forgive you, colonel: the insult was too wounding – but I shall pray, and God may well confer peace on an outraged heart. We'll talk about this again tomorrow, but for now allow me to leave. I'm tired and rather weak…"

"Oh, Foma!" my uncle fussed. "Yes, you must be tired! Do you know what? How about a little something to fortify yourself? Something to eat, perhaps. I can order it at once."

"Something to eat? Very funny! Something to eat!" replied Foma with a derisive laugh. "First you're given poison to drink, and then you're asked whether you'd like something to eat! They want to heal a wounded heart with stewed mushrooms or preserved apples! You're such a pathetic materialist, colonel!"

"But, Foma, really, I was genuinely concerned about you…"

"Well, all right, let's leave it there. I'm off now, and you must immediately go to your mother, fall on your knees and sob your heart out, imploring her forgiveness – that is your duty, your obligation!"

"Oh, Foma, I've been thinking of nothing else the whole time I've been talking to you. I am prepared to stay on my knees before her until dawn, if necessary. But just think, Foma, what it is I'm being asked to do. Surely you can see how unfair, how cruel it is, Foma! Show your generosity of spirit, make me really happy, reconsider, make your decision… and then… I swear…"

"No, Yegor Ilyich, no, it's not up to me," Foma replied. "You know it's none of my business at all, don't you? That is to say, you may be convinced I'm the one to blame for it all, but I can assure you I've never had anything to do with any of this. It has all only ever been your mother's doing – and she, of course, has your interests at heart… Go on, off you go, as quickly as you can, and try to make everything right by promising to be obedient. Let not the sun go down on your anger! As for me… I will spend all night praying for you… I have forgotten what sleep is, Yegor Ilyich. Farewell! I forgive you as well, old fellow," he added, turning to Gavrila. "I know you weren't thinking what you were doing. Yes, and forgive me in turn if I have offended you… Farewell, farewell everybody, and may the Lord bless you!"

Foma left. I immediately dashed into the room.

"So you were eavesdropping?" my uncle exclaimed.

"Yes, Uncle, I was! How could you agree to address him as 'Your Excellency'?"

"What else could I have done, my boy? I am proud of it... it was for such a good cause... but what a noble, selfless, great man! You heard it, Sergei, didn't you? And how on earth could I have offered him that money? I simply have no idea how I could have done that! My dear boy! I was carried away... I was so angry... I didn't understand him... I suspected him, accused him... But no: he could never have been my enemy! I can see that now... And do you remember the wonderfully generous look on his face when he turned down my money?"

"All right, Uncle, you can be as proud as you like, but I'm leaving. I can't stand it any longer! Let me ask you for the last time: what do you want from me? Why did you ask me to come here, and what are you expecting of me? And if it's all over and I'm no further use to you, then I'm off. I cannot bear witnessing such scenes! I shall leave today!"

"My dear boy..." my uncle started to fuss in his usual way. "Wait for only two minutes: I'm just on my way to see Mother... I need to settle something once and for all... such a huge, vitally important matter!... And in the mean time, you can go to your room. Gavrila here can take you to the summer wing. Do you know the summer wing? It's in the garden – I've already seen to it that your suitcase has been taken there. And I'll go to her, beg for forgiveness, settle something very important – I now know exactly what needs to be done – and I'll be with you in a flash, and then I will tell you everything, absolutely everything down to the last detail... I will bare my soul to you. And... and... and then there will be better times for us too! Two minutes, just two minutes, Sergei!"

He shook my hand and hurriedly went out of the room. I had no choice but to follow Gavrila again.

10

Mizinchikov

The wing of the house where Gavrila took me was customarily referred to as the "new wing", but it had in fact been built some time ago by the former owners. It was a pleasant-looking timber building standing not far from the old house, within the precincts of the garden. It was surrounded on three sides by tall, ancient lime trees, whose branches grazed the building's roof. All four rooms in this little building were tolerably well furnished and set up to receive guests. On entering the room that had been put aside to me and where my suitcase had already been brought, I saw, lying on the little table in front of the bed, a sheet of notepaper wonderfully inscribed in beautiful writing in a mixture of styles, embellished with loops, curlicues and various different flourishes. The ornate capital letters and loops were all in different colours. The whole amounted to a delightful illustration of the art of calligraphy. From the very first words I realized that the document was an imploring letter addressed to me, as "the enlightened benefactor". It was headed "The Lamentations of Vidoplyasov". However hard I tried to decipher any of the writing, all my efforts came to nought: it was the most pretentious nonsense, couched in the high style peculiar to lackeys. All I could make out was that Vidoplyasov was in a rather difficult position and asked for my assistance, hoping that I would be able to help him, "in view of my education" – and whether I would be able to intercede on his behalf with my uncle, who was to be prevailed upon with the aid of "my gab",* as he literally put it at the end of his message. I was in the process of reading this when the door opened and Mizinchikov came in.

"I hope you'll permit me to become acquainted with you," he said amiably and very politely, offering me his hand. "I wasn't able to put in a word earlier, but when I first clapped eyes on you I so wanted to get to know you better."

I immediately replied that I too... etc. etc., even though I was feeling so depressed. We sat down.

"What's that you've got there?" he asked, glancing at the sheet of paper still in my hand. "That wouldn't be 'The Lamentations of Vidoplyasov', would it? I thought as much! I knew Vidoplyasov would pester you as well. He's sent me an identical letter, expressing just the same grievances; he's been waiting for you for ages, and he'd no doubt prepared one in advance. You mustn't be surprised: it's a very odd letter, including some quite amusing stuff."

"Merely amusing?"

"Well, it's hardly something to shed tears over, is it? I can tell you the story of Vidoplyasov's life if you like... you'd find it a real hoot."

"I have to confess, Vidoplyasov's not at the top of my mind right now," I replied irritably.

It was clear to me that Mr Mizinchikov's engaging chatter and desire to get to know me was all for a particular purpose, and that he simply needed me for something. Earlier that day he had done nothing but sit in his seat with a glowering, serious expression, but now he was all smiles, prepared to recount lengthy stories. One glance at him and it was immediately clear I was dealing with someone who was fully in control of himself and who had a good knowledge of people.

"Damn and blast Foma!" I said, angrily banging my fist on the table. "I'm sure he's the reason for all the horrors going on here, and involved in everything! Damned brute!"

"Isn't that being a little hard on him?" asked Mizinchikov.

"A little hard?" I shouted, my hackles instantly rising. "I got a bit carried away of course, and anyone has the right to criticize me for that. I know I behaved thoroughly disgracefully, you don't need to tell me!... I am quite aware that that's not how people should behave in polite society. But think about it: how could I *not* have lost my temper? If you'd like my opinion, this is an absolute madhouse! And... and... finally... I simply have to get out of here – so there you are!"

"Do you smoke?" Mizinchikov asked calmly.

"Yes."

"In that case you won't mind if I do. They frown on it there, and I'm dying for a cigarette. I agree," he continued, "it is a bit of a madhouse, but don't worry: I have no intention of criticizing you – not least since, if I'd been you, I would have lost my temper and hit the roof far more forcefully than you."

"Well, then, if you were just as irritated, why didn't *you* say something? In fact, as far as I can recall, you seemed remarkably unconcerned by it all, and I must confess I found it odd that you didn't speak up on behalf of my poor uncle, who is always prepared to be so charitable to everyone!"

"You're right, of course: he's helped and supported many people, but I consider it totally pointless to speak up on his behalf: firstly, it wouldn't have done him any good, and he would have found it somehow humiliating; secondly, I would have been kicked out of the house the very next day. And to be quite frank, my circumstances are such that I can't afford to deprive myself of the local hospitality."

"Well, I certainly wouldn't presume to delve into your personal circumstances... But since you've been here a month already, I'd just like to ask—"

"Please, go ahead, ask away – I'm at your service," Mizinchikov replied eagerly, drawing up his chair.

"How, for example, do you explain the fact that just now Foma Fomich had his hands on fifteen thousand silver roubles, but then turned them down? I saw him do that with my own eyes."

"What? Really?" shouted Mizinchikov. "Please, tell me more!"

I told him what I'd seen and heard, omitting the "Your Excellency" bit. Mizinchikov listened with rapt attention; as soon as I mentioned the fifteen thousand, the expression on his face changed.

"Extraordinary!" he said when I'd finished. "That's the last thing I would have expected of Foma."

"But he turned down money! How do you explain that? It can hardly have been a sudden onrush of generosity, can it?"

"He turned down fifteen thousand to get thirty later. But do you know what?" he added, after a moment's thought. "I somehow doubt that Foma would have had any kind of plan; he isn't a very practical man – in his own way, he's something of a poet. Fifteen thousand... hmm! He would have liked to have taken the money, but he couldn't resist the temptation to cut a dash, put on airs. He's such a sourpuss, I tell you, such a cry-baby... and all combined with the most incredible arrogance!"

Mizinchikov had got all worked up. He was clearly very irritated – he even seemed a little jealous. I looked at him, rather intrigued.

"Hmm! We can now expect considerable changes," he added pensively. "Yegor Ilyich idolizes Foma now. Who knows? Maybe he'll get married, out of the goodness of his heart," he added through gritted teeth.

"So you think that that vile, perverse marriage to that half-witted woman is definitely going to happen, do you?"

Mizinchikov gave me an intent look.

"The absolute scoundrels!" I exclaimed heatedly.

"Yet it's not an absolutely crazy idea: they're saying he has no choice but to go ahead with it, for the sake of the family."

"As if he hasn't already done enough for them!" I exclaimed angrily. "And how on earth can you say that it would be a sensible idea to get married to that vacuous, half-witted woman?"

"I don't of course dispute that she's a halfwit... Hmm! It's good that you're so fond of your uncle; I share your feelings for him... although her money could come in really handy for the estate! But they have other reasons as well: they're afraid that Yegor Ilyich could get married to that governess woman... you know, that rather interesting girl?"

"But that's... that's not really possible, is it?" I asked agitatedly. "I thought that was just idle chit-chat. For Heaven's sake, tell me more: I'd really like to know..."

"Oh, he's head over heels in love with her! Just keeps quiet about it, however."

"Keeps quiet about it? Really, is that what you think he's doing? But what about her? Does she love him?"

"Very possibly. After all, it would be greatly to her advantage: she hasn't a single copeck to her name."

"But what proof do you have that they love each other?"

"It's perfectly obvious, isn't it? Besides, they're meeting each other in secret, I believe. Some people say they're having improper relations. But keep that to yourself, please. I'm telling you in strict confidence."

"But it's hardly possible, is it?" I exclaimed. "Yet you're... you're saying you believe it to be the case?"

"Naturally I can't be certain: I wasn't there. Yet it could be true."

"Could be true!" But what about my uncle's self-esteem, his sense of honour?"

"I agree, but people can get carried away and end up getting married. It happens all the time. I repeat, however: I haven't a shred of actual evidence to confirm the truth or otherwise of this story, particularly since they're doing all they can here to blacken the girl's name. They've even claimed she's had an affair with Vidoplyasov."

"There you are, you see!" I shouted. "With Vidoplyasov! How could that possibly be true? The very thought of such a thing is repugnant! You can't believe that as well, surely?"

"I'm telling you I don't have firm evidence," Mizinchikov replied imperturbably, "but such things can happen – anything can happen in this world. I wasn't there, and, in any case, it's none of my business. But since you're obviously taking such an interest in all this, I really ought to add that this idea of an affair with Vidoplyasov is very difficult to take seriously – it's just Anna Nilovna, that Perepelitsyna woman, fooling about... she's the one here who started such rumours, from jealousy, because she had designs on Yegor Ilyich herself at one point (would you believe it!), on the basis that she was a lieutenant colonel's daughter. Having been turned down, she's incandescent with rage. I think, however, I've already said more than enough about such things, and, I must confess, I hate gossiping like this, particularly since we're wasting valuable time: I came here, you see, to ask you a small favour."

"A small favour? Of course, I'd be pleased to help in any way I can…"

"Very well. I'm hoping in fact you may well be interested in what I'm about to say, since I can see how fond you are of your uncle and seem very concerned about his future and his possible marriage. But before I get on to this, I have another, preliminary, request to make of you."

"And that would be?"

"That would be as follows: whether or not you agree to my main request, before I put it to you I would in any case ask you most humbly to give me your word, as a gentleman of honour and the highest principles, that everything I am about to divulge to you will remain the most closely kept secret between us and that under no circumstances will you ever reveal this secret to anyone or use what I'm going to tell to your personal advantage. Do you agree or not?"

It was a striking preamble. I agreed.

"Well?…" I asked.

"It's essentially a very simple matter," Mizinchikov began. "It's like this, you see: I want to elope with Tatyana Ivanovna and marry her – in short, something like Gretna Green.* Are you with me?"

I looked Mr Mizinchikov straight in the eye, for some time unable to say a word.

"I have to confess I don't understand a thing," I said, "and what's more," I continued, "I assumed I was dealing with someone who had a head on his shoulders, and I never expected—"

"Assumed… expected," Mizinchikov interrupted, "in other words you're saying that what I'm planning to do is stupid, isn't that so?"

"Not at all… yet…"

"Oh, please, feel free to say anything you like! Don't worry: that will make me very happy, as it will mean we'll get to the point more quickly. I agree, of course, that at first glance this can all seem a little odd. But let me assure you that what I am planning to do is not only not stupid, but makes eminently good sense. And, if you would be so kind as to listen to all the circumstances..."

"Yes, of course. I can't wait to hear what you're going to say!"

"Actually, there's really not very much to say. The fact is, you see, I have now run into debt, and am absolutely broke. In addition, I have an unmarried sister of about nineteen living with a family and destitute. That is partly my fault. We inherited an estate of forty serfs, which, as it turned out, coincided with me being commissioned as a cavalry officer. At first I put money by, but then I frittered it all away, on drink and so on. I lived like an idiot... I was a trend-setter, became a veritable Burtsov,* gambled, drank – in short, all very stupid... I'm ashamed even to talk about it. I've now come to my senses and would like to make a totally fresh start. But to do that I absolutely have to put my hands on a hundred thousand. And since I won't be able to earn anything, lacking practical skills and being virtually uneducated, there are naturally only two possible courses of action: steal or get married to a wealthy woman. When I came here – on foot, not in a carriage – I arrived almost barefoot. As I set off from Moscow, my sister gave me her last three roubles. And once here, as soon as I saw Tatyana Ivanovna, this idea came into my head. I immediately resolved to give everything up and get married. You must agree that this is such a sensible idea. In any case, I'm doing it more for my sister's sake than for anything else... well, for my sake, too..."

"But, if you'll permit me, are you intending to propose to Tatyana Ivanovna formally?"

"God forbid! I'd be kicked out of here at once, and anyway she wouldn't agree. But if I were to suggest eloping, running away, she'd do it like a shot. That's the point: so long as it's something romantic, something that catches the imagination. Naturally it would all immediately end up with us getting legally married. But I've simply got to lure her away from here first!"

"But why are you so certain she'll definitely run away with you?

"Oh, you don't need to worry about that! I am absolutely convinced she will. The basic point here is that Tatyana Ivanovna is capable of having an affair with anyone she comes across – with anyone, that is, who cares to respond to her. That's why I asked you to give me your word of honour you wouldn't try to use the idea to your own advantage. But you surely can't deny it would be a sin for me to let this opportunity slip, particularly bearing my circumstances in mind."

"Well, she must be absolutely out of her mind... oh, please forgive me!" I added, suddenly aware of what I'd said. "Since your intentions towards her are clearly—"

"Please don't be embarrassed – there's no need to be, as I've already said. You ask whether she's mad? What can one say? Of course she's not mad – otherwise she'd be locked away in a lunatic asylum. In any case, I don't see anything especially mad about her wish to become romantically involved. After all, despite what you might think, she is an honest woman. You have to understand that, until last year, she was dreadfully poor, having spent her entire life under the thumb of despotic benefactresses. She is an extraordinarily sensitive person, and nobody has ever proposed to her. So, bearing in mind her dreams, desires, hopes, her passionate heart, which she always had to keep caged, together with the constant taunting from her benefactresses, it's hardly surprising that such a sensitive soul should be reduced to such a state. And then, suddenly, she comes into wealth – you will agree that this would turn anyone's world upside down. And now of course she's the centre of attention, much sought after, and all her hopes have risen. You heard her story about that dandy in the white coat – it's a perfectly true story, exactly as she told it. This alone helps to explain everything: just give a sigh, send her billets-doux or little love poems and immediately she's yours – and if in addition you begin talking about silken ladders, Spanish serenades and all such nonsense, then you'll be able to do with her whatever you want. I've already made overtures to her, and immediately been promised a secret tryst. For the time being, however, I've decided to wait for a more propitious moment. But in three or four days' time I'll simply have to get her away from here. The evening before, I'll start cooing and billing – I'm not a bad hand at the guitar, and I can sing a little. That night a rendezvous in the summer-house, and by dawn our carriage will be waiting. I'll entice her in, and off and away we go. There's no risk at all, you understand? She's an adult, and, besides, it will be with her full agreement. And once she's run away with me, then of course she'll be beholden to me… I'll put her into the care of a poor but respectable family – I know of one about twenty-five miles away – and they'll take care of her until the wedding, letting no one in to see her. Meanwhile, I won't lose any time organizing the wedding – that takes only three days. I'll need money first, of course, but I reckon no more than five hundred silver roubles will cover everything, for which I can turn to Yegor Ilyich. He'll give it to me, of course, without knowing what it's for. Is that all clear now?"

"Yes, it is," I said, having understood everything at last. "But tell me, where do I come in, exactly?"

"Ah, you can be a great help, I assure you! I wouldn't have asked otherwise. As I've already said, I've got a poor but respectable family in mind. You can help me in various ways, both here and there, and, finally, as a witness. I must admit, I won't be able to do anything without your help."

"One more question: why have you bestowed such an honour on me by taking me into your confidence like this? After all, you hardly know me… I've only been here for a few hours."

"That's a good point," Mizinchikov replied with the most disarming smile, "a point which I openly admit makes me extremely happy, as it gives me the opportunity to tell you how much I respect you."

"But you're exaggerating, surely!"

"Not at all. You see, I've been studying you quite carefully. You seem a little impulsive perhaps and... and... well, rather wet behind the ears. But I'm quite certain about one thing: once you've given me your word that you won't tell anyone, I have no doubt you'll keep it. You are not Obnoskin – that's the first thing. Secondly, you are an honest person and won't exploit my idea to your own advantage – unless, of course, you should want to come to some kind of friendly arrangement with me. If that were to be the case, then I could well be willing perhaps to let you take over my idea – Tatyana Ivanovna, that is – and I'd do all I could to help you with the elopement, but on the following condition: that one month after the wedding you pay me fifty thousand in cash, interest-free – guaranteed in advance, of course, in the form of an IOU."

"What?" I shouted. "You mean you're offering her to me?"

"Naturally I am quite prepared to let you have her if, after giving it some thought, you should want to accept her. I would lose out, of course, but... it's my idea, and ideas are always worth something, aren't they? Thirdly, and finally, I have turned to you because there is no one else who fits the bill. But bearing in mind everything that's going on here, you'll need to decide quickly. And besides, the Dormition Fast is just round the corner, and weddings won't be possible then.* I trust I've made myself quite clear now?"

"Absolutely, and I once again pledge I won't breathe a word of your secret to anyone. But I see it as my duty to tell you straight away that I cannot be your accomplice in this matter."

"Why on earth not?"

"What do you mean, 'why not'?" I exclaimed, finally giving vent to my bottled-up feelings. "Can't you see just how despicable your idea is? All right, let's agree that your calculations, based as they are on the half-crazed character and neurotic state of mind of that pitiable woman, make perfect sense. But that in itself is more than sufficient reason to stop you, as a man of honour, from going ahead with your idea! Haven't you said yourself that she deserves respect, for all her foolishness? And here you are suddenly taking advantage of her unhappiness so that you can extort a hundred thousand from her! Do you have any intention of being a proper husband to her, of doing your duty towards her? Of course not! No doubt you'll abandon her… It's such a disgraceful idea on your part that, forgive me, I simply cannot understand how it could ever have entered your head to ask me to be your accomplice!"

"My goodness me, what a romantic you are!" Mizinchikov exclaimed, looking at me with unfeigned astonishment. "Well, perhaps not so much a romantic, as someone who simply doesn't understand what's what. You say I'm behaving disgracefully, but actually what I'm proposing will be to her advantage, not mine… Think about it!"

"Well, of course, as far as you are concerned, marrying Tatyana Ivanovna could well appear to be a highly magnanimous act on your part," I remarked with a sarcastic smile.

"Exactly right! Precisely that – a highly magnanimous act!" cried Mizinchikov, getting worked up too. "Just think: firstly, the fact that I am sacrificing myself and agreeing to marry her is not to be sneezed at, is it? Secondly, despite the fact that she undoubtedly possesses a hundred thousand silver roubles, despite that, I shall only be taking that amount in notes, and I have promised myself I won't be taking a single copeck more from her as long as I live, even though I could – that, again, is worth something, isn't it? Finally, just think about it carefully: can she ever have a moment's peace in life? For that to happen, you'd have to take the money away from her and put her in a lunatic asylum, as she'd forever be the target of some layabout or ratbag, or some moustached speculator with a goatee serenading her with his guitar – someone like Obnoskin, who would seduce her, marry her, rob her blind and then abandon her somewhere on the high road. We have a very reputable household here, you know, but they're only allowing her to carry on living here because they're after her money. She has to be freed, saved from all such possible hazards. So, you see, as soon as she gets married to me, all such hazards will disappear. I will ensure that no harm whatsoever comes to her.

In the first place, I will immediately place her with a poor but respectable family – in Moscow, that is, not the one I was talking about earlier, another family altogether; my sister will be with her the whole time, and she'll be kept under very careful watch. She'll have some two hundred and fifty thousand, perhaps even three hundred thousand, in notes: on that kind of money, as you know very well, you can live exceptionally well! All life's pleasures will be hers – balls, masquerades, concerts. I won't even mind if she starts dreaming about having some amorous fling, but I'll always make sure my own interests are protected: 'You can dream as much as you like, but anything beyond that... not a chance!' Anyone can take advantage of her now, you know, but then no one will be able to: she will be my wife, Mrs Mizinchikova, and I will not allow my name to be brought into disrepute, sir! That alone is worth something, isn't it? We won't be living together, of course. She'll be in Moscow, whereas I will be somewhere or other in St Petersburg. I'm telling you this because I want to be absolutely open with you. But so what if we are going to live apart? Think about it, consider her character: would she really be able to fulfil her role as a wife and live with her husband? Could she ever be faithful? She's the most untrustworthy creature on earth, isn't she? She needs constant variety in life; she could get married, become someone's lawful wife on Monday and have totally forgotten about it by Tuesday. And I would make her miserable if we were actually to live together and were to demand my strict marital obligations of her. Naturally I will be going to see her once a year or more often – not to ask for money, I can assure you. I have said I won't be taking more than a hundred thousand from her, and I mean it! As far as the money side of things is concerned, I will behave absolutely honourably. In staying with her for a couple of days or so, I will in fact be giving her a lot of pleasure. She won't find it tedious, as I will make her laugh, tell her funny stories, take her to a ball, flirt with her, give her little presents and souvenirs, serenade her, buy her a little dog, part with her on very romantic terms and keep our relationship alive with love letters. She will be absolutely delighted, having such a romantic, loving and jolly husband! That's perfectly rational, in my opinion: that's how all husbands should behave. Wives only really appreciate their husbands when they're not around, and, following this method, I'll hold Tatyana Ivanovna's heart captive in the sweetest way imaginable for the whole of her life. What more can she possibly want? Tell me! It wouldn't be life: it would be paradise!"

I listened to all this in astonished silence. I realized it would be futile to try to argue with Mizinchikov. He had a fanatical belief in the rightness, not to say the magnificence, of his plan, and spoke about it with the enthusiasm of an inventor. Yet there remained one extremely delicate circumstance that needed to be resolved.

"But have you taken into account," I asked, "that she's practically my uncle's fiancée already? He'll be extremely hurt if you run off with her like that. You'll be taking her away from him more or less the day before their wedding, and, in any case, you'll be borrowing money from him to see your plan through!"

"Aha, that's where you're wrong!" Mizinchikov retorted excitedly. "Don't worry, I expected you to say that. Firstly, and most importantly, your uncle has not yet proposed to her, so I could well have been unaware that they were arranging her marriage. Besides, don't forget that the idea came to me as long as three weeks ago, when I still knew nothing about what was going on here, and so, from a moral point of view, I am absolutely blameless – in fact, strictly speaking, it won't be me taking his fiancée away from him, but exactly the opposite: don't forget we have already had a secret midnight rendezvous in the summer-house. And finally, consider this, if you please: one moment you are outraged at the thought that your uncle is being forced to marry Tatyana Ivanovna, and the next you are standing up for the idea of this marriage and talking about honour and some insult or other to the family! No, on the contrary, I am doing your uncle a very great service: I'm rescuing him, don't you understand? He's dead against this marriage, and, in any case, he loves someone else! I mean, what kind of wife could Tatyana

Ivanovna possibly be to him? And, what's more, she's going to be unhappy with him, since, whatever happens, someone will have to stop her throwing roses at young men. And once I have abducted her in the middle of the night, no general's lady or Foma Fomich will be able to do anything about it: to return with a bride who has fled from the altar would be too scandalous. Surely you'd agree I'd be doing Yegor Ilyich a favour, a good turn, wouldn't you?"

I have to confess that I found this last point especially convincing.

"But what if he were to propose to her tomorrow?" I asked. "It would be too late then, wouldn't it? They would be officially engaged."

"Yes, of course it would be too late! We'll have to try to make sure that that doesn't happen. So why do you think I'm asking for your help? I would find it difficult to do it alone, but together we can sort everything out and prevail upon Yegor Ilyich not to propose. We must do all we can to stop him – even, perhaps, if the worst comes to the worst, by giving Foma Fomich a walloping and thereby distracting everyone's attention away from any thought of a wedding. This would of course only be a last resort – it's just a suggestion. So I'm relying on you now."

"Just one final question: have you told anyone else, apart from me, about your plan?"

Mizinchikov scratched the back of his head, contorting his face into a particularly wry grimace.

"I have to confess," he replied, "that question is worse than the bitterest pill imaginable. The fact is that I *have* told someone else... in short, I have been such a foolish idiot! And who do you think it was? Obnoskin! I can hardly believe it myself. I can't think how it could have happened! He was always nosing around the place... I didn't know him very well at the time, and when the idea first came to me I was naturally in a kind of a feverish state. So, realizing I needed someone to assist me, I turned to Obnoskin... Unforgivable, so unforgivable!"

"Well, what was Obnoskin's response?"

"He leapt at the idea, and early in the morning the very next day he disappeared, only to reappear a couple of days later, with his mother. Not a word to me – he even avoided me, as if he was afraid of meeting me. I realized at once what was going on. His mother's such a crafty woman... knows every trick in the book. I know her of old. He'd told her everything, of course. I'm being watchful now, keeping quiet... they're snooping around, and the situation is becoming rather tense... That's why I'm in such a hurry."

"What is it you're so afraid they'll do exactly?"

"They can't do very much, of course, but they're bound to make my life as difficult as possible. They'll want money for helping me, and for keeping quiet about it – that's what I'm expecting... But I'm in no position to give them very much, and I have decided they're not going to get any more than three thousand. Think about it: three thousand here, five hundred silver roubles for the wedding, all of which I'll have to pay back to your uncle... then I've got some old debts to repay, and I shall need something, just something, however little, for my sister. There's not going to be much left over from the hundred thousand, is there? That means I'm ruined!... The Obnoskins, by the way, have left."

"Left?" I asked, eager to know more.

"Just now, after tea... anyway, to hell with them! But tomorrow you'll see, they'll be back. Well, what about it – are you with me?"

"To be absolutely honest," I replied, with a grimace, "I don't know what to say. It's a rather delicate business... Of course I won't say a thing to anyone... I'm not Obnoskin... but I think it would be better if you didn't rely on me."

"I can see," Mizinchikov said, getting up from his chair, "that you're still willing to indulge Foma Fomich and the old woman, and that, although you are very fond of your kind, generous uncle, you still haven't fully understood the extent to which they are tormenting and persecuting him. You're still new here... But just wait! Stay around tomorrow: you'll see for yourself and you'll have agreed by nightfall. Don't you realize your uncle is finished otherwise? No doubt they will force him to get married. Don't forget he could well propose to her tomorrow. By then it will be too late – you simply have to decide today!"

"I wish you every success, really I do... but as for helping... I just don't know..."

"Well, let's see what tomorrow brings!" decided Mizinchikov with a derisive smile. "*La nuit porte conseil.** Goodbye – I'll see you first thing tomorrow morning... and you think about it..."

He turned and left the room, whistling to himself.

I followed him out almost immediately, to get some fresh air. The moon had not yet risen – it was a dark, warm and airless night. The leaves on the trees were perfectly still. Despite feeling extremely tired, I wanted to go for a little stroll to take a break from everything and gather my thoughts, but I hadn't gone more than a few yards when I suddenly heard my uncle's voice. He was climbing the steps up to the new wing with someone and talking about something with extraordinary passion. I immediately turned and called out to him. He was with Vidoplyasov.

II

Total Bewilderment

"Uncle," I cried, "there you are at last!"

"My dear boy, I was just dashing to see you myself. Let me simply deal with Vidoplyasov first, and then we'll be able to discuss everything."

"What, Vidoplyasov again? Don't waste time on him, Uncle!"

"Just another five or ten minutes, Sergei, and I'm all yours. It's quite an important matter, you see."

"It's almost certainly something silly," I said irritably.

"Well, what can I say, my dear boy? There'll always be somebody pestering you with some trivial matter or other, won't there? Surely, Grigory my dear fellow, you could have chosen some better time for your complaints, couldn't you? So, what can I do for you? You should have pity on me, my dear man; you've totally worn me out, so to speak, eaten me alive, every last bit of me! I'm fed up with the lot of them, Sergei."

And my uncle waved his arms around in a state of profound distress.

"But what's so important that it can't be left for later? There's something I really have to talk to you about, Uncle…"

"Oh, my dear boy, they're always yelling at me that I pay no attention to my servants' morals! I wouldn't be surprised if he began complaining to me tomorrow that I've not bothered to hear him out, and then…"

And once again my uncle threw his arms up into the air.

"Well, then, finish with him once and for all! Perhaps I'll be able to help. Let's go inside. What's the matter with him? What does he want?" I asked, when we'd got in.

"Well, you see, my dear boy, the fact is that he doesn't like his own surname. He's asking for it to be changed. What do you make of that?"

"His surname? What do you mean?... Listen, Uncle, before I listen to him myself, allow me to observe that it's only here, in a house like this, that you could have such absurd things going on," I remarked, spreading my arms in disbelief.

"I agree, my dear boy, I can wave my arms about too, but there's not much point!" my uncle remarked angrily. "Why don't you try to talk to him yourself? He's been going on at me for two months now..."

"It's an unsuitable surname, sir!" declared Vidoplyasov.

"But why unsuitable, for goodness' sake?" I asked in bewilderment.

"Just that, sir. It's offensive."

"But what on earth's offensive about it? And anyway, how can you change it? Whoever changes their surname?"

"Well, sir, have you ever come across such a surname?"

"I agree, it's a little unusual," I continued in total bewilderment, "but what can one do about it now, for goodness' sake? After all, your father must have had that very same surname, mustn't he?"

"That's true, sir," replied Vidoplyasov. "It's my father's fault that I've had to accept a lifetime of suffering, and I'm destined to become the butt of many gibes and endure much grief, sir."

"I bet Foma Fomich had something to do with this, Uncle!" I cried angrily.

"No, my dear boy, not at all – you're wrong. In fact, Foma Fomich has been very kind to him. He has taken him on as his secretary – that's his sole responsibility. And naturally he has broadened his horizons, filled his mind with noble thoughts, so that, in a certain sense, he has come of age... So, you see, I'm being perfectly frank with you..."

"That's right, sir," Vidoplyasov broke in, "Foma Fomich truly is my benefactor, sir, and as such, he has inculcated in me the sense of my own insignificance, precisely what a worthless creature I am, so that, through him, I have become aware of my destiny for the first time in my life, sir."

"There you are, Seryozha, now do you see exactly how it stands?" my uncle continued, prattling away in his usual manner. "He started life in Moscow, from his early childhood, more or less, working for a teacher of calligraphy. You should have seen how he mastered the skill of writing there: coloured and gold letters, surrounded, you know, bordered by cupids – in short, a veritable artist! He's teaching Ilyusha... I'm paying him one and a half roubles a lesson. Foma himself determined that amount. Goes to three local landowners – they pay him for lessons, too. Look at the clothes he wears! Writes poetry as well."

"Poetry! Would you believe it!"

"Poetry, my dear boy, poetry – no, I'm not joking, real poetry, versification on any subject you like, and so well crafted, you know... he can put anything to verse. A real talent! He constructed such a poem for Mother's name day that we could only gasp with admiration... references to mythology, with the Muses flying out of his mouth, so that you could see a certain... damn it, what is it called?... rotundity of form – in short, everything, with Foma's help, rhyming exactly as it should. Naturally I, for my part, didn't disapprove – in fact, it gladdened my heart. Let him write away – just so long as he doesn't play the fool. I'm talking as a father to you, Grigory my dear fellow. Foma heard about it, took a look at his poetry, encouraged him to continue and engaged him as his reader and scribe – in short, educated him. He's quite right when he says that Foma became his benefactor. It explains, you know, the elevated romantic ideas that come into his head and the sense of independence – it's all been explained to me by Foma, and I have to admit I'd quite forgotten I'd planned to give him his freedom in any case, without obtaining Foma's permission. Rather shameful, you know!... But Foma's against the idea... says that he needs him, has grown to like him. And, moreover, as he said to me, I should be very proud that I, as a landowner, have a poet as one of my serfs – there were barons who used to do the same, living *en grand** like that. '*En grand*', that's what he said, '*en grand*'! I, my dear boy, have already begun to respect him, do you understand? But you should see the way he behaves now! What's really bad is the way that, as a poet, he puts on airs in front of the other servants... doesn't even want to talk to them. Don't take offence, Grigory, I'm talking to you as a father. Last winter he promised he'd get married – to one of the serf girls here, Matryona... such a sweet girl, you know – honest, hard-working, cheerful. But now he's completely given up the idea: 'Simply don't want to, no more to be said'... refuses point blank. Maybe he became conceited, or wanted to make a name for himself first, and then find someone else..."

"It's more because of Foma's advice, sir," Vidoplyasov remarked, "since he's my true benefactor..."

"Can't anything ever be decided without Foma Fomich?" I suddenly exclaimed.

"No, my dear boy, that's not the point," my uncle hastily interjected. "You need to understand, things aren't going well for him at the moment. She's a feisty, hot-tempered girl, has set everybody against him... people tease him, jeer at him, even the serf boys take him for a fool..."

"Yes, and it's all Matryona's fault," remarked Vidoplyasov. "She's such a stupid girl, that Matryona, really stupid, sir, and what's more with a mind of her own. She's the one who's made my life so miserable, sir."

"Oh, Grigory, my dear fellow, I told you, didn't I?" my uncle said, giving Vidoplyasov a reproachful look. "You see, Sergei, they've made up some disgusting lines to rhyme with his surname. So he comes to me and complains, asking me whether it might be possible to change his surname somehow, since he's been really unhappy with the way it sounds for a very long time..."

"It's a horrid, disgusting name, sir," interposed Vidoplyasov.

"Hold your tongue, Grigory! Foma's given his approval... well, not so much his approval, but, you understand, one needs to bear in mind the following: if it should ever come to publishing the poetry, as Foma plans, then a surname like that might well be a disadvantage – don't you think?"

"So he wants to publish his poetry, does he, Uncle?"

"Yes, my dear boy. That's already been decided – I'll be paying for it. On the title page it will say: 'The bonded serf of ***', and it will include a foreword from the author, thanking Foma for educating him. It will be dedicated to Foma. Foma himself is writing the foreword. Well, just imagine if the title page were to say: *The Works of Vidoplyasov...*"

"*The Lamentations of Vidoplyasov*, sir," corrected Vidoplyasov.

"You see? It's *Lamentations* now! What sort of a name is Vidoplyasov in any case? It's an offence to one's sensibilities – that's what Foma says. And all those critics, they say, are such a bunch of ruthless scoffers... Brambeus, for example...* They're totally merciless! They just love jeering at writers, for their surname alone... you'll be given such a pasting you'll never get over it – isn't that so? So I say that, as far I am concerned, you can put whatever name you like to your poems – pseudonym, I think they call it... some -nym or other, anyway. 'Oh no,' he says, 'you must see to it that from now on everyone in the household calls me only by my new name – something tasteful, befitting my talent...'"

"And I bet you agreed to do that, Uncle."

"Seryozha, my dear boy, I really don't want to get into an argument with anyone. Let him do as he wants! I had this little falling-out with Foma at the time, you see. And then it all started: every week a new surname, anything with a good ring to it: Oleandrov, Tyulpanov... Just think, Grigory, you wanted to be called 'Faithful' at first: Grigory the Faithful. But then you yourself didn't like that, because some idiot changed it to 'Hateful'. You complained and the idiot was punished. You spent the next two weeks trying to think up a new name for yourself – however many was it? Finally you plumped for 'Uhlanov'. So there you are, my dear boy: tell me, what could be more absurd than the name 'Uhlanov'? However, I agreed to this as well, and gave a second order to the effect that your name was to be changed to Uhlanov. But only," my uncle added, turning to me, "only so that he'd leave me alone. For three days you went around everywhere as 'Uhlanov'. You ruined every wall, every window sill in the summer-house by scrawling your name, 'Uhlanov', in pencil everywhere. So much so that the place had to be redecorated! You covered pages and pages of best parchment paper with 'Uhlanov, specimen of signature', 'Uhlanov, specimen of signature'. But then, in the end, another disaster: someone went and thought up the rhyme 'Bolvanov'.* 'I don't like that,' you said. 'I want another name!' I forget now what your final choice was."

"Tantsev, sir," Vidoplyasov replied. "If I have to represent myself as a dancer through my name,* then it should essentially be something refined and foreign-sounding: Tantsev, sir."

"All right then, Tantsev – I have agreed to that too, Sergei, my dear boy. Except that they have found something that rhymes with that which I simply can't repeat here! He must be here today with another name. I bet you anything he's come up with something new. Am I right or am I wrong about that, Grigory? Come on, own up!"

"Well, in fact, I *have* been thinking of submitting a new refined name to you for some time, sir."

"And what would that be?"

"Essbouquetov."

"Aren't you ashamed of yourself, Grigory? The kind of name you see on a pomade jar? And you call yourself a clever man? How long did it take you to think *that* one up? You can see that sort of thing written on a bottle of perfume."

"For goodness' sake, Uncle," I said in a half-whisper, "the man's clearly an idiot, a total halfwit!"

"What can one do, my dear boy?" my uncle replied, also in a half-whisper. "Everyone maintains he's clever, and that he's been demonstrating his very special qualities…"

"But stop wasting your time on him, for God's sake!"

"Listen, Grigory! Can't you see I've got no time for this… please, my good fellow?" my uncle began to say imploringly, as if he were frightened of Vidoplyasov. "I mean, I ask you, how can I possibly be concerned about your troubles now? You say someone's insulted you again? Well, all right: I give you my word that I'll look into it tomorrow, but for now be off with you... Wait! What was that about Foma Fomich?"

"He's retired to bed, sir. I'm to say that, if anyone enquires, he's intending to spend all night praying, sir."

"Hmm! Well, off you go, my good man, off you go! You see, Seryozha? He and Foma are like hand and glove at the moment, so it makes me particularly wary of him. Yes, and that's why the whole household dislikes him: he reports everything he hears back to Foma. He's gone now, but there's no knowing what kind of slanderous comment he could come up with tomorrow! Anyway, my dear boy, I've now managed to put everything to rights, and it's such a weight off my mind... I was dashing on my way to se you. At last we're together again!" he said with a rush of emotion, shaking my hand. "And there was I thinking, my dear boy, that you were really angry with me and wanted to slink off. I even had someone check on you. But everything's fine now, thank God! What did you think of Gavrila's behaviour just now? And then Falaley, and then you... it never stops, does it? Well, thank God, thank God! Finally I'll be able to say everything I've been meaning to and to open my heart to you. Please don't go, Seryozha – you're all I've got now, you and Korovkin..."

"Yes, but what is it exactly you've managed to put to rights, Uncle? And what's the point of staying here after everything that's happened? I must confess my head's in an absolute spin!"

"And you think mine isn't? It's been going on a merry dance for half a year now, my head has! But it's all been resolved now, thank God! In the first place, I've been forgiven, totally forgiven – on a number of conditions of course... but now I'm not really afraid of anything any more. Sashurka has also been forgiven. My goodness, Sasha, Sasha... such a high-spirited girl! She got a little carried away earlier, but she has a heart of gold! I am proud of that little girl, Seryozha! May the Lord God always bless her! You've been forgiven as well, and do you know precisely to what extent? You can do what you like, go wherever you like in the house and in the garden, even when guests are present – in short, you are absolutely free to do as you want. But there's just one condition: you must on no account say anything at all tomorrow in front of Mother and Foma Fomich – I mean it, not a single word. I have already promised that on your behalf. You are only to listen to what your elders and betters... that is, I mean, to what other people are saying. Their view is that you are still very young. You mustn't be offended, Sergei – after all, you actually are still quite young... That's what even Anna Nilovna says..."

I immediately proved the fact that I was indeed very young by exploding with irritation at such insulting conditions.

"Listen, Uncle," I exclaimed, barely able to contain myself, "could you please put my mind to rest by answering a simple question: do I, or do I not, find myself in an absolute madhouse?"

"I see, my dear boy... finding fault with everything now, are we? You should be a little more tolerant," my uncle replied, clearly saddened by my question. "You're not in a madhouse at all – it's simply that you have both got a little worked up about things. After all, my dear boy, you have to agree that you yourself didn't behave particularly well, did you? Have you forgotten how rude you were to him? A man of his age, worthy of respect?"

"Such people, Uncle, no matter what age, don't deserve respect."

"Now, that's going too far, my boy! That's freethinking! I'm not against freethinking, my boy, provided it's tempered by reason – but that, my boy, is quite beyond the pale. I'm astonished at you, Sergei!"

"Don't be cross, Uncle. I'm at fault, but only in so far as you are concerned. As for your Foma Fomich—"

"I see, it's *your* Foma Fomich now, is it? Come on, Sergei my dear boy, don't be too hard on him: he's a misanthrope, that's all, just a little eccentric! It's wrong to expect too much of him. But he's such an honourable and worthy man... the most honourable of men! After all, you saw that for yourself just now... simply brilliant! Yes, he has his little moments, but take no notice of them. It can happen to anyone!"

"No, Uncle, that's where you're wrong: hardly anyone behaves like that."

"Goodness me, come on! You need to show more compassion, Sergei, be more forgiving!..."

"Well, all right, Uncle, all right! Let's leave it there. Tell me, have you seen Nastasya Yevgrafovna?"

"My dear boy, it was all because of her! Listen, Seryozha, first and foremost: we have all firmly decided to wish him, Foma that is, a happy birthday tomorrow – it really *is* his birthday tomorrow. Sashenka has a good heart, but she's got that wrong. Anyway, we're all going, the lot of us, to see him really early, before the service. Ilyusha will be reading him some poetry, which will be like balm to his soul – in a word, he will be flattered. Oh, Seryozha, it would be so wonderful if you could join us in wishing him a happy birthday! He might well completely forgive you, if you were to do that. It would be so good if you were to make up with each other! Never mind if you've been offended, Seryozha, my dear boy... after all, you yourself have offended him... He's the most honourable of men!"

"But, Uncle, Uncle!" I shouted, my patience exhausted. "Here am I wanting to have a serious talk, while you... Do you know... I repeat, do you know what the situation is with Nastasya Yevgrafovna?"

"Of course I do, my dear boy! No need to shout like that! She was the reason everything flared up just now. It all actually started some time ago, however. I didn't want to talk about it earlier, so as not to alarm you, because they simply wanted to kick her out – in fact, they demanded I send her away. You can imagine the situation I was in... Well, it's all been resolved now, thank God! You see, they thought – I can be quite frank with you now – they thought that I was in love with her and wanted to marry her; in other words, that I was hurtling towards my own ruin – which was precisely, in fact, what I was doing, as they explained to me at the time... so, in order to save me, it was decided to turn her out of the house. It's all Mother's idea, but Anna Nilovna's mostly responsible for it. Foma's keeping quiet for the moment. But now I have manged to persuade them that they're wrong, and, I must confess, I have now told them you're already engaged to Nastenka, and that is why you've come here. Well, that has partly set their minds at rest, and so she's staying – only for the time being, for a trial period, but nonetheless staying. You even went up in their esteem when I told them you were getting engaged to her. Mother seems to have calmed down a little at least. Only Anna Nilovna's still muttering away to herself! I've no idea any more what I can do to please her. And really, what more does she want, this Anna Nilovna?"

"But you've got it completely wrong, Uncle! Don't you know that Nastasya Yevgrafovna is leaving here tomorrow – that is, if she hasn't already gone? That her father came here today precisely so that he could take her away? That it's all been decided once and for all, that she herself told me about it in person today, and asked me, at the end, to say goodbye to you for her? Do you or do you not know that?"

My uncle just stood stock-still in front of me, staring at me open-mouthed. He seemed to give a shudder, and let out a groan.

Seizing my moment, I hurriedly told him all about my conversation with Nastenka, my proposal, her unequivocal rejection, and her anger at my uncle for his presumption in sending me a letter asking me to come. Finally I explained that she was hoping that, by leaving, she would save him from having to get married to Tatyana Ivanovna – in short, I concealed nothing, even deliberately exaggerating any unpleasant details. I wanted to shock my uncle into a decisive reaction – and I certainly did just that. He shouted out and clutched his head in his hands.

"Where is she, do you know? Where is she now?" he said at last, his face pale with fright. "And there I was, idiot that I am, on my way here, quite sure that everything had been settled!" he added despairingly.

"I don't know where she is now, but a little time ago, when all that shouting broke out, she went off to see you. She wanted to say everything she'd said to me, with everybody present. Someone must have stopped her."

"Of course they would! Goodness knows what she might have done! Oh, she's such a wilful, proud girl! But where would she have gone? Where? Where? As for you, you're a fine one, aren't you? Why on earth did she turn you down? Ridiculous! You should have made her fall in love with you. Why didn't you? Come on, answer me, for God's sake! Don't just stand there!"

"That's very harsh, Uncle! How can you be asking me such things?"

"But we can't leave things like this, can we? You have to, absolutely have to marry her. Why did I go to the bother of winkling you out of St Petersburg otherwise? You simply have to make her happy! As it is now, they're going to force her to leave, but if she were your wife and my niece, they wouldn't do that. Where's she going to go otherwise? What's she going to do? Become a governess again! But that would be totally absurd! And where will she live, while she's looking for a position? Her old father has nine little ones to look after, and they're starving as it is. If all this horrible gossip forces her out of here, she won't accept a copeck of my money, nor will her father. In any case, how can she leave just like this?… It's horrible! There's sure to be a scandal, I just know there will. Her entire salary has been paid in advance to cover the family needs – you know she feeds them, don't you? Well, let's suppose I do recommend her as a governess and manage to find an honest, decent family for her… Damn it! Where can one find genuinely decent families nowadays? All right, let us not incur God's wrath, let us suppose that such people exist, even in some numbers if you like! But it's a risk, isn't it, my dear boy? How far can you trust people? And, in any case, when you have little or no money, you're going to be wary: how can you be sure you're not going to be forced to demean yourself for the sake of a crust of bread or a kind word or gesture? They'll insult her… she's a proud girl, and then… goodness knows what then! And then what if, on top of it all, some vile, depraved character should appear on the scene and seduce her? She'd spit in his face – I know she would – but he'd go ahead and seduce her all the same, the scoundrel! Her name would become tarnished, a suspicious shadow would fall over her, and then… My head's reeling at the thought! My God!"

"Uncle, forgive me, but I have to put one question to you," I said solemnly. "Please don't be angry with me, and try to understand that the answer you give may well solve a lot of problems – in fact, I even have the right to demand that you answer me, Uncle!"

"What's that? What question?"

"Tell me, before God, openly and truthfully: do you not feel that you are a little in love yourself with Nastasya Yevgrafovna and would like to marry her? Think about it: after all, that's precisely why they want to get rid of her."

My uncle reacted to this with a violent gesture of impatience.

"Me? In love? With her? Either everyone's completely off their heads or this is some sort of conspiracy against me. Why on earth did you think I asked you to come here, if it weren't to prove that they've gone off their heads? And why, for goodness' sake, am I asking you to propose to her? Me? In love? With her? You've all gone mad!"

"Well, if that's the case, Uncle, allow me to speak my mind fully. Let me tell you, in all solemnity, that I can't see anything wrong at all in such an idea. Quite the contrary: you would make her so happy if you were to love her, and… and may God grant that to be the case! May the Lord love you and guide you well!"

"What are you saying, for Heaven's sake?" exclaimed my uncle, quite taken aback. "I'm astonished you can say such things so calmly… and… in general, my boy, you always seem in such a hurry – I have noticed such a tendency in you! Well, isn't what you've just said totally ridiculous? How, tell me, could I possibly marry her, when I look upon her as none other than my daughter? And yes, I would be ashamed, even regard it as sinful, to look upon her in any other way! I am an old man, whereas she is a little rosebud! Even Foma explained that to me, using the very same words. My heart burns with a father's love for her, and here you are going

on about marriage! It's possible, I suppose, that she wouldn't turn me down from sheer gratitude, but afterwards she would always despise me for taking advantage of her gratitude. That would destroy her, and she'd lose her affection for me! I would give my life for her, my darling little child! In fact, I love her like my Sasha, perhaps even more, let me confess to you. Sasha is my rightful, lawful daughter, but the other I have made my daughter through nothing but love. I saved her from poverty, I brought her up. My angel, may God bless her, loved her and entrusted her to me as her daughter. I saw to her education: she can speak French, play the piano and everything... She has such a lovely little smile! Have you noticed, Seryozha? As if she's laughing at you but yet not laughing at you at all – nothing of the sort, in fact: she's showing her love for you... I thought you would come here and propose to her... they would be reassured I had no designs on her and would stop spreading all those vile insinuations. Then she could have lived with you in peace and calm, and we would have been so happy! You are both my children, both practically orphans, both of you have grown up under my care... I would have loved you both so much, so much! I would have given my life for you, never left your side, followed you everywhere! Oh, how happy we could have been! And why is it that people are so cross, so angry all the time, hate each other so much? If only, oh if only I could knock sense into them! If only I could reveal the whole heart-warming truth to them! Oh my God!"

"Yes, Uncle, that's all very well, except that she's turned me down..."

"Turned you down, has she? Hmm!... You know, I sort of felt she would," he said pensively. "But no!" he cried. "I don't believe it, it's not possible! If that's the case, then everything will unravel! You can't have given it enough thought – perhaps you offended her somehow, or laid it on a bit thick... Tell me once more what happened, Seryozha!"

I told him everything again, down to the last detail. When I got to the point at which Nastenka had expressed the hope that, by leaving, she would save my uncle from Tatyana Ivanovna, he gave a bitter smile.

"Save me?" he said. "Save me until tomorrow!"

"Please don't tell me, Uncle, that you're getting married to Tatyana Ivanovna," I cried in alarm.

"But how else can I ensure they won't kick Nastya out of the house? I shall propose tomorrow – I've made a solemn promise to do so."

"So you've made up your mind, Uncle?"

"What choice do I have, my boy? What choice? It rips my heart in two, but I have made up my mind. I will propose tomorrow – we've agreed the wedding will be a quiet one, family members only... it will be better that way, my dear boy. You'll probably be the best man. I've already tipped them off about that, so they'll certainly allow you to stay at least until then. What can I do, my dear boy? They keep on saying 'The children will be wealthy!' And naturally you're always going to ensure your own children's well-being, aren't you? You'd turn yourself inside out for them – it's essentially the right thing to do, after all. I simply have to do something for the family. I can't just sit there and sponge off everyone!"

"But, Uncle, she's mad!" I exclaimed, quite beside myself, a painful sensation gripping my heart.

"I see... mad now, is she? She's actually not mad at all – she just, you know, finds life a little difficult... What can I do, my dear boy? All right, someone with a few more brains might have been better... but then clever people are not always the easiest to deal with! Oh, if only you knew what a kind, generous heart she has!"

"Good God! He's already resigned himself to the idea!" I said in despair.

"But what else can I do? After all, they are thinking what's best for me – and, in any case, I felt it was bound to happen sooner or later. So why not get on with it now, rather than have another quarrel? Let me tell you frankly, Seryozha, my dear boy: I'm not actually unhappy at the thought. I've made up my mind – so be it... at least it's a weight off my shoulders – it will give me some peace. On my way here I was almost at peace with myself. My future has now been decided! Most importantly, Nastya will be able to remain – I only agreed on that condition. And now *she herself* wants to leave! But I can never allow that to happen!" my uncle shouted, stamping his foot. "Listen, Sergei," he added decisively, "wait here, don't go anywhere. I'll be back in a flash."

"Where are you going, Uncle?"

"Maybe I'll be able to see her, Sergei – it will all be resolved, believe me, absolutely everything, and... and... and you *will* marry her, I promise you!"

My uncle quickly left the room and turned to go into the garden rather than the house. I watched him from the window.

12

Catastrophe

I stood there alone. I was in an intolerable situation: I had been turned down, yet my uncle seemed to be trying to marry me off by force. I was in a totally confused state, unable to think straight. I couldn't get Mizinchikov's proposal out of my head. My uncle simply had to be rescued, whatever it took! The thought occurred to me that I should go and find Mizinchikov and tell him everything. But where on earth had my uncle gone? He said he was going to look for Nastenka, yet he'd gone into the garden. The thought of secret rendezvous flashed through my mind, and my heart was gripped by an unpleasant feeling. I remembered what Mizinchikov had said about a clandestine relationship... After a moment's thought I angrily cast aside my suspicions. My uncle was not capable of deceiving anyone – that was patently clear. With each passing minute I became more and more alarmed. Not thinking where I was going I went out onto the porch and wandered off into the garden, taking the same alleyway as my uncle. The moon was just beginning to rise. I knew every inch of that garden, and was not afraid of getting lost. When I reached the ancient summer-house, standing in an isolated spot on the bank of the age-old, stagnant pond, I suddenly stopped, as if rooted to the ground: I could hear people talking in the summer-house. I can't describe the strange feeling of irritation that overcame me! Convinced it was my uncle and Nastenka, I walked on quite normally towards the summer-house, allaying my conscience with the thought that at least I wasn't trying to creep up on them. Suddenly I could hear the sound of a kiss, then of an animated exchange of words, followed immediately by a woman's piercing scream. At that instant a woman in a white dress came running out of the summer-house and darted past me like a swallow. I even had the impression she was covering her face with her hands so as not to be recognized: she had no doubt seen me from the summer-house. But imagine my astonishment when I saw that the young man dashing out after the terrified lady was none other than Obnoskin – the very same Obnoskin who, according to Mizinchikov, had already left some time ago! For his part, Obnoskin, on seeing me, was highly embarrassed: all signs of his usual cockiness had gone.

"Forgive me, but… I didn't expect to see you here," he said, smiling and stumbling over his words.

"Nor I you," I replied mockingly, "particularly since I'd heard you'd left."

"No, actually… that is… I was merely seeing Mother off to somewhere not very far away. But might I appeal to you as the most honourable person in the world?"

"About what?"

"There are moments – as I'm sure you yourself would agree – when a truly honourable person is compelled to appeal to all that is honourable in someone else, a truly honourable person… I hope you understand me…"

"Sorry to dash your hopes, but I have no idea what you're talking about."

"You saw the lady who was with me in the summer-house?"

"I did, but I didn't know who it was."

"Ah, so you didn't know who it was!… That is the lady I'm shortly going to call my wife."

"Congratulations. But how can I be of any help?"

"Simply by promising you won't ever tell a soul you've seen me with this lady."

"Who on earth could it be?" I wondered. "Surely not…"

"I really don't know," I replied. "You'll have to forgive me, but I cannot promise that…"

"No, for Heaven's sake, please," Obnoskin implored me. "Put yourself in my position… it's a secret. You may want to get married yourself one day, and then I—"

"Shh! Someone's coming."

"Where?"

And indeed, some thirty paces from where we were standing, a shadowy figure hurried past us.

"That... that has to be Foma Fomich!" Obnoskin whispered, his whole body shaking. "I'd know his walk anywhere. Good God! There's someone else coming the other way! Can you hear?... Goodbye! Thank you and... please, I beg you..."

Obnoskin disappeared. A moment later, as if from nowhere, my uncle turned up next to me.

"Is that you?" he cried on seeing me. "All is lost, Seryozha! All is lost!"

I saw that he, too, was shaking all over.

"What's lost, Uncle?"

"Let's go!" he said, gasping for breath, and, grabbing me firmly by the arm, he dragged me after him. He didn't say a word the whole way to the new wing, and wouldn't let me speak either. I was expecting something quite extraordinary, and was not disappointed. When we got inside, he suddenly fainted – he went as white as a sheet. I immediately sprinkled some water over him. "Something terrible must have happened," I thought, "for a man like him to pass out like that."

"Uncle, what's wrong?" I asked him at last.

"All is lost, Seryozha! Foma caught me in the garden with Nastenka, at the very moment I was kissing her!"

"Kissing! In the garden!" I exclaimed, looking at my uncle in astonishment.

"In the garden, my boy. I must have been mad! I just had to go and find her. I wanted to open my mind to her, make her see reason – about you, I mean. She had been waiting for me for an hour already, there by the broken bench on the other side of the pond... She often goes there when she needs to talk to me."

"Often, Uncle?"

"Often, my dear boy! We've been meeting practically every night lately. But they've probably been watching our every movement – in fact, I know they have, and I know that Anna Nilovna is behind it all. For a time we stopped meeting – for about four days, in fact – but we simply had to meet again today. You yourself saw how necessary it was: how could I have said what I wanted to say otherwise? I got there, in the hope of finding her there, and she'd been waiting for me for a whole hour already... she also had something she had to tell me..."

"Good God, that was really careless of you! But you knew you were being watched, didn't you?"

"But it was a critical situation, Seryozha – there was so much we needed to say to each another. During the day I simply don't dare even look at her: she's in one part of the room and I in another. I behave as if I'm unaware of her existence. But at night we get together and talk and talk..."

"Well, Uncle, what happened?"

"I'd hardly had time to say a couple of words, my heart had started pounding away, you know how it is, and I was on the point of tears; I had just begun trying to convince her she should get married to you, when she said: 'You clearly don't love me – obviously you can't see what's happening.' And suddenly she flung her arms round my neck and burst out crying and sobbing! 'I love only you,' she said, 'and will never marry anyone. I have long loved you, but I won't marry you, as I'm leaving here tomorrow and going to a monastery...'"

"My God! Did she really say that to you? So what on earth's going to happen now, Uncle?"

"I looked up, and there was Foma, right there! Where had he come from? He couldn't have been sitting behind a bush the whole time, waiting for the chance of catching us together like that, could he?"

"What a horrible man!"

"I froze to the spot – couldn't say anything. Nastenka took to her heels, while Foma walked on past us without saying a word, shaking his finger at me. Do you realize, Sergei, what a palaver there'll be tomorrow?"

"Of course I do!"

"Do you realize," he cried in despair, leaping up from his chair, "do you realize that they want to ruin her, humiliate her, discredit her? They've just been looking for a pretext to blacken her name so that they can kick her out of the house – and now they've found one! After all, they've always maintained that she's been carrying on with me in a disgusting way, that she's had this fling with Vidoplyasov, the villains! Anna Nilovna was the one who started it all. What's going to happen now? What's going to happen tomorrow? Is Foma going to tell everyone?"

"Without a shadow of a doubt, Uncle."

"But if he does, if he does…" he said, biting his lip and clenching his fists. "But no, he's not going to, he'll understand… he's a highly honourable man! He'll take pity on her…"

"He may or he may not," I answered determinedly, "but either way you absolutely have to propose to Nastasya Yevgrafovna tomorrow."

My uncle stood there staring at me.

"Don't you understand, Uncle, that her name will be ruined if word of this gets about? Don't you understand that you need to avert this disaster as soon as possible, that you need to look everybody boldly and proudly in the eye, openly propose to her, tell them you don't give a damn about their objections and grind Foma to dust if he so much as says a word against her?"

"My dear boy!" my uncle exclaimed. "I was thinking of doing just that, on my way here!"

"And have you made up your mind to do just that?"

"Absolutely! I had already done so, even before coming to talk to you!"

"Bravo, Uncle!"

And I dashed over to embrace him.

We talked for a long time. I set out all the arguments to him, all the compelling reasons why he had to get married to Nastenka – all of which he himself understood perfectly well in any case. I became carried away by my own eloquence. I was overjoyed for him. He would never have stood up for himself if he hadn't been motivated by his sense of duty. He worshipped duty and obligation. Despite this, however, I had absolutely no idea what the end result of all this would be. I knew, and firmly believed, that my uncle would never go back on his word once he recognized where his duty lay – yet I still couldn't bring myself to believe he would actually have the strength to go against the wishes of the others in the household. That was why I was doing everything I could to encourage him and spur him on, using all my youthful fervour to achieve that end.

"Most importantly, most importantly," I said, "you have reached a firm decision and your last doubts have vanished! Something totally unexpected has happened – even though everyone else foresaw it and was already aware of the fact that Nastasya Yevgrafovna loves you! Would you ever," I cried, "have allowed her pure and innocent love to bring shame and dishonour on her?"

"Never! But, my dear boy, is it really true I am going to be so happy?" he cried again, throwing his arms around my neck. "And how could she have fallen in love with me like that? Does she know what she's doing? Does she? I have nothing, it seems, that she could possibly... I'm an old man beside her, hadn't been expecting anything of the sort! My angel, my angel!... Listen, Seryozha, you asked me some time ago whether I was in love with her – did you have any inkling when you asked that?"

"All I could see, Uncle, was that no one could possibly have loved her as much as you did – you loved her and were not even aware of it. Think about it! The only reason you summoned me here, wanting me to marry her, was so that she would become your niece and always be a close part of your life..."

"And you... and you forgive me, Seryozha?"

"Oh, come on, Uncle!"

And he threw his arms around me again.

"Watch out, Uncle, everyone's against you. You have to stand up and go to war – and it has to be tomorrow."

"Yes... yes, tomorrow!" he repeated rather pensively. "And, yes, we'll set about it with courage, with true nobility of spirit, with strength of character... that's right, strength of character!"

"No dithering, Uncle!"

"No dithering, Seryozha! But there's just one thing: how do we begin, how do we go about it?"

"Don't worry about that, Uncle. Leave it until tomorrow. Take it easy today. And if Foma should say anything... kick him out of the house immediately and grind him to dust!"

"But maybe I won't need to kick him out! Here's what I've decided to do, my dear boy: I'll go to him early tomorrow, as soon as the sun's up, and tell him everything you and I have just discussed. He will definitely understand what I'm saying: he is such an honourable man, the most honourable of men! But there is one thing that worries me: what if Mother were to tell Tatyana Ivanovna today that I was going to propose tomorrow? That would be a disaster!"

"Don't worry about Tatyana Ivanovna, Uncle."

And I told him about my encounter with Obnoskin in the summer-house. My uncle was flabbergasted by this. I didn't breathe a word about Mizinchikov.

"Such a weird creature! Really weird!" he exclaimed. "Poor woman! They keep flattering her, planning to take advantage of her simple-mindedness! Obnoskin? Really? But I thought he'd left... Strange, very strange indeed! I find that very odd, Seryozha... I shall have to look into that tomorrow and take steps... But are you absolutely certain that it was Tatyana Ivanovna?"

I replied that although I hadn't been able to see her face, I had very good reason to believe it really had been Tatyana Ivanovna.

"Hmm! But perhaps you were mistaken, and he was actually flirting with one of the servant girls, and not Tatyana Ivanovna at all? The gardener's daughter, Dasha, perhaps? Devious little creature! I say this because she's been caught doing that sort of thing by Anna Nilovna... But no, of course it couldn't have been Dasha – he said he wanted to marry her. Strange! Very strange!"

Finally we parted. I embraced my uncle, giving him my blessing. "By tomorrow, by tomorrow," he repeated, "everything will have been decided... before you get out of bed. I will go to Foma and settle everything with him in an honourable way. I'll be quite open with him, as if he were my own brother, and reveal the innermost workings of my heart. Goodbye, Seryozha. You go to bed, you're tired, though I probably won't sleep a wink tonight myself."

He walked away. I went to bed at once, tired, utterly exhausted. It had been such a difficult day. My nerves were shattered, and before I managed to doze off I kept on starting up awake. But however odd the images that might have flooded my mind as I tried to get to sleep, they were as nothing when compared with the strangeness of my awakening the following morning.

SECOND AND FINAL PART

I

The Chase

I slept soundly, uninterrupted by dreams. Suddenly I felt as if a ten-ton weight had crashed down on my feet. I cried out and woke up. It was already daylight; the sun was shining brightly through the windows. Sitting on my bed – or, more precisely, on my feet – was Mr Bakhcheyev.

There could be no doubt about it: it was Bakhcheyev. Having somehow extricated my feet, I sat up in the bed and looked at him with the dazed bewilderment of someone not yet fully awake.

"Stop looking at me like that!" the fat man exclaimed. "Staring at me as if transfixed! Come on, young man, up you get! I've been trying to wake you for the last thirty minutes – come on, rub your eyes."

"But what's wrong? What time is it?"

"It's still early, young man, but our blessed Fevronia has given us the slip before dawn.* Up you get, we're off in pursuit!"

"What blessed Fevronia?"

"Why, our blessed Fevronia, of course! Slipped away just like that! Before dawn! I thought I'd only need a minute to wake you, my good fellow, but I've frittered a couple of hours away already! Come on, up you get – your uncle's also waiting for you. What a wonderful way to celebrate a festivity!" he added angrily and maliciously, while clearly relishing the situation.

"But who and what are you talking about?" I asked impatiently, nonetheless beginning to guess what his answer might be. "You don't mean Tatyana Ivanovna, do you?"

"Who else, for goodness' sake? Of course I mean Tatyana Ivanovna! I kept on telling you, warning you – but you didn't want to listen! So that's how she's going to celebrate the occasion!

189

Crazy old bat... she's got love on the brain... can't get it out of her head! Pouf! And as for that bearded idiot..."

"What, she's in love with Mizinchikov?"

"Don't be daft! Why don't you wipe the sleep from your eyes and sober up a little, if only for this special day? You must have had one too many at supper last night, if you're still raving like this! Mizinchikov indeed! With Obnoskin, not Mizinchikov. Ivan Ivanych Mizinchikov is an honourable man, and he's about to join us in the chase."

"What are you talking about?" I exclaimed, sitting bolt upright in bed. "Obnoskin? Really?"

"Goodness, you can be so annoying!" the fat man replied, leaping to his feet. "Here I am trying to tell an educated man something, and all he can do is to question what I'm saying! Well, young man, if you want to join us, then get up and put your trousers on. I'm tired of banging on at you, I've wasted quite enough time as it is!"

And he walked out in a strop.

Staggered by what I'd heard, I leapt out of bed, hastily got dressed and ran downstairs. Thinking that I'd find my uncle in the house, where it seemed that everyone was still asleep and quite unaware of what had happened, I cautiously climbed the steps to the main porch and came across Nastenka in the hallway. She had evidently got dressed in a hurry and was wearing some sort of peignoir or dressing gown. Her hair was in disarray; she had clearly only just jumped out of bed and was waiting for someone in the hallway.

"Tell me, is it true that Tatyana Ivanovna has run off with Obnoskin?" she asked in a faltering voice, her face pale with anxiety.

"So I'm told. I'm looking for my uncle; we're planning to go after them."

"Oh, please bring her back, please bring her back, as quickly as possible! She'll be ruined if you don't."

"But where on earth's my uncle?"

"Almost certainly at the stables; they're getting a carriage ready there. I've been waiting for him here. Listen, tell him from me that I definitely want to leave today – I have made up my mind once and for all. My father will take me – I'll leave now, if I can. Everything is ruined now! There is no hope!"

As she said this, she cast a distraught look at me and suddenly burst into tears. She seemed on the verge of hysterics.

"Calm down!" I implored her. "I know it will turn out all right – you'll see... Tell me what's wrong, Nastasya Yevgrafovna!"

"I... I don't know... what it is," she said, catching her breath and unwittingly grabbing my hands. "Tell him..."

At that instant a noise could be heard from behind the door to the right.

She hastily let go of my hand and, without finishing what she was saying, dashed back upstairs in alarm.

I found all of them – that is, my uncle, Bakhcheyev and Mizinchikov – in the courtyard at the back, by the stables. Bakhcheyev was harnessing fresh horses to the carriage. Everything was ready for departure; they were just waiting for me.

"Ah, here he is!" my uncle shouted on seeing me. "So you've heard then, my dear boy?" he added, with a strange expression on his face. There was fear, confusion and, at the same time, something like hope in his eyes, in his voice and in his whole demeanour. He was aware that this was a critical point in his life.

I was immediately informed in detail about everything that had happened. After a most uncomfortable night, Mr Bakhcheyev had left his house at dawn to attend morning service at the monastery some two miles from his village. Right by the turning off the main road he had come across a tarantass, with Tatyana Ivanovna and Obnoskin inside, hurtling along at top speed. Tatyana Ivanovna, seemingly terrified, her face stained with tears, had shouted out and stretched her hands towards Mr Bakhcheyev, as if imploring him to come to her aid – or so it appeared from what he was saying. "As for that bearded wretch of a man," he added, "he just sat there, frozen with fear, trying to hide his face. You got it wrong, my man – you can't hide from me!" Hardly hesitating at all, Stepan Alexeyevich had turned back onto the high road and raced to Stepanchikovo, where he had woken my uncle, Mizinchikov and, finally, me. They decided they would immediately set off in pursuit.

"That Obnoskin, that Obnoskin…" my uncle said, looking at me fixedly, as if wanting to say something else to me. "Who would have thought he'd do something like that?"

"No dirty trick would be beyond that vile little man!" Mizinchikov exclaimed, irritated beyond measure, and immediately turned away, avoiding my look.

"Well, are we setting off or not? Or are we going to stand here the whole day, telling each other stories?" interrupted Mr Bakhcheyev, clambering into the carriage.

"We're going, we're going!" my uncle cried.

"Everything is for the best, Uncle," I whispered to him. "You see how well everything has turned out?"

"That's quite enough of that kind of nonsense, my dear boy… Oh, my friend, they'll now kick *her* out simply as a punishment for the fact that their plans have fallen through! You understand? I can see nothing but disaster ahead!"

"Come on, Yegor Ilyich – how about setting off, rather than standing there muttering all day?" Mr Bakhcheyev exclaimed again. "Or perhaps we should unharness the horses and have a bite to eat? What do you think, a little vodka perhaps?"

These words were spoken with such biting sarcasm that it was impossible not to obey Mr Bakhcheyev at once. Everyone immediately climbed into the carriage, and the horses set off at a gallop.

For a while we all sat there in silence. My uncle kept on giving me meaningful looks, but he was reluctant to say anything to me in front of the others. He frequently lapsed into deep thought – then, as if coming to his senses, he would start up and look around him in alarm. Mizinchikov seemed perfectly calm: he was smoking a cigar and maintaining the dignified appearance of someone who had been wronged. Bakhcheyev, on the other hand, carried on steaming away on behalf of us all, muttering angrily to himself, looking on everything and everybody with the greatest indignation, going red in the face, puffing and snorting, constantly spitting out of the carriage, totally incapable of calming down.

"Are you quite sure, Stepan Alexeich, they've gone to Mishino?" my uncle suddenly asked. "That, my dear boy, is some twelve miles or more from here," he added, turning to me. "It's a tiny little village, of thirty serfs at most. It was recently acquired from its former owners by a retired provincial official. Unbelievably litigious fellow! That's what people say, at any rate… they could be wrong, of course. Stepan Alexeich is convinced that that was precisely where Obnoskin was heading, and that this retired official is now aiding and abetting him."

"There you are! I told you, didn't I?" cried Bakhcheyev, seizing on what he'd just heard. "I said he was heading for Mishino. Except that by now he – Obnoskin I mean – would already have put miles between himself and Mishino! We shouldn't have frittered three hours away back there, in the yard!"

"Don't worry," Mizinchikov countered, "we'll catch him."

"I see… we'll catch him, will we? You think he's going to wait for us, do you? Once he's got his hands on the jewels, he'll be off like a shot!"

"Calm down, Stepan Alexeich, calm down! We'll catch up with them," my uncle said. "They won't have had time to do anything yet – you'll see."

"Won't have had time!" rejoined Mr Bakhcheyev angrily. "Who knows what she may or may not have had time to do – she's so meek and mild! 'Meek and mild!' everyone says. 'Meek and mild!' he added shrilly, as if mimicking someone. 'She's had such a hard life.' And now she's taken to her heels, the poor thing! And here we are chasing her up and down the high road at the crack of dawn, our tongues hanging out! A fellow can't even be allowed to say his prayers on a holy day! I ask you!"

"Yet she's not a minor," I remarked. "She's nobody's ward. You can't bring her back, if she is against it. So what are we to do?"

"That's right, of course," my uncle said, "yet she will want to come back, I assure you. It's just that at the moment she... as soon as she sees us, she'll come back – I can vouch for that. We simply can't abandon her, my boy, to the vagaries of fate... we have, so to speak, a duty..."

"Nobody's ward?" Bakhcheyev yelled, immediately attacking me. "She's an idiot, my dear fellow, a prize idiot – the fact she's not a ward is neither here nor there. I didn't want to say anything to you yesterday, but I happened by chance to walk into her room the other day, and what did I see? There she was, standing in front of the mirror with her arms akimbo, dancing an *écossaise*! And you should have seen what she was wearing... what a sight! I spat and left. I could have foreseen it all there and then, as clear as daylight!"

"But why do you have to be so harsh on her?" I asked a little tentatively. "Everyone knows that Tatyana Ivanovna is not... quite in her right mind... or, rather, she has this obsession... It seems to me that it's Obnoskin who's the only one to blame here, not her."

"Not quite in her right mind? Listen to him, everyone!" the fat man responded, becoming apoplectic with rage. "He's hell-bent on driving me mad! Been at it since yesterday! She's an idiot, my good man, I keep on telling you – a one-hundred-per-cent idiot, and not simply 'not quite in her right mind'. Ever since childhood she's had Cupid on the brain! And now this Cupid has driven her to total distraction. And as for that bearded fellow, he's not even worth talking about! He'll now be laughing all the way to the bank!"

"But surely you don't think he's simply going to abandon her, do you?"

"Of course that's what he's going to do! What, you think he's going to lug a treasure like that around with him? What good is she to him? He's going to take her money and set her down somewhere by the roadside under a bush – it won't be the first time something like that has happened to her, and she'll sit there under the bush sniffing at the flowers!"

"Stop getting carried away like that, Stepan, that's not how it's going to be!" my uncle shouted. "Anyway, why are you getting so hot and bothered? I'm surprised at you, Stepan – why should you care?"

"But I'm a human being, aren't I? It makes me really angry, angry on principle. Perhaps you think it's because I'm fond of her... Oh, to hell with it all! Why have I come here? Why have I got involved at all? What business is it of mine? What business is it of mine?"

Mr Bakhcheyev carried on complaining in this way. But I had stopped listening, as my thoughts had turned exclusively to the person we were pursuing: Tatyana Ivanovna. Here is the brief story of her life, which I was later to compile from the most reliable of sources and which serves as a necessary explanation for her adventures. Brought up as a poor, estranged orphan child in an unsympathetic family, then becoming a poor young girl, then a poor spinster of a certain age, Tatyana Ivanovna had throughout her impoverished existence drunk the entire cup of grief, of isolation, humiliation and recrimination, and somehow had to come to terms with the bitter realization that her survival depended on the charity of others. Inherently cheerful by nature, to the highest degree impressionable and light-minded, she somehow or other managed to endure her bitter lot, even being capable at times of bursting out into the happiest, most carefree laughter. In the course of time, however, fate was eventually to wreak its own particular havoc. Gradually Tatyana Ivanovna began to grow sallow and thin; she became irritable and abnormally sensitive and kept falling into the most profound and boundless trance-like state, frequently interspersed with hysterical tears and convulsive sobbing. The fewer the blessings bestowed on her by real life, the more she would console herself and compensate for such lack by the richness of her imagination. The more definitely and irrevocably her last substantive hopes crumbled, before finally disappearing altogether, the more intoxicating her dreams became, even though they were never to be realized. Unimaginable wealth, undying beauty, elegantly dressed, rich, famous suitors – invariably of princely stock or sons of generals – maintaining the purity of their feelings for her and dying at her feet from their boundless love for her... until, finally, *he* would appear: *he*, the ideal of beauty, combining every possible perfection, passionate and loving, an artist, a poet, a general's son – all this, either at once or in turn, would begin to appear as part of her dreams, or during her waking hours. Her mind was already beginning to deteriorate, unable to withstand such a heady opiate of these constant, secret fantasies... And then, suddenly, fate decided to play her a final trick. In the very last stage of her humiliation, at a moment of the most depressing and soul-destroying circumstances, while acting as a companion to a toothless and unbelievably peevish old woman – invariably to blame for everything, begrudged every piece of bread, every piece of cast-off clothing, abused by everyone, with no one to defend her, worn out by her mind-numbing existence while continuing, in her own way, to derive pleasure from her senseless and febrile dreams – in the midst of all this, she was suddenly to learn of the death of a distant relative, all of whose remaining next of kin had long since passed away (a circumstance about which she had in her light-mindedness never bothered to enquire), a very strange man who had lived as a recluse somewhere far, far away, a lonely, morose individual who had unobtrusively made his fortune through the practice of phrenology and usury. In this way an enormous fortune had as if miraculously fallen like a shower of gold at Tatyana Ivanovna's feet: she had turned out to be her dead relative's sole surviving heir. At a stroke she had acquired the sum of a hundred thousand silver roubles. This whimsical turn of fate was the final blow. For how could an already enfeebled mind not believe in its dreams now, when they were actually starting to be realized? And so the poor woman finally said farewell to the last remaining vestiges of common sense. Overcome by ecstasy, she now totally immersed herself in her enchanted world of impossible fantasies and beguilingly spectral visions. An end to all considerations, all doubts, all the barriers of reality, with its crystal-clear, invariable laws such as twice two equalling four! The thirty-five years of dreams of dazzling beauty, the sad chill of autumn and the whole luxury at the thought of love's endless bliss combined with absolute harmony in her innermost being. If one of her dreams had been realized, why should *all* of them now not come true? Why should *he* now not appear? It was not a question of logic on Tatyana Ivanovna's part, but of belief. Yet in anticipating *him*, the images of her ideal – suitors and admirers of every kind of rank and position, and those of no rank at all, military or civilian, foot soldiers or cavalrymen, grandees or simple poets, those who had been to Paris or those who had stayed in Moscow, with or without beards, with or without goatees, Spaniards or non-Spaniards (but preferably Spaniards) – began to appear, day and night, in such terrifying numbers in her imagination that they gave onlookers serious cause for concern: she was only one step away from the lunatic asylum. She became overwhelmed by a dazzling, intoxicating series of beautiful visions. Her real, everyday life was crowded with just such fantastic dreams: she only had to look at someone to fall in love with him; a man had merely to walk by her to become a Spaniard; if someone died, it was invariably from love for her. All this was as if deliberately confirmed by men such as Obnoskin, Mizinchikov and scores of others who began to prance around her, all with the same intentions. People suddenly began to indulge her every wish, to pamper and flatter her. Poor Tatyana Ivanovna simply had no idea that it was all because of her money. She was totally convinced that, as if with some mysterious wave of a hand, everyone had suddenly undergone a transformation and had become, one and all, happy, sweet, gentle and kind. *Her intended* may not yet have appeared on the scene – but although there was absolutely no doubt that he *would* appear, her life for the time being was so pleasant, so alluring, so full of distraction and delight, that she was quite prepared to wait. Tatyana Ivanovna spent her time eating sweets, gathering the blossoms of delight and reading novels. The novels inflamed her imagination even more and were usually abandoned after the first page. She was unable to bear the thought of reading any further – the first few lines containing the slightest hint of love, or simply even the description of a place, a room or the clothes someone was wearing, were quite sufficient for her to become absorbed in her dreams. New deliveries were constantly arriving at her door: fine dresses, lace, hats, headdresses, ribbons, dress patterns, designs, decorative arrangements, sweets, flowers and lapdogs. Three girls in the female quarters spent days on end sewing and stitching, while she herself filled her time from morning until dusk, sometimes even during the night, trying on her various bodices and frilly dresses, twirling around in front of the mirror. The news of her inheritance seemed somehow to have made her look younger and prettier. To this day, I still have no idea how she came to be related to the deceased General Krakhotkin. I have always been convinced that this was a story concocted by the general's lady, wishing to maintain her hold over Tatyana Ivanovna and to ensure, at all costs, that my uncle married into her money. Mr Bakhcheyev was right when he maintained that Cupid had driven her out of her mind – and my uncle's idea, after he'd heard she'd run away with Obnoskin, to go after her and get her back, by force if necessary, made total sense. The poor woman was incapable of looking after her own affairs, and would immediately have come to grief had she fallen into the clutches of unscrupulous people.

It was after nine when we arrived in Mishino. This was a destitute little village a couple of miles from the main road, situated in a kind of hollow. Visitors found themselves subjected to the baleful stare of six or seven smoke-blackened, rickety peasants' huts, their roofs sparsely covered with sooty thatching. There wasn't a garden or even a bush in sight – simply a solitary willow tree drooping over a greenish puddle that passed for a pond. Tatyana Ivanovna wouldn't have been overjoyed at the thought that this would now become her new home. The master's abode was a newly built, long, narrow wooden structure, with six windows in a row and a hastily covered thatched roof. The one-time government official turned landowner was only just beginning to set up his estate. The yard had not yet even been fenced off, with only the beginning of a new wattle fence that had a few dried-up walnut leaves clinging to it running along one side of the house. Obnoskin's carriage was standing nearby. Our arrival came as a bombshell to the guilty couple. From an open window we could hear the sound of shouting and weeping.

In the hallway we came across a barefoot lad, who quickly turned on his heels and ran off at top speed at the first sight of us. In the very first room we found a tearful Tatyana Ivanovna sitting on a long chintz-upholstered sofa, without a back. When she saw us, she shrieked and covered her face in her hands. Obnoskin was standing at her side in such a pathetically confused and terrified state that he dashed over to shake our hands as if overjoyed to see us. Through the crack of a half-opened door, the edge of a woman's dress could be seen: someone was eavesdropping and spying on us. There was no sight of the owners of the house – clearly hiding somewhere.

"Aha, there she is, our globe-trotter! Look at her covering her face like that!" exclaimed Mr Bakhcheyev as he waddled into the room after us.

"Stop it, Stepan Alexeich! There's no need for that. Yegor Ilyich is the only one of us who has the right to say anything now: the rest of us are completely de trop," remarked Mizinchikov acidly.

My uncle gave Mr Bakhcheyev a withering look and, as if totally unaware of Obnoskin, who had dashed up to him proffering his hand, went over to Tatyana Ivanovna, who was sitting there still with her face in her hands, and started addressing her in the gentlest of tones and with an expression of the sincerest sympathy.

"Tatyana Ivanovna! It is a measure of our love and respect for you that we have come especially to enquire about your plans. Might you be able to come back with us to Stepanchikovo, do you think? It's Ilyusha's name day. Mother is so longing to see you, and I'm sure Sasha and Nastya will have been crying their hearts out all morning…"

Tatyana Ivanovna shyly looked up at him through her fingers and, in floods of tears, flung her arms round his neck.

"Oh, take me away, please take me away from here, as quickly as possible!" she sobbed. "Quickly, as quick as you can!"

"She's had her fling and is now crying over spilt milk!" hissed Bakhcheyev, nudging me in the ribs.

"So it's all over now," my uncle said, drily turning to Obnoskin, barely giving him a glance. "Tatyana Ivanovna, your arm, if you please. Let's go!"

A rustle could be heard in the doorway; the door creaked and opened a little wider.

"Yes, but if you were to look at it from another point of view," Obnoskin remarked anxiously, with a glance at the opened door, "you can judge for yourself, Yegor Ilyich... such behaviour in my house... and, anyway, I come over and say hello to you, while you don't even seem to want to acknowledge me in return, Yegor Ilyich..."

"And your behaviour in *my* house, sir, was outrageous," my uncle replied, with a severe look at Obnoskin. "And, anyway, this isn't your house. You've just heard for yourself: Tatyana Ivanovna doesn't want to stay here a moment longer. What else do you need? Not another word, do you hear? Not another word, if you please! I'm extremely anxious to avoid any further discussion along these lines – something which will be to your advantage as well."

But at this Obnoskin's spirits sank so low that he started spouting the most unexpected nonsense.

"Please don't despise me, Yegor Ilyich," he began in a half-whisper, close to tears from shame and glancing constantly at the door, probably afraid that whoever was there would be able to hear what was being said. "It wasn't my doing at all, it was Mother's. I didn't do it for my own personal gain, Yegor Ilyich... it's simply the way it happened... Of course I did it for my own personal gain, Yegor Ilyich... but it was all with the noblest of intentions, Yegor Ilyich: I would have used my capital to advantage, sir... I would have helped the poor. I simply wanted to further the cause of modern education, and even dreamt of establishing a university scholarship in my name... That was how I wanted to use my wealth, Yegor Ilyich... that was all it was, nothing else, Yegor Ilyich..."

We all suddenly became conscience-stricken. Even Mizinchikov went red in the face and turned away, while my uncle became so embarrassed he was unable to say anything.

"There, there, that's enough, that's enough!" he said finally. "Calm down, Pavel Semyonych! Please don't worry, it could happen to anyone... If you would like to, why don't you come and have dinner with us, my good fellow... I'm so glad... so glad..."

Mr Bakhcheyev, however, reacted rather differently.

"Establishing a university scholarship my foot!" he roared with rage. "Tell me another one! You'd fleece the first person you happened to meet, if you could! You don't even have a decent pair of trousers, and here you are talking about scholarships! You're just a ragamuffin, a ragamuffin! You think you're some Romeo, do you? And anyway, where's your mother now? Bet you she's hiding behind some screen, or has crawled under some bed, out of her wits from fear..."

"Stepan, Stepan!..." my uncle cried.

Obnoskin went bright red in the face, preparing to protest. But before he could open his mouth, the door opened and Anfisa Petrovna herself flew into the room, her eyes flashing, her face flushed with anger.

"What's all this?" she shouted. "What's going on here? How dare you barge into this respectable house, Yegor Ilyich, with your band of ruffians, scaring the ladies and bossing everybody about like this?... Never seen anything like it! I've still got my wits about me, thank God, Yegor Ilyich! And as for you, you prize idiot," she yelled, turning on her son, "why are you snivelling like that in front of everybody? Your mother is being insulted in her own house, and all you can do is stand there and gawp! How can you look on yourself as a proper young man now? You're just a wet rag, and not a proper young man at all!"

Not a sign of yesterday's airs and graces – even the lorgnette had disappeared. Anfisa Petrovna had become quite a different person: she had turned into a veritable fury – a fury without a mask.

No sooner had my uncle caught sight of her than he grabbed Tatyana Ivanovna by the arm and began to dash out of the room, but Anfisa Petrovna immediately barred his way.

"Where do you think you're going, Yegor Ilyich?" she ranted on. "What right do you have to take Tatyana Ivanovna away by force like this? You're angry she's managed to escape the vile snares you've set for her, you and your mother and that idiot Foma Fomich? You'd just love to be married to her yourself, to further your own contemptible self-interest! Forgive me, sir, but we do things rather more honourably in this household! Seeing that your lot were conspiring against her, that her life was being ruined, Tatyana Ivanovna herself put all her trust in Pavlusha. She herself begged him, so to speak, to save her from all your wiles; she was compelled to run away from you in the middle of the night – that's what! That's what you drove her to do! Isn't that right, Tatyana Ivanovna? And if so, how dare you burst in here, into this respectable house, with your gang of villains and forcibly abduct a respectable lady, despite her tears and shrieks of protest? I will not allow it! I will not allow it! I am not crazy!... Tatyana Ivanovna will remain here, because that is what she wants! Come on, Tatyana Ivanovna, let's go; there's no point in listening to them any longer – they are your enemies, not your friends! Don't be afraid, come with me! I'll make sure they'll leave immediately!..."

"No, no!" cried Tatyana Ivanovna, in great anxiety. "I don't want to, I don't want to! That man... my husband? I don't want to get married to your son! I couldn't have him as my husband!"

"You 'don't want to'?" shrieked Anfisa Petrovna, choking with anger. "You've come all this way here, and you 'don't want to'? In that case, how dare you deceive us like this? How dare you make promises like that, running away with him in the middle of the night, thrusting yourself on us in that way, leading us down the garden path and putting us to all sorts of expenses? My son may have lost out on a splendid match because of you!... He could well have lost tens of thousands in dowry because of you!... No, my good woman! You will have to pay for what you've done – you will have to pay now... we have the proof we need: you ran away in the middle of the night..."

But we'd had quite enough of this rant. We all moved as one, grouped around my uncle and marched straight at Anfisa Petrovna and out into the porch. The carriage immediately drew up.

"That is exactly the way only dishonest people, only blackguards and scoundrels behave!" Anfisa Petrovna yelled from the porch, beside herself with fury. "I'll make an official complaint! You will pay for this... you'll be going back to a den of thieves, Tatyana Ivanovna! You can't possibly marry Yegor Ilyich – he'll be flaunting that governess girl as his mistress under your very nose!..."

My uncle shuddered, went pale, bit his lip and hurriedly sat Tatyana Ivanovna down in the coach. I went round to the other side of the carriage and was waiting my turn to take my seat when Obnoskin suddenly appeared next to me and grabbed me by the hand.

"At least allow me to seek your friendship!" he said, eagerly clutching my hand, with an expression of despair on his face.

"What do you mean, 'friendship'?" I said, with my foot already on the carriage footboard.

"Just that! I could see, as clearly as yesterday, that I was dealing with such a highly educated man. Don't be hard on me... It was actually all my mother's doing, nothing to do with me at all. I'm more interested in literature, I can assure you... it was all my mother's doing..."

"I believe you, I believe you," I said. "Goodbye!"

We took our seats, and the horses set off at a gallop, pursued for a long time by the yells and curses of Anfisa Petrovna. Unknown faces suddenly appeared from every window, looking at us in bemused astonishment.

There were now five of us in the carriage. But later Mizinchikov clambered up into the box, giving his place to Mr Bakhcheyev, who had been forced to sit directly opposite Tatyana Ivanovna. Tatyana Ivanovna herself was still weeping, although overjoyed that we had succeeded in spiriting her away. My uncle did what he could to console her. He, for his part, was in a disconsolate and pensive frame of mind: he had clearly been deeply and painfully affected by Anfisa Petrovna's vitriolic comment regarding Nastenka. Our return journey, however, would have passed off reasonably smoothly, had it not been for the presence of Mr Bakhcheyev.

Having found himself sitting opposite Tatyana Ivanovna, he looked decidedly out of sorts. He kept grimacing, shifting uneasily in his seat, his eyes rolling around and his face as red as a lobster. In particular, whenever my uncle tried to console Tatyana Ivanovna, he started growling like a provoked bulldog. My uncle kept casting him anxious glances. Eventually Tatyana Ivanovna noticed that there was something the matter with the man sitting opposite her and began paying him particular attention. Then she looked round at us and suddenly, with a smile, picked up her parasol and daintily tapped Mr Bakhcheyev on the shoulder.

"You mad thing, you!" she said, in a most seductively playful tone, and immediately hid her face behind her fan.

This remark was the final straw.

"Wha-a-t?" the fat man roared. "What did you say, madam? So you're going to make eyes at me now, are you?"

"You mad thing, mad thing!" Tatyana Ivanovna repeated, and suddenly burst out laughing and clapping her hands.

"Stop!" Bakhcheyev shouted up to the driver. "Stop, I tell you!"

They stopped. Bakhcheyev opened the carriage door and hastily started climbing out.

"But what's the matter, Stepan Alexeich? Where are you going?" cried my uncle in astonishment.

"No, that's enough!" the fat man replied, shaking with indignation. "To hell with everything! I'm too old, madam, for such amorous advances. I'd rather snuff it here, on the high road, woman! Goodbye, madam, *comment vous portez-vous?*"*

And, indeed, he had set off walking, with the carriage slowly following behind him.

"Stepan Alexeyevich!" my uncle cried, finally losing his patience. "Stop playing the fool, come on, sit down! We need to get home!"

"You can… go to hell!" Stepan Alexeyevich retorted, puffing with exertion – with his large size he had clearly become unused to walking.

"Off you go, top speed!" Mizinchikov ordered the coachman.

"What are you doing? What are you doing? Stop!" my uncle tried to shout, but the coachman had already set off at a gallop. Mizinchikov had been right: he had immediately achieved the desired effect.

"Wait! Wait!" – we could hear the despairing wail behind us. "Stop, you devil, will you? Stop, you horrible man!"

The fat man finally caught up with us, worn out, half dead from exertion, the perspiration pouring down his forehead, his necktie undone and his cap removed. Silently and sullenly he clambered back into the cab, and this time I let him sit in my place, so that at least he wouldn't have to be sitting opposite Tatyana Ivanovna, who the whole time had been convulsed with laughter and clapping her hands with delight. For the entire rest of the journey she was unable to look at Stepan Alexeyevich with a straight face. He, for his part, kept absolutely silent the whole of the way back to the house, simply staring at the carriage's revolving rear wheel.

By the time we got back to Stepanchikovo, it was already midday. I went straight to my wing of the house, where Gavrila immediately appeared, bringing tea. I was on the point of bombarding him with questions when my uncle came in and immediately sent him out of the room.

2

News

"I've just dropped in for a moment," he began hurriedly, "to tell you the latest... I've found out everything. No one has even been to church today, apart from Ilyusha, Sasha and Nastenka. Mother, so they say, went off into one of her fits. They massaged and pummelled her, and finally managed to bring her round. We're all now supposed to go and see Foma, including me. It's just that I don't know whether I should wish Foma a happy name day or not – such an important point! And what are they all going to say about that whole business today? It's a nightmare, Seryozha, I'm so worried they'll—"

"On the contrary, Uncle," I hastened to reassure him, "everything will turn out wonderfully. Among other things, it means that now there is no possibility of you marrying Tatyana Ivanovna – that in itself is worth quite a lot. I wanted to explain that to you on the way here..."

"That may be so, my dear boy. But that's not the point: God's hand, as you rightly say, is at work here, of course. But I'm talking about something else... Poor Tatyana Ivanovna! She has to go through so much, doesn't she?... What an absolute scoundrel that Obnoskin is! But why am I calling him a 'scoundrel'? Would I not have done just the same in getting married to her?... But again, that's not really the point... Did you hear what that appalling woman shouted back there... Anfisa, I mean, about Nastya?"

"Yes, I did, Uncle. So, *now* do you see there's no time to waste?"

"Absolutely – no two ways about it!" my uncle replied. "The moment of truth has arrived. There's just one point, my dear boy, that didn't occur to us yesterday, something that kept me awake all night: will she agree to marry me? That's what!"

"For goodness' sake, Uncle! Hasn't she herself told you she's in love with you?..."

"Yes, my boy, but then didn't she immediately go on to add that she could never marry me?"

"Oh, Uncle! That's what they all say – besides, the circumstances have all changed now."

"You think so? No, Sergei, my dear boy, we have to tread carefully here – very, very carefully! Hmm!... But do you know? Despite lying awake worrying all night, my heart was bursting with happiness!... Well, goodbye, I must fly. They're waiting for me, and I'm already late. I just dashed in for a little chat. Oh, my God!" he exclaimed, turning back. "I've forgotten the most important thing! Guess what: I've gone and written to him – to Foma, that is!"

"When?"

"Last night. And this morning, first thing, I asked Vidoplyasov to take it to him. I set it all down, my dear boy, on two sheets, told him everything, truthfully and honestly – in a word, that I had to, absolutely had to (you understand), propose to Nastenka. I implored him not to say a word about our meeting in the garden and appealed to all that was noble in him to assist me as far as Mother was concerned. Of course it was a poorly written letter, my dear boy, but it was written straight from the heart and, as it were, bathed in my tears..."

"So? Has he replied?"

"Not so far – except that when we were getting ready for the chase this morning, I met him in the hallway. He was still in his night things – slippers, nightcap and all – on his way somewhere. He didn't say a word – didn't even look at me. I peered into his face like this, from below – no response whatsoever!"

"Don't trust him, Uncle... he'll play a dirty trick on you."

"No, no, my dear boy, don't say that!" my uncle exclaimed, with a wave of his hand. "I'm sure he'll do nothing of the sort. In any case, it's now my final hope. He'll understand – he'll appreciate what I'm trying to say. He's a difficult, fickle man, I agree, but when it comes to showing his real nobility of character, he shines like a jewel… yes, like an absolute jewel. It's all because, Sergei, you've never seen him when he's been at his absolutely noble best… But, my God! If he actually were to tell everyone about yesterday's secret, I simply won't know what to think, Sergei! What will there be left in the world to believe in? But no, I'm sure he could never stoop to such vile behaviour – I'm not fit to hold a candle to him! Don't shake your head, my boy: it's true – I'm not fit!"

"Yegor Ilyich! Your mother is concerned about you," Miss Perepelitsyna's unpleasant voice could be heard calling up from below. She had obviously been able to hear everything we'd been saying through an open window. "People have been looking for you everywhere, sir, and not been able to find you, sir."

"My God! I'm late! There's trouble ahead!" my uncle exclaimed with a start. "My friend, for the love of God get dressed and come down! That's why I came rushing in to see you, so that we could go down together… I'm just coming, Anna Nilovna, just coming!"

Once I was on my own, I recalled my meeting with Nastenka and was glad I hadn't told my uncle about it: he would have been even more upset. I could foresee a really stormy time ahead, and had no idea how he would be able to sort everything out and propose to Nastenka. I repeat: however much I trusted in his generosity of spirit, I was far from certain he would succeed in doing so.

However, I still needed to hurry. Seeing it as my duty to help him, I immediately set about getting dressed. But I was just trying to decide what to wear, wishing to put in as smart an appearance as possible, when Mizinchikov came in.

"I've come to get you," he said. "Yegor Ilyich would like you to come downstairs immediately."

"Let's go!"

When I was fully dressed, we set off.

"What's going on downstairs?" I asked on the way.

"Everyone's gathered at Foma's," Mizinchikov replied. "Foma's behaving himself – he's in a rather thoughtful mood and not saying very much, just keeps muttering something to himself. He even

kissed Ilyusha, which of course absolutely delighted Yegor Ilyich.
He's just asked that Perepelitsyna woman to tell everyone they're
not to congratulate him on his name day – he simply wanted to
test everyone... The old woman is still sniffing her smelling salts,
but she's now calmed down, since Foma himself seems reasonably
composed. Nobody says a word about our little adventure, as if
it had never taken place: they're keeping quiet about it because
Foma is. He hasn't let anyone in to see him the whole morning,
even though the old woman implored him by all the saints to come
down and discuss things. She even tried to force her way into his
room, but he'd locked himself in, telling her he was engaged in
praying for the soul of mankind, or something of the sort. He's
hatching something: you can tell from the expression on his face.
But Yegor Ilyich is in no condition to guess anything from the
expression on a face: he's simply over the moon at Foma's meek
behaviour – just like a little child! Ilyusha has written a poem or
two, and I have been sent to fetch you."

"And Tatyana Ivanovna?"

"What about her?"

"Is she down there? With everyone?"

"No, she's up in her room," Mizinchikov answered drily. "She's
resting and crying. Ashamed, maybe. That... governess is with
her at the moment, it seems. What's that? Not a thunderstorm,
is it? Just look at that sky!"

"You could be right," I answered, seeing the threatening black
cloud on the horizon.

At that moment we were climbing the steps up to the terrace.

"What about Obnoskin, eh?" I asked, just burning to know
Mizinchikov's view.

"Don't talk to me about him! Don't mention the name of that
scoundrel!" he shouted, suddenly stopping, going red in the face
and stamping his foot. "What an idiot! What an idiot! To go and
ruin such a brilliant idea like that! Listen: I am of course such
an ass not to have seen through his dirty little trick – I admit it
quite openly, and you may well have wanted me to make such an

admission. But I swear to you, had he been able to carry everything off properly, I could well have forgiven him! What an idiot! And to think that society sustains and tolerates such people! Why aren't they packed off to Siberia, to some settlement or other, to prison? But they're all wrong! They're not going to outsmart me! At least I know what I'm doing now, and we'll put up a fight. I've got a new plan in mind now… Just think about it: why should I give up my idea simply because some other total idiot stole it and then bungled it? It's not fair, is it? And anyway, this Tatyana Ivanovna just has to get married – it's her destiny. And if she's not yet been sent off to a lunatic asylum, that's simply because she's still an eligible spinster. Let me tell you my new idea…"

"Not now – later, perhaps," I interrupted. "Look, we're there."

"All right, all right, later!" Mizinchikov agreed, his face contorting into a smile. "But now… But where do you think you're going? I've told you: we're going straight to Foma Fomich's! Follow me – you haven't been to his place yet. You're going to see another comedy… Everything's a comedy here nowadays…"

3

Ilyusha's Name-Day Celebration

Foma occupied two large, rather splendid rooms. Strikingly, they were furnished more lavishly than any other room in the house. The great man was surrounded by total comfort. Lovely new wallpaper, the windows hung with brightly coloured silk curtains, carpets, a full-length mirror, a log fire, comfortable, stylish furniture – everything spoke of the tender concern shown by his hosts towards Foma. There were pots of flowers on the window sills and on the little round marble tables by the windows. In the middle of his study there was a large desk, covered in red cloth and stacked high with books and manuscripts. The beautiful bronze inkwell and the array of pens, maintained by Vidoplyasov – all this, taken together, testified to Foma's unsparing dedication to his intellectual work. Let me add here, as something of an aside, that, after spending almost eight years sitting at his desk, Foma had never succeeded in producing anything worthwhile. Subsequently, sorting through his manuscripts after he had departed to a better world, we found that they were in fact filled with unmitigated drivel. We discovered, for example, the beginning of a historical novel set in seventh-century Novgorod; then an utterly appalling epic poem, 'Anchorite at the Graveyard', written in blank verse; then a senseless discussion on the significance and characteristics of the Russian peasant and how he should be treated; and, finally, a high-society tale, 'Countess Vlonskaya', also unfinished. That was all. Yet the whole time Foma Fomich had been compelling my uncle to take out expensive annual subscriptions to all kinds of books and journals. But many of them were to remain uncut.* I myself was to find him on a number of occasions engaged in reading a Paul de Kock novel,* which he would always take care to hide whenever there were people present. In the far wall of the study there was a French window that opened out onto the courtyard.

They were all waiting for us. Foma Fomich was sitting in a comfortable armchair, wearing a long frock coat down to his ankles, but without a tie. He was indeed preoccupied, and spoke little. When we came in, he raised his eyebrows slightly, giving me a quizzical look. I bowed to him; he responded with a faint but nonetheless polite nod. Noting Foma Fomich's cordial attitude, my grandmother acknowledged me with a smile. The poor woman could hardly have expected her darling to have received the news about Tatyana Ivanovna's "little adventure" so calmly that morning – as a result, she was in an exceptionally good mood, notwithstanding her convulsions and swooning fits earlier that very same morning. Miss Perepelitsyna was standing, as always, behind her chair, rubbing her bony hands together, her thin lips pursed into a spiteful, sour, warped grin. Two ancient upper-class ladies, spongers on the general's lady, were perched as usual by her chair. Also in the room was a nun, who had wandered into the house that morning, together with a neighbouring elderly landowner's wife, also silent, who had dropped in after church to pay her respects to the general's lady. Aunt Praskovya Ilyinichna sat almost invisibly in a remote corner of the room, casting anxious glances at Foma Fomich and Mother. My uncle was sitting in an armchair, his eyes shining with an unaccustomed happiness. Ilyusha was standing in front of him in a red festive shirt, his curly hair giving him the appearance of a cherub. To please his father, Sasha and Nastenka had secretly taught him to recite some lines of verse, so that he could demonstrate the excellent progress he had been making in his studies. My uncle was so happy he was almost in tears: Foma's unusual meekness, the general's lady's good mood, Ilyusha's name day, the lines of verse – all this combined to put him in a state of ecstasy, and he had jubilantly sent for me so that I could share in the general happiness and listen to the poetry. Sasha and Nastenka, who had come into the room just after us, stood close to Ilyusha. Sasha was almost helpless with laughter – at that moment she was as happy as a little child. The sight of her made Nastenka also break into a smile, even though, when she had come into the room a moment ago, she had looked pale and unhappy. She had been the only one to meet and calm Tatyana Ivanovna down after getting back from her little excursion, and up to that point had been sitting with her in her room. High-spirited Ilyusha, too, seemed to be scarcely able to refrain from bursting into laughter as he looked at his tutors. All three of them, it seemed, had prepared some uproarious little joke, which they were about to play on all of us... I had totally forgotten about Bakhcheyev: he was sitting on a chair, apart from everyone, still angry and red-faced, keeping silent, puffing and snorting and generally playing a somewhat melancholy role on such a festive family occasion. Nearby, Yezhevikin could be seen mincing about the room – mincing everywhere, in fact – kissing the general's lady's hand and that of the newly arrived guest, whispering into Miss Perepelitsyna's ear, hovering to see if he could assist Foma Fomich with anything... in short, making himself generally busy. He too was greatly looking forward to hearing Ilyusha's poem, and he dashed over to me as soon as he saw me come in, bowing and scraping as a mark of his great respect and devotion to me. There was absolutely no sign he had come to protect his daughter and take her away from Stepanchikovo for good.

"Here he is!" my uncle cried joyfully on seeing me. "Ilyusha has prepared a poem, my dear boy – how about that for a real surprise? Totally unexpected! I'm quite astounded, my dear boy – I sent for you especially, and kept the poem back until your arrival... Come and sit next to me! We can listen together. Come on, admit it, Foma Fomich, my friend: it was your idea, wasn't it, in order to make me happy in my old age? I swear it was!"

The fact that my uncle was adopting such a tone and easy manner in Foma's room might have led everyone to believe that all was well with the world. But the trouble, as Mizinchikov had observed, was that my uncle was quite incapable of reading other people's faces. And one glance at Foma's face was enough to show that Mizinchikov was right, and that we would need to brace ourselves for what was to follow...

"Don't worry about me, colonel," Foma answered in a rather feeble voice, in the tone of someone forgiving his enemy for something. "I can commend the idea: it reflects a certain sensitivity and good manners on the part of your children. Poetry has its merits, not least as an aid to correct one's pronunciation... But my mind has been engaged on matters other than poetry this morning, Yegor Ilyich. I have been praying, as you know... However, I will not find it amiss to listen to some poetry."

In the mean time, I had kissed and congratulated Ilyusha.

"Of course, Foma, please forgive me! I had forgotten... although I feel assured of your friendship, Foma! All right, Ilyushka, fire away! What is it about? Some triumphant ode, no doubt, something from Lomonosov, perhaps?"*

"No, Papa, nothing from Lomonosov," said Sashenka, hardly able to stop laughing, "but since you have been a soldier and fought for your country, Ilyusha has learnt a war poem... 'The Siege of Pamba',* Papa."

"'The Siege of Pamba', eh? Don't remember that one... What's this Pamba, do you know, Seryozha? Something heroic, no doubt."

And my uncle once again assumed a dignified air.

"Off you go, Ilyusha!" commanded Sashenka.

Full nine years now since Pedro Gomez...

Ilyusha began in a small, even and clear voice, without pauses of any kind, in the tone small children usually adopt when reciting poetry.

Full nine years now since Pedro Gomez
Did besiege the fortress of Pamba,
Their only diet was that of milk,
And all the army of Don Pedro,

All nine thousand Castilian troops,
All of them pledged as one
Never to touch a crust of bread,
But to confine themselves to milk.

"What's all this? What's that about milk?" my uncle exclaimed, looking at me in astonishment.

"Go on, Ilyusha," urged Sashenka.

Day after day does Don Pedro Gomez
Weep and bewail his fatal weakness,
Taking refuge, as ever, in his cloak.
And then, when year ten arrives,
The evil Moors win the day,
And of all his troops, in all,
Only nineteen of them survive...

"But this is absolute nonsense!" my uncle exclaimed, highly agitated. "Totally impossible! Nineteen men from the whole army survived, when it had once been a sizeable contingent! What is all this, my dear boy?"

But at this Sashenka could contain herself no longer and burst out into the most unconfined childish laughter – and although there was actually nothing remotely comical, looking at her you couldn't help but start laughing yourself.

"It's comic verse, Papa," she cried, delighted at the success of her idea. "It's meant to be funny – the author wrote it like that to make everyone laugh, Papa."

"Ah, comic verse!" my uncle exclaimed, beaming. "So it's funny?... I *see* now... Precisely, precisely, comic! Hilarious, absolutely hilarious: a whole army surviving on just milk, keeping some pledge or other! As if it was essential! Very witty indeed – isn't that so, Foma? You see, Mother? It's one of those comic poems which people write sometimes – I'm right about that, Sergei, aren't I? Absolutely hilarious! So, Ilyusha, how does it go on?

Only nineteen men left!
Don Pedro Gomez now mustered them
And said to them: "You nineteen men
Unfurl your banners, sound your trumpets
And beat loudly on your drums –
We shall retreat from Pamba,
And though we have not taken the fort,
We can still boldly swear an oath
That in all honour and conscience
We have lived up to our pledge…
That for nine whole years
We've had nothing at all to eat –
Only milk has passed our lips.

"What an imbecile! He thinks that's something to boast about, does he?" my uncle interrupted again. "To spend nine whole years drinking only milk? Where's the virtue in that? He should have given them each a roasted ram to eat, instead of starving them like that! Wonderful, brilliant! I understand now, I can see that it's a satire, or… or… what's it called, an allegory, am I right? Could well be aimed at some foreign general, couldn't it?" my uncle added, turning to me, his eyebrows raised and screwing up his eyes meaningfully. "Eh? What do you think? But of course it's just a harmless, well-meaning satire, not offending anyone! Wonderful! Wonderful! And above all, well-meaning! So, Ilyusha, on you go! And as for you, you naughty girls, you couple of pranksters!" he added, looking lovingly at Sasha and covertly at Nastenka, who was blushing and smiling.

Heartened by these words,
All nineteen Castilians,
As one, swaying on their saddles,
Cried out with feeble voices:
"By Saint James of Compostela,
All honour and glory to Don Pedro!
The mighty lion of Castile!"

But his chaplain, one Diego,
Went and muttered through his teeth:
"Had I been the one in command,
I'd have promised them all meat to eat,
Washed down with finest Turin wine!"

"There you are! Didn't I tell you?" my uncle exclaimed, beside himself with joy. "In the whole of that army there was just one man with a bit of common sense, and he turns out to be some chaplain or other! Who would he have been, Sergei? One of their captains, do you think?"

"A monk, a holy man, Uncle."

"Ah yes, of course! Chaplain, a man of the chapel? I know about them, I remember reading about them – in Radcliffe's novels.* They have various different orders, don't they?... Benedictines, I think... Benedictines, is that right?"

"Yes, Uncle."

"Hmm... I thought so. So, Ilyusha, how does it go on? Wonderful, marvellous!"

And on hearing that, Don Pedro
Pronounced with a hearty laugh:
"Give the man a ram to eat –
He's such a splendid wit!"

"How can he laugh at a time like that? What an absolute idiot! He's simply making a laughing stock of himself! A ram! In other words, there must have been rams there... so why didn't he eat one himself? So, Ilyusha, carry on! Wonderful, marvellous! Extraordinarily original!"

"But it's finished, Papa!"

"Ah! Finished? But of course, there was really nothing else to say, was there? Aren't I right, Sergei? Wonderful, Ilyusha! Phenomenally good! Give me a kiss, my darling boy! Oh, my precious boy! And whose idea was it? Was it yours, Sasha?"

"No, it was Nastenka's. We came across it the other day. She read it and said: 'This is so funny! It'll soon be Ilyusha's name day, so why don't we make him learn it off by heart and recite it? It will be such fun!'"

"So it was Nastenka's idea? Well, thank you, thank you," my uncle mumbled, suddenly going bright red in the face, like a little child. "Kiss me again, Ilyusha! And you give me a kiss as well, you naughty girl," he said, embracing Sashenka and looking tenderly in her eyes.

"Just wait a little, Sashurka, and it will be your name day," he added, as if his feelings of joy were so strong he was unsure what to say.

I turned to Nastenka and asked her who the poem's author was.

"Yes, yes! Who wrote that?" my uncle seconded, leaping in. "Someone really clever, no doubt – don't you agree, Foma?"

"Hmm…" Foma muttered to himself.

Throughout the whole of Ilyusha's recital there had been a caustic, ironic smile playing on his lips.

"I don't quite remember," Nastenka replied, with a shy glance at Foma Fomich.

"It was Kozma Prutkov, Papa – printed in the *Contemporary*," Sashenka hastily intervened.

"Kozma Prutkov? Never heard of him," my uncle said. "But I know Pushkin… Still, he's clearly a poet of some distinction – isn't that right, Sergei? And, what's more, a real gentleman – that's crystal-clear! Even, perhaps, an officer… My congratulations to him! And the *Contemporary* is such a wonderful journal! Definitely have to take out a subscription, if poets of such a calibre appear in it… I do so like poets! Wonderful people! Being able to write everything in verse like that! Do you remember, Sergei, when I was with you in St Petersburg, I saw that literary fellow? The one with the remarkable nose… no, really! What did you say, Foma?"

Foma Fomich, who was becoming more and more engaged in the conversation, suddenly broke out into a loud giggle.

"No, I simply... never mind..." he said, as if only just managing to restrain his laughter. "You carry on, Yegor Ilyich, just carry on! I will save what I have to say for later... I can see how much Stepan Alexeich is enjoying listening to stories of your acquaintance with St Petersburg literary figures..."

Stepan Alexeyevich, who was sitting deep in thought some distance apart from everyone, suddenly looked up, went red in the face and shifted angrily in his chair.

"Don't you start on me, Foma – just leave me alone!" he said, giving Foma a fierce look with his tiny bloodshot eyes. "What do I care about your literature? Just so long as I have good health, that's all I care about," he muttered to himself. "As for all your pen-pushers, I'd like to... nothing but a bunch of Voltaireans!"*

"Voltairean pen-pushers, sir?" said Yezhevikin, immediately turning up at Mr Bakhcheyev's side. "You've hit the nail on the head there, Stepan Alexeyevich. That's just what Valentin Ignatych was on about the other day. In fact I myself have been called a Voltairean... no, it's true! Of course, as everyone will know, I've not written very much so far... but I'm saying that if the well runs dry, then it's all Voltaire's fault! And that goes for all such people as myself."

"Well, no!" my uncle remarked portentously. "You're wrong there! Voltaire was above all a witty writer, someone who ridiculed prejudice and who himself was never a Voltairean – that was a lie spread about by his enemies. Why on earth would they attack him like that, the poor man?..."

Once again Foma Fomich sniggered caustically. My uncle gave him an anxious look, clearly disconcerted.

"No, Foma, you have to understand I was only on about the journals," he said, obviously embarrassed and wishing to recover the situation in some way. "You were completely right, my dear friend, in trying to persuade us to take out a subscription the other day. I myself was precisely of that view! Hmm... they are indeed spreading enlightenment! What's more, if you don't take out a

221

subscription, you can hardly start calling yourself a citizen of the fatherland, can you? Aren't I right, Sergei? Hmm... yes! Take the *Contemporary* as an example... But you know, Seryozha, the best journal of all for science is that thick one... what's it called now? The one with a yellow cover..."

"*Notes of the Fatherland,** Papa."

"Of course, *Notes of the Fatherland* – such a wonderful title, isn't it, Sergei? Giving the idea of the entire country sitting down and taking notes... What a brilliant idea! What a useful journal! And so much contained within it! You just try publishing anything that size! The science simply takes your breath away! Only the other day I came home and found a copy lying there. I picked it up and, curious to see what was inside, I opened it, and there and then read three pages straight off. I was simply staggered, my dear boy! So much information about so many things: the significance of words such as 'broom', 'spade', 'ladle', 'oven fork', for example.* As far as I'm concerned, a broom is a broom, an oven fork an oven fork! No, my dear boy, not a bit of it! It turns out that an oven fork, from the scientific point of view, is not an oven fork at all, but an emblem or some mythical symbol or other, can't remember what exactly, something of the sort anyway... Can you believe it? The things they think of!"

I have no idea what Foma was planning to do or say in response to my uncle's latest venture into the literary world, but at this very moment Gavrila appeared in the doorway and stood there with his head bowed.

Foma Fomich looked at him expectantly.

"Everything ready, Gavrila?"

"Ready, sir," Gavrila replied despondently with a sigh.

"And you've put my things in the cart?"

"I have, sir."

"Right, I'm ready then!" Foma said, and slowly started to get up from his chair. My uncle looked at him in astonishment. The general's lady leapt from her seat and glanced around the room as if she couldn't believe her eyes.

"I hope you won't mind, colonel," Foma began to say in an imposing tone, "if I ask you to desist for the time being from your interesting literary excursion into oven forks – you will be able to continue developing that idea without me. I, for my part, *in taking my leave of you for ever*, would wish to address the following final words to you…"

The entire room became frozen in terror and astonishment.

"Foma! Foma! What is the matter? Where are you going?" my uncle exclaimed at last.

"I am going to leave your house, colonel," Foma said in the calmest of voices. "I have decided to go wherever fate takes me, for which purpose I have hired, at my own expense, a simple peasant's cart. My little bundle of things will be waiting for me there now – there's not very much, just a few of my favourite books, two changes of clothes, and that's all! I may be poor, Yegor Ilyich, but nothing in the world would induce me to take your gold, the gold which I turned down yesterday!"

"But, for Heaven's sake, Foma! What is the meaning of this?" my uncle cried, going as white as a sheet.

The general's lady screamed and looked in despair at Foma Fomich, holding out her hands to him. Miss Perepelitsyna dashed over to support her. The two lady hangers-on froze in their chairs. Mr Bakhcheyev rose ponderously from his seat.

"Well, there's a turn-up for the books!" whispered Mizinchikov in my ear.

At that moment distant rumbles of thunder could be heard – there was a storm on its way.

4

Expulsion

"You were just asking, colonel, I think, what this all means?" Foma said portentously, as if delighting in the general embarrassment. "I find the question astonishing! Pray explain how it is that you are still able to look me straight in the eye? If you are able to explain to me how you can possibly have behaved in such an outrageously shameless way, then I will at least be able to leave here enriched by a fresh insight into mankind's depravity."

But my uncle was in no condition to reply. He stood there gaping at Foma with a totally crushed and terrified expression, his eyes on stalks.

"Oh Lord! Such passions!" Miss Perepelitsyna groaned.

"Do you understand, colonel," Foma continued, "that you are now obliged to let me go, without any fuss or questions? In this house even someone of my age and intellectual abilities has begun to be seriously concerned for his moral integrity. Please believe me when I say that any further questions will merely lead to confirmation of your ignominious behaviour."

"Foma! Foma!" my uncle groaned. Beads of cold sweat appeared on his forehead.

"And therefore permit me, without further explanation, to say a few words of farewell, the absolutely final words I shall have to say in your house, Yegor Ilyich. The matter has been decided and cannot now be reversed! I trust you understand what I am talking about. But I implore you on my knees: if you retain in your heart even a spark of moral sensibility, keep your passions in check! And if the entire building has not yet been contaminated by noxious poison, then you must do your very best to put out the fire!"

"Foma! I assure you you're mistaken!" my uncle exclaimed, gradually coming to his senses, increasingly anxious about the direction in which the conversation seemed to be heading.

"Keep your passions in check," Foma continued in the same portentous tone, as if unaware of what my uncle had just said. "Master yourself. 'If you want to conquer the entire world, then first conquer yourself!'* That is my golden rule. You are a land-owner – you must shine like a jewel on your own estates, but just look what an example of depravity you have set to your inferiors! I have been praying for you night after night, in anguish concern-ing your future happiness. But without success, as happiness can only be found in virtue—"

"But this is impossible, Foma," my uncle interrupted again. "You've got it all wrong, you simply don't understand…"

"And so, never forget that you are a landowner," Foma con-tinued, once again ignoring my uncle's protestations. "Do not imagine that a life devoted to leisure and lasciviousness was ever a landowner's intended calling! Such a pernicious thought! Not leisure, but zealous concern, concern for God, for the Tsar and for the fatherland! Toil, toil and toil again – that is the duty of a landowner, just like the lowliest of his peasants!"

"What, you're saying I have to plough the fields for the peas-ants?" Bakhcheyev grumbled. "I'm a landowner too, aren't I?"

"And now let me turn to you, the household staff," Foma went on, addressing Gavrila and Falaley, who had also appeared in the doorway. "Love your lords and masters and carry out their wishes with meekness and obedience. In doing that, you will in turn be loved by your lords and masters. And you, colonel, should always treat your servants with fairness and compassion. After all, they are human beings too, made in the image of God – little children, so to speak, entrusted to you by the Tsar and the fatherland. Your task is great, but so is your reward!"

"Foma Fomich, my darling! What are you planning to do?" the general's lady shouted in despair, on the point of fainting from the horror of it all.

"Anyway, that's probably enough, don't you think?" Foma cried, ignoring even the general's lady. "Now, let us turn to a few details – trivial, no doubt, but necessary. Yegor Ilyich! You've still not cut the grass on that area of wasteland in Khorinskaya. Don't waste any more time – get on and cut it as soon as you can. That's my advice to you—"

"But, Foma—"

"You wanted, as I well know, to cut down that strip of woodland in Zyryanovsk – but don't do it…. another piece of advice. Leave the trees as they are, because they help to keep the ground underneath them moist… A pity that you sowed the spring crops so late – astonishingly late, in fact!"

"But, Foma—"

"That's enough, at any rate! You can't cover everything, and in any case I haven't the time now! I'll send you my instructions in writing, in a separate notebook. Well, farewell, farewell everybody. May God be with you, and may the Lord bless you! I bless you too, my child," he continued, turning to Ilyusha, "and may God keep you safe from the pernicious poison of future passions! I bless you too, Falaley. Put that Kamarinskaya out of your mind! And you, and everybody… Remember your Foma… Well, Gavrila, let's go! Help me into the cart, if you would, old fellow."

And Foma started walking towards the door. The general's lady shrieked and rushed after him.

"No, Foma! I can't let you go like this!" my uncle exclaimed, and, catching up with him, seized him by the arm.

"So you want to use force, do you?" Foma asked haughtily.

"Yes, Foma… force!" my uncle replied, trembling with emotion. "You have said too much, and you need to explain! You took what I said in my letter quite the wrong way, Foma!…"

"Your letter!" Foma shrieked, instantly flaring up, as if he were waiting for precisely that moment to erupt. "Your letter! Here it is, your letter! Here it is! I'm ripping this letter to pieces – I'm spitting on this letter! I am trampling on your letter and thereby fulfilling the most sacred duty of man! That is what I'm doing, if you're forcing me to explain! Look, here! Here! And here!..."

And scraps of paper flew all over the room.

"I repeat, Foma, there's a misunderstanding!" my uncle cried, his face turning whiter and whiter. "I'm offering her my hand in marriage, Foma – I want to find my happiness..."

"Your hand? You seduce this young girl and you think you can fool me in offering her your hand? When I saw you two together last night, in the garden, under the bushes?"

The general's lady shrieked and collapsed back into her chair in a swoon. There was total uproar in the room. Poor Nastenka sat there as white as a sheet, as if lifeless. Terrified, Sashenka put her arms round Ilyusha; she was shaking all over, as if in a fever.

"Foma!" my uncle yelled in a total frenzy. "In telling everyone this secret, you'll be doing something that is beyond contempt!"

"In telling everyone this secret," screeched Foma, "I am performing the noblest of acts! I have been sent to this earth by God himself, so that I can reveal the world in all its iniquities! I am ready to clamber up onto the thatched roof of the rudest peasant hut and to trumpet abroad to all the landowners in the district and all itinerant travellers just how despicably you have behaved!... Yes, everyone, absolutely everyone should know that last night I came across him together with this young, this most innocent girl in the garden, under the bushes!..."

"Oh, that's such a disgrace!" squeaked Miss Perepelitsyna.

"Foma! Don't do this!" my uncle shouted, clenching his fists, his eyes flashing.

"While he," screeched Foma, "terrified that I had seen him, had the gall to try to beguile such an honest and straightforward man as myself by writing a duplicitous letter in an attempt to get me to condone his crime – yes, his crime!... because you have turned the most innocent of girls into—"

"Just one more word like that against her, and I'll... I'll kill you, Foma – I swear I will!"

"I'm saying that, since you have contrived to turn the most hitherto innocent of girls into the most depraved!"

No sooner had Foma said this than my uncle grabbed him by the shoulders, swung him round as if he were a piece of straw and hurled him forcefully against the French windows that led out of Foma's study into the yard. It was such a violent blow that the windows, already slightly ajar, crashed wide open and Foma rolled head over heels down the seven stone steps, ending up flat on his face in the yard. Bits of broken glass were scattered everywhere, all over the porch steps.

"Pick him up, Gavrila!" my uncle shouted, as white as a sheet. "Sit him down in the cart, and make sure that, within a couple of minutes, Stepanchikovo will have seen the last of him!"

Such a turn of events was no doubt the last thing Foma Fomich expected.

It is not easy to convey what happened during the first minutes after this extraordinary scene: the general's lady's ear-splitting howl as she collapsed into her chair; the dumbfounded look on Miss Perepelitsyna's face as she tried to come to terms with my hitherto docile uncle's totally unexpected behaviour; the oohs and aahs of the lady hangers-on; Nastenka terrified and on the point of fainting, with her father hovering at her side; Sashenka distraught with horror; my uncle pacing about the room in indescribable agitation, waiting for his mother to come to; and finally Falaley's loud wailing at the behaviour of his masters – all this is well beyond the powers of description. I should add that at this exact moment a violent thunderstorm erupted, with increasingly frequent claps of thunder and heavy drops of rain beating against the windows.

"Well, how about that for a party?" muttered Mr Bakhcheyev, looking down at the ground and flinging his arms into the air.

"Things are bad," I whispered to him, also in a state of shock, "but at least they've got rid of Foma, and for good."

"Mother! How are you? Are you feeling any better? Can you hear me now?" my uncle asked, standing in front of his mother's chair.

She looked up, put her hands together and gave her son an imploring look; she had never seen him so angry.

"Mother!" he continued. "You saw for yourself that I simply couldn't take it any longer. I didn't want things to turn out as they did, but the moment had come, and I simply had to act, without delay! You heard his slanderous accusation, so now listen to what I have to say. Mother, I love this girl – she's the most wonderful and sublime person; I have long loved her, and will never stop doing so. She will make my children so happy and will be such a faithful daughter to you. Therefore now, in your presence and that of my relatives and friends, I will kneel down at her feet and solemnly implore her to accord me the immeasurable honour of agreeing to be my wife!"

Nastenka started up in shock, then went bright red and leapt up from her chair. The general's lady looked at her son for a few moments, as if unable to understand what he was saying to her, and then suddenly threw herself on her knees in front of him with a piercing cry.

"Yegorushka, my darling, get Foma Fomich back!" she wailed. "Please get him back at once! Otherwise, without him, I'll be dead before the day is out!"

My uncle froze, seeing his aged mother, his capricious and wilful mother, on her knees before him. An expression of pain flitted across his face. Finally, coming to his senses, he hurriedly lifted her up and sat her back in her chair.

"Bring Foma Fomich back, Yegorushka!" she continued to wail. "Bring him back, the darling man! I can't live without him!"

"But Mother," my uncle cried disconsolately, "didn't you hear what I said to you just now? I cannot get Foma back – please try to understand that! Not only can I not do that, but it would be wrong to do so after his contemptible and base, slanderous attack on this angel of honour and virtue. You have to understand, Mother, that I am now duty-bound, that my sense of honour commands me to see that her virtue is restored! You heard what I said: I am asking for this young lady's hand in marriage, and I am imploring you to give our union your blessing."

The general's lady rose abruptly from her chair once again and threw herself down on her knees before Nastenka.

"My dear, precious girl!" she wailed. "Don't get married to him! Don't do that, but ask him, my dear, to get Foma Fomich back! My dearest girl, Nastasya Yevgrafovna! You can take anything from me, I will sacrifice everything, if you don't marry him. I still have something put aside for my old age – I still have a few crumbs left over from my dear departed husband. All of it is yours, my dear – I will give you everything, and Yegorushka will give you something as well, but please don't put me in my grave just yet... implore him to let me have my Foma Fomich back!..."

And the old woman would have gone on and on pleading and wailing if Miss Perepelitsyna and the lady hangers-on had not dashed forward weeping and groaning to pick her up, indignant that she should be kneeling in supplication before a hired governess. Nastenka herself was barely able to stand from fear, while Miss Perepelitsyna had started weeping tears of rage.

"You'll be the death of your mother, sir," she shouted at my uncle, "yes, you will, sir! And as for you, Nastasya Yevgrafovna, how dare you cause such a rift between mother and son like that? It is against God's will to do such a thing..."

"Hold your tongue, Anna Nilovna!" my uncle cried. "I've had quite enough!..."

"Yes, and I've had quite enough of you, too! The way you reproach me for being an orphan the whole time! How long do you intend going on doing that? I am not your slave, sir! I am a lieutenant colonel's daughter, sir! I cannot stay in this house another day, not another day, sir!..."

But my uncle was not listening. He went up to Nastenka and reverently took her hand.

"Nastasya Yevgrafovna! You have heard my proposal?" he said, giving her an anguished, almost despairing look.

"No, Yegor Ilyich, no! We'd better leave it there!" she replied, now utterly downcast in her turn. "There's absolutely no point now," she continued, holding his hands firmly in hers, in floods of tears. "What happened yesterday was so… but now it cannot be, you yourself must know that. We made a mistake, Yegor Ilyich… But I will always look on you as my benefactor… and… and you'll be always, always in my prayers!…"

At this, her tears prevented her from continuing. My poor uncle had evidently expected such an answer; he didn't even think of objecting or trying to demur. He stood there holding her hand, a silent and broken man. His eyes began brimming with tears.

"I told you yesterday," Nastya continued, "that I couldn't be your wife. You can see for yourself I'm not wanted here… and I knew that would be the case all along – your mother will never give us her blessing… neither will any of the *others*. Perhaps you won't have any regrets later because you are the most magnanimous of men, yet you will be unhappy on my account… you are such a kind person…"

"Yes, that's it – *such a kind person*! You're *such a kind person*, sir! You're right, Nastenka, you're right," her old father agreed, standing on the other side of the chair. "You couldn't have put it any better."

"I have no wish to be the cause of any discord in your house," Nastenka went on. "But please don't worry about me, Yegor Ilyich – nobody will lay a hand on me… nobody will insult me… I shall go and live with my father… today… We should say goodbye, Yegor Ilyich… it's better that way…"

And poor Nastenka once again broke down in floods of tears.

"But Nastasya Yevgrafovna, can that really be your final word?" my uncle said, giving her a look of inexpressible despair. "All you have to say is one word, and I will sacrifice my entire life for you…"

"No, that was her last word to you, Yegor Ilyich, sir, her very last word," Yezhevikin interposed again, "and she expressed it all so well that I must confess it came as a real surprise, sir. You are the kindest of men, Yegor Ilyich, yes, exactly that, sir, the kindest of men, and you have kindly done us such a great honour, sir! Yes, really, sir, a great honour!... Nonetheless, we are not your equals, Yegor Ilyich. You need a bride, Yegor Ilyich sir, who is wealthy, who is distinguished in her own right, who is beautiful, with a fine voice, someone who adorns herself with jewels and ostrich feathers, sir, who is an ornament to your house... Perhaps then Foma Fomich would yield pride of place to you and bless your union, sir! But you should bring Foma Fomich back, sir. You really shouldn't have treated him like that, sir! After all, he only said those things because of his high-minded sense of virtue and through an excess of passion... You'll be the first to admit that yourself later, sir – you mark my words, sir! The worthiest of men, sir. He will be absolutely drenched to the skin by now, sir... It really would be best to get him back, sir... since you'll absolutely have to do it sooner or later in any case, sir..."

"Bring him back! Bring him back!" the general's lady shouted. "He's telling you the truth, my dearest!"

"Yes, sir," Yezhevikin continued, "look at how distressed your mother is – and all so needlessly... So bring him back, sir! And in the mean time Nastya and I will set off back home..."

"Wait, Yevgraf Larionych!" my uncle cried. "Please, I beg you! Let me say one more word, Yevgraf, just one more word..."

On saying this, my uncle withdrew into a corner of the room, sat down in an armchair, bowed his head and covered his face in his hands, as if in deep thought.

At that instant there was a terrible clap of thunder that resounded almost directly overhead. The whole building shook. The general's lady shrieked, followed by Miss Perepelitsyna. The lady hangers-on, accompanied by Mr Bakhcheyev, crossed themselves, numb with fear.

"May the prophet Elijah have mercy on us!" five or six people whispered all at once in unison.

The thunderclap was immediately followed by such a downpour that it seemed as if an entire lake had suddenly emptied itself onto Stepanchikovo.

"But what's going to become of Foma Fomich now, out in the open?" squealed Miss Perepelitsyna.

"Get him back, Yegorushka!" yelled the general's lady despairingly, and she started to rush towards the door like a madwoman. The lady hangers-on restrained her, clustering around her, trying to console her, whimpering and yelping. It was all such pandemonium!

"He had nothing but his frock coat on – he didn't even have his overcoat with him!" Miss Perepelitsyna continued. "Or even an umbrella! He'll be struck by lightning, struck dead – I know he will!"

"That's right!" Bakhcheyev agreed. "And he'll get soaked to the skin."

"Why don't you just keep quiet?" I whispered to him.

"But he's a human being, isn't he?" Bakhcheyev replied angrily. "He's not a dog. Why don't you go out in all this rain and see for yourself what fun it is?"

Foreseeing the possible outcome and anxious to avoid it, I went up to my uncle, who was still sitting in his armchair as if unable to move.

"Uncle," I said, bending down to his ear, "you're not going to agree to get Foma Fomich back, are you? Don't you understand what a mistake that would be – so long as Nastasya Yevgrafovna is still here at least?"

"My friend," my uncle replied, looking me straight in the eye with a determined expression, "I have been weighing everything up while I have been sitting here, and I now know what I have to do! Don't worry: Nastya's not going to be offended – I'll make sure of that…"

He got up from his chair and went over to his mother.

"Mother," he said, "please don't worry! I will bring Foma Fomich back. I will catch up with him, he can't have gone far. But I swear to you that, if he is to come back, it can only be on one condition: that he here, in this room, publicly confesses his guilt and solemnly asks this most noble young lady's forgiveness! I shall see to it that he does that! I shall force him to do it! Otherwise he will never cross the threshold of this house again! I also solemnly swear to you, Mother, that if he agrees to do this of his own accord, voluntarily, then I will be prepared to throw myself at his feet and give him everything, everything that I can afford to give him, but without depriving my own children of anything! I myself will from now on withdraw entirely from everything. The sun of my happiness has set! I shall leave Stepanchikovo. You must all continue to live here happily and in peace. I shall return to my regiment, where I shall live out my unhappy destiny in the heat and storms of the battlefield… Enough! I must leave you now!"

At that moment the door opened, and, much to everyone's consternation, Gavrila appeared, covered in mud and absolutely drenched to the skin.

"What's the matter? Where have you been? Where's Foma?" my uncle cried, dashing over to him.

Everyone else rushed over to Gavrila as well, bombarding the old man with eager questions. Muddy water was literally pouring from him. Every word he said was accompanied by screams, shouts and exclamations.

"I left him by a clump of birch trees, about half a mile from here," Gavrila began in a plaintive voice. "The horse was scared by the lightning and bolted into a ditch."

"My goodness…" my uncle cried.

"The cart overturned…"

"So… what about Foma?"

"He fell into the ditch, sir."

"Well, come on, what happened then? Stop tormenting us like this!"

"He hurt his ribs and started to cry, sir. I unharnessed the horse from the cart and rode back here to tell you what had happened, sir."

"And Foma stayed there?"

"He got up and started walking on further with his stick," Gavrila concluded, then he sighed and looked down on the ground.

The tears and exclamations of the ladies defy all description.

"My horse!" my uncle shouted, and dashed out of the room.

As soon as his horse was brought, he leapt on it, bareback, and a minute later the sound of horse's hooves told us that the chase after Foma Fomich was under way.

The ladies made a dash for the windows. Among all the gasps and groans some sensible advice could be heard. There was talk of the urgent need to run a hot bath, of rubbing Foma down with surgical spirit and then giving him some herbal tea; Foma Fomich "hadn't had a bite to eat since morning, and must now be starving". Miss Perepelitsyna located his spectacles in their case, which he had forgotten to take with him – producing the most extraordinary effect: the general's lady seized on them weeping and wailing, and, keeping firm hold of them, turned back to the window to keep an eye on the road. By this point the sense of expectation in the room had become almost unbearable... In one corner Sashenka was consoling Nastya; they stood there weeping, with their arms round one another. Nastenka was holding Ilyusha's hand and kissing him the whole time, as she said goodbye to her pupil. Ilyusha was in floods of tears, still not entirely sure why. Yezhevikin and Mizinchikov were holding forth about something to one side. It seemed to me that Bakhcheyev was close to tears as he looked at the girls. I went up to him.

"No, old boy," he said to me, "Foma Fomich may well leave here for good sometime, but that time has not yet come: no one has yet provided the gold-horned bulls for his chariot! Mark my words, old boy: he'll send his hosts packing, and he'll be the only one left!"

The storm had passed, and Mr Bakhcheyev had clearly had second thoughts about certain matters.

Suddenly shouts could be heard – "They're here, they're here!" – and the ladies rushed to the door. Less than ten minutes had passed since my uncle's departure – it seemed quite impossible that Foma Fomich had been brought back so quickly, but a simple explanation was very soon forthcoming: on letting Gavrila go, Foma Fomich had indeed "started walking on further with his stick", but then, becoming aware that he was totally alone in the middle of the storm, the thunder and lightning, he had become shamefully terror-stricken, turned back for Stepanchikovo and started running after Gavrila. When my uncle had found him, he was already in the village. They had immediately hailed a passing cart, onto which the now-chastened Foma Fomich had been placed by some villagers who had arrived quickly on the scene. So he now found himself once more in the welcoming arms of the general's lady, who was horrified at the sight of him: he was even more covered in mud and soaked to the skin than Gavrila. There ensued the most utter pandemonium: they wanted to drag him upstairs immediately for a change of clothing; people started shouting about elderberry syrup and other restorative medicines, with everyone rushing around randomly in all directions... But Foma himself seemed not to be aware of anyone or anything. He was led inside, supported by both arms. Reaching his chair, he slumped down heavily into it and closed his eyes. Someone cried that he was dying; this was greeted by agonizing screams. But the one who howled the most was Falaley, as he attempted to fight his way through the crowd of women to get to Foma Fomich so that he could immediately kiss his hand...

5

Foma Fomich Creates Universal Happiness

"Where am I?" Foma Fomich asked eventually, in the voice of a martyr to the truth.

"Pathetic, isn't it?" whispered Mizinchikov standing next to me. "As if he can't see where he is. Prepare yourself for more posturing now!"

"You're back with us, Foma, you're back home, with friends!" my uncle cried. "Cheer up and relax! And you really should get changed, or you'll catch your death... How about a little glass of something warm to buck you up, eh?..."

"I could do with a little Malaga," Foma groaned, closing his eyes once more.

"Malaga? I'm not sure we've got any, have we?" my uncle said, with an anxious glance at Praskovya Ilyinichna.

"Of course we have!" retorted Praskovya Ilyinichna. "We've got four whole bottles left." And, with a clinking of keys, she dashed off straight away to fetch the Malaga, to the accompaniment of exclamations from all the womenfolk, who were clustering around Foma like bees around a honeypot. Mr Bakhcheyev, on the other hand, was in an extreme state of irritation.

"Malaga indeed!" he growled, almost loudly enough for everyone to hear. "Typical to ask for a wine that nobody ever drinks! Well, I ask you: who drinks Malaga nowadays, apart from some scoundrel like him? Pouf, to hell with the lot of them! No idea why I'm still hanging around here! What am I waiting for?"

"Foma!..." my uncle began, stumbling over every word. "Now... now that you've been able to rest and are back with us again... I wanted... that is, I meant to say, Foma, I quite understand that when, just now, you accused, so to speak, the most innocent of creatures—"

239

"Where, where is it, my innocence?" Foma interjected, as if in feverish delirium. "Where have my golden days gone? Where are you now, my innocent childhood, the time when I used to skip about the fields, an innocent and lovely lad, chasing the butterflies of spring? Where are those good old days now? Give me back my innocence, give it back!…"

And Foma, spreading his arms wide, turned to address everyone in turn, as though his innocence were to be found in someone's pocket. Bakhcheyev was on the point of exploding with anger.

"What's he going to ask for next?" he growled furiously. "'Give him his innocence back!' – for goodness' sake! What does he want to do with it? Kiss it? He was probably just as much a scoundrel as a small boy as he is now! I bet he was!"

"Foma!…" my uncle tried again.

"Where, oh where are they, those days when I still believed in love and could love mankind?" cried Foma. "When I could embrace my fellow man and weep on his bosom? But now… where am I? Where am I?"

"You're here, with us, Foma, calm down!" my uncle cried. "But here's what I wanted to say to you, Foma…"

"Why don't you just hold your tongue now?" hissed Miss Perepelitsyna with an angry flash of her snake-like eyes.

"Where am I?" Foma continued. "Who are all these people? Bulls and buffaloes pointing their horns at me. What is this life? You live on and on, only to find yourself a dishonoured, disgraced, belittled and broken man – and it's only when you are buried in the ground that people will come to their senses and crush your bones under a monument!"

"Good grief – he's started talking about monuments now!" Yezhevikin whispered, throwing his arms in the air.

"Don't raise a monument to me!" Foma shouted. "Don't raise a monument to me! I don't need a monument! Raise a monument to me in your hearts, but that's all, that's all I need, that's all!"

"Foma," my uncle interrupted, "that's enough! Calm down! Forget about monuments. You need to listen to me… You see,

Foma, it's like this... I quite understand that when you accused me a little while ago you were aflame with moral indignation, but you got carried away, Foma... you went too far – you were in the wrong, Foma, I can assure you..."

"Stop it, for goodness' sake!" squeaked Miss Perepelitsyna again. "Do you want to kill the poor man just because he's in your clutches again?..."

This remark of Miss Perepelitsyna's set off the general's lady, who followed suit, together with all her followers and hangers-on: everyone began gesturing at my uncle to stop.

"You keep quiet yourself, Anna Nilovna – I know what I'm saying," my uncle replied determinedly. "It's a sacred matter! It's a matter of honour and justice, Foma! You're a sensible man – you have offended this most virtuous of young ladies and you must ask for her forgiveness."

"What young lady? What young lady have I offended?" Foma replied, looking around at everyone in bewilderment, as if he had entirely forgotten about what had happened and had no idea what my uncle was talking about.

"Yes, Foma, and if you now, of your own free will, generously acknowledge that you have done wrong, then I swear to you, Foma, I will fall at your feet and—"

"But whom have I offended?" yelled Foma. "Which young lady? Where is she? Where is this young lady? Tell me something about her, so that I can remember..."

At that moment an embarrassed and frightened Nastenka went up to Yegor Ilyich and tugged him by the sleeve.

"No, Yegor Ilyich, leave him alone, I don't need any apology! What's the point?" she implored him. "Let it be!..."

"Ah! It's coming back to me now!" Foma cried. "My God! Yes, it's all coming back! Oh, help me, help me to remember!" he asked in a voice shaken by agitation. "Tell me: was I really kicked out of here, like some mangy cur? Was I really struck by lightning? Hurled out of here onto the porch steps? Did that really happen? Really?"

The weeping and wailing on the part of all the ladies presented Foma Fomich with the most eloquent answer possible.

"Yes, yes!" he said. "It's all coming back to me now... I can now remember running back here after all the thunder and lightning, and falling down, running back so that I could do my duty and then disappear for ever! Help me to my feet! No matter how weak I am now, I simply must do my duty!"

He was immediately raised from his chair. Foma stood up and adopted the pose of an orator, extending his arm.

"Colonel!" he exclaimed. "I am completely myself again; the thunder has not destroyed my mental faculties; it's true, I'm still a little deaf in my right ear – the result, perhaps, not so much of the thunder as falling down the porch steps... But so what? Who is going to care about Foma's right ear?"

Foma delivered these last words with such ironic pathos and wearing such a self-pitying smile that the assembled ladies were deeply moved and their lamentations broke out again. They all looked at my uncle in such a reproachful and, in some cases, angry way that, confronted by their universal expression of displeasure, he started to show signs of capitulation. Mizinchikov snorted and walked over to the window. Bakhcheyev carried on nudging me more and more violently with his elbow.

"You must now, all of you, listen to my confession," Foma shouted, looking around the entire room with a proud, determined expression on his face, "and, at the same time, decide what to do with the hapless Opiskin. Yegor Ilyich! I have been keeping my eye on you for a long time now with a sinking heart, and have seen absolutely everything, while you haven't had an inkling that that is what I've been doing. Colonel! I may have been mistaken, but, in view of your egoism, your boundless self-love and your unparalleled sensual appetite, is not my instinctive concern for the honour of such an innocent person perfectly justifiable?"

"Foma, Foma!... Please stop, that's quite enough, Foma," my uncle exclaimed, anxiously noting the agonized expression on Nastenka's face.

"What has most concerned me has been not so much the girl's innocence and naivety as her inexperience," Foma continued, as if he had not heard my uncle's warning. "I have observed the tender sentiment blossoming in her heart like a spring rose, and my thoughts have turned involuntarily to Petrarch, who once said that 'innocence is all too often a hair's breadth away from disaster'.* I sighed and groaned, and though I would willingly have offered every drop of blood in vouching for this purest of pure young ladies, where could I find anyone willing to vouch for you, Yegor Ilyich? Knowing of the unbridled nature of your passions, knowing that you would sacrifice anything for their instant gratification, I found myself suddenly cast into an abyss of fear and horror concerning the fate of that most noble of young ladies..."

"Foma!... Did you really think such things?" my uncle exclaimed.

"I have been observing you with a sinking heart. If you should want to find out the extent of my suffering, ask Shakespeare: he will tell you in his *Hamlet* of the state of my soul. I have become fearsome and distrustful. In my anxious and irritated state I saw everything in dark colours, and not the kind of dark colours which they sing about in the famous ballad* – you can be sure of that! Hence my desire at the time, which you yourself saw, to remove *her* from this house. I wanted to save her – that was why you saw me so irritable recently, and so enraged at the human race. Oh! Who will now reconcile me with mankind? I sense I could well have been too taxing and unfair towards your guests, towards your nephew and towards Mr Bakhcheyev and his lack of astronomical knowledge. But who can blame me for the state of my soul at that time? With reference to Shakespeare once again, I can say that I saw the future like some dark, bottomless pit, at the bottom of which lurked a crocodile.* I felt that it was my duty to forestall disaster, that I had been created, placed on this earth precisely for that purpose – with what result? You failed to understand the most noble aspirations of my soul, and all I got from you in return for the whole of this time was hatred, ingratitude, mockery and humiliation..."

"Foma! If that was the case... then, of course, I feel..." my uncle exclaimed in indescribable agitation.

"If indeed you are able to have such feelings, colonel, then would you be so kind as to let me finish and to stop interrupting me? As I was saying, my only fault therefore was that I was too concerned for the fate and future happiness of this child – for that is what she still is, as far as you are concerned. It was my most elevated love for mankind that transformed me at that time into a veritable ogre of rage and suspicion. I was ready to hurl myself at people and to rip them apart. And are you aware, Yegor Ilyich, that your every action, as if on purpose, merely served the whole time to confirm me in my suspicions and justify my mistrust in you? Are you aware that yesterday, when you showered me with your gold so that you could get rid of me, I had the following thought: 'He's using me to salve his own conscience so that it will be easier for him to perpetrate his crime...'"

"Foma, Foma! Surely you didn't think that yesterday, did you?" my uncle cried, horrified at the idea. "Good God, I didn't suspect anything of the sort!"

"It was a suspicion that was inspired from above," Foma continued. "You can judge for yourself – what else could I think when blind chance brought me that evening to that fateful bench in the garden? What other feelings could I have had at that moment – oh Lord! – when I finally saw with my very own eyes that all my suspicions had suddenly been confirmed in such a striking way? But I still harboured a hope – a slight one, of course, but nonetheless a hope. And what do you think? Today, this very morning, you yourself shattered this hope and turned it into dust! You send me this letter stating your intention to get married, and imploring me not to tell anybody... 'But why,' I thought, 'why on earth should he write precisely now, after I had caught them together, and not before? Why hadn't he dashed to see me before, with a face shining with happiness and joy – for faces can be transformed by love – why hadn't he flown into my arms, weeping tears of unbounded happiness, and told me everything,

everything?' Or am I some crocodile who, instead of giving you useful advice, would merely have devoured you? Or some horrible insect who, rather than furthering your happiness, would simply have stung you? 'Am I his friend or the vilest of insects?' – that was the question I asked myself this morning! 'Why, for goodness' sake,' I thought, 'why should he have summoned his nephew from the capital for the purpose of getting married to this young lady if not to deceive us, together with the *frivolous* lad himself, while all the time being secretly engaged on his most criminal of plans?' No, colonel, if anyone has convinced me of the idea that your love for each other was criminal, then it has been you yourself, and you yourself alone! More than that: you are criminally guilty in so far as this young lady is concerned, for you have made her – this pure, innocent girl – vulnerable to slander and the gravest of suspicions through your inappropriate behaviour and selfish mistrust!"

My uncle said nothing, his head bowed: Foma's eloquence had clearly put paid to any further objections, and he was already acknowledging just what a criminal he had been. The general's lady and all her company listened to Foma in silent deference, while Miss Perepelitsyna looked at poor Nastenka with an expression of malevolent triumph.

"Defeated, irritated, destroyed," Foma continued, "I locked myself in my room today and prayed for God to show me the right path! Finally I knew what it was I had to do: to subject you to one final, public test. I may have set about everything in an overzealous way, and allowed myself to have become too irritated, but your response to my noblest aspirations was to hurl me out of the window! As I was falling through the window I said to myself: 'So that's how virtue is always rewarded in this world!' Then I crashed down onto the ground, and I can barely remember what happened to me after that!"

Foma's recounting of this tragic episode was accompanied by groaning and wailing. The general's lady was on the point of dashing over to him with the bottle of Malaga, which she had snatched from the hands of Praskovya Ilyinichna, who had just come back into the room, when Foma imperiously waved both the Malaga and the general's lady away.

"Wait!" he cried. "I haven't finished. What happened after I fell through the window I have no idea. All I know is that I am now standing here, soaked to the skin and about to be struck down by a feverish cold, but intent on being the creator of your mutual happiness. Colonel! For many reasons which I am unable to explain now, I have finally become convinced that your love was pure and even sublime, albeit criminally dishonest. Shattered, humiliated, accused of insulting this young lady, for whose honour I, like a knight from the Middle Ages, was prepared to spill every drop of my blood, I have now resolved to show you exactly how Foma Opiskin wishes to answer the wrongs that have been done to him. Give me your hand, colonel!"

"With pleasure, Foma!" my uncle exclaimed. "And in view of the fact that you have now totally cleared up the question of the honour of this most innocent young lady, then... of course... here is my hand, together with my contrition..."

And my uncle offered Foma his hand, still not knowing what would happen next.

"Give me your hand as well," Foma continued quietly, brushing aside the large group of ladies that had crowded around him and turning to Nastenka.

Confused and embarrassed, Nastenka gave Foma a timid look.

"Come here, come here, my dear, sweet child! It's for your happiness," Foma added affectionately, still holding on to my uncle's hand.

"What's he up to?" wondered Mizinchikov.

The trembling and frightened Nastya slowly went up to Foma and shyly held out her hand.

Foma took her hand and placed it in my uncle's.

"I join you together, with my blessing," he pronounced in the most solemn tones, "and if the blessing of a suffering man shattered by grief can in any way be of assistance to you, then please,

I beg you, be happy. There you have Foma Opiskin's response to the wrongs that he has had to endure! Hurrah!"

Everyone was so astonished by this that it defies description. Such an outcome had been so unexpected that they were all as if stunned, frozen to the spot. The general's lady stood there just as she was, her mouth wide open and still holding the bottle of Malaga. Miss Perepelitsyna turned pale and started shaking with anger. The female hangers-on threw their hands in the air, unable to move. My uncle began quivering and tried to say something, but without success. Nastya turned as white as a sheet, and said timidly, "This isn't right" – but it was already too late. Bakhcheyev, to give him his due, was the first to second Foma Fomich's shout of "Hurrah!", followed by me and then Sashenka, at the top of her ringing voice, as she dashed over to embrace her father – then Ilyusha, then Yezhevikin and then, last of all, Mizinchikov.

"Hurrah!" shouted Foma again. "Hurrrah! And now go down on your knees, children of my heart, on your knees before the most loving and kindest of mothers! Ask her for her blessing – and, if necessary, I too will join you in kneeling down before her…"

My uncle and Nastya, scared and confused by it all, and still not having looked at each other, not having properly understood the implications of what was happening to them, fell on their knees before the general's lady. Everyone crowded around them, but the old lady simply stood there as if bewildered, having no idea what she should do. Foma was equal to the situation here as well: he himself knelt down before his benefactress – an action which resolved her dilemma at a stroke. Finally, in floods of tears, she announced her consent. My uncle leapt up and threw his arms around Foma.

"Foma, Foma!" he said, but his voice betrayed him, and he was unable to continue.

"Champagne!" roared Stepan Alexeyevich. "Hurrrah!"

"No, sir, not champagne!" put in Miss Perepelitsyna, having by now had time to come to her senses and to assess the situation from every angle, including all the possible consequences. "We must light a candle to the Lord and pray to his holy image and receive his blessing, as all God-fearing folk do, sir..."

Everyone rushed at once to follow this prudent advice. There was horrible confusion; the candle had to be lit. Stepan Alexeyevich drew up a chair and clambered on top of it to place the candle close to the icon, but immediately the chair broke beneath him and he crashed down onto the floor – although he managed to stay on his feet. Not at all put out by this, he respectfully handed the task over to Miss Perepelitsyna. Her slight figure did what was required in a flash: the candle was lit. Together, the nun and the lady hangers-on crossed themselves and prostrated themselves before the icon. They took down the icon of the Saviour and carried it over to the general's lady. My uncle and Nastya got down on their knees once again, and the ceremony was concluded to the accompaniment of Perepelitsyna's devout exhortations: "Bow down at her feet... now pay your respects to the icon... now kiss Mother's hand!" After the betrothed, Bakhcheyev considered it his duty to bow down before the icon and also to kiss the general's lady's hand. He was on cloud nine.

"Hurrrah!" he shouted again. "And now let's have the champagne!"

Everyone, in fact, was in a highly elated state. The general's lady was crying, but they were tears of joy: the union, once it had been given Foma's blessing, had now become in her eyes something that was both respectable and holy. But, most importantly, she felt that Foma Fomich had excelled himself and that he would now be staying with her for ever. All the lady hangers-on, at least as far as one could tell, shared the general feeling of elation. For his part, my uncle remained on his knees at his mother's feet kissing her hand, every so often getting up and rushing over to embrace me, Bakhcheyev, Mizinchikov or Yezhevikin. He embraced Ilyusha so tightly that he nearly squeezed the life out of him. Sasha dashed over to put her arms round and kiss Nastenka, while Praskovya Ilyinichna was in floods of tears. On seeing this, Mr Bakhcheyev went up to her and kissed her hand. Overcome by emotion, old

Yezhevikin was weeping in a corner, wiping his eyes with the same check handkerchief that he had sported the previous day. Gavrila was snivelling in another corner, looking at Foma Fomich with a reverent expression, while Falaley was sobbing his heart out, as he too went up to everybody and kissed their hands. Everyone was in a highly emotional state. Nobody had quite said anything yet, nobody had advanced any opinion on what had happened – it seemed there was nothing more to be said; the room was filled only with exclamations of joy. Nobody could yet quite understand how it had all suddenly happened so quickly and simply. Only one thing was clear: that it had all been Foma Fomich's doing, and that that was a self-evident and incontrovertible fact.

But hardly had five minutes passed from the moment the universal rejoicing had begun when Tatyana Ivanovna suddenly appeared in the room. How exactly, by what instinct she could have learnt so quickly, sitting upstairs alone in her room, of the love between my uncle and Nastya and their forthcoming marriage no one will ever know. She fluttered into the room like a little bird, her eyes shining with tears of joy, elegantly and provocatively attired (somehow or other she had managed to get changed in her room), and rushed straight over to embrace Nastenka, exclaiming loudly all the time.

"Nastenka, Nastenka! You loved him, and I had no idea!" she cried. "My God! They loved each other, they suffered in silence, secretly! They were being persecuted! How romantic! Nastya, my darling, tell me the whole truth: you aren't really in love with that madman, are you?"

Instead of replying, Nastya embraced her and kissed her.

"My God, how enchantingly romantic!" exclaimed Tatyana Ivanovna, clapping her hands for joy. "Listen, Nastya, listen, my angel: all these men, the whole lot of them, are ungrateful monsters, not deserving of our love. But perhaps he's the best of them. Come here, you mad thing!" she cried, turning to my uncle and seizing hold of his hand. "Are you really in love? Are you really capable of loving someone? Look at me: I want to look into your eyes; I want to see whether those eyes are lying or not. No, no, they're not lying: I can see the love shining in them. Oh, I'm so happy! Listen Nastenka, my dear friend: you are not rich, and I will give you thirty thousand. Take it, for Heaven's sake! I don't need it, I really don't – I will still have a lot left. No, no, no and no!" she shouted, waving her arms about, seeing that Nastya wanted to turn the offer down. "And you keep quiet, too, Yegor Ilyich, it's nothing to do with you. No, Nastya, I've already decided to give you this money – I've long since wanted to do that, and have been waiting only for you to fall in love with someone... I shall rejoice in your happiness. I shall be hurt if you don't take it – I shall cry, Nastya... No, no, no and no!"

Tatyana Ivanovna was so enraptured with her idea that it would have been discourteous, at least at that moment, to refuse her offer. No one did so, and the whole question was set aside for another time. She dashed over to kiss the general's lady, Perepelitsyna, and then all of us. Bakhcheyev pushed through to her with the most reverential politeness and asked to kiss her hand.

"My dear, my dear sweet lady! Please forgive an old fool for what he did and said yesterday... I didn't know you had such a heart of gold!"

"I've known you all along, you silly man!" trilled the delighted Tatyana Ivanovna playfully, as she touched Stepan Alexeyevich on the nose with her glove and wafted away like a zephyr, her elegant dress brushing against him as she went by. The fat man politely stepped aside for her.

"Such an honourable lady!" he said movingly. "That German's nose has been glued back on, you know!" he whispered confidentially to me with a twinkle in his eye.

"What nose? What German?" I asked in a tone of surprise.

"Well, the one I ordered – the one kissing his lady friend's hand as she wiped away a tear with her handkerchief. Yevdokim repaired it for me yesterday, and as soon as we got back from the chase I sent someone to go and get it... They'll soon be bringing it... A most wonderful piece of work!"

"Foma!" my uncle exclaimed, beside himself with elation. "You are the cause of our happiness! How can I ever repay you?"

"There's no need, colonel," Foma replied sanctimoniously. "*I told you not to worry about me* – enjoy your happiness without Foma."

He was clearly piqued by the fact that, in the general outpouring of joy, everyone seemed to have forgotten about him.

"It's all because I'm so happy, Foma!" my uncle exclaimed. "I hardly know at the moment, my friend, whether I'm coming or going. Listen to me, Foma: I have offended you. Even if I gave my whole life, every drop of my blood, it would not be enough to make amends for that. But if ever you should require my head, my life, I will if necessary throw myself into the most bottomless abyss – all you need to do is ask, and you will see... More than that I can't say, Foma."

And my uncle waved his hand in the air, fully conscious of the impossibility of saying anything that would express his meaning any more eloquently. He simply looked at Foma, his eyes full of tears.

"He's such an angel, isn't he?" trilled Miss Perepelitsyna, wishing to join in the general adulation of Foma.

"Yes, yes!" agreed Sashenka. "I had no idea you were such a good man, Foma Fomich, and I have been rather rude to you. Please forgive me, Foma Fomich – from now on I shall love you with all my heart, you can be sure of that. If only you knew how much I respect you now!"

"Yes, Foma!" Bakhcheyev took up the refrain. "Please forgive me as well... I've been such a fool! I have got you wrong, quite wrong! You, Foma Fomich, are not only a scholar, but simply a real hero as well! My whole house is at your service. In fact, why don't you drive over to my place the day after tomorrow and bring the general's lady – and the bride and groom for that matter! But what am I on about? Why don't the lot of you, the whole household, come? I'll put on such a meal that, though I say so myself, will be fit for a tsar, I tell you! Hand on heart!"

In the midst of all these emotional outpourings, Nastenka also went up to Foma Fomich and without further ado warmly embraced and kissed him.

"Foma Fomich!" she said. "You are our saviour; you have done so much for us that I really don't know how to repay you; I only know that I will be the most loving and affectionate of sisters to you…"

She was unable to finish; her words were choked by tears. Foma kissed her on the top of her head, his own eyes filling with tears.

"My children, children of my heart!" he said. "Live and prosper, and in your moments of happiness don't forget to spare an occasional thought for a wretched outcast! As for myself, I will only say that unhappiness, perhaps, is the mother of virtue. That was said, I believe, by Gogol* – a rather frivolous writer, but who sometimes had some quite pithy ideas. To be an outcast is a calamitous fate! I shall now go off wandering around the world with my staff, and who knows? It may well be that in enduring such a fate I will become even more virtuous! Such a thought is my one remaining consolation!"

"But… where on earth are you planning to go, Foma?" my uncle asked in a state of high alarm.

Everyone shuddered at that and rushed over to Foma.

"But how can I possibly stay in this house after what you did to me yesterday, colonel?" asked Foma with an unusually dignified air.

But he wasn't allowed to say any more – his words became drowned in the general outcry. He was sat down in his armchair, and everyone started pleading with him, tearfully exhorting him to change his mind, and goodness knows what else.

Naturally, he had no intention whatsoever of leaving "that house" either now or earlier in the day, or even the day before, when he had been digging in the garden. He knew that people would zealously stop him from doing so, would cling on to him, especially now that he had made everyone so happy, now that everyone trusted his every word once again, ready to bear him aloft, honouring him for what he had done. But, more probably, it was the cowardly way of his return to the house after being frightened by the storm that had rather injured his pride and prompted him to start playing a heroic role once again. Above all, it had provided him with such a tempting opportunity to show off, to start holding forth once more, to wax eloquent, to embellish and to sing his own praises that he simply couldn't resist the temptation to do so. And so he didn't. He fought to tear himself away from all those clinging on to him, demanded that they give him his staff, implored them to let him go free so that he could explore all the corners of the earth, protesting that he had been dishonoured and beaten unmercifully "in this house", that he had returned simply to make everyone happy, and asking, finally, how he could possibly remain in "such an ungrateful house and eat cabbage soup that, although nurturing, was seasoned with beatings". Eventually, he stopped trying to tear himself away. They sat him down again in his armchair, but his eloquent flow of words never dried up.

"Have I not been insulted here?" he yelled. "Have I not been taunted the whole time? Have you yourself, colonel, not been sneering and jabbing your finger at me, like ignorant, common street children? Yes, colonel! I stand by that analogy, for even though you may not actually have jabbed your finger at me in reality, you did so figuratively – and to do so figuratively is in some cases more offensive than to do it in reality. And that's not to mention the beatings…"

"Foma! Foma!" my uncle cried. "Don't torture me by reminding me of such things! I have already assured you that all my blood would not be enough to wash away such offensive behaviour. Please be charitable! Forgive and forget… stay with us so that you can share in our happiness – in the fruits of your labours, Foma!…"

"…I want to love, I so want to love mankind," Foma shouted, "but I'm not being allowed to see people, I am being forbidden to love people… people are being removed from my presence. Give, oh give me someone so that I can love him! But where is he? Where is he hiding? Like Diogenes with his lantern* I have been looking for him all my life and have been unable to find him, and until I have found him I am unable to love anybody. Woe to the person who has turned me into a misanthrope! I shout out: 'Give me a man so that I can love him' – and what happens? They thrust Falaley on me! Can I love Falaley? Do I want to love Falaley? Will I in fact ever be able to love Falaley, even if I wanted to? No – and why not? Because he is Falaley. Why can't I love mankind in general? Because all I can see everywhere is either Falaley or someone like Falaley! I don't want Falaley, I detest Falaley, I spit on Falaley, I'll utterly crush Falaley, and if I had to choose, then I would rather love Asmodeus* than Falaley! Come, come here, my eternal tormentor, come here," he yelled, suddenly turning to Falaley, who was standing on tiptoe in the most innocent way possible, trying to catch a glimpse of what was going on from behind the crowd of people surrounding Foma Fomich. "Come here! I want to prove to you, colonel," he shouted, dragging Falaley, who was terrified out of his mind, over to him by the hand, "I want to prove to you the justice of what I said about you continually sneering and jabbing your finger at me! Tell everyone, Falaley, and tell the truth: what was it you dreamt about last night? You'll see, colonel, you'll be able to see your handiwork! Well, Falaley, come on, out with it!"

The poor lad, shaking with fear, looked around at everyone despairingly, hoping for someone to come to his rescue, but all they could do was stand there quivering with terror and waiting for him to answer.

"Well, Falaley, I'm waiting!"

Instead of answering, Falaley screwed up his face, opened his mouth and began to bellow like a calf.

"Colonel! Do you see how pig-headed he's being? It's hardly natural, is it? I'm asking you for the last time, Falaley: tell us what it was you dreamt last night."

"About…"

"Say it was about me," prompted Bakhcheyev.

"About all your virtues!" suggested Yezhevikin in his other ear.

Falaley just kept looking around the room.

"About… about your virt… about a white bull!" he mumbled finally, and burst into floods of tears.

Everyone gasped. But Foma Fomich was in an unusually forgiving mood.

"I see you're being honest, at least, Falaley," he said, "something that I don't observe in other people. May God be with you! If you are taunting me with this dream on purpose, urged on by other people, then God will give you, and the others, your just deserts. But if not, then I applaud your honesty, for even in the lowliest of creatures, such as yourself, I have become accustomed to recognize the image and likeness of God… I forgive you, Falaley! Embrace me, my children… I am staying!"

"He's staying!" they all shouted in delight.

"I am staying, and I forgive everyone. Colonel, give Falaley some sugar as a reward: he is not to weep on such a day of general happiness."

Such magnanimity, of course, was met by everyone with surprise. To be *so* concerned, at *such* a moment – and about whom, for goodness' sake? About Falaley! My uncle dashed off to fetch some sugar. Immediately, from Heaven knows where, a silver sugar bowl appeared in Praskovya Ilyinichna's hands. With his hand shaking, my uncle started taking out two pieces, then a third, but then he dropped them, sensing he was too excited to do anything properly.

"Look at that," he shouted. "On such a day! Here, Falaley!" and he tipped the entire contents of the sugar bowl onto Falaley's lap.

"That is for being honest," he added sententiously.

"Mr Korovkin!" announced Vidoplyasov, suddenly appearing in the doorway.

A slight commotion ensued. Korovkin's arrival was clearly rather inopportune. Everyone gave my uncle a questioning look.

"Korovkin!" shouted my uncle in some confusion. "I'm delighted, of course…" he added, with a timid glance at Foma. "But I'm not really sure whether I should invite him in at a time like this. What do you think, Foma?"

"Well, why not? By all means!" Foma said benignly. "Let's invite Korovkin too: the more the merrier."

In short, Foma was in an angelic frame of mind.

"If I might most humbly be granted permission to report, sir," remarked Vidoplyasov, "Mr Korovkin is not really in a presentable state, sir."

"Not in a presentable state? What do you mean? What nonsense is this?"

"Just that, sir: not in a presentable state, sir..."

But even before my uncle had found time to open his mouth, blush, look shocked and squirm with embarrassment, the riddle was solved. Korovkin himself appeared in the doorway, brushed Vidoplyasov aside and stood looking at the assembled and rather nonplussed company. He was a short but well-built man, aged about forty, with dark, greying, closely cropped hair, a round reddish face, small bloodshot eyes, wearing a prominent haircloth necktie fastened by a buckle at the back, an extremely scruffy tailcoat covered in fluff and bits of hay with an enormous tear under the armpit, *pantalons impossibles** and an unbelievably greasy peak cap, which he held out in front of him. This gentleman was totally intoxicated. He walked out into the middle of the room and stopped, swaying from side to side, his head jerking up and down, his mind clouded by drink, then his mouth slowly opened into a wide grin.

"My apologies, gentlemen," he said. "I... seem to have" – at this point he jerked at his collar – "put my foot in it again!"

The general's lady immediately assumed an expression of wounded pride. Foma, sitting in his armchair, gave the eccentric visitor a considered ironic look. Bakhcheyev looked at him in bewilderment, mixed however with a hint of sympathy. My uncle's embarrassment had to be seen to be believed; he was suffering heart and soul for Korovkin.

"Korovkin!" he began. "Listen..."

"*Attendez,** sir," Korovkin interrupted. "May I introduce myself... a child of nature... But what do I see? I can see ladies...

But why didn't you tell me, you scoundrel, there'd be ladies here?" he added with a roguish smile directed at my uncle. "Don't want to say? Come on, don't be shy!... May we introduce ourselves to the fairer sex... Lovely ladies!" he continued, having difficulty in moving his tongue and stumbling over every word. "You see before you an unfortunate man who... well, and so on and so forth... best left unsaid... Musicians! A polka!"

"How about going to bed for a bit?" suggested Mizinchikov, calmly going up to Korovkin.

"Going to bed? Are you trying to insult me?"

"Not at all. You know, to recover after a long journey?"

"Never!" Korovkin replied irritably. "You think I'm drunk? Not a bit of it... Come to think of it, where are the sleeping quarters?"

"Come with me right now, I can show you."

"Where are we going? To the barn? No, my friend, you can't fool me! I've already spent the night there... well, all right, show me... silly not to go with such a decent fellow... I won't need a pillow – a military man has no need of a pillow. Just a sofa would do, my friend, a little sofa... But listen," he added, pausing on the way, "I can see you're a thoroughly good chap... how about fixing me up with a little... you know, something? Just to drown the flies, that's all... just a little glass of something to drown the flies in."

"Of course, of course!" Mizinchikov replied.

"Excellent... But wait a moment, I need to say goodbye... *Adieu, mesdames* and *mesdemoiselles*!... You have, as it were, pierced... But that's quite enough of that! We can talk more later... but make sure you wake me as soon as things get going... or even five minutes before... but make sure you don't start without me! You hear? Not without me!..."

And the jolly gentleman followed Mizinchikov out of the room.

Everybody was silent. The general sense of bewilderment did not die away. Eventually Foma began, little by little, to giggle softly – this grew louder and louder and finally turned into shouts of laughter. Seeing this, the general's lady herself cheered up a little, although retaining her expression of injured pride. Involuntary laughter could be heard coming from all corners of the room. Only my uncle stood there as if dumbstruck, so red in the face that it looked as if he was ready to cry. For some time he was unable to utter a single word.

"My God!" he exclaimed finally. "Who would have thought? But... it could happen to anybody, of course. I can assure you, Foma, that he is the most honest, distinguished and even exceptionally erudite man, Foma... You'll see for yourself!"

"Quite so, quite so, sir," Foma replied, choking with laughter, "exceptionally erudite, exceptionally erudite!"

"He talks so well about the railways, sir," put in Yezhevikin quietly.

"Foma!" my uncle began, but his words became drowned in the loud laughter filling the room. Foma Fomich was splitting his sides. Seeing him, my uncle too burst out laughing.

"Well, so what?" he said animatedly. "You're such a wonderful man, Foma, with such a great heart – you have made me so happy... I'm sure you'll forgive Korovkin as well."

The only person not joining in the general laughter was Nastenka. She was looking at her fiancé with eyes full of love, as if she wanted to say: "You're such a wonderful, kind, generous man, and I love you so much!"

6

Conclusion

Foma's triumph was complete and absolute. Indeed, without him, nothing would have been achieved – an undisputed fact that put paid to any doubts or objections. There was no limit to the gratitude of the happy couple. My uncle and Nastenka simply refused to listen to me when I gently tried to question the process by which Foma had agreed to their getting married. Sashenka kept on shouting "Dear, kind Foma Fomich: I want to sew a worsted cushion for him!" – and even took me to task for being so cruel. The newly converted Stepan Alexeich would, I think, have throttled me if I had so much as dared to say anything disrespectful about Foma Fomich in his presence. He now followed Foma around like a faithful little dog, looking at him in awe and, whenever he said anything to him, always adding: "You are such a wonderful man, Foma! Such a scholar, Foma!" As for Yezhevikin, he was in a state of absolute rapture. The old man had long been aware that Nastenka had turned Yegor Ilyich's head, and all he had dreamt about ever since, awake or asleep, was that the two of them would get married. He had clung on to this hope to the very last, abandoning it only when it was impossible not to do so. And then Foma had transformed everything. It goes without saying of course that, despite his joy at the turn of events, the old man had no illusions about Foma Fomich – in short, it had become clear that Foma Fomich would be reigning triumphant in the house for ever, and that there would now be no end to his tyranny. It is a well-known fact that even the most objectionable, capricious people can mitigate their approach to everything, at least for a time, when their desires are satisfied. That was definitely not the case with Foma Fomich, however: success would make him behave in an even more ridiculous and arrogant way. Just before dinner, having freshly changed his clothes, he ensconced himself in his chair, summoned my uncle and, with the entire family present, proceeded to read him a new sermon.

"Colonel!" he began. "You are now about to be lawfully married, and I trust you are aware of your responsibility as…"

And so on and so forth: picture to yourself a homily of ten sides in the tiniest print in the format of the *Journal des débats*, filled with the most outrageous nonsense, but, rather than including anything about duties, shamelessly praising to the skies the intellect, modesty, magnanimity and selflessness of Foma Fomich himself. Everybody was hungry, everybody wanted to eat – despite that, however, nobody dared to object, and everyone sat there listening deferentially, waiting for him to reach the end of his ravings. Even Bakhcheyev, despite being tormented by an empty stomach, sat through the whole homily not moving a muscle and adopting an attitude of the most profound respect. Delighted with his own rhetoric, Foma Fomich finally cheered up, and he even began to drink too much over dinner, proposing some ridiculous toasts. Then he started joking and making witty remarks – at the expense of the happy couple, naturally. Everyone roared with laughter and applauded. But some of the jokes were so coarse and blatant that even Bakhcheyev was embarrassed. Nastenka jumped up from the table and ran out of the room, to Foma Fomich's intense delight. But he very quickly recollected himself: briefly, and to the point, he depicted Nastenka's virtues and proposed a toast to the absentee's health. My uncle, who just a moment before had been visibly upset and embarrassed, was now ready to embrace Foma Fomich. In general, the bride and groom seemed rather uncomfortable in each other's presence and a little ashamed of their happiness, and I noted that, from the very moment of their being blessed, they even seemed to avoid looking at each other. When everyone got up from the table, my uncle suddenly disappeared somewhere. Looking for him, I wandered out onto the terrace, where I found Foma sitting in a chair at coffee; he was holding forth, fully the worse for wear. Only Yezhevikin, Bakhcheyev and Mizinchikov were there with him. I stopped to listen.

"Why," Foma was shouting, "why is it that I am prepared to go to the stake for my beliefs, whereas none of you seems ready to do the same? Why's that, do you think?"

"But that would be a bit excessive, wouldn't it, Foma – going to the stake, I mean?" Yezhevikin was saying teasingly. "What would be the point? Firstly, it would be very painful, and secondly you'd go up in flames – what would there be left of you?"

"What would there be left of me? My sacred ashes, of course. But I can hardly expect you to understand and appreciate me, can I? As far as you are concerned, great men don't exist, apart from your Caesars or Alexanders the Great! And what have they achieved, your Caesars? Have they made anyone happy? And what about your much-trumpeted Alexander the Great? Conquered the whole world, did he? Well, if you were to give me an army like his, I would be able to conquer the world – so would you, and so would he... Yet he killed the noble Cleitus,* whereas I never killed the noble Cleitus... The little whippersnapper! The scoundrel! I'd give him a good hiding rather than praise him to the skies... and the same goes for Caesar!"

"But you could spare Caesar, couldn't you, Foma Fomich?"

"I never spare idiots!" Foma shouted.

"Quite right, too!" put in Stepan Alexeyevich heatedly – he, too, had had too much to drink. "They don't deserve to be spared: they're just a bunch of upstarts hopping around on one leg! Sausage-mongers! Who was that chap who wanted to establish a scholarship the other day? What is a scholarship, anyway? The devil knows what it is! Some new dodge, I bet. And what about that other chap who staggered into polite society asking for rum? Nothing wrong with having a drink, I say! Drink as much as you like, but keep yourself to yourself, and then have another drink... They don't deserve to be spared! They're all scoundrels, the lot of them! You're the only learned man about the place, Foma!"

Once Bakhcheyev had decided to be loyal to someone, then he did so heart and soul, without any criticism.

I found my uncle in the garden, by the pond, in the most isolated spot. He was with Nastenka. On seeing me, Nastenka dashed into the bushes, as though feeling guilty. My uncle walked towards me with a radiant expression; there were tears of joy in his eyes. He took me by both hands and clasped them warmly.

"My friend!" he said. "I still can't believe my good fortune... neither can Nastya. We can only marvel at it and praise the Almighty. She was crying tears of joy just now. Believe it or not, I still haven't fully grasped what's happened, and am totally bemused by it all: I find myself believing it and, at the same time, not believing it! Why me? Why? What have I done to deserve it?"

"If anyone deserves it, Uncle, then it's you," I said, carried away by emotion. "I have never seen such an honest, wonderful, kind man..."

"No, Seryozha, no, that's too much," he replied, as if regretfully. "The problem is that we can be kind (I'm talking about myself, of course) when all's well with the world, but when it's not, you should steer clear of us! That's just what Nastya and I have been saying. No matter how exceptional Foma was, I couldn't really believe in him fully until today, even though I was trying to convince you just how perfect he was – that was the case even yesterday, when he refused my money! I'm saying that to my shame! My heart skips a beat when I remember how I behaved then! But I was not in control of myself... When he said those things about Nastya, it was as if somebody had stabbed me in the heart. I didn't understand, and behaved like a wild beast..."

"Well, Uncle, maybe it was a perfectly natural thing to do."

My uncle made a dismissive gesture.

"No, no, no, my boy, that's quite wrong! It was all because of my flawed nature, because I'm such a dark, lascivious, selfish character, someone who allows himself to be completely dominated by his passions. That's what Foma says." (What could I say in reply to that?) "Aren't you aware, Seryozha," he went on with deep feeling, "of the number of times I've been short-tempered, cruel, unfair and arrogant, and not merely to Foma! That's why it's all suddenly come flooding back now, and I'm somehow so ashamed I've done nothing until now to deserve such happiness. Nastya was saying exactly the same about herself just now, although I no have idea what faults she possesses, as she is an angel, not an ordinary human being! She said that we were deeply indebted to God, and that we needed therefore to try to behave in as kindly a way as possible and to keep on doing good deeds. And if only you'd heard how passionately and beautifully she said it! My God, what a wonderful girl!"

He paused for a moment, overcome by feeling. Then he went on:

"We've decided, my dear boy, to be especially solicitous towards Foma, Mother and Tatyana Ivanovna. Oh, that Tatyana Ivanovna – such a special person, isn't she? Oh, I've behaved so badly to everyone! Including you, of course... But if anyone should dare to offend Tatyana Ivanovna, oh, then... Enough said, I think!... And we shall need to do something for Mizinchikov as well."

"Yes, Uncle, I've changed my opinion about Tatyana Ivanovna now. You can't help but respect her and feel sorry for her."

"Precisely, precisely!" my uncle agreed wholeheartedly. "You can't help but respect her! And then there's Korovkin, you know – you no doubt find him a laughable figure," he added, giving me an apprehensive look, "as we all did just now. Yet that could be unforgivable, couldn't it?... Could he not perhaps be the kindest, most wonderful man, but then fate... he endured a lot of misfortune... You're sceptical, but maybe that was precisely the case."

"I don't disagree, Uncle – you could well be right."

And I began passionately to advance the view that even the most damaged people can harbour the most elevated human sentiments; that the depth of the human soul is unfathomable; that, rather than despise such people, one should search them out and seek to resurrect them; that the generally accepted definition of goodness and morality is false, and so on and so forth – in short, I started enthusing about all kinds of things, including the Natural School,* and rounded off by quoting the poem

When from the darkness of delusion...*

My uncle was overjoyed.

"My dear boy, my dear boy!" he said, profoundly moved. "You understand me perfectly, and have said everything I myself wanted to express even better than I could. Yes, you're right! Good Lord! Why do men do wicked things? Why do *I* so often do wicked things, when it's such a pleasure and a joy to do good? There was Nastya saying exactly that a moment ago. But just look: what a glorious spot this is," he added, looking around him. "Nature at its finest! Such a picture! And just look at the size of that tree! You could hardly get your arms round its trunk! All that sap, and all those leaves! And the sunshine! The way the sky cleared and brightened up after that storm, and everything was washed clean!... You start to feel that even the trees have an understanding of what is happening to them, are able to feel and to enjoy life... It's possible, isn't it, eh? What do you think?"

"You could well be right, Uncle. In their own way, of course..."

"Well, yes, of course, in their own way... What a prodigious, prodigious creator!... But you yourself must have such wonderful memories of this garden, Seryozha! The way you used to play and run about here, when you were young! You know, I can still remember you as a small child," he added, looking at me with an indescribable expression of love and happiness. "The only thing you weren't allowed to do was to go near the pond on your own. And do you remember how, one evening, my dear beloved Katya called you to her and started cuddling you?... You had just been running around in the garden, and you were all flushed from the exertion – you had such fair, curly hair... She ran her hands in it and said: 'I'm so glad you took him in as an orphan.' Do you remember that?"

"Maybe, just a little, Uncle."

"It was evening, but the sun was still so strong in the sky, and I was sitting there in the corner smoking my pipe and watching you both... Do you know, Seryozha, I go into town every month to visit her grave," he added, lowering his voice, which was trembling slightly, with the hint of suppressed tears. "I was telling Nastya about that just now. She said that from now on we would both be able to go..."

My uncle fell silent, trying to keep his feelings in check.

At that moment Vidoplyasov appeared on the scene.

"Vidoplyasov!" my uncle exclaimed, collecting his thoughts. "Have you come from Foma Fomich?"

"No, sir, I have come on my own business, sir."

"Well, that's wonderful! We'll be able to find out what Korovkin's been up to... I asked him, you see, Seryozha, to keep an eye on Korovkin... So, what's the matter then, Vidoplyasov?"

"If I may make so bold, I would like to remind you, sir, that you promised me yesterday you would do all you could to intercede on my behalf with regard to the insults that I'm subjected to every day."

"I hope you're not going to harp on about your surname again, are you?" my uncle asked in alarm.

"But what am I to do, sir? Nothing but insults, sir..."

"Oh, Vidoplyasov, Vidoplyasov! What am I to do with you?" my uncle said dejectedly. "So, what insults are you talking about exactly? You're simply going out of your mind... you'll end up in a lunatic asylum!"

"Well, as far as my sanity is concerned, sir..." Vidoplyasov began to say.

"All right, all right," my uncle interrupted, "I wasn't attacking you, my dear fellow: I was just trying to help. But I repeat: what insults are you talking about? No doubt some nonsense?"

"They keep pestering me, sir."

"Who does?"

"They all do, but it's mostly Matryona, sir. She makes my life a misery, sir. They've clearly all got very definite opinions, sir; they've

265

all known me since I was a child. They say I'm like a foreigner, sir, largely because of the way I look, sir. And as a result, sir, they won't leave me alone now. Whenever I walk past them, sir, they call me all kinds of horrible names, sir – even snotty little lads who should be given a good thrashing join in, sir... They were shouting at me as I was on my way here just now, sir... I've had enough, sir. Help and protect me, sir!"

"Oh, Vidoplyasov!... But what kind of things are they actually shouting at you? No doubt some kind of nonsense which you can simply ignore."

"Some really indecent things, sir."

"Such as?"

"Too horrible to say, sir."

"Come on, tell me, for goodness' sake!"

"'Grishka the oaf's eaten a loaf', sir."

"Pouf, what an idiot! I thought it would be far worse than that! I'd simply pay no attention if I were you."

"I tried doing that, sir – they just carried on shouting, sir."

"Listen, Uncle," I said, "he's complaining he can't go on living in this house any longer. Why don't you send him away, just for a time at any rate, to Moscow, to live with that calligrapher? You said he used to live with a calligrapher, didn't you?"

"Yes, my dear boy, but that ended really badly."

"Why's that?"

"The man in question, sir," Vidoplyasov replied, "had the misfortune to misappropriate someone else's property, sir, for which, despite all his talent, he was sent to prison, sir, where he most definitely died, sir."

"All right, all right, Vidoplyasov – why don't you calm down a bit now, and I'll see what I can do to put things right?" my uncle said. "I promise! So, how about Korovkin? Still asleep?"

"Oh, no, sir. He's just this minute left, sir. That's what I came to tell you, sir."

"What do you mean, 'left'? What were you thinking of? How can you have let him leave like that?" my uncle exclaimed.

"Out of the goodness of my heart, sir; he cut a very sorry figure, sir. No sooner had he woken up than everything that had happened the previous evening came back to him, sir. He hit himself on the head and started yelling at the top of his voice, sir…"

"Really! Top of his voice!"

"It could be put more decorously, sir: he shouted a whole number of things, like 'How on earth can I look the fair sex in the face again now?' And then he added: 'I don't deserve to be a member of the human race!' – and many such expressions of self-pity, all in very choice words, sir."

"He's such a sensitive fellow! I told you, Sergei, didn't I?… But how could you have let him leave, Vidoplyasov, when I ordered you especially to keep an eye on him? Oh my God, my God!"

"Most of all because I felt really sorry for him, sir. He implored me not to say anything, sir. His coachman had fed and harnessed the horses himself, sir. With regard to the sum of money he was lent three days ago, he told me to convey his most profound thanks and to say that he would be repaying his debt by the earliest post, sir."

"What sum was that, Uncle?"

"He mentioned the sum of twenty-five silver roubles, sir," Vidoplyasov said.

"I lent him that amount at the station, my dear boy: he happened to be a little short of cash. Naturally, he'll return it to me by the first post… Oh my God, I'm so sorry! Should I send someone after him to get him back, Seryozha?"

"No, Uncle, best not to."

"I think you're right. You see, Seryozha, I'm no philosopher, of course, but I think there's far more good in every person than it seems at first. Take Korovkin, for instance: he couldn't bear the shame… But let's go and find Foma! We should have done that ages ago – he might be taking offence at our ingratitude and lack of attention… Let's go! Oh, Korovkin, Korovkin!"

* * *

This is the end of my novel. The lovers were united, and the spirit of goodness reigned supreme in the house, in the person of Foma Fomich. It might at this point be possible to append all kinds of pertinent reasons why this should be so, but all such reasons would be in essence totally unnecessary now. That is my opinion at least. I will confine myself instead merely to saying a few words about the subsequent fate of my heroes – which is now the common practice and without which, as is well known, no novel can be concluded.

The wedding of the "happy couple" took place six weeks after the events I have described here. It was a quiet family affair, without any pomp and ceremony, or even large numbers of guests. I accompanied Nastenka, while Mizinchikov was my uncle's best man. There were some guests, of course. But the most important and esteemed person present was, naturally, Foma Fomich. He was fêted and treated with great respect. But it so happened that, at one point, someone forgot to replenish his glass of champagne. A scene immediately ensued – reproaches, howling and shouting. Foma dashed off to his room, locked himself in, shouting that people despised him, that "upstarts" had now joined the family and that he was therefore a nobody, no more than a little puppy who should be kicked out of the house. My uncle was in despair; the general's lady suffered one of her usual fits... The wedding celebrations started to resemble a funeral. And my poor uncle and Nastya were subjected to seven more years of having to live in the same house as their benefactor, Foma Fomich. Right up to his death (Foma Fomich died last year), he grumbled, moped, postured, raged and cursed, but the feeling of reverence for him on the part of the "happy couple" not only did not diminish, but even grew day by day in direct proportion to his capricious behaviour. Yegor Ilyich and Nastenka were so happy together that they began to feel alarmed, thinking that God had granted them too much – that they didn't deserve such happiness, and that perhaps they would later have to pay the price by bearing the cross of suffering. Living in such a compliant household, Foma Fomich was naturally able to do just as he pleased. And what didn't he get up to in the course of those seven years! The resourcefulness of his overindulgent, idle and corrupt mind in devising, from an ethical point of view, the most refined Lucullan whims* was breathtaking. Three years after my uncle's wedding the general's lady died. The bereft Foma was devastated. People there still talk about the terrible state he was in to this day. When they were scattering earth on her grave, he abruptly jumped down into it, shouting that he wanted to be buried with her. For a full month he wasn't allowed to use knives or forks – and on one occasion four people had to open his mouth forcibly and remove a safety pin he was trying to swallow. One witness claimed that Foma Fomich could have swallowed this pin a thousand times in the course of the struggle, but never actually did so. But this speculative remark was immediately met with a markedly indignant response, and the person responsible was roundly condemned for his callousness and lack of taste. Nastya alone kept silent, with a slight smile on her lips, causing my uncle to give her a rather anxious look. In general, it should be pointed out that although Foma carried on swaggering about and behaving capriciously in my uncle's house as before, he no longer attacked and scolded my uncle in quite the despotic and insolent manner he had adopted previously. He would moan, weep, reproach, rebuke, ridicule as much as ever, but he stopped being quite so coarse and harsh towards my uncle – no more "Your Excellency" episodes, for example, thanks it seems to Nastenka's intervention. She almost imperceptibly forced Foma to concede on one matter and to submit on another. She disliked seeing her husband humiliated and insisted on getting her own way. Foma clearly grasped she had almost entirely got his measure. I say *almost*, because Nastenka too cherished Foma and even wholeheartedly supported her husband whenever he praised his mentor to the skies. She wanted to ensure that other people respected everything about her husband and would therefore openly endorse his attachment to Foma Fomich. And I am convinced that her heart of gold had forgotten about all the insulting things he had once said: she had forgiven Foma all that when he had blessed her union with my uncle – and, what's more, she almost certainly wholeheartedly embraced her husband's belief that it was wrong to expect too much of a one-time "martyr" and former clown, and that, on the contrary, his heart needed to be healed. Poor Nastenka was herself from the ranks of the *humiliated* – she never forgot that she, too, had suffered. It took only a month for Foma to quieten down and become meek and even amiable – but then, very unexpectedly, he started to become subject to other kinds of fits, falling into strange trances – much to everyone's alarm. The poor man would suddenly, for example, say something, even start laughing, and then, at that very moment, freeze in exactly the same position in which he'd been just before the attack. If, for example, he started laughing, he would remain like that, paralysed with a smile on his lips – and if he lifted, say, a fork, it would remain there in his upraised hand, in the air. Foma Fomich would eventually, of course, put the fork down, but he would have no feeling or recollection of ever having done so. He would sit there staring in front of him, even blinking his eyes, but without saying anything, or hearing and understanding anything that was said. He would sometimes stay like that for a whole hour. Quite naturally everyone was transfixed by fear, and went about the place on tiptoe, holding their breath and weeping. Eventually Foma would come to, feeling extremely exhausted and assuring everyone he'd heard and seen nothing at all that time. He somehow thought it necessary to posture and pose, and deliberately put himself through whole hours of torment, solely so that he could say later: "Look at me, my inner life is so much richer than yours!" Finally he started berating my uncle for his "never-ending insults and affronts" and moved out in order to live with Mr Bakhcheyev. After my uncle's wedding, Stepan Alexeyevich had had many quarrels with Foma Fomich (always ending, incidentally, with him asking for the latter's forgiveness), but now he fervently accepted the idea, welcomed Foma enthusiastically, fed him a splendid meal, at which he there and then proposed a formal severance of all ties with my uncle and even taking out a writ against him. There was somewhere a small joint plot of land whose ownership they had disputed, but which in fact had never caused a quarrel between them, as my uncle had always totally accepted the fact that it belonged to Stepan Alexeyevich. Without saying a word, Mr Bakhcheyev ordered a carriage to be harnessed, galloped into town, where he put in a claim for the piece of land to be formally made over to him, together with full compensation for any costs and damages, as just punishment for my uncle's arbitrary and rapacious behaviour. Meanwhile Foma, having by the very next day become bored at Mr Bakhcheyev's, forgave my uncle, who had arrived to offer his apologies, and set off back to Stepanchikovo. Mr Bakhcheyev's anger, on returning from town to find Foma no longer there, knew no bounds, but he turned up three days later at Stepanchikovo with an apology, asking for my uncle's forgiveness with tears in his eyes, and destroyed his claim. On the very same day, my uncle reconciled him with Foma Fomich, and Stepan Alexeyevich started following Foma around like a little dog once more, repeating after every word as before: "You're such a clever man, Foma, you're such a learned man, Foma!"

Foma Fomich is now resting in his grave, by the general's lady's side. The grave is marked by a magnificent marble headstone, engraved with lachrymose quotations and laudatory inscriptions. From time to time Yegor Ilyich and Nastenka visit the churchyard on one of their little walks to pay their respects to Foma's memory. They are still unable to speak about him other than in tones of deep emotion; they remember his every word, everything that he used to eat and loved to do. All his personal belongings are preserved and treasured. In their bereavement, my uncle and Nastya have grown even closer to one another. God has not blessed them with any children, something they find very distressing, but they do not dare complain. Sashenka has long since been married, to a wonderful young man. Ilyusha is studying in Moscow. Consequently my uncle and Nastya are now living on their own and continue to dote on each other. Their concern for one another is so strong that it has become almost pathological. Nastya is constantly on her knees, praying. If one of them were to die, then the other, I think, would hardly last a week. But may God grant them both a long life! They welcome all visitors to the house in a very cordial manner, and are always ready to share what they have with any who are less fortunate. Nastenka loves to read the lives of the saints, remarking with regret that kind deeds are still so rare in life, and how necessary it is to give everything to the poor and seek happiness in poverty. Had it not been for the need to provide for Ilyusha and Sashenka, my uncle would have long since done that, as he fully agrees with his wife on this. Praskovya Ilyinichna still lives with them, taking delight in meeting their every need; she is responsible for managing the household. Mr Bakhcheyev proposed to her soon after my uncle's wedding, but she flatly turned him down. As a result, it was assumed that her intention was to go to a nunnery, but this didn't happen either. One remarkable trait about Praskovya Ilyinichna's character is that she totally effaces herself with regard to those people she has come to love: she will remain almost invisible in their presence, looking them straight in the eye, putting up with all their possible whims, taking care of them and always being at their beck and call. Now, with the death of the general's lady, her mother, she sees it as her duty to stay by her brother's side and to fulfil Nastenka's every wish. Old Yezhevikin is still alive, and has recently begun to visit his daughter more and more often. At first he had greatly upset my uncle by almost totally keeping himself and his "teeny-weenies", as he called his children, away from Stepanchikovo. He ignored all my uncle's invitations, being not so much proud, as touchy and oversensitive. This self-centred sensitivity was sometimes so marked that it almost became pathological. He found the thought that he, a pauper, might be accepted in a wealthy house purely out of charity, that he might be seen as importunate and annoying, utterly humiliating – to the extent that sometimes he would even refuse to accept any help from Nastenka, agreeing to take only what was absolutely essential.

As for any help from my uncle, that was totally out of the question. Nastenka had been quite wrong when she had told me in the garden that time that her father acted the fool *for her benefit*. True, at the time he was really anxious to see that she got married, but if he forced himself to act the clown it was merely because he needed an outlet for his pent-up anger. The need to mock and to ridicule was absolutely essential to him – it was in his blood, so to speak. He projected, for example, a caricatured image of himself as the basest, most grovelling of flatterers – yet at the same time he made it perfectly clear that he was only doing it for show – and the more humiliating and obsequious the flattery, the more evident the biting nature of his mockery. That was his manner. He managed to find places for all his children in the very best Moscow and St Petersburg schools, but only once Nastenka had assured him that it would all be at her expense – paid out, that is, from the thirty thousand that had been given her by Tatyana Ivanovna. In fact, they had never actually taken that thirty thousand from Tatyana Ivanovna, but so as not to offend her or hurt her feelings, they had softened the blow by promising that, as soon as any unexpected family needs became apparent, they would turn to her for help. That is what they did: for the sake of appearances they negotiated two separate sizeable loans at different times. But then Tatyana Ivanovna died three years ago, meaning that the thirty thousand came to Nastya in any case. Poor Tatyana Ivanovna's death was very sudden. The whole family had gathered for a ball at a neighbouring landowner's house, and she had only just been able to attire herself in her ball gown and adorn her hair with a delightful wreath of white roses when she suddenly felt faint, sat down in a chair and died. She was buried wearing that very same wreath. Nastya was extremely upset. Tatyana Ivanovna had been very much loved by all the people in the house, and they had cared for her as if she had been a little child. She astonished everyone by leaving a remarkably sensible will: apart from Nastenka's thirty thousand, all the rest, nearly another thirty thousand in cash, was set aside for the education of poor orphan girls and for cash emoluments on graduation from their educational establishments. The year of her death also saw the marriage of Miss Perepelitsyna, who, on the death of the general's lady, had stayed on in my uncle's house, hoping to lick Tatyana Ivanovna's boots. In the interim period, the former clerk and landowner of the tiny little hamlet of Mishino, which had witnessed the episode involving Obnoskin, his mother and Tatyana Ivanovna, had become a widow. This inordinately litigious man had six children from his first wife. Suspecting that Miss Perepelitsyna must possess money, he began to approach her with offers of marriage, and she accepted with alacrity. But in fact she was as poor as a church mouse, having no more than three hundred silver roubles to her name – and even that had been given her by Nastenka for her wedding. Now the two of them do nothing but spend the whole day bickering with each other. She pulls his children by the hair and boxes their ears; she also has a go at her husband by scratching his face, or so people say, and is constantly reminding him that she is the daughter of a lieutenant colonel. Mizinchikov has also found his niche in life. Having sensibly abandoned any intentions he might once have had towards Tatyana Ivanovna, he embarked, a little tentatively at first, on the study of agriculture. My uncle recommended him to a wealthy count, a landowner with an estate of three thousand serfs some fifty miles from Stepanchikovo which he would occasionally visit. Noting that Mizinchikov was not without talent and taking my uncle's recommendation into account, this count offered him the position of estate manager, having dismissed the existing incumbent, a German who, notwithstanding his nation's much celebrated honesty, had swindled his master at every opportunity. In the space of five years the estate had changed beyond recognition: the peasants had prospered, projects hitherto considered impracticable were initiated, and the income from the estate had very nearly doubled – in short, the new manager excelled himself, and word of his business shrewdness soon spread throughout the province. Imagine the count's bewilderment and vexation when, after serving for five years, Mizinchikov, despite all kinds of pleas and promises that his salary would be increased, firmly resolved to give up his position and retire! The count thought he must have been lured away by another landowner from the neighbourhood or even another province. But then, much to everyone's astonishment, two months after Ivan Ivanovich Mizinchikov had retired, he suddenly became the owner of a most excellent estate of a hundred serfs situated at a distance of around twenty-five miles from the count's estate, which he had purchased from a former friend, a hussar who had become destitute having frittered away his money! He had then immediately mortgaged those hundred serfs and within a year acquired sixty more from the surrounding area. Now he himself is a landowner, with an estate second to none. People are astonished, wondering where on earth he had obtained the money – some merely shake their heads. But Ivan Ivanovich takes it all in his stride, feeling that it was perfectly within his rights. He has asked his sister to join him from Moscow – the very same sister who had given him her last three roubles to enable him to buy a pair of boots when he was setting off for Stepanchikovo. She is the sweetest soul imaginable, no longer in her prime – an unassuming, loving, well-educated but extraordinarily nervous woman. She had previously somehow managed to make a living in Moscow by acting as a companion to some wealthy patroness; now she worships her brother, manages his household, does whatever he asks of her, and is perfectly content. Her brother does not overindulge her, and in fact adopts quite a strict attitude towards her, but she doesn't seem to mind. Everyone at Stepanchikovo has become extremely fond of her, and people say that Mr Bakhcheyev is not indifferent to her. He would like to propose to her, but is afraid she might refuse him. With regard to Mr Bakhcheyev, however, it is my intention to say more about him in more detail in another story.

That then would seem to cover everybody... No, not quite! Gavrila is now an extremely old man and has totally forgotten how to speak French. Falaley has become an extremely competent coachman, and poor Vidoplyasov was sent to a lunatic asylum a long time ago – where, apparently, he has died... One of these days I will go to Stepanchikovo and make a point of asking my uncle about him.

Note on the Text

The text for this translation has been taken from F.M. Dostoevsky, *Polnoe sobranie sochinenii v tridtsati tomakh*, Vol. 3 (Leningrad: Nauka, 1972), pp. 5–168. We have also made use of the supplementary material in the same volume, pp. 496–516.

Notes

p. 10, *sundry Ivan Yakovleviches*: The reference is to Ivan Yakovlevich Koreisha (1783–1861), a *yurodivy*, or holy fool, who became famous in Moscow in the 1820s for his so-called prophetic powers. He was to be the model for the figure of the *yurodivy* Semyon Yakovlevich in Dostoevsky's novel *Devils* (1871–72).

p. 16, *such works as The Liberation of Moscow... etc. etc.*: Titles of adventure novels that had flooded the book market in the 1830s and 1840s.

p. 16, *such tasty dishes for the wit of Baron Brambeus*: "Baron Brambeus" was the pseudonym of the Polish-Russian journalist and writer Osip Ivanovich Senkovsky (1800–58), a prolific writer on a range of topics, and the editor of the journal *Library for Reading* (*Biblioteka dlya chteniya*), known for its lively and humorous style.

p. 17, *the Kievan caves*: The reference is to the Kyivo-Perchers'ka Lavra (the Kiev Monastery of the Caves), one of the holiest centres of Eastern Orthodox Christianity, dating to the early eleventh century.

p. 22, *Pushkin... "such a brave man that the Tsar loved him"*: A loose quotation from a passage in *Table Talk* (1834–36) by Alexander Pushkin.

p. 22, *Foma Fomich..."your shrewd Russian peasant"*: Dostoevsky is here parodying Nikolai Gogol (1809–51), who, in his 'Selected Passages from Correspondence with Friends' (1847), recommends to landowners that they address their peasants using just such language.

p. 22, *the Kazan fire*: The city of Kazan, the capital of Tatarstan, suffered a major fire in 1842.

p. 23, *Mais répondez donc*: "Please do reply" (French).

p. 24, *Mais, mon fils...*: "But, my son..." (French).

p. 39, *he hasn't got... even the most miserable one*: In 1722 Peter the Great instituted a Table of Ranks (see p. x), a hierarchical list of fourteen positions and ranks in the military, government and court of Imperial Russia.

p. 43, *cochon*: "Pig" (French).

p. 55, *Frol Silin*: 'Frol Silin, a Virtuous Man' was a short story by the Russian writer, historian and critic Nikolai Karamzin (1766–1826).

p. 60, *like some Talleyrand, so to speak*: A reference to the French statesman and diplomat Charles-Maurice de Talleyrand-Périgord (1754–1838), the chief French negotiator at the Congress of Vienna.

p. 70, *voltigeur*: "Acrobat" (French).

p. 71, *The Simpleton*: The debut novel of the Russian writer Alexei Pisemsky (1821–81), published in 1850.

p. 82, *I have as many children as the Kholmsky family!*: The reference is to the five-volume novel *The Kholmsky Family* (1832) by the Russian writer and politician Dmitry Begichev (1786–1855). Reflecting the world view of the Russian gentry, the novel was regarded as an antecedent of Tolstoy's *War and Peace*.

p. 93, *the Kamarinskaya*: A famous traditional Russian folk dance and song, also referred to as 'The Peasant from Kamarin'. It was popularized in the eponymous overture by the Russian composer Mikhail Glinka (1804–57). The word "Kamarinskaya" is thought to have derived from Kamarichi, a district of the province of Oryol.

p. 95, *a holy fool*: See note to p. 10.

p. 96, *Donnez-moi mon mouchoir*: "Give me my handkerchief" (French).

p. 97, *just like Martin with soap*: An expression picked up by Dostoevsky during his time in exile in Siberia during the 1850s.

p. 101, *The band would consist... a tambourine*: The composition of this band is reminiscent of the one Dostoevsky heard while he was in prison in Siberia, and described by him in *The House of the Dead*.

p. 105, *à l'enfant*: "Like a child's" (French).

NOTES

p. 106, *Only a society idiot could conceive of such senseless niceties*:
Dostoevsky has taken this phrase directly from a letter by Nikolai
Gogol on the subject of *Dead Souls*.

p. 109, *Borozdnas*: Ivan Petrovich Borozdna (1804–58) was a minor
Russian poet.

p. 111, *I respect the immortal Karamzin… for his Frol Silin*: Nikolai
Karamzin's eleven-volume *History of the Russian State* was writ-
ten between 1816 and 1824; his short historical novel *Martha the
Mayoress* was published in 1802; his historical work *Memoir on
Ancient and Modern Russia* was written in 1811. For *Frol Silin*, see
note to p. 55.

p. 112, *The Mysteries of Brussels*: A poor imitation by Édouard Suau
de Varennes (1809–72) of the novel *Les mystères de Paris* by Eugène
Sue (1804–57). It appeared in a Russian translation in 1847.

p. 112, *the 'Scribe'*: The pen name of the writer and critic Alexander
Druzhinin (1824–64), who wrote articles in the journal the
Contemporary (*Sovremennik*), representing the views of an enlight-
ened country landowner.

p. 114, *Krasnogorsk*: A town situated some fifteen miles from Moscow.

p. 115, *active state councillor*: The fourth class in the Table of Ranks
(see p. x).

p. 119, *like Orpheus… singing*: The mythical poet and musician
Orpheus was said to be able to charm living and inanimate things
with his music.

p. 119, *Monsieur Chematon*: "Mr Useless", "Mr Good-for Nothing"
(from the French *chômer*, "to idle, loaf about").

p. 119, *that monster Pugachev*: Yemelyan Pugachev (1742–75), the leader
of a major popular uprising in the region east of the River Volga and
south of the Ural Mountains. He was eventually captured, sent to
Moscow and executed.

p. 121, *Journal des débats*: The *Journal des débats* ("Journal of
Debates") was a French political newspaper founded in 1789, with a
large literary section.

p. 134, *fifteen thousand, in silver roubles*: A very large sum, worth more
than £200,000 in today's money.

p. 144, *Mercadante*: The Italian opera composer Saverio Mercadante (1795–1870).

p. 147, *"my gab"*: Another expression picked up by Dostoevsky during his time in exile in Siberia.

p. 152, *Gretna Green*: A Scottish town just north of the border with England which had become a popular destination for eloping couples due to Scotland's exemption from the Clandestine Marriages Act of 1753, according to which parental consent was required for marriages between those under the age of twenty-one.

p. 153, *became a veritable Burtsov*: Alexei Petrovich Burtsov (d. 1813) was a Russian officer of the hussars renowned for his excessive drinking bouts and generally licentious behaviour.

p. 156, *the Dormition Fast... possible then*: According to the Orthodox tradition, a period of fasting takes place during the first two weeks of August. Weddings are not permitted to be held during this period.

p. 162, *La nuit porte conseil*: "The night makes you wiser" (French) – the equivalent of the idiomatic English notion of "sleeping on" a problem.

p. 166, *en grand*: "In grand style" (French).

p. 167, *Brambeus, for example*: See second note to p. 16.

p. 168, *'Bolvanov'*: "Bolvan" is the Russian for "blockhead", "dimwit".

p. 168, *represent myself... my name*: The Russian for "dancer" is *"tantsor"*.

p. 189, *our blessed Fevronia... before dawn*: St Fevronia (*c.*1175–1228) was the wife of St Peter, Prince of Murom (*c.*1167–1228). The couple are among the most venerated saints in the Orthodox Church. According to a sixteenth-century legend ('The Tale of Peter and Fevronia'), Fevronia, a wise young maiden who has become the princess consort of Murom, is asked to leave by the boyars, who are unhappy to have a woman of low origins as their ruler.

p. 204, *comment vous portez-vous?*: "How are you doing?" (French). An absurd use of the language here, typical of Bakhcheyev.

p. 213, *uncut*: Unopened (that is, with pages still attached along the top and fore-edge – a result of the traditional method of printing several pages on a single sheet and then folding and binding them).

p. 213, *a Paul de Kock novel*: Paul de Kock (1793–1871) was a prolific and popular French writer of sentimental stories.

p. 216, *something from Lomonosov, perhaps?*: The Russian polymath, scientist and writer Mikhail Lomonosov (1711–65), author of more than twenty solemn ceremonial odes.

p. 216, *'The Siege of Pamba'*: The poem 'The Siege of Pamba' was written by "Kozma Prutkov" and published in the satirical supplement to *Sovremennik* in 1854. Kozma Prutkov was the collective pen name of the writers Alexei Tolstoy (1817–75) and his cousins Alexei (1821–1908), Alexander (1826–96) and Vladimir (1830–94) Zhemchuzhnikov during the 1850s. Under this name they published aphorisms and fables, together with humorous and nonsense verse.

p. 219, *in Radcliffe's novels*: Ann Radcliffe (1764–1823) was an English novelist and pioneer of Gothic fiction. Her best-known work is *The Mysteries of Udolpho* (1794).

p. 221, *Voltaireans*: Followers of the French philosopher and writer Voltaire (1694–1778), famous for his wit and his anticlericalism, and an advocate of freedom of speech.

p. 222, *Notes of the Fatherland*: *Otechestvenniye Zapiski*, a Russian literary journal published in St Petersburg from 1818 to 1884.

p. 222, *the significance of words such as… for example*: Dostoevsky is here parodying the ideas put forward in the article 'The Pagano-Religious Significance of the Slav's Hut' by the Russian Slavist, folklorist and ethnographer Alexander Afanasyev (1826–71).

p. 226, *'If you want… conquer yourself!'*: A variant of the famous Latin saying "*Vincit qui se vincit*" ("He conquers who conquers himself").

p. 243, *Petrarch, who once said that 'innocence… from disaster'*: The quotation appears to be either fictitious or misattributed.

p. 243, *the famous ballad*: A reference to a popular sentimental ballad of the time, 'Dark Colours, Gloomy Colours'.

p. 243, *With reference to Shakespeare once again… lurked a crocodile*: This image should be attributed not to Shakespeare, but to the French diplomat and writer François-René de Chateaubriand (1768–1848), who wrote in his novella *Atala* (1801): "That heart which is most apparently serene is like the natural well in the Alachua savannah: on the surface it is calm and pure, but peer into its depths, and you will see a huge alligator, which feeds in its waters."

p. 252, *That was said, I believe, by Gogol*: No exact quotation can be found in Gogol's works.

p. 253, *Like Diogenes with his lantern*: A reference to the ancient Greek Cynic philosopher Diogenes (*c.*404–323 BC). He was once observed walking through the streets at midday carrying a lighted lantern. He told people who asked what he was doing that he was "looking for a human being".

p. 254, *Asmodeus*: Asmodeus, or Ashmedai, the prince of demons and of hell in Judaeo-Islamic lore.

p. 256, *pantalons impossibles*: "An outrageous pair of trousers" (French).

p. 256, *Attendez*: "Wait" (French).

p. 261, *Cleitus*: Cleitus the Black (375–328 BC) was an officer in the Macedonian army who saved Alexander the Great's life at the battle of Granicus (334 BC), but who was killed by him in a drunken quarrel six years later.

p. 264, *the Natural School*: The literary movement founded by the critic Vissarion Belinsky (1811–48), which insisted that literature should focus on social problems.

p. 264, *When from the darkness of delusion…*: An 1845 poem by Nikolai Nekrasov (1821–78). Its theme, the rehabilitation of a fallen creature, was close to Dostoevsky's heart.

p. 269, *the most refined Lucullan whims*: Lucius Licinius Lucullus (*c.*117–56 BC) was famous for his wealth and his fondness for a luxurious life of self-indulgence.

Extra Material

on

Fyodor Dostoevsky's

*The Village of Stepanchikovo
and Its Inhabitants*

Fyodor Dostoevsky's Life

The family name Dostoevsky was derived from the village
Dostoev in the Minsk region. It was granted by the Prince of
Pinsk in perpetuity to the boyar Danil Ivanovich Rtishchev
in 1506 for services rendered. The city of Pinsk goes
back to the eleventh century and forms the heartland of
Belorussia. No fewer than four nationalities – Belorussian,
Russian, Ukrainian and Polish – go into the composition of
the Dostoevsky family tree, and the end result is about as
multinational as was possible at the time. The Rtishchevs
were Russian, the setting was Belorussian, the suffix "-sky"
is predominantly Polish, and over the years some of the
Dostoevskys moved and settled in the Ukraine, while others,
like Fyodor Mikhailovich's branch, ended up in Moscow.
Dostoevsky's father, Mikhail Andreyevich (1789–1839), was
the son of a Ukrainian Uniate priest, Andrei Dostoevsky.
Fyodor Mikhailovich himself, of course, never considered
himself anything other than Russian. The eminent Dostoevsky scholar, Ludmila Saraskina, was recently asked if the
writer was not of Polish blood, and she responded: "The
Dostoevsky lineage presents a fascinating and unusual
mixture of nationalities: in a family where the father was
Lithuanian, the mother Ukrainian, there was a cult of Russian
literature and history, the cult of reading. The atmosphere
was one of devotion to the spoken word, and it is precisely
this which above all else shaped the author's creative make-
up. Hence, Dostoevsky's Russianness is a wholly cultural
rather than ethnic phenomenon." The concept "Lithuanian"
must, of course, be understood in the traditional sense as in
the Grand Duchy of Lithuania, which has precious little to
do with modern Lithuania.

Birth and
Early Years

Fyodor Mikhailovich Dostoevsky was born in Moscow on 30th October 1821. In 1831, his father had bought a small estate, Darovoye, and two years later, the neighbouring Chermoshnya, which would acquire lasting fame as Chermashnya in the violent murder plot of Karamazov senior in *The Karamazov Brothers*. Speaking of Darovoye, Dostoevsky confessed: "This small, insignificant place left in me the deepest and most memorable impression for life." Fyodor was the second in a family of six siblings. His mother, Maria Fyodorovna (née Nechayeva, 1800–37), a religious-minded woman, came from a merchant family. She taught him to read from an edition of *One Hundred and Four Old and New Testament Stories*, and within the family circle there were readings from Karamzin's *The History of the Russian State*, as well as from the works of Derzhavin, Zhukovsky and Pushkin. Dostoevsky often sought the company of peasants, and his discussions with them proved to be a rich source of material for his future compositions.

Education

In 1832 Dostoevsky and his brother Mikhail were educated at home by visiting tutors, and from 1833 they were placed in various boarding schools. Dostoevsky found the atmosphere in these establishments oppressive and uncongenial, and his only solace was extensive and intensive reading. From late 1834 to early 1837 the two brothers attended one of Moscow's best private boarding schools, run by the Czech-born Leonty Ivanovich Chermak, a man of little or no education, but a brilliant, intuitive pedagogue and a humane and understanding father figure. State-run schools, on the other hand, had an overall unflattering reputation for frequent application of the disciplinary rod and staple bad food. The teacher of Russian, Nikolai Ivanovich Bilevich, turned out to be something of a role model and allegedly served as the prototype for Nikolai Semyonovich in *The Adolescent* (variously known as *A Raw Youth* and *An Accidental Family*), whom the hero Arkady picked at random as an appraiser of his autobiographical notes. "At long last I decided to seek someone's counsel. Having cast around, I chose this gentleman with purposeful deliberation. Nikolai Semyonovich was my former tutor in Moscow, and Marya Ivanovna's husband..." (*The Adolescent*, penultimate chapter.)

Parents' Death

By all accounts Dostoevsky's father, Mikhail Andreyevich, was an upstanding, hard-working family man – his one failing, however, being his touchy, short temper. After the death of his

286

wife in 1837, he retired and settled in Darovoye, where he died on 6th June 1839. Officially the cause of death was recorded as apoplexy, but by all popular accounts he perished at the hands of his peasants, forming a possible clue to the origins of the plot involving the mysterious death of the head of the family in *The Karamazov Brothers*. The loss of his mother in 1837 coincided with the shattering news of Pushkin's fatal duel, which Dostoevsky perceived as a personal bereavement too. Dostoevsky's adulation of Pushkin continued all his life, and reached its apotheosis in 1880, only months before his own death.

In May 1837 he enrolled at the Koronad Filippovich Kosto- *Central Military* marov cramming institute, prior to applying to the Central *Engineering Academy* Military Engineering Academy, where he got to know the highly colourful Ivan Nikolayevich Shidlovsky, subsequently a poet and church historian. Originally the name of the principal character in *The Idiot* was to be Shidlovsky, and when responding to Vladimir Solovyev's request in 1873 for some biographical material for an article, Dostoevsky enjoined him to mention his friend. "Make sure you mention him in your article. It does not matter that no one knows of him and that he has not left behind a literary legacy. I beg you, my dear chap, mention him – he was a *major* figure in my life, and deserves that his name should live on." Dostoevsky attended the Engineering Academy from January 1838; unfortunately his brother Mikhail had failed to qualify for entry. The gruelling, soul-destroying military regime was to a large extent relieved by the company of close and devoted friends, the writer Dmitry Vasilyevich Grigorovich being one of them. It was he who first noted Dostoevsky's reticence and unsociability, and who later recorded the tumultuous effect upon Dostoevsky of his rift with Belinsky and his circle, particularly with Ivan Turgenev.

The vast bulk of information on Dostoevsky's early life comes from the *Reminiscences* of his younger brother Andrei. He was an architect, and also a meticulously scrupulous and tidy worker in everything he undertook. His *Reminiscences* are well executed, detailed and informative. Quaintly, and for an architect not inappropriately, the book is conceived as a mansion, and the chapters are termed *rooms*.

Dostoevsky's first literary projects were conceived at the *Early Literary* Engineering Academy. In 1841, at a soirée organized by his *Works* brother Mikhail, Dostoevsky read out excerpts from some of his dramatic compositions – *Mary Stuart* and *Boris Godunov* – none of which have survived. On graduation, and having served just under a year in the St Petersburg Engineering Corps, he resigned with the rank of senior lieutenant (поручик) to devote himself entirely to literature.

His first published work was a translation of Balzac's *Eugénie Grandet*, which appeared in 1844. In the winter of the same year he started writing the epistolary novel *Poor People*. Dmitry Grigorovich and the poet Nikolai Nekrasov were so taken with it that they spent the night reading it in manuscript. They then headed for Belinsky's and on the doorstep announced, "We've a new Gogol!" to which Belinsky retorted, "Gogols sprout like mushrooms with you!" But having read the work, his enthusiasm knew no bounds: "The novel reveals such profundities of characters and of life in Russia as no one had ever dreamt of before." It was accepted for publication by the *St Petersburg Anthology*, edited by Nekrasov. The praise lavished on the novel obviously went to Dostoevsky's head, because he requested that each page should have a black border to make the work stand out; the astonished Nekrasov refused point blank, and it was published without the borders. It was an overnight success.

At the end of 1845 at a soirée at Belinsky's, Dostoevsky read out selected passages from *The Double*. Belinsky was quite interested at first, but later expressed his disapproval. This marked the beginning of the rift between the two men. Dostoevsky took it very badly and, stressed as he was, the very first symptoms of epilepsy, which were to plague him for the rest of his life, began to manifest themselves.

Arrest and Sentencing   In spring 1847 Dostoevsky began to attend (on a far from regular basis) the Friday meetings of the revolutionary and utopian socialist Mikhail Petrashevsky. The discussions, which included literary themes, bore on the whole a political and sociological slant – the emancipation of the serfs, judicial and censorship reforms, French socialist manifestos and Belinsky's banned letter to Gogol were typical subjects of debate. In 1848 Dostoevsky joined a special secret society, organized by the most radical member of the Petrashevsky Circle, one Nikolai Speshnev, by all accounts a colourful and demonic figure, whom Dostoevsky imagined to be his Mephistopheles. The society's goal was to organize an insurrection in Russia. On the morning of 23rd April 1849, the author, together with other members of the group, was arrested and confined in the Peter and Paul Fortress. Many of them, including Speshnev, found themselves depicted twenty-three years later in the pages of *Devils*.

After eight months in the fortress, where Dostoevsky wrote his story *The Little Hero*, he was found guilty of "plotting to subvert public order" and was initially sentenced to death by firing squad, which was at the last moment commuted to *mort civile*, amounting to four years of hard labour and subsequent conscription into the army. His experiences as a convict in the Omsk Fortress are poignantly recorded in *The House of the Dead* (1860–62) and the theme of execution itself is treated in some detail in *The Idiot*.

After January 1854 Dostoevsky served as a private in Semipalatinsk, eastern Kazakhstan. Even before his departure for the army, he wrote to Natalya Dmitrievna Fonvizina, the wife of one of the Decembrists (members of the ill-fated uprising in December 1825):

> I seem to be in some kind of an expectation of something; I can't help feeling I'm ill, and that soon, very soon something decisive will happen. I feel that I'm approaching a turning point in my life, that I've reached a state of maturity and am on the verge of something peaceful, blithe – perhaps awesome – but certainly inevitable.

These were prophetic words. Almost immediately on arrival in Semipalatinsk he made the acquaintance of a minor clerk, Alexander Ivanovich Isayev, an impoverished customs-and-excise officer and alcoholic, and his wife, Maria Dmitrievna. *Maria Dmitrievna* Mrs Isayeva was then twenty-nine years old. Dostoevsky fell head over heels for her, although his love was not always requited and she considered him to be "a man with no future". He was no doubt attracted by what he perceived to be her vulnerability and spiritual defencelessness. Dostoevsky's own life was not the happiest, and the two revelled in bouts of self-pity. And then came a terrible blow: Isayev was transferred to Kuznetsk, some six hundred versts from Semipalatinsk. Dostoevsky took the parting indescribably badly.

In August 1855 Maria Dmitrievna informed Dostoevsky that *Marriage Proposals* her husband had passed away. She was in dire straits – alone, without means, in an unfamiliar town, without relatives or friends to help her. Dostoevsky proposed to her immediately, but Maria Dmitrievna demurred. He realized, of course, that it was his own lowly status that was at the root of the problem. However, with the death of Nicholas I and the enthronement of Alexander II, there was hope in the improvement of the fate of the Petrashevsky Circle convicts. In December 1855 he was made a warrant officer; this elated him so much that in early 1856 he wrote to his brother of his intention to tie the knot: "I've taken my decision and, should the ground collapse under me, I'll go through with it... without that, which for me is now the main thing in life, life itself is valueless..."

Dostoevsky was so desperately short of money that he implored his brother for a loan of 100 roubles or more, or as much as he could afford. Begging for money was to become a way of life for Dostoevsky. Almost in desperation, he made a daring move. Having obtained official leave to go to Barnaul, he took a secret trip to Kuznetsk. But, to his surprise, instead of being greeted with love and affection, he found himself in a situation such as is depicted in *White Nights* and *Humiliated and Insulted*. Maria Dmitrievna flung her arms round his neck and, crying bitterly and with passionate kisses, confessed that she had fallen in love with the schoolteacher Nikolai Borisovich Vergunov and was intending to get married to him. Dostoevsky listened in silence to what she had to say, and then sat down with her to discuss her prospective marriage to a man who had even less money than he, but had two incontestable advantages – he was young and handsome. Maria Dmitrievna insisted the two rivals should meet and, like the Dreamer in *White Nights* and Ivan Petrovich in *Humiliated and Insulted*, Dostoevsky decided to sacrifice his own love for the sake of others. This fairly bowled Maria Dmitrievna over: Dostoevsky wrote to Wrangel, quoting her words to him: "'Don't cry, don't be sad, nothing has yet been decided. You and I, and there's no one else.' These were positively her words. I spent two days in bliss and suffering! At the end of the second day I left full of hope..."

But he had scarcely returned to Semipalatinsk when Maria Dmitrievna wrote to him that she was "sad and in tears" and loved Vergunov more than him. Dostoevsky was again absolutely distraught, but still found it in him to continue to stand by the love of his life. He would seek to obtain for her an assistance grant on the basis of her deceased husband's government service record, try to enrol her son in the cadet corps and even assist Vergunov in securing a better position.

In those turbulent times, when Dostoevsky imagined he had lost Maria Dmitrievna for ever, there was suddenly new hope. On 1st October 1856 he was promoted to officer, and his dream of being able to return to St Petersburg became a distinct reality. It is unlikely that this was the only cause – Maria Dmitrievna had probably always loved him after a fashion, though obviously never as strongly as he loved her – but her resistance to him suddenly broke down to the extent that Vergunov simply melted into the background and was heard of no more. Later that month Dostoevsky went to Kuznetsk, sought and obtained Maria Dmitrievna's hand and was married to her on 6th February 1857. *Marriage to Maria and Return to St Petersburg*

His happiness knew no bounds, but a major blow was just round the corner. On their way back to Semipalatinsk, when the newly-weds had stopped in Barnaul, Dostoevsky, as a result of all the emotional upheaval, had a severe epileptic fit. This had a shattering effect on Maria Dmitrievna. The sight of her husband staring wildly ahead, foaming at the mouth and kicking convulsively on the floor must have been disconcerting and frightening in the extreme. She burst into tears and began to reproach him for concealing his ailment. He was actually innocent; he had been convinced that what he suffered from were ordinary nervous attacks, not epilepsy – at least that's what doctors had told him previously. All the same, he hadn't told her even that much.

They settled in St Petersburg, but the local climate was too uncongenial for her, and she moved to Tver. From then on they saw each other only sporadically, moving, as they did, from town to town and from flat to flat. On 7th June 1862 he made his first trip abroad – alone. He felt he had his own life to lead. Maria Dmitrievna had little to do with it, and she was fast approaching death as she had contracted tuberculosis.

Dostoevsky returned to Russia in September. At the beginning of November 1863 the couple settled in Moscow. Maria Dmitrievna was fighting for her life, but on her deathbed she was getting more and more irritable and demanding. Dostoevsky looked after her assiduously, yet at the same time he was riveted to his writing desk. Her suffering and moodiness are reflected in the description of Marmeladov's wife in *Crime and Punishment* and of Ippolit in *The Idiot*. Maria Dmitrievna died on 14th April 1864. *Maria's Death*

On his return from Siberia in 1859 Dostoevsky published *Uncle's Dream* and *The Village of Stepanchikovo*, neither of which met with much success. *The House of the Dead* began its life in 1860 in the daily newspaper *The Russian World* (*Русский мир*), but only the introduction and the first chapter were printed, for Dostoevsky had to keep a wary eye on the censor, as he had pointed out to his brother Mikhail in a letter in 1859: "It could all turn out nasty... If they ban it, it can all be broken up into separate articles and published in journals serially... but that would be a calamity!" Chapters 2–4 were published in subsequent issues in 1861, but it was serialized no further in *The Russian World*. With some notable alterations, the early chapters were reprinted in the 1861 April issue of *Time* (*Время*), a journal he founded jointly with his brother, and the concluding chapter of Part II came out in May 1862. Certain passages, deemed subversive, were excised on the grounds that "morally regressive individuals, who are held back from crime by the severity of punishment alone, may be misled by the *Notes* to form a distorted impression as to the lack of efficacy of the legally prescribed sanctions" (Baron N.V. Medem, Chairman of the St Petersburg Board of Censors.) *Humiliated and Insulted* was also serialized in *Time* during 1861, and *Notes from Underground* in *Epoch* (*Эпоха*), the second journal that the Dostoevsky brothers had founded in 1864.

In 1866 Dostoevsky was in dire financial straits and, in what could have been a moment of carelessness, but more likely for fear of being thrown into a debtors' jail, he concluded one of the most dishonest and unfavourable contracts in recorded literary history. The other contracting party was the publisher Fyodor Timofeyevich Stellovsky, by all accounts a ruthless and unprincipled money-grubber. According to the terms of the contract Dostoevsky had to deliver a brand-new novel by 1st November 1866, or lose all rights in all his subsequent compositions for a period of the next nine years. Dostoevsky was to receive three thousand roubles, but contingently on the new novel being completed and delivered within the prescribed period. Over half of this money was already spoken for; it was needed for the discharge of promissory notes, the irony being that most of these – unbeknown to Dostoevsky – were already in Stellovsky's hands. The wily Stellovsky knew perfectly well that Dostoevsky was a sick man and that the epileptic attacks, which occurred on a regular basis, made him unfit for work for days on end; besides, he was also aware that Dostoevsky was committed to completing *Crime and Punishment* and would be unable to write two novels simultaneously. It was very much in Stellovsky's interests that the contract was not fulfilled.

Right up to the end of September Dostoevsky worked flat out on *Crime and Punishment*. This was a novel on which many of his hopes were pinned. It was to be a heavyweight: most of the fiction he had written previously was shot through with humour and had a tongue-in-cheek quality about it, but for whatever reason his best efforts had failed to find wide acceptance, let alone a demand for more either from the public or the critics. He was not giving his readers what they wanted, so *Crime and Punishment* was to change all that. But then came the end of September, and not a word of the contractual novel had yet been penned. The significance of this suddenly hit him. The as yet non-existent – and very likely to remain such – novel was, not inappropriately, to be called *The Gambler*. His friend, the writer Alexander Milyukov, on hearing the sad story, suggested that a few of his fellow writers should pool their efforts and write a chapter or so each, the more so since Dostoevsky had already sketched out a plan; or, if he didn't wish to sacrifice that plan and wanted to keep it for his own use later, they'd work out something new themselves.

Crime and Punishment and The Gambler

Dostoevsky declined, saying that he wouldn't put his name under anything he hadn't written himself. Milyukov then came up with the idea of using a stenographer. It was thus that the twenty-year-old Anna Grigoryevna Snitkina, who by chance had just recently completed a course in the new-fangled (for Russia, at all events) skill of stenography, came on the scene. They started work on 4th October 1866, and on 30th October the manuscript was ready for delivery, the deadline being midnight.

But Stellovsky had one more dastardly trick up his sleeve. He arranged to be out of his office on the day, and there was no one to receive the manuscript. On legal advice, they found out that it would be enough for the script to be lodged at a police station and signed for by a senior officer. Dostoevsky and Snitkina rushed to a police station, and luckily found an officer – usually, come the afternoon, senior officers were in the habit of disappearing without notice. Even so it was not till after 10 p.m. that they obtained the sought-after receipt. And so the novel – a manic, surcharged paean to reckless abandon and desperation – was finished from scratch in twenty-six days flat.

Marriage to Anna Snitkina

Dostoevsky married Anna Snitkina, twenty-five years his junior, on 15th February 1867. Exactly two months after their wedding, they both went abroad. Anna had taken charge of Dostoevsky's business affairs efficiently, and by and large successfully. She was proving herself indispensable on a second major front, making up for Dostoevsky's inadequacy in dealing with day-to-day practical affairs. But there was a limit even to her frugality, acumen and, above all, the positive influence she could exercise, when she encountered Dostoevsky's incurable penchant for gambling. This had manifested itself during his previous European tour with his mistress Apollinaria Suslova, immortalized as the enigmatic tease in *The Gambler*, whose story Anna was herself ironically obliged to set down on paper from the lips of her future husband.

While gambling with the devil-may-care Apollinaria had a romantic edge to it, indulging the habit on honeymoon with his level-headed, home-making wife Anna – impecunious as they were – became a cruel and pathetic, not to say sordid, human tragedy. He would find himself down to the last penny, dashing over to the tables, staking that very penny, losing it, running back home to pawn his cufflinks, his last remaining possessions, his wedding ring, his winter overcoat, his young wife's lace cloak, on his knees in front of her, beating his breast, with tears in his eyes accusing himself and imploring for forgiveness, and yet begging for just another louis or two from their common purse to go and break even. And it was in these circumstances, his frame continually convulsed by epilepsy, constantly on the move across Europe – like a veritable Flying Dutchman, flitting from one foreign resort to another – that he deliberated over, planned and eventually completed *The Idiot*. Not least of his handicaps was separation from Russia and its living language, which he himself considered essential in maintaining the momentum of his creative process.

Children

On 5th March 1868 the couple experienced their first joys of parenthood with the birth of their daughter Sofya, but two months later followed the devastating blow of the infant's death on 24th May. On 26th September 1869 their second daughter Lyubov was born (*d*.1926). The Dostoevskys had two more children: Fyodor, born 16th July 1871 (*d*.1922), and

Alexei, born 10th August 1875, who died before he reached the age of three on 16th May 1878.

On their return from abroad to St Petersburg the Dostoevskys were beset by creditors for debts incurred before their departure. Fortunately the plucky and quick-witted Anna was able to fight them off, and the author went on to embark upon and complete the last four of his great works more or less undisturbed. *Devils* was published in 1871; *The Diary of a Writer* was begun in 1876 and, at intervals, continued till 1881; *The Adolescent* came out in 1875, followed by *The Karamazov Brothers* in 1880.

On 8th June 1880 Dostoevsky delivered his famous speech at the unveiling of the Pushkin memorial in Moscow, organized by the Society of the Friends of Russian Letters. It had a most electrifying effect upon his audience, and has been subsequently referred to as "well nigh the most famous speech in Russian history". Tolstoy declared it a farce, and point-blank refused to attend. It therefore fell to the two remaining pillars of Russian literature, the arch rivals Dostoevsky and Turgenev – who had had it in for each other ever since they first met some thirty years previously – to occupy the centre stage. *[margin: Address at the Pushkin Memorial and Rivalry with Turgenev]*

Of the two, his imposing, patrician physical presence aside, it was Turgenev who, by dint of his reputation abroad, coupled with his progressive, enlightened Western ideology at home, felt that precedence to occupy the throne of Russian literature should be accorded to him, rather than to the reactionary, stick-in-the-mud Slavophile Dostoevsky. Moreover the replies to such RSVP messages as had been received from Western celebrities, notably Victor Hugo, Berthold Auerbach and Alfred Lord Tennyson, were all addressed to Turgenev – doubtless confirming him as the only Russian writer known abroad – though it later transpired that all three prospective guests from abroad had politely declined the honour to attend.

Still, home-grown honours were not to be spurned, and the two writers, in true prize-fighter fashion, retired to their respective camps to prepare and hone their speeches – Turgenev to his magnificent country seat Spasskoye-Lutovinovo, Dostoevsky to his modest house in Staraya Russa.

The festivities were spread over two days. Turgenev spoke on 7th June, Dostoevsky on the 8th. Of all the numerous speakers on the occasion, it was only Turgenev's and, above all, Dostoevsky's performances that have gone down in history. Turgenev, ever the aristocrat, did not indulge in any personal gibes in his speech. But what he did, as far as Dostoevsky was concerned, was equally hurtful. Having given Pushkin his rightful due, he permitted himself to express some doubt as to whether the author of *Eugene Onegin* might be regarded as a truly national and consequently world poet such as Homer, Shakespeare and Goethe. This question, Turgenev remarked, "we shall leave open by and by for now". Subsequently, in his letter home to his wife, Dostoevsky remarked that Turgenev had humiliated Pushkin by depriving him of the title of national poet.

Dostoevsky himself was not present at this speech – he had been preparing his own. His famous speech was given the next day. He delivered an electrifying performance, passionately arguing for the greatness of Pushkin as *the* national writer. He claimed that Pushkin was not only an independent literary genius, but a prophet who marked the beginning of Russian self-consciousness and provided the paramount illustration of the archetypal Russian citizen as a wanderer and sufferer in his own land. Dostoevsky's speech culminated in a plea for universal brotherhood and was met with rapturous applause.

That evening, Anna Grigoryevna records in her *Reminiscences*, after Dostoevsky returned to his hotel late at night, utterly exhausted but happy, he took a short nap and then went out to catch a cab to the Pushkin Memorial. It was a warm June night. He placed a huge laurel wreath at the foot of the memorial and made a deep, reverential bow to his great mentor.

Later Works On his return from Moscow in the summer of 1880, Dostoevsky embarked on a burst of writing activity that knows no precedent in Russian literature. In the course of a few months he finished the bulk of *The Karamazov Brothers*, continued his *Diary of a Writer* and kept up an intensive correspondence, all the while suffering shattering, debilitating fits of epilepsy. But it was not all doom and gloom. The summer of 1880 was particularly warm, perhaps reminding him of gentler climates. His correspondence, going back to these balmy, final days, is characterized by being written in bursts – several letters at a time without a break – during strategic gaps in his work. On completion of *The Karamazov Brothers* in 1880, Dostoevsky made far-reaching plans for 1881–82 and beyond, the principal task being an ambitious sequel to the novel; yet at other moments at the end of that year, he confessed to a premonition that his days were numbered.

Tolstoy, says Igor Volgin, left the world defiantly, with a *Death* loud bang of the door, which reverberated throughout the world. By contrast, Dostoevsky's death was very low key. The author Boleslav Markovich, who came to see Dostoevsky just before he died, wrote: "He was lying on a sofa, his head propped up on a cushion, at the far end of an unpretentious, dismal room – his study. The light of a lamp, or candles, I can't remember, standing on a little table nearby, fell directly onto his face, which was as white as a sheet, with a dark-red spot of blood that had not been wiped off his chin... His breath escaped from his throat with a soft whistle and a spasmodic opening and shutting of his lips." Dostoevsky died on 28th January 1881, at 8:36 p.m., according to Markovich's watch.

Dostoevsky's own universal legacy is, of course, indis- *Legacy* putable, in the way that Shakespeare's is – meaning that, adulators aside, both have their eminent detractors too. Henry James, Joseph Conrad and D.H. Lawrence, to mention but three, famously disliked Dostoevsky.

Among the lesser known of Dostoevsky's legacies in the West is what is termed in Russian *достоевщина* (Dostoevshchina). A dictionary definition of *достоевщина* would be: psychological analysis in the manner of Dostoevsky (in a deprecating sense); tendency to perversion, moral licence and degradation in society. This topic falls outside the scope of this account, but readers of his novels would see how in a traditional society, dominated by religion, such as was the case in nineteenth-century Russia, and also in the eyes of such fastidious arbiters as Turgenev, his repeated delving into the seedier aspects of human behaviour could easily attract severe censure. It is therefore fitting to end with the words – expressing Dostoevsky's essential ambiguity – of Innokenty Annensky, one of Russia's foremost Silver Age poets and literati: "Keep reading Dostoevsky, keep loving him, if you can – but if you can't, blame him for all you're worth, only keep reading him... and only him, mostly."

Fyodor Dostoevsky's Works

Poor People (*Бедные люди*, 1846), Dostoevsky's debut epistolary *Poor People* novel, with which he conquered Belinsky's heart and entered upon the St Petersburg literary stage, is in choice of subject firmly rooted in Gogol. However, in emotional substance and character delineation it goes way beyond anything that the author of *The Greatcoat* ever attempted. "People (Belinsky and others) have detected in me a radically new approach, of analysis rather than synthesis, that is, I dig deep and, delving to the level of the atoms, I reach further down to the heart of the matter, whereas Gogol's point of departure is the heart of the matter itself; consequently he is less profound." Although Dostoevsky's self-analysis may not be altogether convincing, the novel itself – an exchange of heart-rending letters between two lost souls – is artistically persuasive. It is set wholly in the stifling bureaucratic, class-ridden Russia of the early-nineteenth century, but in spite of the passage of time has lost none of its universal appeal. The events could easily have been taking place in any epoch, in any society – a lowly official exchanging messages with an unfortunate, repressed female living in the house across the way.

The Double   Dostoevsky's next major work, *The Double* (*Двойник*, 1846) is by any standards a most unusual and inventive piece of novel writing. According to Dostoevsky's own evaluation, it was "ten times better than *Poor People*". This opinion, however, was not shared by the vast majority of contemporary critics, who had trouble accepting its blend of fantasy and realism. Mr Golyadkin, an ordinary, perfectly unremarkable, naive and helpless nineteenth-century man, is overwhelmed by the pace of progress in a modern metropolis with all the latest waterproof galoshes, open-plan offices, luxury soft-sprung carriages, dazzling gas streetlights and the hectic pace of social life all round, and begins to inhabit another world or, to put it in clinical terms, slowly but surely to lose his mind. The author does not state this in so many words – Mr Golyadkin's mental disintegration is never explained or accounted for. The reader is plunged *in medias res* into a mad world from the word go. As a result Golyadkin's predicament gains in authenticity because specifics do not stand in the way of the reader identifying himself with the hero; each one of us can supply our own catalogue of examples that threaten our sanity and therefore there is a pervasive atmosphere of "there but for the grace of God go I".

The Double was hugely controversial, and on the whole was pronounced to be stylistically inadequate, a judgement with which Dostoevsky himself tended to agree, though with important reservations. In 1846 he wrote to his brother: "absolutely everyone finds [*The Double*] a desperate and unexciting bore, and so long-drawn-out it's positively unreadable. But, funnily enough, though they berate me for bringing on tedium, they all, to a man, read it over and over again to the very end." This very early novel was already full of innovative, arresting characteristics: agitated, strained dialogue, always disordered, always rambling; madness predominating over method; a perplexed, pathetic soul cruelly disorientated amid confused perspectives of time and place; heart-rending tragedy compounded by a welter of manic Hollywood-type slapstick comedy – this off-the-wall tale of galloping schizophrenia took contemporary readers by storm and left them quite bewildered. Some critics hailed *The Double* as profound, others found it so permeated with the mentally aberrant spirit of Gogol's story 'Diary of a Madman' that it was no longer a question of influence, but of blatant imitation. However, if it was imitation, it was imitation of the highest order.

Like much in Dostoevsky, *The Double* was too far ahead of its time, and it would only find a reading public ready to appreciate and enjoy it to the full much later. For Vladimir Nabokov, who was no fan of Dostoevsky, *The Double* was "the best thing he ever wrote... a perfect work of art". Time and again Dostoevsky expressed, probably under the influence of outside pressures, his intention to "improve" *The Double*; a partially revised version appeared in 1866.

Netochka Nezvanova (*Неточка Незванова*, 1849), a novel- *Netochka Nezvanova* la which was originally conceived as a full-length novel: in its present form it should be considered as an unfinished work. Dostoevsky deals here with what was to become one of his favourite themes – the psychology and behaviour of an unusually precocious child. The plucky child-heroine Netochka has much in common with Nelly from *Humiliated and Insulted*, particularly in her capacity for boundless love, self-sacrifice and indomitable will-power. They are both fighters who refuse to succumb to life's vicissitudes whatever the odds.

Although the novella still captures the imagination today thanks to its dramatic intensity – which, for example, prompted a successful theatre adaptation at the New End Theatre in London in 2008 – it is generally considered to contain tedious and long-winded passages, which one outspoken contemporary critic, A. Druzhinin, characterized in 1849 as reeking of perspiration. These words must have rankled with Dostoevsky, because he recalls them with dramatic irony in the epilogue to *Humiliated and Insulted*.

The Village of Stepanchikovo   In *The Village of Stepanchikovo* (*Село Степанчиково*, 1859), Dostoevsky again found himself irresistibly drawn to Gogol, who had by then become an obsession. Set on a remote country estate, the story concerns a household completely dominated by the despotic charlatan and humbug Foma Fomich Opiskin, whose sententious utterance contains a good deal of satire on the reactionary Gogol. The owner of the estate, the retired Colonel Rostanev, is a meek, kind-hearted giant of a man, cruelly dominated by Opiskin. With deftly controlled suspense, the novel builds up to a confrontation between these two.

The chief asset of the work is its rich, dramatic dialogue – *The Village of Stepanchikovo* was in fact first conceived as a drama. It is through their words that Dostoevsky gives flesh and blood not only to the protagonists but also a host of unforgettable minor characters – the perspiringly loquacious and hypochondriac landowner Bakhcheyev, the literary valet Vidoplyasov, the dancing peasant household pet Falaley, the scheming poseur Mizinchikov and the unfortunate heiress Tatyana Ivanovna, touchingly confined in her fantasy world.

Humiliated and Insulted   Dostoevsky was thirty-nine when in January 1861 *Humiliated and Insulted* (*Униженные и оскорблённые*) began to be serialized in the first issue of *Time* (*Время*), the literary periodical which he founded jointly with his brother Mikhail. A much revised version came out in book form in autumn of the same year. It was his fourth novel to date after *Poor People* and *The Double* (1846), and *The Village of Stepanchikovo* (1859), neither of the last two being originally designated as novels, but given the stylized titles of "poem" and "tale" (*повесть*) respectively. However, *The Village of Stepanchikovo* and *Humiliated and Insulted* have this in common: that they were written in close succession, straight after his return from the ten-year period of penal servitude and exile in Siberia, and were meant to serve as passports for re-entry to the literary scene from which he was debarred for so long.

The House of the Dead   *The House of the Dead*, literally and more accurately *Notes from the Dead House* (*Записки из мертвого дома*, 1862), is Dostoevsky's fictionalized record of four years of unremitting hardship and privation suffered as a convict in one of Tsar Nicholas I's Siberian penal institutions. In 1854 he wrote to his brother: "The different folk I met in the settlement! I lived amongst them and got to know them well. The stories I heard from the vagabonds and felons – about their nefarious deeds and gruelling way of life – would be enough to fill several tomes. What an amazing set of people!" Dostoevsky looked upon penal servitude with the eyes of an artist, making imaginative generalizations and giving the narrative a deliberately fictional intensity and tone. And yet its genre category is unclear. Without a coherent plot or storyline, it is hardly a novel. Attempts to call the work a memoir are fundamentally wrong. Dostoevsky had a particular penchant for "notes", which is perhaps the most appropriate term.

Tolstoy had read it three times, and in a letter to the critic Nikolai Strakhov, he wrote: "I was a bit under the weather the other day and reread *The Dead House*. I'd forgotten a lot... I know of no better work in the whole of modern literature, including Pushkin... If you see Dostoevsky, tell him I love him." In his response, Strakhov informed Tolstoy that Dostoevsky was very pleased to hear the words of praise and asked to be allowed to keep Tolstoy's letter, only he was taken a little aback at the implied note of disrespect for Pushkin.

Notes from Underground (*Записки из подполья*, 1864) is a work which holds an enduring fascination for critics and readers. It opens, rather famously, with a burst of angry, personal observations: "I am a sick man... a spiteful man... an unattractive man, that's what I am." Having introduced himself in this manner, the narrator describes his current situation, having retired early from a low-ranking civil-service job thanks to an inheritance that enables him to survive in misery and seclusion. He explains that, due to a heightened consciousness of his own motives and emotions, he has retreated to a life of inertia and boredom. He also expounds his theory that man, out of a desire to exercise his free will, intentionally acts against his own interest and the dictates of logic – contrary to the claims of conventional rationalist doctrine. While he exposes his arguments, the narrator frequently interpolates his imaginary audience's potential objections, and often backtracks and revises his opinions.

In the second part of the *Notes*, the narrator relates anecdotes from his past, ostensibly to illustrate the points

Notes from Underground

he has made in the first part. The first story deals with his obsessive plans to get revenge against an officer who offended him by pushing him out of his way in the street. After weeks of fantasizing he finally acts by intentionally bumping into the officer, only to find, to his annoyance, that his victim is not in the least bothered by this assault.

He then tells of a farewell dinner for his former classmate Zverkov, a pompous and boastful high achiever, along with other former school friends. Even though he dislikes them all, especially Zverkov, and is destitute and shabbily dressed, he decides to attend out of spite. He is infuriated when he arrives at the agreed time but has to wait for an hour because they have neglected to tell him that they had delayed their arrival. Civilities are quickly cast aside, and he launches into a diatribe against them and mankind in general. The others leave to go to a brothel without him, and he eventually follows them, but they are gone by the time he arrives. There he meets the prostitute Liza.

The scene continues later on, in the same setting, with the narrator delivering an impassioned moralistic lecture about Liza's lifestyle and bleak prospects. She is moved by his apparent concern for her plight, and he gives her his address and leaves. The narrator begins to regret having left his details and is haunted by the possibility of her coming to see him. When she finally does arrive, she catches him at an undignified moment, which prompts a cruel outburst from him, before he breaks down and owns up to his own sense of humiliation. She embraces him out of pity, but he cannot help taking advantage of her, and she leaves, never to be seen or heard from again. The narrator's truthful confessions end on this regretful note.

Unlike those of Rousseau and Heine, these alleged confessions are unsparing in their detail and self-criticism. The narrator parades convictions, sentiments and soul-searching observations which would normally be subconscious, or at least not consciously acknowledged by normal people.

These amount to negative attributes such as envy, jealousy, the inability to empathize, insecurity. The only positive attribute is frankness, but frankness leads the narrator to own up to and to illustrate his own self-centredness, cowardice and moral cruelty – characteristics which he suggests are the inevitable concomitants of being hyper-sensitive and over-educated. "Here," as the underground man concludes in his *Notes*, "are *deliberately* gathered together all the characteristics of an anti-hero."

Crime and Punishment (*Преступление и наказание*, 1866) is one of the four of Dostoevsky's major novels, which Nabokov referred to as "the *so-called* major novels" (my italics). The arguably much greater, but less well-known Nobel-Prize-winning author Ivan Bunin had a similarly low opinion of Dostoevsky's great novels, or novels of ideas, as they are also not infrequently referred to. Valentin Kataev recalls that Bunin raged over the hero, Raskolnikov: "Dostoevsky obliges you to witness impossible and inconceivable abominations and spiritual squalor. From here have come all Russia's ills – Decadence, Modernism, Revolution, young people who are infected to the marrow of their bones with *Dostoevshchina* – who are without direction in their lives, confused, spiritually and physically crippled by war, not knowing what to do with their strengths and their talents..." *[right margin: Crime and Punishment]*

At the heart of *Crime and Punishment* is the student Raskolnikov's premeditated murder of a miserable old woman moneylender with the manic idea that this act would somehow make him into a superman, raise him above the law and enable him to identify himself with Napoleon. Around this idea, Dostoevsky, armed with a marvellous title, manages to spin a truly fascinating tale. Issues of crime and punishment are always calculated to arouse interest, and he manages to score some significant firsts, such as his creation of the detective Porfiry. "Wilkie Collins and Dickens portrayed Victorian detectives, but no one had yet shown the 'master' detective, capable of deducing facts from psychological observation: in the twentieth century the super-detective was a close rival of the criminal for the status of hero," writes Professor Richard Peace.

As mentioned above, Dostoevsky was addicted to gambling, and he channelled this personal experience into his next novel, *The Gambler* (*Игрок*, 1866). The action takes place in the spoof town Roulettenburg, where a bunch of Russian prize idlers have fetched up to feed their habit and indulge in conspiracies and sterile romantic pursuits. As was to be expected, no one gets any richer, just the opposite, and all personal relationships end in frustration and heartache. *[right margin: The Gambler]*

In a letter to his favourite niece Sofya Alexandrovna Ivanova, to whom he dedicated *The Idiot* (*Идиот*, 1868), Dostoevsky wrote: "I have been nurturing the idea of this novel a long time now. It is a particular favourite of mine, but is so difficult that I have not dared to tackle it... The main aim is to portray *[right margin: The Idiot]* a positively good man. There's nothing more difficult than this in the world, especially nowadays. All writers, not only ours, but even the European ones too, who tried, had to give up, for the simple reason that the task is measureless."

The hero of the novel, Prince Myshkin, is a Christ-like figure. He is mentally distinctly unstable, indeed he brands himself an idiot. The question arises, can saintliness survive in the real world? Russia being the real world, the novel's answer is no, because it is synonymous with some kind of mental deficiency, which is bound to lead to disaster. At the beginning of the novel Myshkin returns from a Swiss sanatorium after a lengthy treatment, hopefully on the way to complete recovery. Abroad he had witnessed public executions by guillotine, and the memories continue to haunt him, especially the gruesome ordinariness of the preparatory ritual. What goes through the condemned man's head as he hears the swish of the descending blade? In St Petersburg he finds no solace. On the day of his arrival, without a respite, he is thrown into a vortex of events that would have unsettled a much stronger man. Representing the darker side of humanity is the volatile, passionate, reckless merchant Rogozhin, whom Myshkin gets to know on the journey. It is a fateful meeting. As the action unravels both come to grief in their rivalry and quest for happiness, Rogozhin's fate being, if anything, the more heart-rending, because he ends up with blood on his hands beside the lifeless corpse of the woman they both loved to distraction. As for Myshkin, he returns to the sanatorium, we fear permanently.

The novel is conceived on a large scale with numerous sub-plots and a host of secondary characters. True to form they are all colourfully depicted, invariably with customary Dostoevskian humour and wit. However, some critics have found the structure of the novel problematic, and it is not the most popular choice among a wider readership.

Devils   In the work *Devils* (Бесы, 1871–72, also known as *The Possessed* and *Demons*), one of Dostoevsky's main concerns is nihilism: this is embodied in the novel to devastating effect through its memorable characters. The great Russian critic and novelist Dmitry Merezhkovsky argues in *Gogol and the Devil* that the suave, smooth-talking, clownish con man Chichikov in Gogol's *Dead Souls* is the devil par excellence, because he is one of us who goes about deceiving people left, right and centre with impunity, hiding under his mask of normality and ordinariness – a point worth noting in relation to *Devils*.

The novel boasts some of the most blood-curdling episodes imaginable, but at the same time the translator Michael R. Katz writes: "*Devils* is without doubt Dostoevsky's most humorous work. It has more irony, more elements of burlesque and parody, more physical comedy and buffoonery, more exaggerated characterizations and ambiguous use of language than any of his other works." We are indeed not miles away from the Marx Brothers' *Night at the Opera*. Stepan Trofimovich Verkhovensky, with whom the novel opens and who continues to play a significant role to the very end, can, improbably enough, be seen as a Groucho Marx figure with a touch of Don Quixote thrown in. The picture is completed with the former's inimitable screen foil Margaret Dupont, who is represented in the novel by the grand and unapproachable Varvara Petrovna Stavrogina.

Dostoevsky based his story on a Russian press report of a brutal murder by a follower of the revolutionary anarchist Ivan Bakunin. He uses that as a paradigm for depicting a ruthless nationwide conspiracy, incidentally directed from abroad, to bring down the existing order in Russia. Acts of terrorism and extreme violence are used as political tools. But the events, despite being narrated by an apparently non-committal chronicler, are by no means a factual record of reality. The highly mysterious chronicler's very protestations of veracity are a novelist's ploy to draw the reader into a fantasy world that is blatantly of his own creation. At the centre of it are the demonically beguiling figures of Nicolas Stavrogin, a self-confessed paedophiliac and sadist, and his utterly unprincipled sidekick Peter Stepanovich Verkhovensky. Besides the motif of rampant terrorism, there is the theme of suicide, not as a desperate solution out of a psychological impasse, but as a supreme manifestation of one's will.

Dostoevsky had always been keenly interested in all aspects *Diary of a Writer* of publishing. Even his fictional characters are bitten by the bug. Vanya in *Humiliated and Insulted* talks to a publisher or entrepreneur, as he facetiously styles him, and appears to know his role and what motivates him; Liza Drozdova in *Devils* comes up with a serious proposal to bring out a digest, "an illuminating overview" of current affairs, and she waxes lyrical over the benefits and commercial viability of the prospective undertaking. Dostoevsky himself was a prolific journalist and the founder and editor of several periodicals. Liza's idea in fact goes back to Dostoevsky's plans of 1864–65 to found *Notebook* – a fortnightly periodical which failed to materialize – and looks forward to *Diary of a Writer* (*Дневник писателя*, 1873–81), which did materialize in 1873. In both cases Dostoevsky was to be the sole contributor. It is for this reason that *Diary of a Writer* can, indeed should, be regarded as a free-standing literary work. In essence it is a ground-breaking, wide-ranging pot-pourri of all types of literary genres, "an illuminating overview" of all that continued to preoccupy the writer till the end of his days, and some of the issues touched upon were further reflected in his Pushkin speech and in *The Karamazov Brothers*.

The Adolescent   In 1876 Dostoevsky wrote: "When, about a year and a half ago, Nikolai Alexeyevich Nekrasov asked me to write a novel for *Notes of the Fatherland*, I was on the point of starting my version of *Fathers and Sons*, but held back, and thank God for that. I was not ready. All I've been able to come up with so far is my *Adolescent*."

Just as in Turgenev's *Fathers and Sons*, the theme of the generation gap is at the heart of *The Adolescent* (*Подросток*, 1875). Incidentally the narrator-hero rejoices in the name of Arkady (Dolgoruky), the same as one of the principal characters, Arkady (Kirsanov), in Turgenev's story; the other – the more important of the two – being Yevgeny Bazarov. The similarity does not end there. Both Arkady Dolgoruky and Yevgeny Bazarov are kindred spirits, rebels at heart and ardent champions of liberalism and truth. This ideological confluence is quite remarkable because on most points the two authors could not see eye to eye at all.

Also, the theme of relationships with serf women is tackled head on by both authors, especially Dostoevsky, who of course extracts every ounce of drama from the controversy associated with such liaisons. Arkady is illegitimate: he is the son of the serf Sofya, wife of the bonded serf Makar Dolgoruky, and the gallivanting nobleman, Andrei Versilov. Dostoevsky is immediately on home ground – the trials and tribulations of a thoroughly dysfunctional family. After his wife has been taken away from him, Makar Dolgoruky leaves his village to wander off and walk the land as a penitent, surfacing only at the end of the story. Young Arkady, at nineteen – having been knocked all his life from pillar to post – is back with his biological father, whom he has hardly met since birth, eager to get to know him closely. It's a love-hate relationship from the start: Arkady is fascinated by Versilov, and is drawn to him inexorably. Versilov shares a good few characteristics with the devil of Ivan's nightmare in *The Karamazov Brothers*, who, in line with Dostoevsky's intertwining of good and evil, is of quite an affable, genial sort. Arkady wants to live up to his father, and in his young heart he nurtures a grand, but in his view eminently attainable and realistic idea. He lusts after money, and above all, power. As he says in the novel, he wants to become a Rothschild. Father and son also lust after the same woman almost to the point of committing murder. In the background there is the ever-present mother figure of the saintly, long-suffering Sofya, and what with Makar Dolgoruky bearing a strong resemblance to Father Zosima, the similarity between Dostoevsky's last two novels is striking. Yet the atmosphere is altogether different. Perhaps the chaotic, topsy-turvy, structurally unbalanced *Karamazov Brothers* is more action packed and stimulating, intellectually intriguing and humorous too, which is what counts with readers in the end, even the more sophisticated ones. *The Adolescent* is, in that case, arguably too sophisticated and refined for its own good. One way or another *The Adolescent* has been overshadowed by his other great novels both in Russia and the Anglophone West.

Sigmund Freud wrote that *The Karamazov Brothers* (Братья Карамазовы, 1879–80) was "the most magnificent novel ever written". Indeed, the novel played right into his hands, above all as regards the Oedipal connection. The work blends together literature, philosophy and entertainment in a way that has held a strong appeal for many intellectual readers. *The Karamazov Brothers*

At the heart of the novel is a dysfunctional family, four sons – one illegitimate – and the father, a dissolute, cunning, mistrustful old man, who is in a running feud with the eldest over money and the favours of the local siren. The conflict gets out of hand and Dmitry Karamazov is accused of patricide. Bound up with this intense family drama is Dostoevsky's exploration of many of his most deeply cherished ideas. The novel is also richly comic and philosophically challenging. One chapter, entitled *The Legend of the Grand Inquisitor*, in which the churchman, in a confrontational dialogue with Christ, argues that freedom and happiness are incompatible, is styled a poem, and for its content and form occupies a unique place in literature.

Miscellaneous   This account of Dostoevsky's works is by no means
Short Fiction exhaustive, but has had to be limited to some of the most famous and pivotal novels and novellas. During his career Dostoevsky wrote many other shorter works of fiction, not to mention articles, essays and travel writing, and among his short stories one could mention the following, among many others: *White Nights* (*Белые ночи*, 1848), a story of isolation and heartbreak spanning four nights, during which the protagonist realizes his love for a young girl called Nastenka must always remain unfulfilled; *The Eternal Husband* (*Вечный муж*, 1870), which compellingly describes a recently widowed man's encounter with his dead wife's former lover; *A Gentle Creature* (*Кроткая*, 1876), the tale of a widowed pawnbroker's turbulent relationship with a young customer who eventually becomes his wife; *The Dream of a Ridiculous Man* (*Сон смешного человека*, 1877), which recounts the spiritual journey of its suicidal protagonist, who finds salvation in an encounter with a young girl and a subsequent dream.

– Ignat Avsey

Select Bibliography

Biographies:

Carr, Edward Hallett, *Dostoevsky, 1821–1881: A New Biography* (London: Allen & Unwin, 1931)

Dostoevsky, Anna, *Dostoevsky: Reminiscences*, tr. B. Stillman (Liveright, Dutton, 1974)

Frank, Joseph, *Dostoevsky*, vols. 1–5 (London: Robson, 1977–2002)

Grossman, Leonid Petrovich, *Dostoevsky: A Biography*, tr. Mary Mackler (London: Allen Lane, 1974)

Magarshack, David, *Dostoevsky* (London: Secker & Warburg, 1962)

Mochulsky, Konstantin, *Dostoevsky: His Life and Work* (Princeton, NJ: Princeton University Press, 1967)

Simmons, Ernest Joseph, *Dostoevsky: The Making of a Novelist* (London: John Lehmann, 1950)

Yarmolinsky, Avrahm, *Dostoevsky: A Life* (New York: Harcourt, Brace & Co., 1934)

Other books by FYODOR DOSTOEVSKY
published by Alma Classics

The Adolescent (tr. by Dora O'Brien)

Crime and Punishment (tr. by Roger Cockrell)

The Crocodile (tr. by Guy Daniels)

Devils (tr. by Roger Cockrell)

The Double (tr. by Hugh Aplin)

The Eternal Husband (tr. by Hugh Aplin)

The Gambler (tr. by Hugh Aplin)

The House of the Dead (tr. by Roger Cockrell)

Humiliated and Insulted (tr. by Ignat Avsey)

The Idiot (tr. Ignat Avsey)

Notes from Underground (tr. by K. Zinovieff and J. Hughes)

Poor People (tr. by Hugh Aplin)

Uncle's Dream (tr. by Roger Cockrell)

Winter Notes on Summer Impressions (tr. by Kyril FitzLyon)

EVERGREENS SERIES
Beautifully produced classics, affordably priced

Alma Classics is committed to making available a wide range of literature from around the globe. Most of the titles are enriched by an extensive critical apparatus, notes and extra reading material, as well as a selection of photographs. The texts are based on the most authoritative editions and edited using a fresh, accessible editorial approach. With an emphasis on production, editorial and typographical values, Alma Classics aspires to revitalize the whole experience of reading classics.

For our complete list and latest offers visit
almabooks.com/evergreens